The
Canasta
Capers

The
Canasta
Capers

STEVEN SWERDFEGER

Star Cloud Press
Scottsdale, Arizona

The Canasta Capers
Copyright © 2005 by Steven Swerdfeger

originally published in 1996 under the title
Thursday's Child

cover art
© 2005 by Lucy Swerdfeger

Cover by Trisha Hadley

Published by

~ STAR CLOUD PRESS ~

6137 East Mescal Street
Scottsdale, Arizona 85254-5418

www.StarCloudPress.com

ISBN: 1-932842-07-1 — (cloth) — $ 29.95
ISBN: 1-932842-08-X — (paper) — $ 21.95

Library of Congress Card Catalog Number: 2005908827

Printed in the United States of America

For Martha

and
Monica, Lucy, Sarah, Michael
Matthew, Patrick, and David

Monday's child is fair of face,
Tuesday's child is full of grace,
Wednesday's child is full of woe,
Thursday's child has far to go,
Friday's child is loving and giving,
Saturday's child works hard for a living,
But the child that's born on Sabbath day,
Is blithe and bonny and good and gay.

Chapter One
The Wakening

He felt himself falling and jolted awake. His heart was pounding, his breathing shallow, the percale sheets of his bed and his pajamas damp from the warmth of his sweat.

The dream was the same. It loomed over his consciousness like an executioner, its images haunting his waking thoughts: the cold, icy, snowy, windy January evening of the accident, the corner store, the lights of his parents' car, the advancing truck, all too terrible, too wrong.

"DAVID, IT'S TIME TO GET UP. Mr. Dewey will be here by nine," called Aunt Lillian.

The enticing aroma of eggs and sausage wafted through the dining room and up the stairwell into David's bedroom. Max, his Husky-Collie, a most capable actor with deep brown eyes, would soon bound upstairs and escort David to the kitchen. Although fully fed and watered, Max was always eager for the curtain to rise on the ritual drama of *OH, BUT FOR A TASTE FROM THE MARVELOUS HIGH TABLE.*

The percale sheets smelled like wind and sunshine because Aunt Lillian always dried them on her clothesline in the summer. David lay between the waking world and the world of dreams, debating which direction he would travel, a choice between the smooth, cool, and inviting light blue sheets or the breakfast he smelled downstairs. There was a hollowness in his belly, initially from his dream but now from the succulence of sausages, eggs, and browned potatoes. He stretched lazily one last time, sat up, yawned, turned and lifted himself into the waking world. As he brushed his teeth, Max bounded into the bathroom, nuzzling his nose against David's leg, trilling with excitement and happily wagging his tail. Still not fully awake, David lumbered downstairs with Max at his heels.

Aunt Lillian's ruffled, long-haired gray cat, dubbed many years before as *Her Majesty, The Queen*, owing to her ability to sit up like a person when grooming herself, was reclining against the bathroom door, warily eyeing Max. Having been a denizen of Her Majesty's kingdom for only a month and still, therefore, an interloper, poor Max was now drawing what David called *the look*, which conveyed the words, "If only you were dead, my kingdom would be a happy one."

"Morning, your Majesty," David bowed to the Queen. Turning to Max, he teased, "And I'm sure you're hoping for a little of my sausage and eggs." Max lifted his ears and wagged his tail expectantly. David sniffed with approval, "Home-fries, too! Don't worry Max, I won't forget you. Her Majesty's relationship with Max is quite a bit different here than it was at my parents' house, isn't it Aunt Lillian? There Max ruled the roost; here she rules her kingdom."

"Yes, I remember how tentative Her Majesty was when we came to live with you for those months after the accident. All in all, I think Max was more welcoming of her there than she has been of him here, but they seem to have worked out a truce of sorts. Today, I decided to add home fries to our breakfast because we have a big day ahead of us,"Aunt Lillian smiled.

"It's an absolutely fantastic breakfast!" exclaimed David, taking his cloth napkin from its holder and tucking it under his shirt as he sat down. Aunt Lillian insisted on using cloth napkins, hoping that it might help to save a few trees here and there. 'It isn't a big thing, but it *is* one small thing we can do,' she had explained.

"I am glad that you and Mr. Dewey will be assembling shelving for your parents' books today. We'll finally have a real library for them."

2

In front of his place, David saw the quotation Aunt Lillian had written for their game OWAQ [O-wok]. OWAQ was an acronym for 'Oh! What a quote!' The recipient could agree, disagree, or defer. The game had been a favorite of his parents, and David was glad Aunt Lillian had consented to play, for it lent a familiar structure to the day and reminded him of the holidays they had shared together. Aunt Lillian and David and his parents had lived less than two hours away from each other in their respective upstate New York villages, but had seen each other only during holidays, although David had for many years visited Aunt Lillian for a few weeks each summer.

David unfolded the quotation Aunt Lillian had chosen and read aloud, "No man can be wise on an empty stomach.—George Eliot." Smiling, he took a small paper from his shirt pocket, handing it to Aunt Lillian who was pouring herself a second cup of Earl Gray. She opened it and read aloud, "If any man seeks for greatness, let him forget greatness and ask for truth, and he will find both.—Horace Mann."

"You go first," David insisted. He most enjoyed looking at her when she mulled over a quotation, for it was then that she looked most like a wren contemplating the location of her nest. Her brown hair was only beginning to turn gray, her deep brown eyes accentuated by laughter lines and large dimples. She looked fifteen years younger than her actual age except when she was sad, and then she looked fifteen years older.

"Well, David," Aunt Lillian began, closing her eyes in contemplation, "I think I agree with Mr. Mann."

David nodded as he salted his home-fries.

"The best that any of us can do is to plod through life naming truth insofar as we can see it *and* live it, yet always remaining open to encountering greater light. However, the world is often not kind to people who have the courage to seek truth or to hold onto the truths that they find."

David poured some more ketchup on his egg and plopped part of the yolk and some home-fries into his mouth, nodding in agreement.

"David, shame on you. You're trying to make a philosopher out of me! Perish the thought!" Aunt Lillian teased.

"You'd be great!" David managed, swallowing his food. His Aunt had always seemed like a wonderful, patient, little wren to him when he was younger. He had discovered that although she was short in stature, she amply made up for any lack of outward height with an interior, enduring optimism and joy. David swallowed and cleared his throat, saying, "I agree with you that when we try to follow truth as we see it, we risk getting in trouble with the forces of the world, especially if we challenge society."

"I suppose people who don't march lockstep with society's whims seem dangerous to the authorities because they threaten the *status quo*," sighed Aunt Lillian. She motioned to the many boxes of books stacked in the living room, adding, "Just as people who own and read books can't always be trusted to do the popular thing. David, you look sad. Is anything bothering you?"

"I had my same dream last night," confided David, "the one about my parents' accident. For a while, I thought it was going away."

"I'm sorry. It seemed to be coming less frequently, didn't it? I miss your mom and dad, too. Did you know that I taught your mom how to sew and crochet? She was a little younger than you are, and she developed a fascination for making candles. We even tried making some together, and they turned out credibly well, not so much for their form, but certainly for their function. She always insisted on candle light at dinner."

4

"I know. It has seemed sort of strange not having candles at dinner time," said David.

Aunt Lillian suddenly looked very sad and, as she lifted her napkin to wipe a tear from her eye, she whispered, "I know. But I still don't think I could bear it. Candles remind me so much of your mom and dad, and all the light and love they shared with those they knew. I'm sorry, David, to get teary-eyed like this. These watery moments still come and go for both of us, I know, and it's been more than seven months. I don't think it's ever possible to get over such a loss. The important thing, though, is to treasure our memories of the wonderful times we did share together, and to honor them for all the love that they gave. I know they would want us to go on enjoying candles, so let me try to find a little more courage, and maybe we can start having candles during dinner sometime this fall. How would you like that?"

"I really would. The accident is beginning to seem like a dream, so far away, so many changes, and it only happened in January. I'm so glad you were willing to come and live with me until the end of the school year. It gave me a chance to say 'good-bye' to my friends, not to mention selling off most of the furniture and the house."

"I'm glad you decided to keep your parents' books, David," said Aunt Lillian.

"Well, that *was* their life. They were good librarians, too."

"That's certainly what everyone in Long Lake said at the memorial service."

"Bits and pieces of that service still come back to me. Everyone was so kind. And right before we moved back here to Midville, their renaming of the library in my parents' honor touched me more than anything else ever has."

"It was certainly most deserved, David," smiled Aunt Lillian.

"I really appreciate your turning your music studio into a library, Aunt Lillian" said David. "That means a lot to me, too."

"This is *your* home now, David. We still have each other, but I sometimes wish our family were larger, so you'd have other family after I'm gone."

Tears glistened in David's bright green eyes as he asked, "Is Mr. Dewey going to put shelving all over the music room?"

"Only two walls of it, David. I haven't used the studio since I gave up teaching piano. I am very grateful that my arthritis has now abated, and I don't want to encourage its return with the kind of practice it takes if one is going to be a good teacher. I count the addition of your books more than a fair trade for my loss of a music studio."

"Anybody home?" called a cheerful voice from below the kitchen window.

"Hello, George," replied Aunt Lillian. "Come in the rear garage door and have some tea."

Aunt Lillian poured a cup of tea and put a teaspoon of sugar in it, stirred it, and set it on the place-mat next to David.

George Dewey was a small stocky man in his late sixties, with silver hair and thick black eyelashes that accentuated his sympathetic gray eyes. There was a certain nobility about his manner, even though he had been a tradesman most of his life. Early in his career, he had become Aunt Lillian's jack-of-all-trades, and she relied on his expertise for everything from refrigerators to furnaces, including plumbing and carpentry.

"I don't mind assembling these prefab shelves, but real ones would have looked a lot nicer in that studio, Lillian," he said after taking an appreciative sip of the tea Aunt Lillian had prepared for him.

"It's not my studio any longer, George," she admonished, "and you created a splendid addition when you built it. My piano will dress up the room, so it will seem more like a formal library, even if we have inferior shelving."

"Now, don't get me wrong. I'm not saying they don't look nice, but real wood is real wood, after all."

"Well, the piano can embellish them," Aunt Lillian smiled.

"No room for that monster anywhere else in the house. I remember the day we moved it in. Good thing I reinforced the subfloor under the studio to make sure it was extra strong."

"The books will now enjoy their own dedicated place, and my former music room will be transformed."

"Aunt Lillian, why did we get prefab bookshelves?" asked David.

"Because you will be able to dismantle them and take them with you should you ever want to relocate your books."

"They are *our* books," David said gently.

Aunt Lillian smiled at George Dewey. "I am blessed to have a thoughtful and generous grandnephew. Don't you think so, George?"

"One in a million. That's what I say David is. One in a million."

"George, shh! We mustn't talk this way in his presence lest he become full of himself."

"No chance of that. He's too good-hearted and generous."

David blushed.

"See, we've embarrassed him," chided Aunt Lillian.

"Well, give credit where credit's due is what I say," said George, turning to David. "I didn't know your mom and dad very well, but I liked them. And I know that the village where they served as librarians liked them a lot, too. I have a cousin who lives near Long Lake. She'd go on and on about them. The only thing that surprises me is that I would have thought two librarians would have had more books."

"Well, they sort of felt they had the best of both worlds," explained David. "They'd read the library's books, and they'd buy only the very special ones for our home library. They often told me it would be one of their most important legacies." David felt tears welling in his eyes, adding, "I didn't think it would come this soon."

"Drunken drivers kill thousands of innocent and decent people like your mom and dad each year. And I know that doesn't help much, and it shouldn't. It's a damnable shame, if you ask me," lamented Mr. Dewey, shaking his head.

"George, will the shelves be finished by noon?" inquired Aunt Lillian, gently changing the topic.

"Yes, Lillian, but I need to tell David something else. It's one thing to know the reality of death as a statistic, another as a personal tragedy. My tragedy, David, was a little baby daughter my wife and I lost before she was even ten weeks old. We cried for her, night after night, for many, many months. Mercifully, the Lord gave us another child, a new daughter, who has since given us grandchildren. What I'm trying to say, and probably am not saying very well, is that even though the mind may know death is a part of life, it's a lot harder for that to sink into our emotions. Time doesn't allow us to forget, but it does somehow manage to lessen the burden. I'm sorry. I've gone rattling on, and it's really time for us to get those shelves up."

"How long, George?" called Lillian from the kitchen.

"I think we'll have the last shelves assembled by noon or one o'clock, just in time for a late lunch."

"Mr. Dewey," began David, "thank you for sharing your pain."

"I just wanted you to know I've been there, too."

"Thanks."

"These shelves will be beautiful, David."

"That's for sure. I really will be glad when can get all those books in the living room in place."

"Do you have any special way you want them organized?" asked Aunt Lillian, returning from the kitchen.

David thought for a minute. "No. Mom and Dad never really had a formal system at home, but they always knew where every book was. I suppose just anywhere."

"You'll be sorry," warned George Dewey.

"No, I don't think I will," replied David. "It won't take me more than a week to memorize where everything is. Let's go for it."

"He does have a remarkable memory, George," said Aunt Lillian.

"Very well," he replied, standing and taking his empty tea cup to the sink to rinse it. "The sooner we get started and all that ... "

* * * * *

Later that afternoon all three of them, fully exhausted, sat sipping lemonade in the new library.

Lillian beamed, "Organized or not, the books are beautiful."

"Wait until you want to find one," cautioned George.

"I'll ask David to get it for me, George," Lillian grinned.

"What if he isn't here? Maybe he'll be at school."

"Maybe Mr. Dewey is right, Aunt Lillian," suggested David.

"Why David, to hear you say that *after* we've shelved all your books!" exclaimed Aunt Lillian.

"*Our* books," corrected David. "And by the way, while we were shelving everything this afternoon, I remembered why my parents never organized our library at home."

"Why was that, I wonder?" asked George.

"Their small village library had a larger than average number of books," explained David. "Finally, they decided they needed to convert from the Dewey Decimal System, no offense, Mr. Dewey, to the Library of Congress system. They closed the library and spent hundreds of hours redoing everything. That was their vacation that year. In fact, I recall Mom brought me here to be with you during those many weeks, Aunt Lillian."

"You know, David, I'd forgotten the circumstances of that summer's visit, except that it was longer than usual. Mostly I remember the fun we had exploring the field up behind the Methodist Church, and how you found a small brook and tried to catch some polliwogs and fell in—"

"And you got your blue and white skirt all wet when you stepped in to help me out," David laughed.

"David, you couldn't have been more than five or six when that happened. What a fine memory you have. You won't have any trouble knowing where these books live," Aunt Lillian smiled.

"Mr. Dewey, thanks for all your help," said David. "I really like the shelves."

"Thanks for saying so, David."

"And I don't know what I would do without you, George. I've relied on you for everything practical for so many years. I'm glad you're younger than I am," said Aunt Lillian.

"Not by much, my dear, not by very much," laughed George.

"Well, we've had a wonderful day of hard work and, on balance, an ample lunch. I don't think I'll manage my regular afternoon nap, but I'll probably try to get to bed a little early."

After George Dewey left, Aunt Lillian and David sat down to enjoy some English muffin toast amply coated with garlic butter and accompanied with some chicken noodle soup. Lillian aptly described it as a light meal for a heavy day. Both were tired and their arms ached, for they had worked hard, but their fatigue held the satisfaction that comes from having met a robust challenge. Dishes were done up quickly, and David and Lillian soon found themselves sitting in the library, watching the evening twilight forming the rich and long shadows of summer evenings. Neither one of them spoke a word; they sat in silence and listened. A warm summer breeze blew through the large casement windows which faced on to Aunt Lillian's garden. Crickets chirped in the fading light. An occasional voice could be heard in the distance. Finally, when they heard the Methodist Church tower clock strike nine, each looked at the other and smiled.

"I love you Aunt Lillian," said David.

"And I love you, David."

David closed his eyes. He felt a familiar gnawing, dull pain—an empty pit in his stomach. "I don't know if I'll ever get over missing them."

"We won't, and we shouldn't, you know. It's quite understandable that we should miss those we have loved."

Again David felt his heart warmed. —I'm just beginning to know and to understand this woman who is my very own Great Aunt Lillian, he thought.

"Not a day passes that I don't think of your mom and dad, David. We shared some good times together. Do you remember the time we went to the Collier farm to pick corn?"

"The time with the hornets?"

"Yes."

David's grin broke into a hearty laughter.

"David? What's so funny?"

"*You* were," he laughed.

"Why on earth?"

"Remember when Mom stepped on the hornets' nest, and they started swirling around her, and she started to run?"

"Yes. I remember she got stung five or six times, poor dear."

"And it would have been worse if she hadn't run for her life," declared David.

"I suppose so."

"Well, when she screamed and started running, you turned around from your row and yelled, 'Stand still, Margaret. Don't run!'"

"Well, I had always been told that bees don't bother you if you remain still."

"Yes, Aunt Lillian, that may be true. But these weren't bees, they were hornets."

"Well, I must have thought they were bees."

"But then one small hornet flew over around your head and do you remember what you did?"

"No. I don't think I remember, but it must have been hilarious."

"I'll never forget the way you uprooted an entire cornstalk and started swinging at that one, lone hornet."

"Well, I suppose I panicked."

"But it was so funny to see you swinging that cornstalk at that hornet especially after you had yelled at my mom to stand still and not to run."

David laughed again.

Aunt Lillian smiled. "Incongruity, David, is one of the ingredients of humor. You have a good eye for human behavior, and you have a remarkable memory for what people say ... down to the smallest detail. I suspect most people aren't as fine-tuned or as precise as that. And now that you're thirteen, you're entering adolescence. That is an age when one is particularly tuned to life's incongruities, especially when evaluating the behavior of adults. Please be kind, though, and remember that we all have our own little quirks and eccentricities."

"I know. One of mine is that I love to read. I guess I get that from Mom and Dad. I learned early on that my love for reading made me a little strange. Most kids would rather watch TV or play computer games. But because Mom and Dad insisted that I read instead of watching TV, I discovered a whole new universe. *Now* I'm glad my parents allowed TV only on the weekends."

"Well, since the shelves are finished, why don't we plan to sleep in tomorrow morning? I won't wake you. And I won't start breakfast until you've come down for a big glass of orange juice."

"Cool," said David.

* * * * *

David woke uneasily at 1:30 a.m. to a blinding flash and loud thunderclap. Rain was spattering on his screen, wetting the paint on the windowsill. He got up from bed and closed the window. He heard Aunt Lillian quickly moving from room to room downstairs, also closing windows. Max whimpered and nuzzled David.

A sudden, brilliant flash brought an intense and prolonged rumble that literally shook the house.

"Aunt Lillian, you okay?" David called.

There was no answer, but David could hear her closing windows in the kitchen. He shouted, "Aunt Lillian, are you okay?"

"David, is that you?"

"Yes. Are you all right?"

"Yes. I've just closed all the windows downstairs. Are yours closed?"

"Yes. I only had the big one open."

The light in the hallway clicked on. "David, come down and I'll make you some mint tea—that is, if we don't lose the electricity. It's a pretty fierce storm."

David donned his blue silk bathrobe and started downstairs. Max followed like a shadow, not wanting to be left alone with the thunder.

The hall light flickered at the next crash of thunder.

"That must have gotten a transformer somewhere," announced David, entering the kitchen.

Aunt Lillian patiently watched the kettle.

"Watched pots don't boil," warned David.

"Especially if we lose power. And we don't have a gas stove backup, either."

Curls of steam lifted from the pot's spout. Aunt Lillian deftly pour the hot water into a blue and white china teapot.

"It will take a few minutes for it to steep. Would you like some crackers or cookies? I think I may have some graham crackers. It feels like a graham cracker night."

"How do you know it's a graham cracker night?" asked David.

"Well, whenever I find myself hungry for something, *then* it's *that* kind of night, at least for me. It might be a chocolate ice cream night for you."

David brightened. "I feel an ice cream wave washing over me."

Aunt Lillian smiled, "I think you might find an emergency reserve of the double chocolate in the freezer in the cellar."

As David went to the cellar, an especially bright flash of lightning and loud thunderclap interrupted the electricity.

"Wow! That was a close one!" David called up to Aunt Lillian.

"Yes. I hope we don't lose any of our big maple trees. Hazel Schumacher lost one of her lovely pine trees last year."

The power flickered on and off. "Lightning must have hit some other transformer. What a storm!" said David. Almost in answer, normal power was restored.

David returned to the kitchen carrying a half gallon container of double chocolate.

"This would go well with your graham crackers," he suggested.

"Wish I had the courage to risk it. Chocolate isn't kind to my arthritis," Aunt Lillian lamented.

David dished out three large scoops for himself. Chocolate was a serious business and ensuring ample portions was important.

"Storms are a lot scarier if you're all by yourself," said David.

Aunt Lillian reflected for a moment, and then asked, "Were you ever by yourself in a storm?"

"Last summer, Mom and Dad went to take Max to the vet for a flea treatment and a really violent thunderstorm came across the lake. I'll never forget how the hail pelted the windows and how the wind and thunder rattled the house. I felt scared all by myself during that storm. I'm glad you're here, Aunt Lillian."

"So am I," replied Aunt Lillian, adding, "And I'm glad you're here, David. And I am also glad that you can still enjoy chocolate."

"Me too," mumbled David, his mouth full of ice cream.

"There are different kinds of storms, David, and I hope we can weather many of them together."

David nodded in agreement.

Max watched every bite, fervently hoping David might allow him to lick his bowl.

"It will be good to sleep late," Aunt Lillian continued. "Shelving the books exhausted me, and this storm has disturbed our sleep. I'll send Max to fetch you for a late breakfast."

"Sounds great," said David, "Can I please have some more of the double chocolate for breakfast?"

"Certainly not!" said Aunt Lillian. "Perhaps for lunch."

One of the many things that David liked about his Aunt Lillian was that her humor rarely seemed to fail her.

* * * * *

As he drifted off to sleep that night, David wondered what part of his dream would haunt him. He assumed it had something to do with what others had called the mourning period. He thought about the day, Aunt Lillian's and Mr. Dewey's kindness, and about how right Mr. Dewey had been. It hadn't helped him in the slightest to know that drunken drivers kill thousands of people every year. Ironically, it had been Mr. Dewey's sharing of his own loss that had seemed to lessen David's. Maybe it was just knowing that he had been there, too. Who can understand loss through death *unless* they've experienced it? His imagination conjured up the dark shadow of a menacing truck approaching the intersection, picking up speed in defiance of the stop sign. In one solitary instant, his life had been fractured, twisted, and torn. He still felt like a limp dishrag. A weariness descended that could not be softened by natural sleep.

Chapter Two
Waking to Help

David's sleep was not haunted by his recurrent dream after all. As he woke, he had only the faintest recollection of a beautiful oak tree being blown by the wind and then falling into a lake. He had slept restlessly, for he was sweating, and as he apprehended the world he was now entering, he felt a vague uneasiness, as if the other shoe was about to fall.

D AVID HAD DRESSED and was brushing his teeth when he heard Max barking frantically. He raced downstairs, through the dining room, and into the kitchen, noticing that Aunt Lillian had set the breakfast table with his favorite cereal, *Grandma's Granola*. The barking was coming from the steps that led from the kitchen to the basement. As he reached the door, David gasped to see Aunt Lillian sprawled at the bottom of the stairs. Max moved aside as David edged his way to the bottom.

"Aunt Lillian! Are you all right?"

"No. I slipped and fell at the top of the stairs and tumbled down here. I think I may have broken my right wrist. It really hurts and I can't move it."

Lillian noticed tears in David's eyes.

"Now, don't worry, dear. I'm going to be all right," she reassured him, "but I need to get to the hospital. Please go check the card file and ring up Dr. Wayne Smith. Tell him that I refuse to be transported to the hospital in an ambulance, but that he should send a taxi. Say that I said to tell him, 'I may be down, but I'm not defeated!' Now help me over against that wall, and then go call."

Dr. Smith's answering service promised to relay the message, and David returned to Aunt Lillian with some cold wash cloths and a plastic bag full of ice.

"What did he say?"

"I only got the answering service. They promised to deliver the message."

"Did you tell them everything I said?"

"Yes."

"Good."

The telephone rang. David bolted up the steps.

"Hello?"

"Hello? This is Dr. Smith calling for Lillian Biggs. To whom am I speaking?"

"I'm David Andrews, her grandnephew. I'm living with her now."

"Oh, yes. I remember her telling me you would be coming back to live with her. Is Lillian all right? How did she fall?"

"She was starting to go down to the basement, but slipped near the top, and she thinks she's broken her right wrist. I've already applied ice to the swelling."

"I'm glad you're there, David. Does she still refuse to ride in an ambulance?"

"That's right. She wants you to send a taxi."

"I'm coming myself. I should be there in about fifteen minutes. You and I will take her to the hospital for X-rays. Can she walk?"

"I think so. She's sitting up against the basement wall right now."

"Get three aspirin from the medicine cabinet in the bathroom next to the kitchen, and take them to your aunt. They will help to relieve her pain. If she is able to move, bring her up the stairs and let her sit at the kitchen table. Have her lay her wrist on a pillow on the table."

"Yes, sir. Thank you."

David hung up the receiver and turned, shocked to see Aunt Lillian standing at the top of the stairs, her right arm dangling at her side, her admiring gaze studying him.

"Don't stand there looking as if you've seen a ghost. It's only your Aunt Lillian. What did Wayne say?"

"He's on his way over to take us to the hospital."

"Good boy, that lad. Wayne used to be one of my piano students. One of my best, in fact. He could have had a career in music, if he hadn't been captivated by medicine. He's one of the few bright ones ever to return to Midville. Most of the best students graduate, and then you never see them again. Because of that, we have become a little inbred, and outsiders are suspect until they prove themselves."

"Here, Aunt Lillian. Please sit in this chair. I'll be right back."

"Thank you."

David returned in seconds with a fluffy pillow.

"Dr. Smith said you should put your wrist on this."

"Yes, dear."

"He also said you should take these aspirin. Here's some water."

Aunt Lillian obliged.

"Do you want more ice?"

"Please, if you don't mind. I couldn't bring up the other."

"That's okay. I'll get that bag later."

Aunt Lillian shook her head, "Such a stupid accident! It's so frustrating. I'm sorry, David. It's going to be inconvenient for awhile."

David grinned and shrugged, "So ... it will be inconvenient. Big deal. I'll take care of you. I know where the store is, and I already know how to make soup and sandwiches. I only want you to get better."

Lillian studied David's eyes.

"I know you do, dear. I want to get better, too, and as soon as possible. Each of us is the only family the other has and we need to stick together. I can't guarantee anything, but I am nearly seventy and in reasonably good health, so, God willing, I hope to be around when you graduate from college, which is at least seven or eight years from now, should you *choose* to go to college. Have you given any thought as to what you'd like to do?"

"I've thought about lots of things, but I don't really know yet."

"That's well and good. No rush. Lots of people change careers throughout life. The most important thing is to like what you do. Now Wayne Smith is a good example of someone who enjoys what he does."

"How can you tell?"

"Because he radiates an inner peace and harmony. He's a born healer. I saw that even before he did. He is what the French would call *entier*."

"*Entier?*"

"Yes. It means 'whole, complete, having integrity'. Tell me if you don't notice something like that in his manner when he comes. To be sure, we are all mixtures, and no one is completely *entier*, but some are closer than others."

"Okay, but I'm not really sure what I'm looking for."

"We'll talk about it after we've been to the hospital. But be sure to notice *everything*."

* * * * *

Wearing his stethoscope over his blue scrubs and sporting a beeper at his waist, Dr. Wayne Smith looked no older than a first year resident, a healer who had discovered the fountain of youth.

David met him at the garage door, and felt the immediate power of the physician's confident, dancing blue eyes. His brown brush cut lent the impression of a babyface, yet with a certainty that could move mountains. A cheerfulness and optimism emanated from him. Handing David his bag as he entered the garage, he asked, "Where is she?"

"In the kitchen," answered David. "She walked upstairs by herself when I was talking to you, and I've got her wrist on a pillow."

"You've done very well."

Entering the kitchen, Dr. Smith looked at Lillian, raised the index finger of his right hand, and scolded, "You're too young to be flinging yourself down the stairs. Leave that to attention-getters like the late painter Salvador Dali. How's that wrist?"

"The aspirin is beginning to help, but I'm sure my wrist is broken."

"Sorry if this hurts, but I need to feel it."

Lillian grimaced slightly.

"You would have been a first-rate physician. Your diagnosis is absolutely correct, and although it's broken, the good news is that your wrist will heal, and your exquisite piano playing will not suffer. Just don't plan to tickle the ivories before Christmas."

"You should have been a concert pianist; that way, you could have tickled them for me."

Their eyes met in silent laughter.

"We will keep your wrist on this pillow until we get to the hospital for X-rays."

"Thank you for taking us, Wayne," said Lillian.

"I was just getting ready to attend my daily rounds when David's call came through. You have impeccable timing."

"How long do you think it will take for my wrist to heal?"

"I want to see the X-rays before I commit."

"How about worse case scenario?"

"Lillian, my dear. You are intrepid, come what may. We will hope that the break is nothing more than a compression fracture, which would mean you will probably be able to do most things by early September."

"Early September!"

"Yes. Early September, and that is *only if you are good,* and do what I say, and most especially *whether or not David gives me a good report.* As of now, David and I are in cahoots with each other."

"Stop forming alliances! A good report!" sighed Aunt Lillian.

* * * * *

The emergency room had no patients waiting. Dr. Smith wrote the necessary orders for Lillian's X-rays and left to make his rounds. The nurse admitted Lillian and asked her and David to wait until called.

"I like him," said David. "He seems to know what he's doing."

"Yes. He's very focused," said Aunt Lillian. "What else did you notice?"

"When I answered the door, he looked much younger than I had expected, yet somehow I knew everything would be all right."

"Yes. One could drown in those rather disarming, blue eyes."

"Drown?"

"Another way of saying that Dr. Wayne Smith is *entier.*"

"Aunt Lillian, are many people *entier*?"

A silence followed. Aunt Lillian sighed.

"David, I believe," she answered, "that we are all *entier* to a certain degree. We are all striving to be *entier,* and because it is a journey rather than a destination, no one ever completely arrives. The human condition is our common bond, but each of our journeys is quite unique."

"What is the opposite of *entier*?"

"In French, it would be *brisé,* which means broken."

"Broken?"

22

"Yes. Like my wrist. Incomplete. Lacking."

"Lacking what?"

"I suppose it varies with the person. But you will notice, if you begin to look for it. Sometimes it appears as an absence of inner peace or inner harmony."

"How can you see something like that?"

"At first it is difficult, and one is frequently wrong. What is required first is for the intuition to discern the real individual beneath the surfaces and façades. Often what, at first, passes for *entier* is little more than compensation."

"Compensation?"

"Yes. You sensed a certainty in Wayne, didn't you? A firmness? A resolve? A strength that was quietly connected to an inner harmony?"

"I didn't sense all of that, but he certainly seemed confident about what he was doing."

"Well, to complicate our search for *entier*, I must warn you that I have found, in my own experience of people, that overt strength of personality is more often *brisé* than *entier*. Some people need to present themselves as being very sure about something because they, in truth, are not very sure at all. We live in a world where the bluster of leadership initiative is highly prized. Most people feel more secure in the presence of someone who *seems* to be very sure."

"And that person may not be sure at all?"

"Yes. It all depends on the attending signs, like the presence of the inner harmony we talked about. Sadly enough, appearances can be deceiving, and their unexpected convolutions throw us into muddles where it is hard to see clearly."

"I wish life weren't so complicated."

"Me, too. Part of the price we pay for living in society is finding ourselves embroiled in a muddle that is swirling with mistaken appearances. Unwittingly, we call things by their wrong names. For example, I believe we live in a society where gentleness is often mistaken for weakness. Gentleness and weakness are not the same thing, and to confuse one for the other bespeaks a blindness that comes from strutting and blustering about as if we knew everything and were very, very sure of ourselves."

"Aunt Lillian, for me, this is a whole new way of seeing things."

"Yes, David. But you have eyes to see such things. This tends to be a provincial community, unaccepting of new ideas and newcomers. I sometimes fear you may find yourself an outsider when school begins."

Lillian was called in for X-rays. David insisted on accompanying her. The injury proved to be a compression fracture, and Lillian was outfitted with a fiberglass cast so that she could shower with ease.

* * * * *

David went outside to watch for the taxi. Dr. Smith had returned.

"Now, Lillian," Dr. Smith cautioned, "you need to let David do most of what needs to be done. He's very competent. It's fortunate he's here, although its terribly sad how he lost his parents. How is he managing?"

"Fairly well, although we do share some teary moments. Perhaps now that David is needed, he may begin to focus outward. That will certainly help some."

"It wouldn't surprise me if you planned this accident."

"Wayne! How could you even suggest such a thing?"

"As long as I have known you, you have always had the good of others foremost in your heart."

"But certainly not at such personal expense, my dear. No, this is merely an instance of potential good coming out of adversity."

"Do you promise to be a good patient?"

Lillian nodded.

"Then I will look in on you once a week. If you need anything more for the pain, call me."

* * * * *

David was rinsing the lunch dishes. The afternoon was lazy and humid; thundershowers had been predicted, but had not yet arrived to purge the oppressive air of its moisture. Aunt Lillian was sitting hunched over the kitchen table, her brow furrowed. Sighing, she said, "David, I hate being an invalid. I must ask you to go to the grocery store again. I'm sorry."

"That's okay," said David, as he finished rinsing the dishes. "It's only up through the field, past the Methodist Church. It won't take me more than twenty minutes."

"Well, it would be impossible to push a cart through that field and there is the hill by the fellowship hall, so I'm afraid we're confined to random small trips rather than our normal weekly shopping."

"Where's the list?"

"Here. I find that we are fresh out of ginger tea. I also forgot to look before you went this morning to see if we needed more ice cream." Aunt Lillian smiled at David, adding, "Let's not forget your double chocolate ice cream. And let's pick up three or four of those extra special dark chocolate bars. Two liters of ginger ale for me, please. Is that too much?"

"No way. We should call it our special treats trip."

"When you are gone I will select a book for you to read to me after you get back. Find me in the library. I can't think of a better way to pass a sultry summer afternoon. The floor fan will prove a great comfort to us."

* * * * *

David returned in half an hour and put away the groceries, calling out from the kitchen, "Aunt Lillian, how about a nice cool glass of ginger ale?"

"I'd love it, dear. Thank you."

"Coming up," returned David.

The cold wet glasses felt good to his hands. He took them with two coasters into the library, placing one on the table next to the easy chair where Aunt Lillian was reclining, fanning herself with a book that had a red, white, and blue cover.

"David, I have been thinking about the quote you recently shared at breakfast, and I have found a book that tells us about greatness and truth, or more specifically one that tells us about some of our country's statesmen who had the courage to make brave choices. It's called *Profiles in Courage*. Have you ever read it?"

David shook his head.

"It was written by the thirty-fifth president of the United States."

"Wow! By JFK!"

"Yes, when he was still a senator. Let's see how far we can get with it this weekend. It's much too hot to go to church, so we may now choose our preferred reclusion."

David loved the way Aunt Lillian played with words. He nodded, reached for the book, and opened it eagerly.

"David, before you begin, let me suggest that this book may help us to understand the Horace Mann quote we discussed with last week, *If any man seeks for greatness, let him forget greatness and ask for truth, and he will find both.*"

David nodded again and began to read, *"THIS IS A BOOK about the most admirable of human virtues—courage. 'Grace under pressure,' Ernest Hemingway defined it. And these are the stories of the pressures experienced by eight United States Senators and the grace with which they*

endured them—the risks to their careers, the unpopularity of their courses,
the defamation of their characters, and sometimes, but sadly only sometimes,
the vindication of their reputations and their principles."

* * * * *

Thunderstorms descended Saturday night, releasing the humidity, and Sunday proved a much more comfortable day to read. They finished the book Sunday afternoon, and as David closed the volume with obvious admiration and approval, Aunt Lillian asked, "Of these eight senators, whom did you most admire, David?" A gentle August breeze stirred the air and a bumblebee bumbled against the screen.

After reflecting, David said, "I liked them all because they stood up for what they believed in even though most people were against them. And they were willing to risk their careers and fortunes for the truth as they saw it. They weren't afraid to make their opinions known, even though it put them at odds with the crowd."

"Yes, the pressure to go along with the crowd. There is a lot of talk about peer pressure in the middle school and high school, but the pressure to conform can be found at all levels and ages. I have always admired Walter Lippman's celebrated quote, 'Where all think alike, no one thinks at all,' or something very much like that," observed Aunt Lillian.

"These senators weren't afraid to go against the crowd, were they?"

"No. They prized truth and integrity more than popularity."

David closed his marble green eyes in contemplation.

"Yes," he said to himself. Opening his eyes, he looked at Aunt Lillian, declaring, "For me, it was George Norris, the Senator from Nebraska who dared to stop Speaker Cannon, the one they called the Czar."

"Why is Senator Norris your favorite?"

"Because of the way he did things. In a quiet, unassuming way, he worked against a kind of tyranny."

"Tyranny?"

"Speaker Cannon had absolute power, Aunt Lillian. That's not right. No one should have so much power. But Mr. Norris also cared about the Speaker as an individual person and voted against the Speaker's offer to resign. I liked that a lot. It showed that George Norris had a good heart.

"And when he thought he might be able to prevent us from going to war, he didn't like the filibuster, but he supported it. But then President Wilson called Congress back into session, and Norris' group failed, and everyone who knew him didn't want to talk to him. In fact, no one had the guts to chair the big meeting Norris called in Lincoln. Over three thousand people attended that meeting! George Norris walked in, took the platform and said, 'I have come to tell you the truth.' I was so glad when all those people applauded him. I also admired the way Norris stood up for Al Smith, saying that the real issues were about power and farm relief, rather than Al Smith's religion or his stand on prohibition."

"Would you say that Mr. Norris was *entier*?"

"Definitely!"

That night, as David fell asleep, he thought about the life of Senator George Norris and prayed that he would have the courage to meet such moments of decision, should any ever come his way.

Chapter Three
Old Kids, New Kids

When David woke he felt a soothing, fresh breeze blowing through the window of his bedroom. A vestige of his recurrent dream still haunted his consciousness. He remembered watching his parents as they pulled out of the IGA parking lot in the heavy snow squall just as a large, dark truck began to run the stop sign. This time there had been a faintest glimpse of someone riding in the truck's cab. David had tried, in vain, to repress this dream, although it intruded now less frequently, even as it afforded him new impressions of his imagined version of his parents' deaths. This new, vague detail of someone's face, apparently a passenger, was eerily disconcerting, for the real driver had been killed, and was riding alone in the cab.

THE LAST THURSDAY OF AUGUST was a near perfect summer day. Eighty degree sunshine radiated everywhere as a gentle breeze played through the trees, causing occasional leaves to break off and meander to the earth. David was returning home from the grocery store, and had come to love this field through which he walked almost every day. The path, worn from frequent pedestrian traffic, wove its way through what had now become tall yellow grass. The planks of wood straddling the small brook had survived the onslaughts of spring and summer rains in their dogged determination to serve walkers. Butterflies lilted above the field.

As he descended the hill that lay between the store and the Methodist Church parking lot, David noticed that there were three boys standing near the brook at the opposite end of the field. They appeared to be waiting, but for what?

As he approached them, he got the uneasy feeling that they were waiting for him. They were, in fact, blocking the path that led to the planks of wood that afforded walkers safe passage over the brook. The stockiest boy was broad shouldered, of medium height, wore grubby clothes, and had curly black hair. His eyes smoldered with hostility and his pug nose lent a decidedly canine flavor to his appearance. He had a small scar near his left ear and a bruise on his neck.

"Ain't you the new kid livin' with that old dame over in the green house on Biggs Street, just over there?" It was clear he spoke, and perhaps even thought, for his two companions, the slightly taller one with slicked back black hair and a weak chin, the other about the same size as the leader, but lankier and with piercing blue eyes and a pony tail of ratty blond hair that strung down over his shoulders.

David took a breath, answering, "Yes, but she's not an old dame. She's my great aunt, if it's any of *your* business."

"Hey, guys, Mr. Freckles Redhead here has a little more spunk than we thought," said the leader, grinning at his friends. "Maybe he's lookin' for trouble."

—Definitely *brisé*, thought David, clearing his throat, "I'm *not* looking for trouble."

"What grade you goin' into?" asked the leader.

"Eighth grade."

"Well, me and my gang will be in the ninth grade, but you look more like a seventh grade runt to me."

David felt an empty pit forming in his stomach, as he answered, "What's it to you?"

The leader grabbed David by the collar of his shirt, saying, "Don't give me no wise stuff. What's it to me? Let me tell ya somethin', Freckles. THIS is OUR field, where we chill when we ain't in school, and we ain't takin' no likin' to the way you've been burnin' up the path five, maybe six times a week. The field is named for me. It's called the BOBBY PERKINS field, and I ain't gonna permit any little runts crossin' it. Say, maybe it's time for us to start chargin' you for usin' our field. What's in the bag?"

Bobby released David's collar and peered into the bag.

"Nothing for you," said David.

"Oh, yeah? Guys, look, here's a big Hershey bar. That's gonna be our pay today, Freckles," said Bobby as he grabbed the bar and turned to go.

"No!" cried David, reaching for the bar.

"Tough runt, eh?" said Bobby, turning back to face David. "Here's a wee sample of what you'll get if you dare tell on us!"

Bobby's fist connected with a thump against David's nose. David reeled back as he felt a warm splatter and knew he was bleeding. Then someone shoved him off balance and into the mud by the brook. The bag of groceries fell next to the planks.

As David looked up at the blue sky, he could hear the mocking retreat of his attackers. He saw blood all over his shirt and his nose was still bleeding and stinging. He picked up the groceries and put them in the torn bag and limped home. —Fortunately, he thought, —it's only a short way.

Aunt Lillian looked up in disbelief as David stumbled into the kitchen.

"David! Good Lord! What's happened? Are you all right?"

"I think so," he panted, out of breath.

"Here, come over to the sink. I'll fetch some towels to get that blood off. Is your nose still bleeding?"

"A little."

* * * * *

31

Max nuzzled into David's lap as David, now sitting at the kitchen table, described his attackers, as best he could remember them, to Aunt Lillian.

"That mean bully!" Aunt Lillian grimaced. "Bobby Perkins has quite a reputation for trouble in this town, and I can't say much for the ones who run after him. They've been a constant problem. Last Halloween they smashed pumpkins all around town, and even spray-painted some street signs. Bobby's father owns a run-down garage over on East Hatfield Street. He used to have a lot of business, but his work got rather slipshod, so people stopped taking their cars to him. I'm going to call him right now."

"Bobby said he'd get even if I told anyone."

Aunt Lillian studied David, who now held a washcloth over his nose.

"Do you mean you *don't* want me to call?"

"Well, not exactly. I just don't want to get beat up again."

"David, we can't be intimidated by threats. Think of the senators we just read about."

"Yeah. But they didn't have to worry about getting punched it the nose."

"All punches are not physical, David. The worst, in fact, are not physical."

David sat looking at the bloodstained grocery bag.

"Okay," he consented.

Aunt Lillian returned looking a little grim. "They apparently don't have a telephone, so I've called the police department to take this note over to Mr. Perkins."

"Isn't that a little drastic?" asked David.

"Not at all. The Chief used to be one of my students."

* * * * *

The next morning Aunt Lillian gave David the shopping list, saying, "Why don't you take Max with you? Tie his leash to the bicycle rack outside the store when you're getting groceries."

"That's a brilliant suggestion, Aunt Lillian. Thank you."

As they strode up through the field, David felt a knot in his stomach as he saw Bobby Perkins and his two friends running to head them off before they reached the hill by the Methodist Church's fellowship hall.

"Get ready," he warned Max.

The boys blocked the path.

Bobby's left eye was very black and puffy. Glaring daggers at David, he chided, "So Freckles is a little low down ratter!"

Max gave a low growl.

Bobby noticed Max for the first time. "So you hauled along a little protection. It ain't gonna do ya no good. Just remember that!"

The boys ran off into the trees.

David and Max continued up the hill, through the parking lot, to the store.

"Here Max, stay here for a little bit. I won't be long."

David was a careful shopper. He checked the list to see that he was buying exactly what Aunt Lillian had requested, making sure he was getting the coupon items. Although he only bought tea, he walked by the coffee grinder because he loved the smell. Occasionally, he would buy something not on the list, such as gum, and on the next list it would magically appear. Aunt Lillian was very thorough.

David had gotten the tea, lettuce, carrots, chicken, tomato puree, and two large Hershey candy bars and was rounding a very tall display of fruit juice cans when he heard a woman shriek, "A snake! A snake!" Suddenly the pyramid of cans cascaded toward him, several hitting his right knee, with others tumbling on the floor, making a loud racket.

33

"What's going on there?" called a clerk, advancing from the meat counter.

"I was just coming round the corner and I heard a woman yell 'A snake, a snake!' and then these cans tumbled down," replied David.

The manager, a rotund man with a florid face, arrived. "I'm Mr. Cassidy, the manager. Do you have anything to do with those three boys who just ran out of the store?"

"No, sir," said David. "I'm shopping by myself."

"Are you *sure?*"

"Yes, sir."

The manager glared at the clerk. "They apparently threw a rubber snake in front of Mrs. Weston. Larry said he thought one of them may have been lurking in this aisle, and maybe that explains these all these cans getting pushed over."

"Can you tell me anything more?" asked Mr. Cassidy.

David gulped. He didn't want to get beaten up again, but he also knew he would not be telling the whole truth if he said, 'No.'

"Those three boys beat me up yesterday, sir," he said, "and they just met me again when I was coming here from across the field. My dog, Max, growled at them, and they said they were still going to get me. I bet they shoved the cans over."

Mr. Cassidy's face clouded. "Do you know any of their names?"

"Only the leader, Bobby Perkins."

"Is he that broad-shouldered kid with curly black hair?"

"Yes. I'm sorry. I didn't know they would follow me in here and cause trouble."

"Do you know Bobby's father's name?"

"Only that he runs a garage over on West Hatfield Street."

"That would be Edward Perkins. I hope I don't get you in any more trouble, but I'm going to call the police and lodge a complaint."

"That's okay with me," said David, adding, "I'll help pick up these cans."

"No. You go along home. Larry, you set them up again."

While checking out, David was momentarily afraid the boys might have done something to Max, but he was relieved to find his Husky-Collie wagging his tail and prancing in place. David untied him and they enjoyed an uneventful walk home.

* * * * *

David was lying in bed reading when Aunt Lillian gently knocked on his door.

"Come in."

Aunt Lillian entered, royally clad in her blue satin nightgown and bedslippers. She smiled in David's direction, approached the bed and sat on its corner.

"David, I know it's late. In fact, it's almost midnight. I wouldn't have bothered you, but I was going down to the kitchen for some warm milk when I noticed your light on. I'm afraid I couldn't sleep for worry over that bully Bobby Perkins."

"That's okay. I'm not afraid of Bobby Perkins."

"I know that, but I also know that you believe in non-violence, and I'm afraid that makes you especially vulnerable to bullies."

"*Mine* is a moral victory."

"Yes, but a moral victory doesn't keep you from getting your nose bloodied or your teeth knocked out. I know you don't believe in an eye for an eye, a tooth for a tooth, but that doesn't stop mean-spirited people who insist on punching those who refuse to fight."

"I hate fighting and I'll avoid it if I can. I don't think there's any real solution in trying to batter someone who's trying to batter you. Maybe I can find a way to get to know Bobby Perkins, although I

35

honestly don't want to. Sometimes, though, when people who don't like each other get better acquainted, they make peace."

"A bully is really a coward underneath, David," sighed Aunt Lillian.

"I know. I don't back down from them either, but I usually pay with a punched in nose or a black eye."

"Did this happen much at your other school?"

"No. I was established there. It happened a little bit a long time ago when I was in the third grade, but that was pretty trivial compared to this."

"David, I'm worried about you."

"Don't worry. I won't be the goat. I promise."

"Do you want me to call the middle school principal? He's fairly new there, since last year I think. A word or two to him might be helpful."

"No, thanks, Aunt Lillian. Let's see what happens. I'm in the eighth grade; Bobby and his friends are in ninth. I probably won't see very much of them."

"I hope so. I truly hope so," said Aunt Lillian bending down to kiss David's forehead.

* * * * *

David slept in until nine the next day. He showered and dressed and moseyed downstairs. Aunt Lillian was reading the morning paper and sipping some grapefruit juice.

"Good morning, David," she smiled.

"Morning. I always make it a point to sleep late on Labor Day. Second to last chance before the end. With school starting Wednesday, I'll have to adapt to a new schedule," sighed David.

"Yes, you'll have to stop reading by nine or ten, instead of twelve or one, or is it two?" observed Aunt Lillian. "Here, help yourself to the paper during breakfast. I'm going to get our flag. Will you please help me put it up later?"

"Sure. Glad to," said David.

* * * * *

After breakfast, David got out the stepstool and positioned the flag in the eagle mount to the right of the front door.

"There! That's wonderful!" cheered Aunt Lillian. "Come inside now. I have a surprise for you."

They entered the front hallway and walked to the library. A cool breeze blew through the open windows. Aunt Lillian seated herself in her recliner as David sat in the leather swivel chair.

Aunt Lillian looked as if she were straining not to tell a secret.

"David," she began, "here's my surprise." She handed David an advertisement flyer which read: 'Midville Village Inn—Labor Day Ham Dinner—ALL YOU CAN EAT!'

"Wow!" exclaimed David.

"I've got reservations for us at five o'clock. George and Evelyn Dewey will come here about four o'clock for some lemonade and then take us to the Village Inn. The food is generally very good."

"That's wonderful," said David.

"It's *my* treat to you for having been so wonderful to me during my illness, and also my special thank you to George for the wonderful job he did with your, I mean our, bookshelves."

"You're still not completely better yet," admonished David.

"You sound just like Wayne Smith, David. Don't try to wrap me in cotton wool."

"Okay. Deal," said David as he studied the elegant typeface on the announcement. "Is this a formal restaurant?"

37

"Yes. We'll have to dress up. But won't that be fun? I also propose that we go very lightly on lunch so we get our full money's worth."

"It isn't *very* expensive, is it?" David asked cautiously.

"No. For what you get, it's very reasonable. I'm sorry we haven't gone there for dinner before now, but better late that never. By the way, we forgot to exchange our quotes for the day. What's yours?"

David closed his eyes for a few seconds. "From Ralph Cudworth, an English clergyman: 'Truth and love are two of the most powerful things in the world, and when they both go together they cannot easily be withstood.'"

"David, that's beautiful ... just marvelous," said Aunt Lillian, nodding her head.

"What's yours?"

Aunt Lillian laughed. "I'm afraid I was so busy worrying about you and that bully Bobby Perkins that I forgot to pick one. I owe you one."

"Okay, but I want it before we go to dinner," laughed David.

Chapter Four
First Day at School

DAVID PAUSED TO CONSIDER the enormous three story, rectangular, yellow brick building that stood before him. He had vaguely noticed it in passing several times before today, but now he would enter its doors and become a member of its student body. A moderately tall brick smokestack from the building's center reflected the early morning sunlight, and lent the impression that this ancient pile of brick and glass had once been a passenger liner that had run aground, with time gradually converting its steel casings into brick and its portholes into large windows that now displayed antiquated green shades. The school faced onto Proctor Street, across which there lay an athletic field including a track, two baseball diamonds, and a neglected playground. The building's sheer size and early Depression architecture suggested that it might support a Draconian faculty, but David hoped otherwise. Upon entering the building, David smelled the faintest hint of fresh paint. The brick stairwells had also been mopped with some sort of cleaning fluid or turpentine, and in his homeroom the familiar smell of chalk dust and sharpened pencils mixed with the faint odor of musty books. David had resolved the evening before, during his prayers, that he would look for the *entier* in every person he met on this first day of school. He knew there would also be the *brisé* part as well, for everyone, without exception, was a mixture of the two; however, some people, like Aunt Lillian and Dr. Smith, seemed to radiate a lot more *entier* than *brisé*.

David reported to Homeroom 302. Mrs. Donovan, a stern, full-faced woman in her mid thirties, sat at a desk surrounded by students.

"Please, class," she commanded, "tell me your names one at a time and I will show you your place on my chart."

"And who are you?" she inquired.

"David Andrews."

"Let me see, Andrews, Andrews, Andrews ... oh, yes, here you are right in the front row, second seat from the door. You will be in charge of turning off the lights and shutting the windows in the event of a fire drill. You will also take the lunch count to the office on your way to your first period class, since you're going in that direction anyway. Let me see. Oh, yes, I have also assigned you to be in charge of conducting any kind of survey that may be required. Sometimes the student council canvasses us to assess interest for some activity or other."

"What do you teach?"

"Math. Are you good in math?"

"Sort of."

"What do you mean 'Sort of'?"

"Well, I can do it if I put my mind to it, but I'd much rather be reading. I find stories a lot more interesting. I find math a little on the dry side."

"I see. Well, if you should ever take math with me, we'll have to see what we can do to make it a little more palatable."

"Thank you."

"You must be new to Midville?"

"I am. How did you know?"

"Most students I've taught here do not like to read. They like math even less. But you, you seem unusually focused."

"Perhaps it comes from reading a lot," David smiled.

Mrs. Donovan shrugged, saying very tentatively, "Perhaps ... "

After students had found their assigned seats, Mrs. Donovan announced, "Welcome to Homeroom 302. I hope you like this room as much as I do. In the spring we can smell the blossoms of the large apple tree over in the park. It is also a sunny room, and I like a lot of light. Our homeroom period has been extended this morning so that we can fill out a number of important records. Let me ask David Andrews to pass out these green medical forms."

The required forms were distributed, completed, and collected. David arranged them in order and placed them on Ms. Donovan's desk. She was hard at work on some sort of report herself, and David sat down at his desk. The other students were chatting with the excitement that the first day of school brings, and all of them obviously had known each other from the year before. No one made an effort to help David feel welcome. He sat at his desk, looking at his schedule and a small school map that had been sent to him in the mail. His first class was American history with a Mr. Thatcher Pennythorpe.

"Attention, all students and faculty," interrupted a deep voice on the public address system, "This is Mr. Ferlinghausen, your principal. The passing bells are not synchronized to accommodate our extended homeroom period today, so we will announce from the office when it is time to pass to each class. On behalf of the faculty and staff of Midville Middle School, I want to welcome all students to what I am sure will be a splendid school year. Most especially, I want to welcome our new students and to remind them that we have a clockwise traffic pattern when we pass to classes and that the two east stairwells are reserved for upward traffic only, just as the two west stairwells accommodate traffic that is moving to lower floors. You will find reminder arrows near each stairwell entrance. Please do not travel against the normal traffic pattern. I also invite all new students to take a moment this week to drop by my office, or to stop me in the hallway, to say hello and to introduce themselves. You may now pass to your first period classes."

David looked at his schedule and map as students poured out of the homeroom. Mr. Pennythorpe's classroom was number 102 which was adjacent to the office. He reminded himself to drop off the lunch count at the office.

The corridors were flooded with students. David realized from the map that he would have to descend at one of the first two stairwells and then travel the rectangle on the first floor in order to pass the office, since ascending stairwells lay on the side of the building opposite from his homeroom.

The corridor walls had been freshly painted with a myriad of pastel colors, brightening the halls considerably. Wondering if time-honored institutional green had ever been the previous color, David wasted no time in taking the first east stairwell down to the first floor and then advanced around the rectangle, through double doors, past a sunken basketball court called 'The Girls' Gym', and then around by a main lobby entrance to leave the lunch count at the office.

Entering the office, David saw a tall, heavy-set man wearing black glasses that matched the black fringe of hair surrounding a shiny bald head. He was dressed in a dark blue suit and wore a red and green tie over a yellow shirt.

—Only the principal would dare dress like this, thought David, who had decided to take the bull, or rather the Ferlinghausen, by the horns. Stepping up to the counter, David thrust his hand out, saying, "Hi. I'm David Andrews, one of the new students you asked to say hello. I assume you're Mr. Ferlinghausen."

A genial smile emerged on the principal's patrician face. "Why yes, thank you. I have decided to tell all the new students this year that I, myself, was new here only a year ago, and that there *is* life after a few months of getting to know people."

"Thanks. I needed to hear that. I just sat through a lonely homeroom period."

"Well, at least you and I know each other. So, you've made at least one new friend today. Where do you come from?"

"I used to live up along Long Lake, but my parents were killed in a car accident in January. They had made arrangements for me to move here to Midville to live with my Aunt Lillian if anything ever happened to them. So ... here I am."

Mr. Ferlinghausen's face clouded with sadness, his eyes visibly moist. "David, isn't it?"

"Yes, sir."

"David, I'm very sorry. I lost my father when I was about your age. I can't even imagine what it's like to lose both parents."

"Pretty awful," said David.

"Yes. A nightmare."

"Well, I'd better go or I'll be late."

"Drop by any time, David. What grade are you in?"

"Eighth."

"If you ever need anything, just stop by. Have a good first day."

"You, too, sir. Thank you."

David strode twelve paces, advancing into room 102. A small man with a bald head and fringe of white hair that draped to his neck was writing on the chalkboard. His hands were gnarled, his profile wizened, and to all appearances it would have seemed a gnome had invaded the classroom. He wore dark trousers, a white shirt, and a maroon bow tie. A maroon blazer hung over the chair beside the teacher's desk. On the chalkboard he had written: HISTORY 8 — Period 1 — The United

States — Mr. Pennythorpe, your guide. All Seekers of Truth welcome on this journey.

—Wow! David thought. —Mr. Pennythorpe is posing some of the same ideas Aunt Lillian and I are talking about.

Mr. Pennythorpe turned to the class. He looked incredibly ancient and fragile, but still he smiled, and announced in a mellow, rich voice, "Good morning, students. My name is Pennythorpe, and I will be your guide through some of the adventures of American history, and there are many amazing things we will discover together. Each of you has a textbook on your desk, a list of course requirements, and an assignment schedule for the first marking period. There is also a seating chart with your names on it. Please take ten seconds to find your proper desk and, at my signal, move to that desk as quickly as possible."

Mr. Pennythorpe looked at his watch, muttering to himself, "Now if this is a *good* class, we can accomplish seat adjustment in twenty-five seconds. GO!"

Students scrambled to their new seats, occasionally colliding with each other and, remarkably, all were in their assigned seats in twenty seconds.

"Twenty seconds!" exclaimed Pennythorpe. "This *is* a most remarkable class indeed! Perhaps it is because it is so early in the morning. What do you say to that, Mr. ... er ... " here he glanced at his seating chart, "... er ... Andrews?"

David responded, "I think we *are* a most remarkable class, Mr. Pennythorpe."

"Right on!" rejoined a voice from the back of the room.

The class laughed, and so did Mr. Pennythorpe. —He can laugh, thought David. —A good sign that there's a lot of *entier* in him.

Mr. Pennythorpe stopped laughing and suddenly looked very sad. Silence fell on the room. Inhaling deeply, Mr. Pennythorpe took out his handkerchief and mopped his hoary brow. Holding its collective breath, the class hoped that this strange, little ancient being who stood before them was not about to take his leave from this earthly environ. Even an unstudied glance would convince most viewers that Pennythorpe had at least a foot, if not a leg and arm, already in the grave. Generally, for most middle school students, daily witness to such a tottering between life and death would prove absolutely thrilling, especially if the subject were to die, but somehow in a few short minutes Pennythorpe had managed to galvanize History 8, Period 1, into something greater than the sum of all its members.

"A glimpse," he whispered, still breathing deeply.

Everyone strained to hear, some even cupping their ears.

"Beg your pardon, sir?" said an attractive girl sitting in the back of the classroom, wearing long brown hair combed into a pony tail.

"A glimpse," repeated Mr. Pennythorpe more forcefully. "We have had, just now, my friends, a glimpse of what we could be together. Something more than your average class—something more profound than rote learning and memorization of facts—something that rarely happens—but ... something wondrously beautiful when it does occur."

The class sat spellbound, listening.

Mr. Pennythorpe retired his handkerchief, moving forward into the middle row of students, everyone's attention hanging on his words.

"A glimpse," he repeated. "My friends, what we could become together is absolutely amazing. But we can't go *anywhere* together unless everyone," and here he looked around again to catch everyone's eye, "*everyone*, I repeat, every single one does his or her part. We will be united by what we read. If we choose not to read, then the common foundation for our dialogue is lost. And it's truly a matter of choosing, not a matter of can or can't, but rather a matter of will or won't. Do you agree?"

The class sat in rapt attention, many nodding their assent. No teacher had ever broached the topic of homework in quite this way.

Mr. Pennythorpe breathed more heavily, continuing, "Some of you agree, but do you *all* agree? Do you, each and every one of you agree? Please tell me—tell me now, so I don't entertain false hopes."

The entire class was nodding its assent.

Mr. Pennythorpe sighed to himself. "Telling me by nodding your heads is a start, but I would like to hear your 'yes' from your very own lips. Can anyone bring himself or herself to say 'yes' to this query —and, mind you, don't dare say it lightly, for much effort and work and travail is involved in this commitment. Do *not* say it lightly, but *only* if you really mean it—I ask you—do we have agreement, do we have an unanimous 'yes'?"

"Yes," said the attractive girl with the long brown pony tail, her braces showing.

"Yes," answered David, repeating, "Yes, yes, yes, yes."

Others began to join the chorus, at first almost a whisper but then growing to a fortissimo—"Yes! Yes! Yes! Yes! Yes!"

Mr. Pennythorpe retrieved his handkerchief and mopped his brow again.

The class looked at him in expectation and he, in turn, looked solemnly at them.

He drew a deep breath and intoned, "So now we have said it, so now we have claimed it, so now we have made it our very own." Closing his eyes, Mr. Pennythorpe folded his hands to his chest.

The class was hanging on his every breath and gesture. Silence fell on the room. It was almost as if the teacher had gone to sleep.

"And having made this glorious commitment," Mr. Pennythorpe slowly whispered, as he suddenly stretched his arms wide as if in praise, and shouted, "I WILL NOT LET YOU DOWN!"

Nearly everyone jumped several inches. It was so unexpected but, at the same time, so clever and dramatic. History class would never be the same again, and no one would ever know quite what to expect from this intense, mysterious, gnome-like entity that most people called 'Mr. Pennythorpe'.

"My home telephone number is at the top of the assignment schedule. If you have any confusion, any misunderstanding, any trouble at all, please call me so that I may offer help. I also hope that you'll rely on each other's strengths, taking turns pulling each other through the hurdles we must scale. Please work together as much as possible to achieve the best understanding that you can of the material you are asked to master. Those readings will serve as our common foundation to the glorious dialogue that we will begin tomorrow. Please write down answers to all questions after each chapter in your History 8 notebook. I will check these from time to time, and you may be asked to read what you have written. Now we historians know better than most people that time is precious, so don't waste a moment, but turn to the chapter assigned for tomorrow and begin reading. Please write your names in your textbooks. I have already recorded your book numbers according to the seating chart. If you have any questions, please feel free to come forward to speak to me. Good luck."

The class immediately settled into its reading assignment.

David wrote his name in his book and turned to the first chapter.

Mr. Pennythorpe sat at his desk, making notes. Several students in turn approached the desk, and were invited to sit down to ask their questions, to which Mr. Pennythorpe responded with interest and enthusiasm.

David felt in Mr. Pennythorpe's bearing a delight and a joy that seemed to transform the learning process. The instructor's enthusiasm seemed to be contagious, and David wondered if this unusual love for reading and learning, so atypical in most classes in most schools, would continue. If it fizzled out, he wondered whether it would cause the frail, retiring Mr. Pennythorpe to fizzle out as well. But intuition suggested to David, that as ancient and frail as Mr. Pennythorpe seemed, that he was actually tougher than nails beneath all appearances. —Definitely *entier*, thought David. —And wonderfully eccentric as well.

Mrs. Dixon, the office secretary, gave the announcement for all classes to pass to second period. David had to trudge up to the third floor to room 308 for Science 8. Bertha Smiley was a woman in her late forties, with unkempt dirty brown hair that strung to each side of her face, which was accentuated by a sharp nose and earnest eyes. David felt uncomfortable when he saw her give an unsympathetic smile to a student who dropped her books.

"Sink or swim," Ms. Smiley intoned, "You all must learn to swim or sink. Life will pass you by if you don't learn to swim—so you will either sink or swim this year in this course." It was hardly the best of beginnings for class and teacher, and the onus of it screamed painfully in David's mind in the wake of the extraordinary overture to learning given by Mr. Pennythorpe. Ms. Smiley's nasal twang did not lend credibility or warmth to her injunctions to the class. In fact, her nasality suggested that if she could possibly torpedo most students' efforts to swim, she would be glad to see them sink. The week's assignments were written on the chalkboard. When Ms. Smiley was asked questions after explaining the curriculum and work involved, she launched into her tirade about sinking or swimming.

"I will keep a daily class record of work performed by you as indicated by your answers *in class* to your homework. If you do not get the problem entirely correct, you lose your plus. This is followed by a check, followed by a check minus, followed by a check minus over a zero, followed by a zero, and last by a zero filled in with dark pencil.

Anyone getting more than three zeros marked in dark pencil will automatically receive a fat 50 for the marking period. You must all learn to sink or swim. *If* you work very, *very* hard — you may be able to swim. If you do not pay attention or do not do the work, you will sink. The lazy *should* sink; the industrious *will* swim."

David couldn't resist raising his hand.

"Yes, young man. Please identify yourself."

"My name is David Andrews. My question is this: what if someone works very, very hard and still can't get the answers?"

Ms. Smiley's face twitched. "I will not hear of that. If any student works, he or she will swim."

"But what if the student is blind to science?" David persisted.

"Blind to science? Then that student is a dumbbell and should consider taking a different course. All of you who have been placed in this class are capable of swimming. The choice is yours. Sink or swim! You must learn to swim, or you will sink."

Ms. Smiley's nasality had by this time caused most of the class to commence gritting their teeth, for which presumably their respective dentists would be happy. If a poll had been taken, to a person the students would have gladly escorted Ms. Smiley to a large cruise ship, namely the *Titanic*, where she herself could learn to sink or swim. But brittle as she was, she rigidly bore the protective mantle of tenure and, thus having herself once learned to swim, had now found a sinecure in which to put young fish through their respective wiggles.

—Definitely *brisé*, thought David, relieved to hear Mrs. Dixon announce that the time had come to pass to third period classes. It was going to be a long year in Science 8.

The next class was Math 8 and that was in room 206, which meant David would have to perambulate the entire rectangle as well as descend one floor.

Upon entering the room, he saw a seating chart meticulously crafted and lettered on a large piece of tag board. Mr. Wendel Paxton, a dapper middle-aged man dressed in gray trousers, light blue shirt, yellow sweater, and aquamarine bow tie, sat on a stool in front of a podium, making notes. What caught David's attention as he located his assigned seat was how very well-groomed Mr. Paxton looked. A fastidious cat could not have done better. Mr. Paxton's black hair was severely parted and tightly combed back. A small moustache, with what must have been an exact number of hairs on each side, accentuated a noble nose, much like a Senator of ancient Rome. Mr. Paxton's blue eyes smoldered with quiet worry. The desk in front of him was immaculate. The chalk in the trays were all of the same length. The window shades were pulled to exactly the same middle level on each of the four windows. David suddenly had the impression that he had not so much entered Math 8, as he had been thrust into an entirely conforming world of order and exactitude, leaving no room for mystery, or paradox, or even imagination.

—Feels like climbing into a coffin, David thought to himself, regarding Mr. Paxton and considering what a charming waxworks corpse he would make.

When Mrs. Dixon finally announced that classes should pass, David breathed deeply as he left the room, feeling that he had just been released from a subtle kind of straight-jacket.

David's schedule called for a period 4 study hall that alternated with gym class. The sixty students who were assigned to room 216 were noisily speculating who would serve as their study hall monitor. David's schedule had merely listed STAFF under the faculty appointment column, and it was to his great surprise and delight that none other than Mr. Pennythorpe entered the room carrying a large stack of books.

A student followed, carrying an equally large stack of books and, at Mr. Pennythorpe's direction, placed them on the teacher's desk.

Mr. Pennythorpe stepped forward and clapped his hands with experienced authority. A hush fell over the room. "My name is Thatcher Pennythorpe and I teach history here at Midville Middle School. I have only been here since last spring, but I recognize many of you and I am glad to have you in my study hall. I think we understand each other well enough to know that this is an ideal opportunity for you to do your homework. Mr. Lowery informs me that the library will be open daily, in about a week's time, for the first twenty-five students who sign up. Mr. Henry is a ninth grader who is assisting me today; he will call out names for your assigned seating chart. A copy of this seating chart will also be posted on the bulletin board above the pencil sharpener and beneath the fire drill plan. Now if you have any problems, that's what I'm here for. I daresay I will try to help you or, at least, find someone else who can, if you are having difficulty with one of your subjects. We're all here to learn and, quite honestly, I confess that I learn more from you young people than you learn from me. Normally I do not allow social visitation during study hall—we *all* have work to do. But today *is* the first day of school, and I know you're exploding with enthusiasm for your friends ... so, kindly remember the advice of William Shakespeare: 'The friends that thou hast and their adoption tried, grapple them to thy soul with hooks of steel.' For this first day only, you may visit *quietly* with your neighbors, if you choose to do so. I have much of my own work to do up here, but please do not hesitate to seek me out if I may be of assistance. Now, I will help Mr. Henry start the seating plan."

Mr. Pennythorpe handed the seating plan to Mr. Henry, and looked at David. "The first student to be seated in the front row here by the door is Mr. David Andrews, an eighth grader who is new to our school. Mr. Andrews, please come forward and take your seat."

David promptly obeyed. Student Henry then began to call names, following Mr. Pennythorpe's example of using Mr. or Ms. before each student's surname. Many students, if they were not relocating themselves, fell into quiet conversations. Others preferred to read or to work on assignments they had already received. David opened up his history text and began reading. When Student Henry finished designating seats, he reported back to Mr. Pennythorpe, who thanked him and motioned for him to have a seat in a chair next the teacher's desk. The hum of quiet conversation continued.

"He's awesome, isn't he?" observed an attractive girl sitting next to David. She was wearing a salmon blouse and a green dress. Her long blond hair was captured in back by a pretty barrette. Her eyes were honest and blue and alive.

"Yeah!" whispered David. "Have you had him before?"

"Last spring he came to substitute for Mrs. Levine, who took maternity leave, but then decided not to come back. He's by far the *best* teacher I've ever had. And just wait. You'll see. Everybody will buckle down and work in this study hall. And he's always wonderful about helping, if you ask him."

"There aren't very many teachers like that!" exclaimed David, thinking of Ms. Smiley and Mr. Paxton.

"And the amazing thing is how interesting he makes history. I never liked it before I had him. It was boring and dull. Somehow, he makes it live."

"He's certainly been around a long time," observed David.

"*I* heard that he knew President Roosevelt."

"Really? Which one?"

"I don't know. Probably whoever was the oldest Roosevelt."

"No way. He couldn't be *that* old."

"Well, just look at him. How old do you think he is?"

"I don't know. I'm not a very good judge of age."

"Well, someone told me he's at least ninety, and they can't make him retire because he was teaching before they even granted teaching certificates, so he falls under some sort of grandfather clause."

"Well, that's really cool, for sure. What's your name?"

"Kim Evans. I'm in the ninth grade. I remember your name is David. And you're new here, aren't you?"

"Yeah. I came to Midville in early July. Do you like it here?"

"I suppose so. I've only lived here for four years ... before my mom and dad broke up. We used to live in Chicago. My dad is an architect. When my parents got divorced, my mom brought me and my sister back here to Midville where she grew up. My grandparents still live here. What brings you here?"

David felt a tightness in his chest. "My parents were killed in an automobile accident. I've come here to live with my Aunt Lillian."

"Oh, I'm so sorry."

"That's okay. I can't bury it forever."

"If there's anything I can do, David, please— "

" —Students may now pass to their fifth period class," interrupted Mrs. Dixon's voice over the loudspeaker.

"Thanks, Kim. See you Friday."

"You have gym, too?"

"Yeah."

"Me too."

David decided he would not stop at his locker before lunch. He soon joined the cafeteria line, which was rapidly growing longer. He would have been in sooner except that a dozen students budged in line and as a result kept the ones behind them waiting even longer. David felt angry at this injustice, but decided not to object on the first day of school.

No matter where you purchase it, school cafeteria food is appallingly poor. The hot dogs were of rubbery texture. The beans were lukewarm and the french fries dry. David found an empty table and sat down. Most of the other students were eating and chatting with their friends.

—I really hate to eat by myself, thought David. He surveyed the cafeteria to see if anyone else was eating alone. Suddenly he noticed a girl reading in a corner. Yes. It was the girl with the long brown hair and glasses from his history class. —Well, here goes, he thought. —Nothing to lose.

Advancing to her table, he placed his tray at the opposite corner of the table. As he sat down, he looked over and greeted her, saying, "We might as well eat alone together."

"I wouldn't come closer if I were you," she warned.

"Why not?"

"I've got the plague."

"Bubonic or pneumonic?"

The girl's crystal blue eyes met David's. Some sort of door had opened because she was smiling, braces and all. Perhaps it was because David had taken her warning in stride.

"Readonic. I love to read mysteries. Can't put them down. That certainly makes me an odd sort around here. Most of our classmates spend their time watching TV or playing videogames or sports. Some play musical instruments. Only a few kids read."

"I *also* suffer from the readonic plague. Guess they'll have to quarantine us together in the library," said David.

"Really? Personally, I'd be just as happy to be excused from classes if I could read all day," the girl brightened. "My name is Lisa Jones. And you're David Andrews."

"Gosh! How did you remember?"

"From the seating chart in History 8. Mr. Pennythorpe believes names are important. He knows the names of practically everybody in the school, and he *never* forgets anything you tell him. And the kids don't give him any guff. There's something different about him. I'm not sure what it is. Somehow it seems he really doesn't belong in middle school, but everyone says he's terrific. I know some kids who never do their homework but who work their butts off for his class."

"A girl in my study hall said she'd heard he knew Roosevelt, although she wasn't sure which one."

"Well, *I* heard that he walked with Lincoln."

David grinned, and Lisa laughed, once again showing her braces.

"Amazing how rumors inflate, isn't it?" he said.

"You mean how rumors *age*, don't you?" Lisa smiled.

"Hey. I've an idea. Since we're both taking History 8 with Mr. Pennythorpe, why don't we become study partners? We could use our lunch hour to help each other through," suggested Lisa.

David bit into the rubbery hot dog, deliberately chewing and trying to swallow. "This hot dog isn't so bad if you put a lot of mustard on it."

"They slice them off the tires of old cars at the junk yard on Route 321, and then they paint them red to fool you," retorted Lisa.

"The food was just as bad in my last school," confided David.

"Where was that?"

"I used to live on a hill overlooking Long Lake, and I went to school in a village near there. It was mostly a summer tourist town."

"Why did you move here?"

David felt the familiar sinking feeling in his stomach. "My parents were killed in an automobile accident in January. I came here to live with my Great Aunt."

Lisa averted her eyes. "I'm really sorry. I wouldn't have asked—"

"No. That's okay. How were you to know? Anyway, I can't forget it happened, although some days I wish I could."

David took another bite of his hot dog, chasing it down with a large gulp of milk.

"Who do you have for your other classes?" asked Lisa.

"I think I started at the top with Mr. Pennythorpe. I got Ms. Smiley for science—"

"Oh, no! Sink-or-Swim Smiley. Almost everyone has to go through that torture."

David laughed, "Do they really called her Sink-or-Swim Smiley?"

"Of course. What else would you call her, except maybe a little brown toad?"

"Lisa, you've got a wicked streak."

"I'm entering into my adolescent rebellion. It's is my solemn obligation to rebel."

"Usually that rebellion starts at home against the parents," reproved David.

"Well, I can't rebel at home. It would kill my parents. They own a little restaurant just near the village limits, and they each work sixty hours a week. They never managed to graduate from high school, and they desperately want me to go to college. And I really want to. But I feel so much pressure from them. They don't like to see me reading mysteries, and nothing makes them happier than to see me pick up an encyclopedia. They don't realize that mysteries can broaden one's experience, too. Anyway, I try to read my mysteries away from home. I hate to see the way they worry with their eyes."

"They only want you to have more advantages than they had," said David.

"I know, but it still can be pretty hard. Who else do you have?"

"Mr. Paxton for Math."

"Picture-Proof Paxton."

"Do you have names for all of the faculty?"

"Most of them. Some of these nicknames are used by a lot of the students, that is," Lisa cautioned, "when the faculty aren't there. Another one is Dandy-Pandy. That's for Mr. Dandy, our guidance counselor. When he used to visit the elementary classes, he would come in and introduce himself by saying, 'Hi, my name is Dandy. It rhymes with candy.' He's a funny little man. I've also made up a few nicknames of my own. 'Picture-Proof Paxton' is mine, and no one else's, although I'll let you share it, if you like."

"Why Picture-Proof?"

"Did you notice how he ties his tie and parts his hair?" Lisa laughed to herself, continuing, "It's just a little *too* perfect. You'll notice it in the painful precision of his enunciation and language, too, as well as how he letters on the board. Everything has to be *absolutely* perfect."

David reflected for a moment. "It's almost as if he's on stage."

"Yes! That's it. It's as if a movie camera were following and recording his every word and action."

"Each to his own," said David.

"But for the grace of God," nodded Lisa. "Who else do you have?"

"I lucked out by getting Mr. Pennythorpe for study hall. I still have to report to computer lab, and then to English. I have 'Staff' for computer lab and Mrs. Riley for English."

"Retiring Riley," sighed Lisa.

"Why retiring Riley?" inquired David.

"She announces her retirement each year on the first day of school, but then she comes back each September."

"Probably wishes she *could* retire."

"Probably. She's not too bad, if you don't get on the wrong side of her."

"Wrong side?"

"Yeah. I've heard if you mouth off or throw spit wads, you'll be staying after for weeks. She's one of the old school types, and getting older each year."

"Yes. But I agree with that. Don't you?"

"Yes, I do. A lot students try to get away with murder. It's a game. No wonder she wants to retire. Maybe she hopes her announcement will make them take pity on her."

"Maybe. I'll let you know tomorrow if she does it."

"She will. Trust me. Or, at least, that's what I've heard."

"Do you bring your lunch every day?"

"Remember, my parents run a restaurant. Leftovers are great compared to Midville cafeteria fare. But I still have to wait in line to get milk."

"Maybe I'll pack a lunch, too, to save going through line."

"You'll still need to get milk—the same way I do."

"That's right. Doesn't seem fair to stand and wait just for milk. I saw half a dozen students budging in line today. That really burns me."

"What are you going to do? Call the local TV station to do an exposé on it?" asked Lisa.

"I wish I could," sighed David, "It just isn't right."

"Guess you're stuck," commiserated Lisa.

"Wait, I've got a great idea. I'm going to write an article for the school paper," brightened David.

"Don't bother. She won't publish it."

"Who won't?"

"Gertrude Coachman, our published poet."

"Wow! We have a real poet teaching here?"

"Not really. She *thinks* she's a poet. The local paper prints her poems; she probably even talked their poor editor into giving her a free subscription. I really like poetry but, personally, I think her verse stinks. I suppose she must think it's wonderful, though."

"What does she teach?"

"Mostly English 9 classes. Be glad you don't have her. I've heard she's really bad. Would you believe that she used to work in the cafeteria before she got her teaching certificate? Now she's sort of a self-appointed prima donna. Everything in her classroom is all sweetness and light and 'what a good poet I am'. I hear she really murders the grammar and doesn't even realize it."

"Something to look forward to next year," sighed David.

Chapter Five
Old Student, New Friend

THE PORK LOIN AND GERMAN POTATO SALAD sat waiting, David brought the lemonade to the table.

"What was this girl's name?"

"Lisa Jones."

"Lisa Jones!" exclaimed Aunt Lillian. "Why Lisa used to be one of my piano students. She was very shy at first, but a good student. Definitely *entier*, David. Don't you agree?"

"Yes. At least that's my first impression. I don't really know her very well yet," said David, dishing out potato salad and cutting the pork loin for Aunt Lillian. "Do you want more pork?"

"No, thank you. That's just right," said Aunt Lillian, reflecting and adding, "I suspect you will like Lisa more and more as you get to know her. She used to read a lot. I wonder if she still does?"

"Yes. That's how we met. I saw her reading by herself, so I went over and asked her if I could sit down and read while I ate my lunch. She warned me that she had the plague. So I asked, 'What plague?' and she said she had the readonic plague. Don't you love the pun? So, of course, I said I had the readonic plague, too. That's when her eyes got bright, and she gave me the biggest smile, braces and all."

"Please pass the salt, David," said Aunt Lillian.

"We talked for a lot about school. We're in American history together. It was great. She likes to read mysteries, but her parents sort of frown on it. From what she told me, they seem a little paranoid about whether or not Lisa will go to college."

Aunt Lillian smiled. "Yes. I remember them quite clearly. There always seemed to be a shadow of worry on their brows. Too bad."

"Lisa told me they never graduated from high school, so they *really* want her to go to college."

"Does *she* want to go?"

"I don't know. I expect she does, but right now she prefers English mysteries to reading the encyclopedia. Her parents insist she read the encyclopedia every night for an hour. That's a little much, isn't it?"

"For Lisa, yes, but obviously not for them. Perhaps it is *they* who need to read the encyclopedia, or even go to college."

"But they can't go if they never even graduated from high school, can they?"

"Well, maybe to one of these very fine culinary institutes, then," rejoined Aunt Lillian. "After all, the Statler is right in their back yard."

"Well, until that time comes, I think *they* should read the encyclopedia and let Lisa read mysteries."

"David, people often prescribe for others the very medicine they themselves most need, and you, my dear, are sounding absolutely protective of Lisa."

David frowned, adding, "I *am*? Well, maybe I am. But why do people try to get others to do what *they* want?"

"I don't know. You tell me. All I've learned is that people have to work out solutions to their own problems. I can't solve someone else's problems," suggested Aunt Lillian.

"But can't we help others? What if they ask us to help?"

"Helping and butting in are two different things. Even if people ask advice, generally they are only asking to be listened to."

"I believe people should be able to read whatever they want to read."

"I agree. What business is it of ours what others choose to do, as long as it doesn't hurt anyone?"

"Aunt Lillian, I'm grateful you are like my mom and dad and let me have my freedom."

"Thank you, David. And I'm glad you've met Lisa. I remember her as a delightful girl. Why don't we invite her to come over for dinner when my wrist is better, and then we can drive her home?"

"Wow! That would be great. Thanks!"

"Wayne says I'm doing better than I should be. I hope to have the cast off in a week or two."

"Betrthnamnth," said David, chewing his food.

"David, dear, please don't talk with your mouth full."

"Sorry," gulped David.

"I know you're excited," laughed Aunt Lillian. "I am, too. I look forward to seeing Lisa again. It's been a few years, you know."

David nodded, helping himself to more potato salad.

"I'll make a special invitation for her. I'll write a funny poem."

"I didn't know you wrote poetry."

"A little, here and there. I was literary editor for my school newspaper last year. Our computer and laser printer really came in handy. I'm glad there's room in my bedroom for all that equipment."

"I'd love to see the poem when you're done," said Aunt Lillian, smiling, "that is, if you don't mind."

"Sure. I'll share it in the morning, if I like it. Okay?"

David thought he caught a twinkle in Aunt Lillian's eyes as she nodded her agreement.

At the end of dinner, Aunt Lillian looked appreciatively at David as he cleared the table and rinsed the dishes for the dishwasher. "You know, I owe you many weeks of dishes and dinner."

"No you don't. It's a partnership. You're just under the weather. All I'm doing is filling in for you until we can help each other," David grinned.

Aunt Lillian took her napkin and wiped the corner of her right eye.

* * * * *

David enjoyed a bedroom of moderate size and his computer and laser printer fit neatly into the corner opposite the door. Aunt Lillian had given him one of the fluorescent lights she once had used for raising African violets for the annual bazaars of Christ Episcopal Church, where she had served as organist for thirty years.

David stationed himself in front of the computer, hearing the familiar grinding whir as he turned it on. His mastery of computer skills during his tenure as layout editor for his former school's newspaper had acquainted him with the almost limitless kinds of fonts and graphics that are possible. Greeting cards had also been fun to create, personalizing them to particular friends and occasions.

Selecting the greeting card program, David picked a dagger icon for the front of the card and began typing the text for the inside:

> To Bobby Perkins, Bully—
> Roses are red; violets are black;
> You'd look better
> With a knife in your back.
> —signed, Anonymous

David frowned at the screen and then scolded himself, saying, "Never do anything anonymously, except good deeds." His parents' injunction had served him well. He erased 'Anonymous', and typed in 'David Michael Andrews', and then deleted the card.

Selecting a new card format, David picked for its cover an icon of several books on a table. —Now the tough part, he thought. —What to write?

> Readonics is an awful plague
> And cures are very few:
> It causes us to miss our play
> For a mere page or two—
> Bringing new wonders and delights
> To spark the imagination,
> I say Readonics really is
> A cause for celebration.

David made a hard copy of the card and, taking some color pencils, added soft color to the cover. —I hope Lisa likes this, he thought, —maybe she'll write a poem for me.

* * * * *

David poured himself a second bowl of cereal while stroking Max with his left hand. Max always finished David's breakfast, although Her Majesty would have dearly loved the privilege.

"David, your poem is delightfully fun," Aunt Lillian exclaimed, adding, "I'm sure Lisa will like it, too. It may even open up a discussion about whimsical verse."

"I doubt it."

"Why do you say that?"

"Well, I sort of made a covenant when I sat with Lisa yesterday. Essentially, we will spend our lunch time eating and reading at the same table. I want to respect and honor that understanding."

"Wise of you. Eventually there may be time for visits; understandings *do* change."

"I hope so. Lunch time is short enough as it is. I have a two-fold theory about it. The first fold is that the school wants to ease the students' pain at having to eat the lousy food, so they rush us through."

Aunt Lillian lifted her left eyebrow.

David heartily ate his cereal.

"David?"

"Yes?"

"What's the second fold?"

"Oh!" said David, who could sometimes be absent-minded, "I'm sorry. I was thinking of Lisa. The second fold is that all the fast food chains are in cahoots with the managers of school cafeterias, who subversively prepare students to like fast food, because the stuff they dish out is so awful."

"Isn't that a little severe?"

"The hot dogs are rubber, the peas are cold, and the milk is almost always warm."

"Oh, dear!" exclaimed Aunt Lillian, adding, "You could take your own lunch."

"Not a bad idea. Let me think about it. I would still have to wait in line for milk."

"Does Lisa bring her lunch?"

"Yeah. Leftovers from her parents' restaurant. But she still has to wait in line for milk."

"Maybe you could suggest whoever gets in line first gets milk for both?"

"Good idea. But if I'm at the end, the milk would be warm and vice versa."

"Well, how about taking a thermos?"

David brightened and grinned.

"Capital idea, milady. Absolutely capital!"

* * * * *

David was scheduled for gym class on Tuesdays, Thursdays, and alternate Fridays instead of fourth period study hall. The relative distance to the cafeteria meant that he always found himself standing near the end of the lunch line on gym days. He was eager to see Lisa, and the line didn't seem to be moving at all. Then he noticed that line cutters were delaying his advance.

"That just burns me up!" he said to the boy standing in front of him.

"What?"

"Those budgers," David replied, pointing to two just cutting in.

"Oh, that. It's the ones who think they're really special and swell who do it. They either get in front of their friends, or they step in front of some underclassman."

"Doesn't anyone object?"

"No. It just goes on. It's always been that way."

* * * * *

David entered the cafeteria, saw Lisa wave from her table, and advanced to her location, slamming down his tray.

"Bad day?" she greeted him.

"Line cutters! I hate them. I'd hoped we'd have more time for lunch. Now the period is half over."

"I was afraid you were absent or something."

"I've got gym on the off days and I'm always last. Tomorrow I'll be one of the first in line, so I guess it's only fair, but the budgers still bug me. Anyway, I've got a surprise for you."

David handed Lisa the card on which he had written his poem.

"David! It's lovely. Thanks. I'm glad we share the same plague."

"Yes. We also have a mutual friend, who just happens to be my only living relative."

"No kidding! Who?"

David smiled, proudly proclaiming, "Lillian Biggs."

"Miss Biggs, my piano teacher?" exclaimed Lisa. "Wow!"

"She sends her best regards, and we both want you to come over for dinner when her wrist is better. She broke it a few weeks ago."

"Oh, please tell her I'm sorry about her wrist and that I'd love to come visit. Be sure to tell her, too, that I miss my piano lessons."

Lisa's face suddenly darkened.

"What's wrong?" asked David.

"I'm so sorry. I can't help but think of you not having a Mom and Dad the way most kids do."

David took a deep breath, and said, "I'm glad I had them for as long as I did. Anyway, quality is more important than quantity."

David felt tears welling to his eyes.

"Oh, I didn't mean to ... " began Lisa.

"Please ... don't. I'll be all right. I just can't help it. Whenever I think I'm getting over it, a hollow pain comes back even stronger."

Lisa closed her eyes for a few seconds, then picked up her mystery and resumed reading. David ate his lunch in silence.

When the passing bell sounded, Lisa looked up at David who was just finishing his dessert.

"Thanks," he said.

She nodded and smiled, saying, "See you tomorrow."

* * * * *

The next day, because his study hall was next to the cafeteria entrance, David was second in line.

The hamburgers and french fries were tolerable and David had eaten most of his lunch before he saw Lisa enter the cafeteria. David raised his hand, but he saw immediately that she had already seen him and was now walking toward what was becoming *their* table. Her eyes danced above a confident smile.

"I was worried that *you* weren't coming," greeted David as Lisa sat down.

"Budgers in line," Lisa frowned.

"It's not fair. Something should be done."

"This is a small school. There are lots of cliques. It's hard to fit in, especially if you like to read. That's not considered 'cool'. New kids get the business, too."

"The business?" questioned David.

"You know, pushed around, made to feel at the bottom of the heap. Hasn't that happened to you yet?"

"A little," said David, thinking of Bully Bobby, adding, "Here, I got two ice creams. Which one do you want?"

"How nice. Chocolate, please. Thanks."

"Sorry that it will be half melted before you get to it."

"No, it won't. I'm going to eat it now."

"Unorthodox," warned David, shaking his head. "We're already in enough trouble now because we read while we eat lunch."

Both laughed.

"It's funny how something like reading can be scorned," said David. What do others do, I wonder?"

"Glued to the idiot lantern or to video games," observed Lisa.

David nodded in agreement, savoring and swallowing his strawberry ice cream.

"And some kids can be cruel," Lisa continued. "I had a bad case of acne last year, and some of the kids kept calling me 'Salami Face'."

"That's awful," said David, frowning.

"It didn't help my self-image. Mom and Dad said just to say to them, 'Sticks and stones ... ', and they might stop."

"Did they?"

"No. I don't think they knew what I meant. One of them is that girl over there with the giddy laugh?"

"The one with the long black hair?"

"Yes. That's Audrey Vanderkamp. She thinks she's just the latest fashion model, and she even tries to dress like one, lipstick and all."

—Definitely *brisé*, thought David, observing Audrey's rapid jaw movement. Wanting to cheer Lisa up, he dryly observed, "Boy, Lisa! That kind of surface beauty, when it goes, it goes out like a light!"

Lisa smiled at David and asked, "Do you want to know something really funny?"

David nodded as Lisa continued.

"Our bus picks Audrey up about ten minutes after I get on. We turn a sharp corner and come up over a hill before we get to the estate."

"The estate?"

"Yes. Her father is a rich and powerful lawyer. She lives in a huge house that sits on acres and acres of land."

"Must be nice."

"I don't know. I wouldn't want to trade places if it meant I had to be like she is. Anyway," Lisa continued, "when our bus makes the crest of the hill we can sometimes see her waiting by her mailbox. It's so funny, like 'mirror, mirror on the wall' from *Snow White*."

"*Snow White?*"

"When a really strong wind is blowing toward the bus, Audrey can't hear it coming, and we sometimes catch a glimpse of her preening herself in the reflection of their aluminum mailbox."

David laughed and whispered, "Mailbox, mailbox on the post: who's the beauty, who's the most? Do I have to preen and preen to look my best, the beauty queen?"

Lisa burst out laughing so loudly that she caught annoyed stares from students at surrounding tables. David loved hearing her laugh. It was a rich, full, hearty laugh. He hoped his jest would serve some small recompense for Audrey's cruel acne slights.

Pulling out her mystery, Lisa thumbed to her bookmark and glanced at the clock.

"Oh, darn," she said, "We only have five minutes left."

"It just burns me," said David. "And it's because of those line cutters. We'd have more time if they didn't steal places."

"It's always been that way."

"It doesn't always need to be that way. It's a form of tyranny."

"What do you mean?"

"I mean, I don't think we should become victims to a convention that is unfair. Perhaps tyranny is too strong a description. Certainly line budging is unfair, yet no one ever dares to complain. Unless people say something, the line cutting will continue."

"I guess nobody wants to rock the boat," observed Lisa.

"I *do*," rejoined David, "and I *will*."

"If you make a fuss in line, someone will probably punch you."

"I'm sure of that. No, I want to use the power of the press."

"Power of the press?"

"Yes. Like in colonial times ... Thomas Paine and all that."

"I still don't follow."

"Do we have a school newspaper?"

"Sort of."

"What do you mean, 'Sort of'?"

"It's really more like a literary magazine. The faculty advisor is Mrs. Coachman. As I told you, she gets some of her poems published in the local newspaper. Most people think they're pretty horrible, but she thinks they're wonderful. The school newspaper is called *Just the Best*. I don't think she'd be happy to get any controversial material."

"Well, I'm going to try. If she won't help me, I'll publish my letter myself and post it at key places around the school. We need to rally the support of other students if we are going to make a difference. I think we should probably try to organize a petition."

"A petition?"

David's eyes shone brightly. "I've got it! I bet we could get Mr. Pennythorpe to help us. This is really sort of a parallel to the American Revolution, in a small way, perhaps, but a genuine way."

"David, settle down. We're only talking about a little line cutting."

"We're talking about basic individual rights, and the dignity of each and every single human being."

David looked longingly at the remainder of the quiche on Lisa's plastic plate. Noticing his interest, she offered, "Would you like the rest of this quiche?"

"For sure! Thanks!"

"Be my guest."

"Mmm. This is delicious. You're so lucky to have parents who run a restaurant."

"It has it's drawbacks. What did your mom and dad do?"

David gulped and answered, "Librarians. They were never really into the culinary scene. Food for thought nourishes the soul *and* the body, and all that."

Lisa's eyes widened, and she asked, "They never starved you, did they?"

David laughed, replying, "No. It was never that intentional, but I usually got hungry before they did. My mom would cut up vegetables and leave them in the refrigerator. That must explain my good eyesight. If I've eaten one, I've eaten a million carrots!"

"I am *very* nearsighted," said Lisa, adding, "take my glasses off and I'm completely lost."

"Have you ever tried carrots?" asked David.

"Not in such vast quantities, but maybe I should, if you think it would help."

David shrugged.

"I know," said Lisa, "I could bring extra food, if you'd like."

"That would be great, but we don't get in here at the same time."

"Thanks to the line cutters," sighed Lisa.

"You know, I'm going to do something about that. Give me a little time. Wait 'til you see my article for the school newspaper."

"I don't think they'll accept it. They aren't looking for controversy."

"Then I'll publish it myself."

Lisa laughed. "Like Thomas Paine."

"Perhaps," rejoined David. "But I would rather people compare me to Senator George Norris, a man who had the integrity and courage to speak out against tyranny. He was not afraid to go against convention."

"Good luck."

"Thanks. See you tomorrow."

Chapter Six
A Letter to the Editor

"**L**ISA SENDS HER LOVE, AUNT LILLIAN," said David, after he and his aunt had shared a silent blessing for their dinner.

"She is such a sensible young girl. One of my better students, too. I was eager to know when you came home how your luncheon went."

"Why?"

"One never knows how other people will strike one's fancy. It seems that lunch went well, then?"

David recounted his luncheon conversation in great detail, still finding himself upset at the inequity of line budging.

"Don't you agree it's wrong, Aunt Lillian?"

"Yes, I do. Why should anyone presume to step in front of another person? We are all supposed to be equal under the Constitution. It's a marvel that young people feel compelled to follow the example of some of their foolish elders by proceeding to put on airs."

"What would *you* do about it?"

"I think I would try to call attention to it, naming it for the injustice it is," said Aunt Lillian, mulling over the problem.

"I agree. I'm going to write an editorial for our school paper. Lisa said it is called *Just The Best*. A Mrs. Coachman is the advisor."

"I don't want to discourage you, but I will be very much surprised if Gertrude Coachman prints your letter."

"Not publish a letter to the editor? That's not right."

"David, you must remember this is a rather provincial community. One of the unwritten rules around here, as I'm sure it is in many places, is that no one should rock the boat."

"That's absolutely awful!"

"I agree. But Midville is Midville. Our forebear Jonathan Biggs had the same frustrations, and he was a champion against slavery."

"It seems to me that line budging, when tolerated, results in a different kind of slavery. It's really being bullied by a minority that thinks itself pretty swell. That's not right, and someone should say so."

"All you can do is try, David," encouraged Aunt Lillian.

"No. I can do *more* than that. If the school paper won't print my letter, I'll publish it myself. I've got my parents' computer and printer, and I've got the weekend to work on it," said David, pausing to add with a grin, "and I've got the words."

* * * * *

Monday was unseasonably warm for September. David waited with several other walkers for the front doors of Midville Middle School to open. After the doors were unlocked, David went directly to the office.

Mrs. Dixon, the school secretary, peered out at David from under a shock of curly brown hair, which made her look like a leftover from the Beatles' generation. Her horn-rimmed glasses emphasized her alert blue eyes, strengthening a rather soft face, which rested on a prominent double chin.

"Yes, what may I help you with?"

"I'm David Andrews."

"Oh, yes. You're one of the new eighth graders. I remember when we received your school records in late July because I have a sister who lives near your old town. How do you like school so far?"

"Most people have been friendly. I'm getting to know more and more kids. Would you please put this letter in Mrs. Coachman's mailbox?"

"Glad to."

"Thank you."

"You're welcome. Have a good day."

* * * * *

David had waited next to Lisa's locker for five minutes before a new wave of bus students flooded in. Among them was Lisa, who was wearing a sky blue jumper and white blouse.

"Lisa!"

"Hi, David. How are you?"

"Fine. I want you to read a copy of this letter I wrote to Mrs. Coachman for the school paper. I just had the original put in her mailbox."

The warning bell rang.

"Okay. See you next period. I hope you'll get some justice out of your letter."

As David climbed the southwest stairwell, he encountered Bobby Perkins and two of his gang on the landing.

"Hey, guys! If it ain't Howdy Doody in person! Long time no see," said Bobby reaching out to pull David back. "Slow down, Red. What's the rush? You ain't got your mangy dog to protect you."

"Lay off," said David, pushing Bobby's arm away.

Bobby grabbed David's shirt by the lapels and shoved him hard against the brick wall, warning him, "Don't you never dare do that again, do you hear me, or you'll be lookin' out a window of blood all over your rotten little freckled face."

"Hey, give me those books," David shouted as Danny Taylor and Zeke Minturn tossed his books and notebook from the top of the stairwell, yelling, "Finders keepers!"

David tried to catch his notebook as it fell, the other books striking the stairs. As he knelt to pick them up, the homeroom bell sounded. David was now officially late, no matter what he did.

—What a way to start my third day of school, he sighed to himself. Mrs. Donovan gave him a reproving glance as he entered in the middle of the pledge of allegiance, admonishing him afterward, "David Andrews, two more tardies and you will receive a detention."

* * * * *

Lisa had not encountered any difficulty in arriving at her homeroom on time. She mumbled the words to the pledge of allegiance and during announcements carefully opened David's letter, which read:

Dear Mrs. Coachman:

My name is David Andrews and I wish to submit the following letter for publication in this year's first issue of *Just The Best*. I am a new student in the eighth grade, and I have had considerable experience working on the staff of school newspapers. I would like to help with your paper, if there is room on the staff.

AN OPEN LETTER CONCERNING INEQUITY

Classmates, we are allowing a form of tyranny in our school, namely line budging during lunch periods. I believe it is UNFAIR for anyone to cut in front of someone else. We must consider and respect the rights of all students. I write this letter to urge you to join with me and other students to discourage those who currently budge in front of us. Sometimes students who take their places in the middle of the lunch line end up at the end! Next time, say to anyone who tries to cut in front of you: "Look, friend, I don't cut in line, and I don't allow budging ahead of me. Please take your rightful place at the end of the line!" —David Andrews

* * * * *

The bell for B lunch rang. David waited for Lisa and they joined the line together.

"It's a good letter, David. Do you think it will help?"

"I hope so."

"You could have gotten a table for us right after study hall."

"I didn't want you to wait in line by yourself," David smiled. "Anyway, I wanted to see who was budging. Look, there go two girls now; one of them is that Audrey you pointed out on Friday. Who let them budge?"

"Oh, that's Sylvia White. They use her like that all the time. She wants to be in their little crowd, and the bone they throw her is to let her sit at the end of their table."

"There goes another one."

"That's Zeke Minturn. He's—"

"I know. One of Bobby Perkins' gang."

"How do you know that? You're new here."

"Let's just say we all got acquainted in August."

"David, be careful. They're really tough, and they don't care what they do. Everyone gives them a lot of room."

"Maybe that's the wrong thing to do," said David. "Bullies are usually asking for some form of limit. Somewhere inside they really *want* to be stopped. Maybe Bobby doesn't get stopped at home."

"I've heard his dad really beats him up sometimes."

"Really? Why doesn't he report it?" wondered David.

"He lives alone with his dad, although rumor has it his dad has a steady flow of girlfriends. I heard Bobby's mother died when he was born. His father runs a really dumpy garage. Bobby just seems to get into more and more trouble," explained Lisa.

"I don't want trouble, but I'm not going to back down to any bully."

"David, please promise me you'll be careful."

"I promise. What's for lunch. Oh, I see it now. Rubber hot dogs."

"David, they're not *that* bad."

"I don't see you eating them," David observed slyly.

"It's *most* convenient that my parents run a restaurant."

"You're lucky, Lisa."

"Do you really think Mrs. Coachman will publish your letter?"

"I hope so. It will save me publishing it myself."

"You really *are* serious about this, aren't you?"

"You bet. In the meantime, I've got to figure out who does most of the line budging. If it's the bullies or the swell crowd, I need to know whose tail I'm pulling."

"You got it in one," Lisa smiled. "But what do you mean by pulling their tails?"

"It seems to me I'll be waking up a couple of sleeping tigers. They enjoy a certain kind of invisible power, or maybe it's really a kind of potential power. The bottom line is that they've never been challenged, and people are afraid to cross them. But I'm not afraid. What's there to lose? We're standing here near the end of the line anyway."

"I see," said Lisa. "They're accustomed to the *status quo*, which has until now, conveyed to them the illusion that somehow they're a little more important, so they can budge in front of others."

"Exactly," grinned David. "I have a feeling that the *status quo* around here, as it pertains to line budging, is going to change. We're going to raise the consciousness of many of the unwitting victims."

Chapter Seven
A Paper Tiger

TUESDAY MORNING BROUGHT A DRIVING AUTUMN RAIN, renting brilliant leaves from their branches. David sat in history class listening to Mr. Pennythorpe hold forth on the cultural seeds of the American Revolution. So intense and dramatic was the performance, the instructor had to apply a handkerchief regularly to the beads of sweat emerging on his high forehead, as he gesticulated about the British abuses of Colonists.

"And to all these protests," continued the inspired lecturer, "King George lent only a deaf ear, not to mention his reinforcement of troops to quell any type of colonial rebellion. But our forefathers, God bless them, were working for freedom and liberty and equality."

David could be still no longer. If history were to have any relevance at all, it must be compared to the present. Raising his hand and clearing his throat, he attracted Mr. Pennythorpe's attention.

"Yes, Mr. Andrews?"

"You mentioned that our forefathers were working for equality, among other things?"

"Yes, that's correct. The Founding Fathers intended that people, in all their diversity, be seen as equal under the law, enjoying the same rights, while accepting the same responsibilities."

"I have an example of inequality that exists here at Midville Middle School that flies in the face of what the Constitution guarantees our citizenry."

"And what is that?" asked a curious Pennythorpe.

"It may seem a trivial example, but I believe it is an inequity that should be addressed. I speak of line budging during lunchtime. I don't believe any student has the right to paw in front of another, thereby denying all who follow in the line their rightful places."

"Is there very much of this?" asked Mr. Pennythorpe.

"Yes. It happens to me and to many others *every* day."

"And what," beamed Mr. Pennythorpe, "do you propose we do about it?"

"I propose that we launch a petition," suggested David.

"A petition? Yes, why *not* a petition?" encouraged Mr. Pennythorpe, adding, "That's what the Colonists did. And Mr. Ferlinghausen is certainly not as severe as King George was, so I suspect we'll get some positive action for our efforts."

"Mr. Pennythorpe, would you please draw up a proper petition for the class to sign?"

"Wait a minute!" interrupted a brazen voice from the back of the room. Audrey Vanderkamp glared at David as she stood up, "*This* isn't history. We're supposed to *learn* about history in this class, not waste a lot of time on silly petitions."

Having had her say, Audrey sat down in a huff.

"Ah, my dear Miss Vanderkamp," responded Mr. Pennythorpe with a studied eye, "What we're doing here right now might well *become* history, at least a part of Midville Middle School history. In this small exercise, we have the opportunity to bring equity to a situation where inequality seems to hold sway."

"I don't think any of this makes sense," Audrey grimaced. "We are just getting carried away by a lot of emotion. Maybe some of the people who budge only want to sit with their friends. What's wrong with that?

Maybe they had to stop and check their makeup before going to lunch. What's wrong with that?"

Before Mr. Pennythorpe could respond, David took the offensive, saying, "What's wrong with it Audrey is that no person is better than anyone else when it comes to waiting in line, whether it's for lunch or for voting."

A faint ripple of applause caused Audrey's face to redden.

"Well, David, dear," she answered mockingly, "you have another *think* coming if you think a new student can barge in here and upset the way things are done. There's never been anything wrong in saving a place for a friend."

"But there *is*," David persisted, "and if you ever had to wait in line longer because of someone else's rudeness, maybe you'd feel differently about it."

"Let Mr. Pennythorpe draw up a petition," proclaimed Lisa, to the reception of general applause and whistles.

Mr. Pennythorpe took a long sheet of paper and began writing, speaking as he wrote, "We, the undersigned, do hereby present this petition to Mr. Ferlinghausen, expressing our growing concern for the inequity caused by line budging during the lunch hour. We do not believe any student is entitled to step in front of another, thus wrongfully assuming the latter's rightful place in line. We, accordingly, do request that a line monitor be appointed to ensure this inequity is stopped, thus ridding ourselves of a subtle tyranny now present in our daily routine. Signed, Thatcher Pennythorpe."

Looking up at his students, Mr. Pennythorpe announced, "I will now circulate this petition in this and all of my classes. Please sign it if you agree with it; pass it on if you don't agree. For the remainder of class, I invite you to take one of these blank pieces of paper I am now distributing and, with your pen, write a few short paragraphs about your own personal view of line budging, whether you favor it or oppose it, and whether or not you see it as a violation of the common rights we share under the Constitution. You need not place your name on this opinion should you prefer to remain anonymous."

Ten minutes remained before the bell. David wrote three paragraphs and then observed his classmates. Most were still writing their considered opinions. Gazing back at Audrey who, instead of writing, had been fuming at her desk, he caught her attention long enough to be the recipient of several stared daggers. Yawning and cupping his mouth with his left hand, he crossed his arms and smiled at her. So nonchalant was his response that Audrey, in smoldering fury, grabbed her sheet of paper, crumpled it loudly, and advanced to the front of the room, tossing it into the wastepaper basket. Upon returning to her desk, she threw herself so violently into her seat that she inadvertently knocked her books off her desk. Containing an amused smile, David merely raised his eyebrows in mock surprise. Audrey gave him, in return, her best hateful look as she mouthed the words *Shut up!* As soon as the passing bell rang, she stomped to front of the room, and flung the door wide, profoundly startling a timid seventh grader, note in hand, waiting to enter.

"You're off your rocker if you want to go in there," she growled as she flounced out of the room.

Mr. Pennythorpe beckoned the seventh grader to his desk, taking the note.

"David," he announced, "Mr. Dandy would like to see you immediately in his office. Please take this note with you and, yes, I would like to read what you've written."

Looking at the remaining class members, who were passing their papers forward, Mr. Pennythorpe grinned and, giving a confidential wink, announced, "Class dismissed!"

* * * * *

The Guidance Office was adjacent to the cafeteria-auditorium. Here Mr. Melvin Dandy reigned supreme, together with his dour and no nonsense secretary Mrs. Amelia Fullerton.

As David entered the office, Mrs. Fullerton was typing a letter and didn't notice him for more than a minute after he had placed himself beside her desk.

"May I help you?"

"Yes. I'm David Andrews, and I just received this note," he replied, handing her the slip.

"Ah, yes. So *you're* David Andrews. Let me announce you to Mr. Dandy at once."

Picking up her telephone, she pushed a button that sounded a strident buzz behind a closed door which displayed the sign 'You Can Only Be Your Best'.

"Mr. Dandy, David Andrews is here."

The door to the office swung open.

"David, David, there you are. I'm sorry we haven't gotten together before now. The opening of school is so busy, you know. I sometimes don't manage reviewing the records of our new students until October. And I know," he continued, as he waved an admonishing finger, "there's no excuse for it. But please take pity on me, and remember it's quite a challenge to be the only counselor for over 550 students."

"Five hundred and fifty-seven," Mrs. Fullerton smiled.

"Yes," agreed Dandy. "And everyone of them individuals in their own right, too. Right down to the socks they wear. But, be that as it may, I do need to visit with you for a few minutes David. Please enter my sanctum sanctorum."

As Melvin Dandy laughed at his own little joke, David entered the office and sat down in one of two red leather chairs which faced a large mahogany desk. The window shades were drawn shut, and the florescent light flooded the office with an unnatural hue. Some sort of certificate or award and two framed degrees were prominently displayed on the wall behind Mr. Dandy's desk. On an adjacent wall, David noticed an enormous collection of insects, pinned and labeled to a huge mounting board that was encased in glass. The library shelf also displayed several volumes on the insect kingdom. Although David had heard of butterfly collectors before, he had never heard of anyone who collected beetles.

Mr. Dandy sat down in his large, black leather swivel chair with an air of utmost authority. He smiled at David as he took a transcript from his desk, announcing, "David, let me come to the point quickly, for time is money, you know, and in *your* case, wise use of time and talent is why we're here. I have, as of late yesterday afternoon, thoroughly reviewed the transcript and records we received from your former school. I must confess to you that I was sorry not to have gotten to them earlier. Oh, yes, I did glance at your academic average in August when Mrs. Fullerton and I sat down to make out your schedule, but what I failed to notice was that you have already taken English 8. And it was an honors course, at that. You have been, and are, an exceptional student. Quite impressive, really quite impressive."

"Thank you."

"I don't know if you know anything about your file, David. Did anyone ever take time to talk to you before?"

"My parents always encouraged me to read a lot."

"Oh, yes. Your parents. Let me add my condolences regarding their most untimely deaths. It must have been very hard."

"It still is, sometimes," said David.

"Did they ever talk to you about your abilities?"

"They only told me they always wanted me to do my best and that, if I did, I would never be disappointed."

"Ah, yes! Did you notice the sign on my door?"

"Yes."

"So we're not too far off, are we?"

David reflected briefly, swallowed, and answered, "Your sign says 'You Can Only Be Your Best'. But my experience tells me that when you really try to be your best, you can actually be *better* than your best. That may sound ironic, but I believe it's true."

"Semantics, David. Mere semantics. Perhaps you *think* too hard sometimes."

"But the word *only* in your sign is a limitation, isn't it?"

"David, that sign has been with me for many years and it has helped countless students to aspire to their highest potentials. Let's not argue about signs. I have not called you in here for that."

"I wasn't arguing, sir. Only trying to be clear."

"Ah, yes. Your anecdotal records talk a lot about your sharp focus and drive to 'be clear' about things. I don't think it wise to reveal the details of those records, but you may take my word for it that you will most probably become successful at any career you might choose."

David was slowly deciding that he didn't want to take Mr. Dandy's word for anything.

The piercing buzzer broke the silence.

"Yes?" answered Dandy. "No, tell him I'm busy. No, I'll call him back later. What? He only wants to give me the new numbers for the computerized report cards? Oh, all right, I'll take it since he'll be out later."

Taking a yellow legal pad, the counselor took a pencil, looked at David apologetically, saying, "Please excuse me. This shouldn't take very long."

Pushing the flashing telephone button, he announced, "Hello, Harry. This is Melvin. Let me have the numbers."

As David waited for Mr. Dandy, he studied the office. The insect display by its size and ugliness made him feel a little sick. A photograph of a much younger Mr. Dandy hung next to the display. The background looked like a rain forest, and the younger Mr. Dandy was showing some specimens to several older men who were obviously smiling their approval. But something in the picture seemed different. David searched to discover the anomaly. Standing and walking over to the photograph, he studied it intently. The much younger Melvin Dandy had curly black hair and a pronounced receding hairline. The current Mr. Dandy who now sat at his desk taking dictation had a much lower hairline and straight black hair. A toupee! That was it, at least in part. Mr. Dandy was really bald, but had decided to cover his bald head with a toupee.

David returned to his seat and studied the face and hairline of the man sitting across from him. Yes. It was definitely a toupee. David pondered the Mr. Dandy who sat before him in a crumpled tweed suit and polka dotted tie, his light blue shirt showing rings around the collar. The sad truth was that the toupee didn't really flatter the man. But something else was lacking, perhaps a certain warmth of personality. The expected words were there, of course, but they rang hollow. —Pretty *brisé*, thought David, as he pondered the paradox, —Yet here he sits trying to help others.

"Thank you, Harry," said Dandy, concluding his telephone conversation, adding, "See you next week."

Pushing the intercom button and returning the rude buzz to Mrs. Fullerton, Mr. Dandy ordered, "I will not accept any more calls until I have concluded my conference with David."

Sighing as he replaced the telephone receiver to its cradle, Melvin Dandy looked at David; David, in turn, studied the man's restless eyes.

"David, I'm sorry we were interrupted, although that may have been just as well since we were heading off on some tangent or other. Now what I brought you here to tell you is that, having just now thoroughly reviewed your records, I am transferring you immediately to English 9 honors. Fortunately, it is taught during the fourth period, so we can exchange it for your present study hall and gym, and switch those to seventh period. Quite a minor change, actually. I'll notify your study hall and gym teachers. You, in turn, should report directly to English 9 honors fourth period today."

David, feeling a definite sinking feeling in his gut, asked, "Who teaches that course, sir?"

"Why, Mrs. Coachman, of course."

"Mr. Dandy, I don't think I want to take English 9 this year."

"Nonsense. You're a bright student, a rare specimen, a real find."

David wondered if the poor insects on the mounting board had ever received similar accolades just prior to being impaled.

"Couldn't I take some sort of elective instead?"

"Nonsense. You'll benefit from Mrs. Coachman. She is a *published* author."

David could only mutter, "I've heard about her poems."

"And you have already managed to get Mrs. Coachman's attention, David. She brought your letter to me yesterday after school, asking my opinion."

"And?" prompted David.

"We *both* agree that you have better things to do with your talents and time than to write letters that might upset our school community. School is a microcosm of society, with its own unique values, mores, and codes. You are a newcomer, and you will have to learn this school's system as you make your way through Midville. Part of learning is recognizing that there will always be opportunistic people, no matter where one goes."

"But *that* isn't right!"

"David, David," said Mr. Dandy in a forebearing tone, "you can't change an established system and, if you try, it *might* change you."

"It *still* isn't right! And if I don't try, it will change me even more."

"Okay, let's talk specifics. Who are these so-called line budgers?"

"I'm just getting to know some of them. It's only the second week of school. But Audrey Vanderkamp is one."

"Ah, Audrey. Not surprising. Do you know who her father is?"

"Should I?"

"Now, don't be brash. It was a silly question, since you are so new to our community. Audrey's celebrated father is Horace Vanderkamp, our county's most successful lawyer. Rumor has it he may be appointed to a judge's chair by the Governor in another year or two."

"That still doesn't change anything!"

"David, this is becoming tiresome. Mrs. Coachman will *not* publish your letter and that is *that*."

"I'll publish it myself, then," said David.

"Now *where* will you get with that? You'll only make yourself into a laughing stock. Schools are charged to prepare their students for the real world which is, I remind you, full of cliques and opportunists."

"Why should schools wink at inequity?"

"Now, I never said that they should," sputtered Mr. Dandy.

"No, not directly. But between what you suggest be done, which is to accept inequity as a part of society, as opposed to taking positive action against an identified inequity, I really wonder which direction the framers of the Constitution would call more pusillanimous?"

Melvin Dandy sat spellbound, unable to answer, but not because he didn't want to answer. The sad truth was that he did not know the meaning of the word 'pusillanimous'. Choking back his nervous cough, and reaching for what dignity he could muster, he intoned to David that he had had enough nonsense, and that David would begin English 9 studies with Mrs. Coachman fourth period.

As David left the inner sanctum sanctorum, he heard its high priest intone a last dictum, "David, I would strongly advise you to pull your horns in and try to cooperate with those of us who are trying to help you."

Chapter Eight
New News, Debate, & Resolution

"**D**AVID, WHAT *WILL* YOU DO?"

"I don't know, Aunt Lillian. May I please have some more beans? Thank you. I don't mind going into ninth grade English, except that I don't think I'm going to like Mrs. Coachman."

"Maybe it's better to get it over with," suggested Aunt Lillian.

"What bothers me most is the whitewash Mr. Dandy tried to give to line budging. I mean, I really think it's wrong. After hearing him say I should go with the flow, I wondered if I wasn't overreacting. But having thought about it, I know I'm right," lamented David.

"David, I'm sure Mr. Dandy was trying his best to help you, although I must confess I have come to feel very tentative about some of these counselor types. I'm sure *most* of them mean well, but my experience has told me that, whenever anyone like Mr. Dandy attempts to help others, his own blind spots hinder his efforts. And I certainly don't agree with Mr. Dandy's stance on not rocking the boat; more to the point, I think we owe an enduring debt to those individuals who have gone before us who have mustered their courage *to* rock the boat. Such rocking often helps us to steer to clearer waters."

"If I wasn't sure about my petition against line cutting when I went in to Mr. Dandy's office, I am *very* sure of it now," confided David.

"Well, he's done at least one good thing, then. Please pass me the tea pot. I think I'd like a little more. Thank you."

"Any thoughts that might help me now that you've heard about my day's exploits?"

"I have two concerns, David. The first is related to your rather prodigious vocabulary."

"Look, Aunt Lillian, I can only be who I am, nothing more, nothing less."

"That's true. I just don't want you to get hurt. Some people are put off by those whose abilities are more obvious."

"I've read a lot. And I love language and literature."

"I know. It's your teachers I'm worried about more than your peers. Some adults are very insecure around younger people who are brighter and more imaginative than they are. I begin to wonder if Mr. Dandy might be a little like that. Such adults don't take kindly to being found in error, or in ignorance, by a young and pert upstart with red hair."

"Aunt Lillian!"

"Oh, yes. I forgot to mention your charming freckles and marble-green eyes."

"Please don't. I get enough razing already about my complexion from Bobby Perkins and his gang. They call me Howdy Doody."

"And what's wrong with Howdy Doody? He was a perfectly affable character for an entire generation of young people. And *he* had his own television show. These boys must have seen him on one of those channels that specializes in airing programs from the fifties."

David laughed. "Maybe you're right. I'll try a little humor next time they call me Howdy Doody by offering them my autograph. Maybe that's one way to defuse anger."

"You have a very generous heart and a very quick mind, David. Have you used any of your fifty cent words in school yet?"

"I don't know. I just use words as they come into my head. Wait! I did it today. I used the word pusillanimous with Mr. Dandy. I'm afraid it flummoxed him. He started coughing and got really red in the face. Then he said there had been enough nonsense, and that I would be transferred to English 9 immediately. He even predicted that I would some day return to thank him when I was in high school."

Aunt Lillian surveyed David with a studied gaze.

"My second concern, David, is your new teacher."

"Do you know Mrs. Coachman?"

"Oh, perhaps we have met a half dozen times. I doubt if she would remember me. She's very self-absorbed. Many years ago I used to substitute teach every so often, and I remember at that time she was employed as a dishwasher in the school cafeteria. That's when it was both a high school and a middle school. She's always impressed me as being a little crude and ill-educated, and I'm afraid her poems do not reflect the work of a towering intellect or literary genius."

"Aunt Lillian, you don't have to couch your opinion in hyperbole. Mrs. Coachman really murdered the language in class today, at least a dozen times."

"Oh, David, I see a storm brewing on the horizon. Your parents always wanted you to have the greatest respect for language and its proper use. Do you want me to see if I can get you transferred to a different class?"

"Not yet. Let me see how it goes. I'm going to try to make Mrs. Coachman's class as positive an experience as possible."

"That may be a tall order."

"I know. But I need to. I feel she betrayed me when she took the letter I intended for the newspaper to Mr. Dandy. I'm trying to get over that feeling. I guess she thought she was doing the right thing. Anyway, let me try her class."

David stared at his plate and stirred the mashed potatoes.

"David, forgive me for worrying," began Aunt Lillian, "but I hate to see you as the victim, either of a bully or of someone's weak ego."

"Don't worry, Aunt Lillian. I'll try to stay away from Bobby Perkins. He's the kind of kid who will punch you even if you don't hit back."

Aunt Lillian sighed. "He must really hurt inside to do that."

"Why do you say that?"

"Because people who hurt other people usually are hurting, too, perhaps even more than the people they hurt."

"Untrue, untrue!" protested David. "*I* was in deepest pain when Bobby and his gang beat me up in August."

"Oh, David, dear, I know that. I don't *minimize* that, but I'm talking about inner pain, and that is much different from the physical sort. The only way I've found to stop that kind of pain is to bring it to light and to face it."

David looked at Aunt Lillian and waited.

Aunt Lillian stared at her tea cup for what seemed a long time.

"Many years ago when I was at the conservatory, I made a friend whom I trusted and believed. His name was Frank. I didn't really know the true person that was in Frank, but I thought I did. He was preparing for the ministry at the university's divinity school. In time, and it was a very miserable time, I learned that the real Frank was not the kind, generous person he pretended to be, but rather one bent on lies and egotism. I broke off the relationship when I discovered he had been two-timing me, but the pain and suffering he caused me and my friends continued to haunt me. It was like suffocating in a little box of anger and hurt, and I couldn't get out of it by myself. I needed someone who would listen to what had happened, someone who wouldn't judge my words in any way. That person's name was Rachel.

She's dead now, poor dear. I will be forever grateful to her for caring enough to listen to me in one of my darkest hours."

David and Aunt Lillian sat in silence for a few minutes. He somehow felt closer to her. She sat and waited.

"I still feel a lot of anger at the man who killed my parents. Sometimes I'm glad he died. Other times I wish he had lived so he could suffer from the guilt. I know it's not good to have those kinds of feelings, but I can't help it."

Aunt Lillian, her eyes sadder than David had ever remembered them, continued to listen.

"I don't feel that way every day now, only most days."

"Have you forgiven the man?"

"No. I don't even want to."

"You're hurting yourself by not forgiving him, David."

"Could you forgive him?"

"I don't know, David. I just don't know. But I do know that if you don't forgive someone who's hurt you, the enmity inside of you acts like a poison that chokes off your love."

"I understand that intellectually, Aunt Lillian. I just can't do it emotionally."

"Please bring it to mind from time to time. It took me over two years before I could forgive Frank. I don't say it's easy, and you can only do it in your own time. Just take it out and look at it every so often, okay?"

David grinned. "Okay, provided you do the dishes. I need to work on my EXTRA edition of my paper."

"It's a deal," Aunt Lillian smiled. "By the way, have you picked a name for your paper?"

"Yes. I'm going to use a computer logo of a grizzly bear and call it BARE FAX, fax being spelled f-a-x instead of f-a-c-t-s."

"Do you think people will get the pun?"

"Most will. Mr. Dandy won't."

* * * * *

David hardly noticed the Methodist Church clock striking eleven. He had stayed up past his usual bedtime to complete his special edition of *Bare Fax*. The document would be suitable for posting on homeroom bulletin boards and at key locations around the school. —This should get the word out, David thought. —I'll need to get in to school before everyone else. I'll try the entrance that faces onto the faculty park lot.

As David applied the mint flavored toothpaste to his toothbrush, he imagined the look of surprise on Mr. Dandy's face when he saw the extra edition of *Bare Fax* taped to his office door. —Maybe his toupee will fall off, he chuckled to himself.

* * * * *

The next morning the school's back door was unlocked, just as David had surmised. Having posted his newspaper in a number of high traffic areas, David was just taping a copy of it to Mr. Dandy's door when he heard a cough behind him. Starting and turning, expecting to see Mr. Dandy himself, David was relieved to be facing the school's custodian, a short man with white wavy hair who was looking at him curiously.

"Good morning," David blurted. "I'm David Andrews, and I was just posting some copies of my *Bare Fax* extra edition. There are a lot students who budge in lunch line, and I'm letting people know there's a petition to stop it."

"I'm Walker, the custodian. Students don't usually come in until we unlock the main doors at twenty of eight."

"I know, but if I had waited, I couldn't post these in time for people to read them. We just signed the petition in Mr. Pennythorpe's class, and the other students need to know."

"Oh, you're with Pennythorpe, are you? Well, you're okay then, because Pennythorpe is all right."

"He doesn't know yet about this *Bare Fax* edition. I don't want to mislead you."

"Would he approve?"

"Yes. I'm sure he would."

"Don't worry, then. If I get any flack about your coming in, I'll just tell them how polite you were. It's a free world, isn't it?"

"I'm hoping this will help make it a little freer," grinned David.

* * * * *

The main entrance to Midville Middle School was opened at precisely twenty to eight. The ripple of student voices and click of shoes grew to a cacophonous rumble as students fetched books from their lockers.

David sought out Mr. Ferlinghausen, who was greeting students in the lobby, as they entered the building.

"Mr. Ferlinghausen, do you remember me? I'm David Andrews."

"Of course, David. I just had a note about you from Mr. Dandy, about your promotion to ninth grade English. How's it going?"

"Too early to tell, sir. But I really do like American History with Mr. Pennythorpe. Yesterday I brought up a school problem in class, and he helped us to write a petition."

Mr. Ferlinghausen's black eyebrows furrowed. "What problem is that?"

"Line budging during lunch period."

"Really? That's not so good, is it?"

"No, sir. I wrote an article for the school's regular newspaper, but Mrs. Coachman, without telling me, referred my letter to Mr. Dandy, who then called me in to counsel me. Here's a copy of my letter. I decided my only alternative was to publish it in my own paper. I brought you a copy."

Mrs. Dixon appeared at the door to the main office. "Mr. Ferlinghausen, telephone."

"Excuse me, David. I don't condone line budging, but I wish you had come to me first before going to all this trouble. I think we can find a solution."

"Thank you, sir."

"Don't worry any more about it," called out Mr. Ferlinghausen as he walked into the office. He turned, adding, "Justice *will* prevail."

* * * * *

Melvin Dandy prided himself on the many hours he worked after school. Generally, he wouldn't leave his office until after five o'clock. Paperwork required time, and Melvin Dandy was one of paperwork's most creative and sustaining partners. In compensation for late hours after school, Melvin Dandy would rarely enter the building until after homeroom period had begun. He hated the disorder, confusion, and noise students brought into the building as they entered. The rumblings of their early morning onslaughts made him nervous and ill at ease. Passing between classes was one thing; there was a definite beginning and end signaled by the passing bell. Never having quite conquered his irritation of before-school-chaos, Melvin Dandy had resolved long ago to exempt himself from its unpleasantness. On this crisp, fall morning, he strode purposefully up to his office door, just as morning announcements were being read over the public address system.

Before opening the office door, he paused, noting a sheet taped on the door frame. A closer examination of the sheet caused in him a sudden surge of blood pressure, not severe enough to cause a stroke, but intense enough to cause rapid heart palpitations. Ripping the document loose, Mr. Dandy stalked into his office and waved the paper at Mrs. Fullerton, growling, "Didn't you see this?"

EXTRA! EXTRA!

BARE FAX

a newspaper dedicated to publishing
NEWS *that students want*.

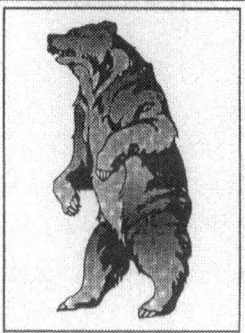

Classmates unite! Line budging during lunch period is wrong! We must respect and consider the rights of each and every student. If students will join together to discourage line budging, then fairness to all will prevail. This will keep students who start at the middle from ending up at the end! I do not cut in line, and I do not allow it ahead of me! Please join in helping to eliminate line budging!

Sincerely, \signed\ *David Andrews*

MR. PENNYTHORPE'S CLASSES SIGN PETITION!

Many students in Mr. Pennythorpe's American history classes have submitted a petition to Mr. Ferlinghausen asking for his help in solving the problem of line budging. The petition urges that a faculty monitor be assigned to protect the rights of those students who lose their rightful place because of line budging. Mr. Pennythorpe's first period history class drew up the petition and Mr. Pennythorpe himself was the first to sign the document, much in the style of John Hancock. Mr. Pennythorpe noted that the students were probably on the cusp of making their own small bit of history here at Midville Middle School.

GROSSLY TEASED — ANSWER IN NEXT ISSUE

Question: Approximately how long does a cockroach live after its head has been severed? Debate this fascinating query with your friends and watch for the answer in our next issue. [Hint: the answer to this is *really* gross, so plan to be surprised!!!]

THIS PAPER INVITES SUGGESTIONS
FROM ITS READERS!

Please contact David Andrews, Homeroom 302. Thank you.

"What?" she asked blankly, looking up from her typewriter.

"Oh, never mind. Call Ferlinghausen and tell him I am coming down to see him immediately. We've got trouble."

"Yes, sir."

Entering his inner sanctum and throwing off his coat, Mr. Dandy began to read the document, mumbling to himself, "That little red-haired scourge!"

* * * * *

As David entered American history class, he noticed one of his *Bare Fax* extra editions prominently displayed on the front bulletin board.

Mr. Pennythorpe stood rubbing his hands and gazing out the window, looking like a little gnome warming his hands over a fire. The tardy bell sounded.

All eyes turned to Mr. Pennythorpe, who still gazed out the window.

Mr. Pennythorpe turned to the class and pointed to the window, saying, "I see a new horizon from this window today. It is a horizon grounded in a rediscovered responsibility that goes beyond our society's usual selfish norms. This new consciousness springs from our discussion yesterday. That new consciousness identified line budging as wrong, and we petitioned the principal requesting that it be ended. Part of the lesson to be learned is that if you don't ask, you don't get. Yesterday we were provoked enough to ask, and today we have received. Mr. Ferlinghausen stopped in here during homeroom period to tell me he has read our petition, and that he will appoint a faculty hall proctor today to monitor the situation so as to insure line budging doesn't continue. He wants you to be the first to know."

Cheers and hoots filled the room. Audrey Vanderkamp scowled and took out her makeup pack, peering at the shadow under her eyes.

100

David was pleased. Now he and Lisa would have more time together during lunch. David was so excited he could barely concentrate on Mr. Pennythorpe's special lecture, which offered a historical view of petitions, beginning with King John and the Magna Carta.

When class was over, Mr. Pennythorpe beckoned David to his desk as the class left.

"Good work, David. I congratulate you," offered the teacher, hand outstretched.

David shook his hand, saying, "Thank you." Mr. Pennythorpe muscled a firmer grip than David had expected from a little gnome.

"Oh, yes," Mr. Pennythorpe added, "David, Mr. Ferlinghausen asked me to request that you stop and see him after class."

"When?"

"You may go right now. The office will give you a tardy pass to your next class."

* * * * *

Thirty seconds later David entered the office. Mrs. Dixon was at her desk typing.

"Mr. Ferlinghausen wants to see me," David announced.

Mrs. Dixon looked up. "Oh, yes, David. He's expecting you. Please go right in. Don't bother knocking, just walk in."

David did so and as he entered, he saw Mr. Ferlinghausen seated at his desk, frowning over a faculty schedule.

Looking up, Mr. Ferlinghausen said, "David, thank you for stopping. Come have a seat. I assume Mr. Pennythorpe announced the news to your class that we will now be posting a hall monitor to prevent line cutting during the lunch period."

"Yes, sir. Thank you."

Mr. Ferlinghausen smiled. "David, your special edition of *Bare Fax* caused me some minor problems this morning."

"'I'm sorry, sir."

"Don't be sorry. Problems are what my job is all about. I don't mind the territory, as long as I know who all the players are and what the stakes are. Right now I'm trying to fit all the pieces of the puzzle together, and I need your version."

"My version?"

"Yes. As it turns out, you seem to be the principal player."

"I'm afraid I don't understand."

"Well, the petition was your idea, wasn't it?"

"Yes. Completely. Mr. Pennythorpe sort of played into my suggestion during history class."

"Mr. Pennythorpe is as solid as a rock, isn't he?"

"Yes, sir. He's my favorite teacher."

"I was not aware of your petition or this problem until this morning. The entire matter took on a somewhat exaggerated proportion when Mr. Dandy stormed in here shortly after homeroom period, denouncing both the petition and special edition."

Mr. Ferlinghausen picked up an issue of *Bare Fax* and smiled at David. He had kind and gentle eyes, accentuated by dark circles.

"Mr. Dandy was waving this, and his face was so red I was a little worried about his health. He acquainted me with the problem as he saw it, and also gave me a short review of your background and abilities. Apparently you and he have not, shall we say, quite hit it off?"

"I don't feel he listens to me. He may hear my words, but not what I'm really trying to say."

Mr. Ferlinghausen sighed and nodded.

"Confidentially, I don't feel he listens to me, either, David."

David's eyes widened as he heard this intimate revelation.

"When I first assumed this principalship a year ago," Mr. Ferling-hausen continued, "it was like coming aboard a large ship, the crew already having been signed on. There are a number of faculty members with whom I work that I would not have personally chosen to be part of my crew, but who continue here because they enjoy the privilege of tenure. Now, I am not against tenure *per se*. It offers many healthy and important protections. In any case, Mr. Dandy told me about his initial interview with you. Everything he said contradicted my very clear first impression of you, as well as my impression of you this morning just before school. Such intuitions help me to keep things in balance."

"Mr. Ferlinghausen, I wanted to have my letter published in our school paper, but Mrs. Coachman refused."

"I also got a full report about that. As you know, we have a few people around here who don't like having their boat rocked. Of course, if the boat isn't rocked a little now and again, it merely drifts aimlessly in the water, never getting anywhere."

David was gratified Mr. Ferlinghausen understood.

"David, I think you should seek out a faculty advisor for your *Bare Fax* paper. I suspect Mr. Pennythorpe would be delighted to assist you in any way."

"I'll ask him later today," David agreed.

"There is only one other matter that bothers me, David, and I hope you will help me."

"What's that, sir?"

"I dare not tell you how many students stopped me in the hallway after homeroom period to ask if I knew how long a cockroach lives after its head is severed."

David smiled.

"Please feel free to come see me any time, especially if there is a problem I can help you with," Mr. Ferlinghausen continued. "I tell all of my students and their parents or guardians that my door is always open to them."

"Thank you, sir," said David.

"Are there any concerns that come to mind right now?"

"I had a bad scrape with Bobby Perkins and his gang in August. Every time I see them now, they call me Howdy Doody and push me around a little. I'm not afraid of them, but personally I refuse to use any form of violence. So for them, I guess, I'm just an easy mark."

"I want to know immediately if they give you any more trouble. I will see Bobby Perkins later today and make it abundantly clear to him that he and his gang had better lay off."

"Please don't, sir. I'd rather fight my own battles for now. Anyway, I think your involvement would only fan the flames."

"Very well. But please keep me informed. Do you have any other concerns?"

David looked at the tan carpet and then at Mr. Ferlinghausen's desk.

Mr. Ferlinghausen waited.

"Well," David began, "I'm not sure how to say this. There may be a problem with Mrs. Coachman. I don't think I'm going to like her class very much. I'm trying to like it. We sort of got off on the wrong foot when she took my letter to Mr. Dandy. But it's not just that. It's really because she doesn't use the language very well, and I don't think she even realizes it. I mean, she really murders it sometimes."

David looked up at Mr. Ferlinghausen who was listening intently. His eyes looked very sad, and he looked very sorry.

"I understand what you're saying, David. I don't know what to tell you. It's a situation I inherited. Sometimes students, such as yourself, are called to be their teachers' teachers."

David looked up with interest, as Mr. Ferlinghausen continued.

"It goes back to that old expression that 'to those whom much is granted, much is expected'. You have been granted exceptional gifts; others are not as fortunate."

David thought Mr. Ferlinghausen's assessment very generous.

"Under such circumstances, David," continued the principal, "the one with the greater gifts may be the *real* teacher. Do your best, and let me know how it's going. Right now, I need to review this faculty schedule to find a monitor for the lunch line. I appreciate your stopping."

"Thank you, sir. I feel much better about being at Midville Middle School now that I've gotten to know you. Thanks for your honesty."

"Thank you, David. That makes it all worthwhile for me."

* * * * *

David could hardly wait to share the news with Lisa at lunch. Their lunches would be longer now, and Midville Middle School had taken its first step. Perhaps it was only a small step, but the first step in the right direction is always the hardest.

Chapter Nine
From Bad to Worse to Awful

DAVID SAT IN GERTRUDE COACHMAN'S ENGLISH 9 CLASS gazing out the window. Large fluffy flakes of snow were falling, adorning trees, bushes and buildings with a delicate white lace.

David turned to consider Mrs. Coachman, who was writing the week's assignment schedule on the chalkboard. Her flabby hands did not flatter her, but only accentuated her considerable girth. Her iron gray hair was severely parted down the middle, and combed back tightly on each side. The style reminded David of someone, but he wasn't quite sure. The classroom clock was at the rear of the room, and every few minutes Mrs. Coachman would peer at it with furtive eyes.

Having resolved to try to understand this boorish woman, David now felt a growing distrust and dislike for her. Was there any common ground for their relationship? One didn't necessarily have to like one's teachers. As he studied the back and side of her head, David concluded in his own mind that Mrs. Coachman deserved her surname for, with her severe iron gray hair and stocky frame, she looked not unlike the frumpy coachman seen old lithographs riding at the rear of the seventeenth and eighteenth century English coaches. But something else tweaked David's mind. Suddenly he had it! —Yes, he thought, —she parts her hair just like Emily Dickinson! And her dresses are sort of dark and plain, just what one would expect. I wonder if her Dickinson imitation is conscious or unconscious? There was something pathetic in a barrel trying to wear the garb of a sylph.

"Now class," announced David's new English teacher, "we will begin our poetry unit tomorrow. As most of you know, I am the school's *only* published author. I may even bring in some of my own work to share with you, provided your creativity and enthusiasm is up to snuff. Now, as I make final preparations for our studies in poetry, which will begin tomorrow, please take time to read the poems in your textbook found on pages 85 through 110."

* * * * *

That evening Gertrude H. Coachman sat at her antique mahogany writing desk in the stylish Victorian house that she had inherited from the spinster Countess Anastasia Sperling, having served as that recluse's companion for twenty years.

—Hardly a companion, more like a vassal, thought Coachman, as she peered at a rare photograph of herself and Anastasia, which had been taken shortly after her appointment as companion to minister to the needs of the aging recluse.

Coachman reflected on their agreement, which had seemed sound and attractive at the time. For a modest salary, she had agreed to live with and take care of Anastasia until the latter's demise, at which time she would inherit the large, stone Victorian house and sufficient monies left in Trust dedicated specifically to paying taxes on what her mistress had once called an old, cold pile of stone. To say that Anastasia had been welcoming would be the height of hyperbole. From beginning to end, their relationship had been as cold as the mansion itself got on the deepest day of winter, with few words spoken, yet many more repressed. First there had been the signed contract, specifying the terms of their mutual obligations, witnessed by Anastasia's lawyer and his secretary.

With the stroke of a pen, the Countess, a confirmed and crotchety old recluse, who desired little in attention, and even less in conversation, condemned herself to living with the uncultured victim of a deprived childhood who needed, more than anything, the blind affirmation and unconditional acceptance as could be regularly found in the tedium of endless and idle conversation.

Gertrude Coachman reflected on those first months of her employ, on that fateful evening during which the Countess had stared coldly at her throughout the meal, asking her icily at its conclusion, "Why don't you just SHUT UP?!"

That was the last meal they were to share together. Cold silence descended on the house, the Countess opting to write notes for almost all of their communications. In its devolution, their relationship lasted nineteen years too long. Coachman, having received nothing in the way of inheritance from her own parents, each of whom had been plagued with financial problems, had always felt singularly cheated. It hadn't mattered that there was no estate to inherit; it only mattered that she had been cheated, and at the relatively young age of twenty-three, after a brief but failed marriage, she resolved to make her own way in the world, as well as to make the world pay what it owed her.

When Gertrude Coachman signed on with the Countess, she had sold her trailer and invested the resulting ten thousand dollars in several promising stocks. Fulfilling her domestic duties required the better part of her time, the few remaining hours left to reading and talking to herself. By happenstance, she discovered the writings of Vachel Lindsay, and used some of her dividends to begin a small, personal library. She also began to fancy herself to be a budding author, in fact, a poet, and she dedicated herself to daily versifying.

—I'll show 'em all, thought Gertrude Coachman, as she grudgingly remembered those lonely years.

"The Countess got hers in the end," she snorted, "'Cause I didn't even bother to go to her miserable little funeral."

A snicker shook the desk as Coachman remembered the pneumonia that killed her late Mistress. —Served her right, she thought.

Growing suddenly sober, she frowned and scowled, adding aloud, "But the last laugh was on me, by golly. Some day I'll unload this little tub of stone on to some unsuspecting idiot. Then I'll retire in real style." The harsh laugh returned. "True to her every word. I got the house and barely enough for taxes. Hope it doesn't fall down before I sell it. No real maintenance in over thirty years! Looking the worse for wear, too. Should probably try to unload it in the spring."

The lack of a regular salary after the Countess' death had forced Gertrude Coachman to seek outside employment. Soon to discover she lacked for marketable talents, she accepted a job as cafeteria dishwasher at the former Midville High School, which later became Midville Middle School. Owing to her cultivated habit of talking to herself as she washed dishes, her supervisor had more than once suggested sarcastically that, in light of her interminable loquacity, she should become a member of the school's English department, and thereby created a monster of prediction and prophesy.

—And why not an English teacher? Coachman chortled to herself as she pored over her month's bills. —Pays a lot finer than any dishwasher. Showed 'em, showed 'em all.

The proximity of a nearby community college and state college had allowed Gertrude Coachman the opportunity to complete her degree, during evenings and summers, in only six and one half years. That she was nearing fifty when she had been hired to replace an English teacher who had gone on maternity leave mattered not at all. She had "showed 'em", as she would chortle to all who would listen.

When the new mother decided not to return to teaching, no suitable replacement could be found, and the position fell by default to Gertrude H. Coachman. The principal who hired her had been desperate, and had already in his own mind retired from education; his inattentiveness vastly increased Coachman's prospects for tenure, which she was awarded after the customary three years of trial service.

"Indentured servitude," she laughed to herself, thinking of those first few years, adding, "Never worked so hard in all my life."

If her trial period had been the summer of her teaching, her tenure period proved to be the fall. Soon there were fewer and fewer assignments for her students and more and more free reading days. A sudden onset of influenza once caused her to miss three weeks of school, over a full year of sick leave.

Refusing to heat her inherited stone house to more than sixty degrees, and shutting off rooms she didn't use, she came to feel herself especially vulnerable to colds. Whenever she was heard to say "I'm feeling coldie today", one could be sure she would be absent from her duties for at least the next three.

—And why not? she mused ruefully to herself, checking in her mind the number of sick days still available to her this academic year. —I have 'em comin' to me, and I won't be cheated out of what's my due, I'll have 'em know." Another snorted laugh echoed through the frigid room. An electric heater near her writing desk labored in vain to reduce the chill that pervaded the room.

The awarding of her tenure had also instilled a rapid change of focus, namely toward a hitherto unannounced and long postponed ambition of becoming a published author. She paid a visit to the editor of the local Midville paper, who gave her little encouragement that any space would be found for her poems, having browsed over the several examples she had proffered. After five more visits repeating the same request, a small space was made available to her once a week, entitled, "Verse from A Local Writer". —Should have read 'from The Local Poet', grudged Coachman as she remembered her encounters with the editor, who had later that year retired from his job, as had her own principal. —Not enough moxie, thought Coachman. —Education and publishing is no place for the fainthearted. I showed 'em. Brought myself up by my own boot-straps: classic flight from cafeteria dishwasher to English professor. Maybe I should write an autobiography to inspire the goats of the coming generation.

For Gertrude Coachman the 'p' in published was for PROFIT. At first, she had been mildly peeved that no financial offers had arrived for large printings of books containing her poems. Her smoldering anger gradually turned into a firestorm of rage, wherein she finally flounced down to the newspaper's new editor, demanding a free subscription for as long as she continued to allow her poems to be published. This concession she had quickly won, almost as if it had been worth the price of getting rid of her. The sad truth about her weekly offering of verse was that very few people even read it, and of those who did, very few did so again. Her poems proved themselves to be a hyperbolic antitheses of her own life's struggle, and thus were ladened heavily with flowers, sweetness, light, beauty, hackneyed rhymes, painfully obvious conclusions, and extremely strained language; such were the ditties that had arrived to litter the Midville *Courier's* weekly landscape.

"Never has been any respect for the great artists," grumbled Gertrude Coachman, as she sat filling out the application on her desk. She had recently received an advertisement promising to include one of her poems in a comprehensive volume of poetry to be entitled *Our Nation's Greatest Living Poets*. There was absolutely no charge for this courtesy, so said the advertisement, which also proceeded to announce the sale of said book for a bargain-basement hardcover price of $ 45.00.

It was clear, however, that the submitted poem and book order *must* accompany one another, since only a limited number of books would be printed.

Coachman had decided that this was now her ideal chance to go national, especially since the Midville intelligentsia had obviously fallen asleep, failing to proclaim the presence of her enormous artistic talent from the town's rooftops.

—Maybe I should order two books, she pondered, carefully examining her checkbook. Ample resources were available. —I wonder if I gave the book to the library, would it be tax deductible? I can get the school to order one for its library, but the public library is another kettle of fish. I don't have any influence there. Darn fools forbade me to give free poetry readings. No real support. They'll be sorry once I'm nationally published and famous. I'll show 'em.

Sighing heavily as she wrote the ninety dollar check, she closed her eyes after sealing the envelope, visualizing her poem in print. Having been restricted to a twenty line maximum, she had decided to write a new poem about writers, the better to inspire the next generation of authors striving for recognition. She closed her eyes and contemplated how her poem would appear on the printed page. Now she would finally become a published author in more than that local rag of a paper. She would have her name and work in a nationally published volume of verse. Since she couldn't accurately remember the poem she had just submitted, she studied her copy of the text, visualizing how it would appear on the printed page.

—Better give my poem a good billing, or I'll sue 'em, she chortled to herself, wondering if she might be able to get her money back.

She look admiringly at the poem that lay before her eyes.

Writing A Way Today

I come to this native land of flowers and rhymes,
To bring to the reader's mind that which is sublime.
No one ever more cares to read about the light's sway:
That is why authors have very little more to say.
This sonnet rings clear to all who hear and read
Of one's life's work that is truly well-conceived.
Little more, little more than walking through a garden,
Why don't you call and fetch me to your pardon?
"We are so sorry to have not noticed your talent;
You are cleverer than those who invent."
"It is nothing," I now modestly proclaim,
"Rather it is our society we must blame."
So that, like this, since Shakespeare wrote on earth,
Never again shall you fail to mourn this poet's worth.

—If life won't recognize me, thought Coachman,—history will. Smiling smugly to herself, Gertrude Coachman reviewed the short autobiographical statement she had submitted for publication with her newly fashioned poem:

Gertrude H. Coachman, author, educator, was born in Midville, New York, and grew up attending local schools, including the nearby community college and state university. Ms. Coachman's poems appear regularly in the Midville *Courier*. Ms. Coachman is a fond fan of the poetry of Mr. Vachel Lindsay. She once presented a workshop on Mr. Lindsay's work at a New York State Humanities Conference.

"That'll teach 'em of my notoriety," she chortled. Taking a tissue from a box in front of her, she said to herself, "Now poor Gertrude, don't get coldie until after you've taught this marvelous poetry unit. Then you'll have earned your right rest."

Yawning, she looked at the clock, which showed that it was well past midnight. Sealing her poem and biography in the envelope, together with her check, she applied a return address label and placed it in her briefcase, "Darn school can pay the postage," she grumbled.

Rising slowly, she pulled her frayed bathrobe tighter as she hobbled up the circular staircase to the second floor. She brushed her teeth, took two pills for her arthritis, and then rinsed her mouth. Gazing at the haggard face she saw in the mirror, puffy and jowled, she rejoiced that she looked better than all the old crowd, the beautiful ones, the special ones. That swell crowd, in her imagination and memory, had always been the pretty ones, the absolute rage. She gleefully reviewed their faces in her mind. All of them now had passed middle age and looked all the worse for wear, their youthful beauty and charm having diminished much more than her own.

—Not so *special* now, she grimaced. —And what did *special* mean, she wondered. What was it that they had that she lacked? Or had *they* ever even had it, whatever it was? They seemed to have had *something*, but maybe *it* had only been an illusion.

Turning into the hallway, she wondered what still bothered her. Something still pricked at her like an ice pick, causing her impatience and temper to smoulder. There was something she hadn't yet seen, something that haunted her memories. It had something to do with the word *special*, although she did not know what. —What? she thought.

Puffing as she approached her bedroom, she paused at the hallway thermostat to reduce the temperature to fifty degrees. The device's cold, clammy metal caused her to shiver. For the slightest instant she felt chilled to the bone. The warmth that she craved in that flash of unconscious recognition was not the kind that any furnace could provide. A familiar emptiness stirred within her, causing her to close her eyes and to breathe deeply, wondering if she might be having those old familiar heart palpitations that had enabled her to direct so much of her attention to her own health. Those twitterings, however, had never presented themselves in this way. Still, the emptiness at her center implored her attention as surely as a vacuum stifles a flower, but she summoned sufficient strength to shove it down once again into an oblivion she dared not travel through, nor even acknowledge.

Entering her bedroom, she placed a second comforter on the bed before removing her bathrobe, slipped between the sheets and, after turning out the light, she thought to herself, —I'll sure as hell show 'em. I'll show 'em all.

* * * * *

David sat in English 9, bored and frustrated. —Mrs. Coachman can't help looking dowdy, he thought. —She simply *is* dowdy.

Perhaps it was an internal carelessness that did not flatter her general appearance, which ran from slovenly to sloppy. The drabness of her dresses, which were never completely ironed, suggested their origin lay in a previous century. It seemed to David, however, that even something more was lacking in her character.

—Out of focus, he thought, as he watched her write on the chalk board. —Almost like a blur or a scribble.

The unit on poetry had been worse than David had first feared. On the previous Thursday, Mrs. Coachman had asked the class to open their books to Robert Frost's poem "Stopping By Woods On A Snowy Evening". Admittedly, she had picked a war-horse to ride, and her explication of the poem included cliché after cliché about the poem, casting its mood of potential suicide against the poet's struggle in his deepest soul, whether or not to surrender to the darker forces. David sighed to himself, for he had heard a much better explication of the poem the year before, by a more competent teacher of literature, who herself at one time had even met Mr. Frost's daughter.

David later lamented the question he would ask, which had bestirred this strange woman, causing her much consternation.

"Mrs. Coachman," he had ventured, "Don't you think the poem's form succeeds for the simple reason that he broke it?"

"Broke it? Broke what? What do you mean?"

"Well, the poem is written in iambic pentameter and follows the rhyme scheme of a rubaiyat. But the last line doesn't bring in a new rhyme word, it simply repeats the line before it. In a sense, the form becomes more profound when departed from."

"What is this gibberish? Broken forms? What absolute nonsense! I would have you know, young man, that I am a published author, and I know a good deal more about writing poetry and studying poetry than you do, so don't get beside yourself and put on airs. I'll thank you to keep such questions to yourself in the future and not to disrupt my lecture. You have a long way to go in learning good manners around here, dearie."

David had sat silent in the face of this unjust and undeserved reproof, sorry that he had even asked the question, and wondering whether Aunt Lillian might have been right after all that he should never have consented to enter Gertrude Coachman's English 9 class.

—Well, that was last week, David thought. —Let bygones be bygones.

Yet David had had as full a taste as he cared to of Gertrude Coachman's desiccated pedagogy, which was very dry bones indeed. David remembered how she had clutched the teacher's answer book the previous Friday, during the review just prior to the weekly quiz. There had been something in the way she had held the book that conveyed an air of uncertainty.

The first twenty-five minutes of each Monday's English class was given to "the bliss of creative writing". During these sessions, Gertrude Coachman seemed a bit more animated. Tugging at her rumpled dress, she would purse her lips, blink a lot, lick her lips, and then exhort her charges to enter with her into the "mystic realm of creativity". Her eyes fluttered, as if charmed by some magic lantern, after which Gertrude Coachman, published author and teacher of literature, would help to usher in the next generation of writers.

The writing exercises proved nondescript, with students being asked to write about overgeneralized topics such as "My Best Day" or "My Favorite Color" or "My Pet of Pets" or "Buttons", calling forth trite and hackneyed results, many of which Mrs. Coachman would praise as both exceptional and promising. Occasionally she would place a big red star on a student's work and, after reading it to the class, would tack it to the bulletin board until the next week. Then she would fling these "precious pearls" into her "folder of the ages".

"Now class," intoned Gertrude Coachman, "take out paper and pencil for this week's creativity exercise and complete the sentences I have just written on the board."

David took pen in hand and started the exercise.

    1. My hope in life is to be _____.
    2. Perhaps I'll try _____.
    3. Who let _____?
    4. I wonder _____.
    5. To me the world at large _____.
    6. I admire Shakespeare the man for plays and _____.

"Now we'll hear what you've written," announced Mrs. Coachman, taking her place at the wooden podium sitting on the desk next to the board.

"Jennifer, sweetie, you go first ... read your sentences slowly so everyone can understand them."

Jennifer, a shy and slender creature with long brown hair as fine as silk falling over her purple blouse, took her paper and began:

"My hope in life is to be as good a student as I can be."

"Tremenjus," pronounced Coachman, her eyes closed, again pursing her lips for the next sentence.

"Perhaps I'll try to become a teacher of geography."

"Ah," exclaimed Coachman, her eyes still strained shut, wetting her lips as if she were having some ecstatic religious experience.

"Who let the cows out of the barn?"

"Yes, sweetie, go ahead. You're doin' good."

"I wonder if they'll do some harm?"

"Just excellent, sweetie. Just excellent."

"To me the world at large seems great."

"Yes, ah, yes," Coachman continued, eyes still shut, pursing her lips for the last sentence.

"I admire Shakespeare the man for plays and poems."

"Tremenjus, just tremenjus, sweetie. You're doin' really good!"

"Well," corrected David, not able to stand it any longer.

Mrs. Coachman started, as if ripped from a trance, and looked coldly at David. "Well, well what?" she demanded.

"Isn't it more appropriate to use the adverb 'well' when describing how one is doing?"

Coachman scowled at David, groping for an answer.

"Well, in one sense, dearie, well is proper if you're describing an action, but I was describing what she had written, with the word 'work' to be inferred after good."

David heard the words but they felt hollow, and he felt himself roll inside, his gut instinct telling him this was a lie designed to save face, and that he had now become the goat for having interrupted Mrs. Coachman's precious creative writing session.

Clearing his throat, David answered, "Thank you for your clarification."

"You're certainly welcome, dearie. That's what I'm here for."

"I have another question."

"Yes, dearie. Go ahead."

"Don't you think an appositive is required for emphasis in sentence number six?"

If Gertrude Coachman had ever known what an appositive was, she had long forgotten this intricacy of language, yet we must give her credit for taking the offensive.

"I always try to be positive with my students, dearie."

David suspected that dearie was the underside of sweetie, although while the latter carried no warmth of feeling, the former seemed even more forced.

"No," replied David. "I mean an appositive in the grammatical sense."

"I also try to be positive with grammar, when I'm not bombarded with irrelevant questions. But let's see how you completed your sentences, dearie. Read them to me."

Abandoning any hope of securing a 'Tremenjus', David began:

"My hope in life is to be a hungry and a humble flea."

Silence. So David decided to plunge ahead.

"Perhaps I'll try for meals of cacophony. Who let the cats and dogs escape? I wonder why my meal is late. To me the world at large is huge. I admire Shakespeare, the man, for plays and muse."

The class laughed, and David smiled in acknowledgment as Mrs. Coachman glared at him.

"And what makes you think that yours is so funny, dearie?"

David thought a moment. "Well, it has the strength of continuity. The point of view is consistently from that of the flea mentioned in sentence one. It also turns on rhyme. It also makes a pun."

"Pun? What pun?" asked Coachman blankly.

"Well, the flea is hungry, and wonders where the dogs and cats have gone, and acknowledges how very tiny it feels. Then, when thinking of Shakespeare, it admires the playwright for his plays and Muse, meaning the goddess of his art, and also muse, meaning to think, if there are any fleas referred to in the body of the bard's work."

"Did you really intend all of that or are you just making it up?"

David smiled in triumph. "It wasn't accidental. I meant all of it. I was bored with these infernal exercises, and I was trying to have a little fun with this one. John Donne wrote a poem about a flea, albeit a far grander one. Some critics have suggested it might be one of the best seduction poems written in the 17th century. So there *is* an established literary precedent."

"Fleas aren't important," scoffed Gertrude Coachman. "What have fleas to do with English class? Anyway, the literature of the 17th century had lots of flaws and shortcomings, I'll have you know, including many mistakes in spelling," Mrs. Coachman pontificated.

"But they weren't really mistakes," corrected David, whose omnivorous reading habits had picked up interesting tidbits of information over the years, "because it wasn't until Samuel Johnson published his dictionary in 1755 that any standardization in spelling had even *begun* to happen. And what's even more interesting is that the Old English language wasn't even written down until around 600 A.D., and then it was corrupted by the influences of language that William the Conqueror brought from France in 1066, so that now only about half of our words are derived from Old English with most of the others coming from French or Latin. Did you know that some authorities believe that Shakespeare had a really wicked huge vocabulary?"

David's burst of scholarship was too much for Gertrude Coachman, who pursed her lips and then wet them with her tongue and looked at the class, which for once had given her its undivided attention owing to the unusual nature of this teacher-student interchange. Giving a condescending smile, she spoke with great restraint and patience, as if she were addressing a slow learner, saying, "Now, David, dearie, since you know so much about the history of the language, I want to see if you can do as well by completing a poem I have written for publication in our local newspaper. They insist that I submit my poems at least three weeks ahead of time. Published authors, as you probably don't know, must work well ahead of their deadlines. *This* should be interesting. Now take out another piece of paper while I write my poem for next week's *Courier* on the board. I would like the class to see how you would complete it, and then how, in fact, I completed it. Anyone in class is welcome to try this little contest, if you'd like."

Taking the poem from a folder in her desk, Gertrude Coachman wrote the following on the chalk board. A smiling David dutifully copied and filled in spaces as he went.

THESE ROSES CAN'T BE SEEN AT NIGHT,
BUT GIVE THE SMELLER SWEET _____;
THIS GARDEN FORMS THE MIGHTY ORB
OF MEMORY'S FADED _____;

WHAT BRINGS THE MIND TO PAST EVENTS
IS WHAT WAS NOTICED IN A _____;
THE WALL THAT FAILS AS WISDOM GROWS
IS ONE WHERE THOUGHT BECOMES A _____.

"Now," gushed Coachman, "I will read mine to all of you and then we will hear David's." Completing this poem had taken her several hours, but she did not allow David more than an iota of time.

"David, you may stop writing. Attention, Sweeties, here is my completed poem:

THESE ROSES CAN'T BE SEEN AT NIGHT,
BUT GIVE THE SMELLER SWEET DELIGHT;
THIS GARDEN FORMS THE MIGHTY ORB
OF MEMORY'S FADED CATALOG;
WHAT BRINGS THE MIND TO PAST EVENTS
IS WHAT WAS NOTICED IN A DREAMT;
THE WALL THAT FAILS AS WISDOM GROWS
IS ONE WHERE THOUGHT BECOMES A ROSE."

Looking up smugly, Mrs. Coachman added, "Class, please note that I took poetic license with the word dream. Published authors can do that, you know. I changed the verb 'dream' to its past tense: dreamt. It rhymes that way, and it also shakes the reader a little."

"It sounds nice, but what does your poem mean?" asked Adam Blake, as he brushed his hand through his brown curls.

"It means, Sweeties, that we remember things from our senses, such as smell. And when we dream, our unconscious selves return to earlier memories where smells can remind us of things we've forgotten, like the fresh smell of gingerbread and sweet whipped cream remind me of

Christmas when my grandmother would make a gingerbread house for a candy Santa Claus."

"I like your poem," announced Melanie Richards.

"Thank you, Melanie. I must say, in all modesty, it's one of my better poems. Perhaps a little deep for most of you, but in time you'll understand its meaning. But now, just for the fun of it, let's hear what David has managed."

Smiling, David stood and advanced to the front of the room. Clearing his throat, he read:

> *These roses can't be seen at night,*
> *But give the smeller sweet insight;*
> *This garden forms the mighty orb*
> *Of memory's faded analogue;*
> *What brings the mind to past events*
> *Is what was noticed in a scent;*
> *The wall that fails as wisdom grows*
> *Is one where thought becomes a knows.*

"And that's 'k-n-o-w-s' instead of 'n-o-s-e'," explained David.

The class sat spellbound. No one had expected very much, yet here was a poem far better than the first, and everyone knew it.

"Just *see* what can be accomplished when you are given most of something ahead of time!" puffed a very distraught Gertrude Coachman, salvaging what credit she could for David's work.

David accepted the backhanded compliment with a quiet smile, looking directly at Coachman.

"Now, David, dearie, why don't you explain to us why you wrote what you did."

"I like puns, so I tried to write my poem on several levels at once. The roses are likened to insight, which brings the reader to the road of self-inquiry and self-knowledge. In using the word analogue, I go beyond mere cataloging of thoughts to imply that senses, events, choices, actions are all analogous to the formation of memory, that it is not a simplistic process. When I suggest that memory can be tapped through the recollection of a smell, I make it deliberate when I say 'a scent' which also is meant to mean 'ascent', which brings us along further on our quest for self-knowledge and truth. The wall that fails as wisdom grows is the wall of repression that has muddled our thoughts whereby thought becomes a new kind of knowing, a certainty that goes beyond proven fact. Some might call it mystical knowledge. But there is also a pun on 'knows' and 'nose', since the poem tries to extol the importance of smell and memory."

The class broke into spontaneous applause as David returned to his seat and sat down. Mrs. Coachman was wearing an upside-down smile that threatened to extend her jowl into one additional double chin, if such a phenomenon were possible.

Looking at David warily, she quickly advanced, snatched his paper from him, studied it intently, wetting her lips several times. Finally she announced, "You did good, dearie, I must admit. You're a buddin' bloomin' poet and a bit of a maverick to boot. Of course you *were* given the advantage of a good foundation on which to build your poem, so it wasn't too hard, with all that preliminary work already done, for you to come off so spectacular. Anyone in here would 've done the same thing."

David generously accepted this second backhanded compliment, wishing he had had his own foundation on which to build.

Mrs. Coachman flung David's paper on his desk and plodded to her own desk, heaving herself angrily into her chair. Taking three tissues from a large box on which was scrawled ONE *ONLY* PLEASE!, she blew her nose and sniffed several times.

"I'm afraid I'm feeling a little coldie."

By this, as most of the class had come to understand, she meant she might possibly be getting a cold, and that they would be doing group work or individual reading for the next day or two while Mrs. Coachman sat at her desk and prepared for their Friday exam.

"Tomorrow you will discuss the story that has been assigned in small groups, reading your written answers to each other. I fear I am not at my best today. I really am beginning to feel coldie. I will do my planning when you discuss the assigned story. On Wednesday, we will discuss your discussions. And remember: be sure to have all of your vocabulary words learned by Thursday. We will have a brief review of the words on Thursday and our usual vocabulary test on Friday."

Mrs. Coachman sat down at her desk and scribbled out a note. Melanie was then dispatched to the library, soon to return with a small brown book which she gave to Mrs. Coachman, who began to pore through it intently, pursing and wetting her lips as she pored over it.

David thought he recognized the book as a volume of the collected works of John Donne.

* * * * *

"I do not think you will learn much in English class this year, David," sighed Aunt Lillian, as she poured more tea.

"No. And that's exactly what happened today. Can you believe it? I checked later, and the book she requested was the Oxford collection of poems by Donne. I think she was checking to see if Donne really did write a poem about a flea, hoping to catch me in a mistake."

"Do you really think she had *never* heard of it?"

David closed his eyes. When he opened them, they reflected resolute certainty.

"My best guess is that she has a very shallow knowledge of literature, but the funniest thing is that she seems to be all wrapped up in appearing to be creative. Why doesn't someone tell her that she only writes rubbish?"

"We shouldn't be too harsh, David. Not everyone has *your* gifts. Would you like me to insist that you be returned to your eighth grade English class?"

"Let me think about that. I'm certainly not happy where I am. But let's give it until the end of the month to see if something good comes of it. I'll try to take a mountain of salt and a kinder humor into the tragedy called English 9 with Gertrude Coachman."

* * * * *

The group discussions on Tuesday had been interesting to David, largely because Mrs. Coachman sat at her desk, reading and writing for the entire period. Several students had, in fact, approached him, wondering if he would consider becoming their teacher during the group work.

On Wednesday, leaders from each small group reported to the larger class a summary of their discussions, during which time Mrs. Coachman sat at her desk taking notes, occasionally saying, "You did good ... really good" and "Tremenjus."

On Thursday the class was given a practice vocabulary test, and then exchanged papers to correct errors and to report their classmates' grades to Mrs. Coachman, who called names and recorded the scores in her book. David was the only one who had received a perfect score, and fully without benefit of having studied the words the class had learned in September.

"You did really fine, dearie," Mrs. Coachman had remarked.

David felt that "dearie" was still several pegs below "sweetie", and that "sweetie" was several pegs below "Hello, stranger".

"We will now have a vocabulary bonus exercise, so you can earn some points to help bring up your grades." Although Mrs. Coachman's vocabulary test had been called "preliminary", the subsequent scores were not, counting by a factor of two as against the major factor of five for Friday's test. Something, after all, had to be inserted into all those little spaces on the classroom register, for the end of the marking period would require the reporting of grades, and compositions took such a very, very long time to read, and even longer to evaluate.

Words on the bonus exercise plumbed the subtle differences between similar words, and David noticed that Mrs. Coachman was taking them from a book with an '11' marked on it.

Henry Major was asked the difference between furtive and elusive, and although it was apparent he didn't know, he managed to talk himself into extra credit by virtue of sheer nervous enthusiasm and Mrs. Coachman's help.

Annette Hesburg was asked to explain the difference between languish and deteriorate, responding, "Well, if something languishes, it sort of, um, like fades away, while if something deteriorates, it falls apart, like an old house or car."

"Tremenjus," was Mrs. Coachman's response as she marked a plus in her book. "Um, let me, er, see. Now for a really difficult one for double extra credit—and any takers must raise their hands."

As well as being bored, David was also beginning to feel that the subtleties of vocabulary explication were being slighted, so he promptly raised his hand.

"Dearie, you don't need the bonus points because you did so good on the preliminary test, but since you were first, I'll give you the first go."

A dramatic pause ensued as Mrs. Coachman scanned her book for two words.

"Ah, I've got 'em. David, dearie, what is the difference between harass and harangue?"

David reflected for an instant, but suddenly a flash of wicked wit got the better of his sober judgment, and he replied, "Well, she usually wears her 'rangue' on her finger ... "

Silence ensued for several seconds, before the class erupted in raucous laughter. Mrs. Coachman sat dumbstruck, her mouth wide open in disbelief, and showing a full red face above the quivering jowls.

"How, how, how ... " she sputtered, "dare you! Such insolence! Such rudeness! Go to the office immediately. I will not tolerate such language in this classroom!"

David took his books, left the classroom, and went to the office. Mr. Ferlinghausen was, as it turned out, at a meeting at the high school. Zeke Minturn was also waiting to see the principal, and watched with keen interest when he overheard that David had been referred to the office by Mrs. Coachman for disciplinary action. David waited until the period was over, and then went to meet Lisa at lunch.

Chapter Ten
Rock Bottom

THE SIGHT OF AUNT LILLIAN LAUGHING during dinner warmed David's heart.

"Your pun was wonderful! It's too bad Mrs. Coachman couldn't enjoy it."

"I didn't think she would take it so personally. Mrs. Fullerton, the Guidance Office Secretary, brought me a note from Mr. Dandy during seventh period stating that I had been transferred out of Coachman's English 9 honors course into the another section of English 9. The best thing is that Mrs. Martin's class meets during the same period, so my whole schedule doesn't need to be changed, because everything else is okay."

"David, I am pleased you will no longer have to suffer the whims of Gertrude Coachman. Whatever your new situation, it can only be better. I will be thinking of you all day tomorrow."

"Thanks. It can only get better from here on out," agreed David.

* * * * *

Melvin Dandy stood in front of Otto Ferlinghausen's desk. The principal was staring incredulously at his counselor's attire, which consisted of black pants over which he wore a bright orange sport jacket, accented by a dark maroon shirt that was itself accentuated at the neck by a gaudy, chartreuse bow tie. Otto had been asking for a clarification in the report he had just received.

"And after Gertrude asked David what the difference was between harass and harangue, then what happened?"

Dandy sputtered, "Then that little-freckled-faced scourge had the utter audacity to say, 'She wears the ring on her finger'."

A scowling Melvin Dandy watched a broad grin on the face of Otto Ferlinghausen give way to a hearty laugh. "The boy was only making a pun, for heaven's sake, and a pretty grand pun at that."

"But, Otto, I don't think *you* appreciate the hostility this has engendered between Gertrude and the boy," rejoined a persistent Melvin Dandy.

"Gertrude wouldn't know a pun if one ran over her."

"That is not for me to say, sir. But I do believe this incident is most unfortunate. In the best interests of all concerned, I have transferred David to Miriam Martin's English 9 section."

"Good Lord! That's the remedial group, isn't it?"

"Yes. But any other change would have wrecked his entire schedule. And Gertrude will have nothing more to do with the boy. She made *that* very clear to me yesterday during her lunch period."

"I've seen that very real obstinate streak before. We've also learned that there is very little hope for change once she has closed her mind to something," reflected Otto.

Dandy nodded grimly, adding, "Well, look at it this way. Miriam is an excellent teacher who won't stand in David's way. She'll probably have him do lots of independent study work in the library, or maybe even invite him to assist her in teaching the others. That should keep the lad occupied, idle mind the devil's playground and all that."

"Melvin, Melvin. I think you grossly underestimate David's abilities. He's probably sharper than most of our faculty."

"I don't disagree. But we've got to hold the line somewhere."

"The line? What line?"

"The line of dignity, decorum, and discipline. You don't know David as well as I do. There's an anti-authoritarian streak in that boy that could prove very unsettling to our entire school, should he ever put his mind to rocking our little boat."

Otto Ferlinghausen considered the counselor before him. "Perhaps David is against unjust authority; Einstein is said to have been the same way, and so were many others who saw through all that muck. In any case, I most certainly agree that Miriam is much more flexible than Gertrude, and she will certainly work to further David's strengths. That independent study idea may be the best answer yet to this problem. I wouldn't be surprised if Gertrude felt threatened by David's superior imagination and intellect."

"Threatened?" sputtered Dandy. "Why should she be threatened? She's over three times his age."

"Melvin, age and intellect don't always reflect each other. You're the counselor. You are supposed to see these personality traits. Gertrude Coachman has one of the most fragile egos I have ever encountered. For some reason, she thinks *everything* is her due. Look at those inane poems she submits to the paper. They don't reflect well on our otherwise very accomplished English department."

"But she's a *published* author."

Otto looked into Melvin Dandy's eyes, smiled, and said firmly, "Melvin, she's about as much a 'published author' as I am the King of Bavaria. "David made a funny pun that most people would have laughed off. Gertrude, in her insecurity and with her Victorian sensibilities, pulls out all the stops and throws David out of her classroom. I suspect they're *both* relieved. Let's see what happens. Better apprise Miriam that we have a very special student coming."

"Already have, sir."

"Good. I will make a point to talk to David a week from today to see how things are going. If he's unhappy, we'll have to try something different. With someone like David, you've got to play it by ear."

"Odd, isn't it?"

"What's that?"

"David is a problem to us because he's so bright, yet most of our problems come from students who don't have his abilities."

"Melvin, abilities have very little to do with it. Most of our problems come from a lack of love."

"A lack of love? We have a very caring faculty."

"I know. I'm not berating them in the slightest. I speak of a lack of love in the home as well as in the world—and, yes, by extension, here in school."

"But we bend over backwards ..."

"Yes, I know, and still we seem to have our fingers in an enormous dike that is leaking like a sieve."

* * * * *

David entered his new English classroom and handed his guidance office slip to Mrs. Martin, noticing a twinkle in her eyes as she smiled at him.

"Thank you, David. I'm glad you've come to join us. I think much of our work bore you, so I hope you will consider contracting for a lot of independent study in the library. I would also welcome any ideas you might have on how to make the basics of English a little more interesting to your classmates, who perfectly loathe it."

All David could respond was, "Thank you." He began to wonder if he hadn't arrived in heaven.

"You're welcome, David. Why don't you take the fourth seat in that row by the window."

The passing bell rang.

Students began to open their notebooks.

The door flew open and, with a raucous laugh, Bobby Perkins and Zeke Minturn sauntered in.

David quickly revised his estimate of this new English class in regard to its similarity to heaven; in fact, shades of another place now clouded his thoughts.

"That will be a detention for both of you tonight," announced Mrs. Martin. "This is the third time you've been late to class. Here are your slips. I will sign you up when I go to the office."

The boys took their slips. Bobby suddenly noticed David. His eyes ignited with anger as he scowled at David, "What's he doin' here?"

"This is David Andrews, a new student."

"He's in eighth grade. He ain't supposed to be in ninth."

"David is a year ahead in English. I think you will find him more than equal to the task, which reminds me that you still owe me some back assignments."

Bobby ambled to his seat, slamming his books down on his desk, and flinging himself into his seat as he glowered at David.

The class settled into its work. Mrs. Martin assigned David his new books, gave him an assignment schedule, and knelt beside his desk as she explained the class routine.

"Look over all this material and let me know what you've already mastered. Then we can begin to build an independent study schedule for you. Okay?"

David nodded.

The bell finally rang. David was eager to meet Lisa for lunch, but as he entered the stairwell, he felt a hostile hand grab the back of his shirt, throwing him against the brick wall, bumping his head.

"Ow!" he yelled.

Bobby Perkins sneered at him, "Well, if it ain't Howdy Doody, the new ninth grader."

Somehow, to David, it didn't seem quite the time to make fun of the Howdy Doody accolade, as he had once fancied himself doing—at least not after he studied the fierceness in Bobby Perkins' eyes.

"Leave me alone," announced David. "What's it to you, anyway?"

Bobby grabbed David by his shirt lapels and pulled him closer, "Listen to me, you green-eyed, freckle-faced runt. You better mind your p's and q's if you want to live to see the ninth grade. I'm just waitin' for you to mess me up again, and then you're dead. Understand? I already got a detention 'cause of you."

"You got detention because you were late for class."

"Yeah, and if you hadn't been there, she would've let it slide like the other times."

"I doubt it. She's made of stronger stuff than that."

Bobby suddenly thrust David back against the wall.

"Ow! My head."

"A lot more than your head will hurt when I'm finished with you. What are *you* made of? Can you *break*? You've got a lot comin' to you. I'm gonna be keepin' my eye on you. Understand?"

"You'd might do better to keep your eyes on your school work."

Bobby drew his fist back, ready to paste David in the mouth, but stopped short when he heard, "Hey. Get along there, Perkins. Don't loiter in the stairwell."

The passing bell rang. Mr. Besio, the shop teacher, advanced and grabbed Bobby's shoulder, saying, "Pick on someone your own size."

"Ain't you heard?" snorted Bobby. "This here's the *new* ninth grader. I was just welcomin' him to our class."

"Sure you were. Now move along."

Glaring at David, Bobby gave a heavy sigh and moved along.

"Are you all right?" asked Mr. Besio.

"Yes, thanks. I'm afraid that kid has a grudge against me."

"Bobby Perkins? He's mad at the world, and you just happened to get in his way."

* * * * *

David, the last to join the cafeteria line, was grateful there was still some macaroni and cheese waiting for him when he got his plate.

He placed his tray across from Lisa, who was lost in a book.

"Oh, David! I thought you'd skipped lunch for something."

"Sorry I'm late."

"David," Lisa confided, "you missed all the excitement!"

"Excitement?"

"Yes, in lunch line. Bobby Perkins tried to elbow his way in front of Conrad Bowles. You know him—he's the little shrimpy seventh grader with the big thick glasses."

"Sort of nerdy? I think I've seen him," David nodded.

"Well, Bobby shoved in front of him, and suddenly Conrad started screaming about his rights and yelled for Mr. Lynch, the line monitor."

"Gosh, what happened?"

"Mr. Lynch came right over and pulled Bobby out of line. Bobby shook Mr. Lynch's hand off his arm, yelling that he had *his* rights, and nobody was going to take him out of line, especially since he had been late because of some sort of unfinished business."

"I think *I* was the unfinished business," groaned David.

"No way, David. Are you serious?"

"I'll explain later. What happened to Bobby?"

"Mr. Lynch pulled him again *really* hard, saying, 'Don't you dare be insubordinate with me! Get to the end of the line.' And Bobby yelled,

'Screw you.' And Mr. Lynch grabbed him by the scruff of his neck and walked him down to the office. It was a real spectacle!"

"Did Bobby come back?"

"No. He's probably suspended by now. David, are you all right? You look a little pale."

"Well, as I was saying, I think *I'm* the unfinished business Bobby was talking about. He tried to bully me after my first English class with Mrs. Martin. *He's* in the class. Can you believe it? He was blaming me because he got a detention slip; now he'll blame me for his problems in trying to cut line."

"Don't be silly. You didn't have anything to do with it."

"Not directly, but I made the stink so we could get line monitors."

"Bobby will never put that together in a million years."

"Why not?"

"Because I doubt very much he ever reads anything, much less anything connected with school."

David smiled weakly.

Lisa was doing her best to be upbeat about the whole mess, but David couldn't help wonder how ugly Bobby would be with no lunch. David had a sinking premonition and stumbled, "I ... I ... don't think I want to walk home from school today."

"Why don't you call your aunt to come and get you?"

"Good idea. Maybe I'm a chicken, but Bobby beat me to a pulp once in August, and I *never* want to go through that again."

"David, please, PLEASE call your aunt."

"Okay. I will, right after last period. Mrs. Dixon will let me call."

* * * * *

David pushed the office telephone's redial for the third time.—Aunt Lillian must be out shopping, he thought.

136

"David, is everything all right?" inquired Mrs. Dixon.

"I'm not sure. I was trying to call my aunt to ask her to come pick me up, but she's not home."

"I'm sorry. Is there anything I can do for you?"

"Thanks, anyway. I guess I'm just going to have to walk home."

Having stopped at the office, David was one of the last students to leave the building. —Maybe I should take a different way home, he thought. Then he remembered the book he and Aunt Lillian had read together in August. —No, I will go my usual way, come what will.

Having advanced safely for several blocks, David began to wonder whether or not his apprehensions had been misplaced. As he turned the corner by the wooded lot, Bobby Perkins emerged from behind a tree and stepped in David's way.

"Well, if it ain't Mr. Howdy Doody. Fancy meetin' you here."

Prickles chilled David's spine and his knees began to feel like rubber.

"What do *you* want?"

"You *know* what I want, sport," sneered Bobby, "and what I'm gonna do because there ain't no one to protect your little freckled face out here in the *real* world. And there's gonna be a lot more red on your face when I get done with it. 'Cause of you, I got two weeks of detention, but I ain't gonna go, so I'll probably get suspended, and it's all the same to me, anyways."

Part of David wanted to turn and run, but his knees felt like water and he couldn't move. It was also a foregone conclusion that Bobby could easily catch him.

"You ain't nothin' but a weak sister dressed up like Howdy Doody," taunted Bobby, his eyes cold with hate, "'cause you ain't got the balls to fight like a man."

"A *real* man wouldn't resort to violence."

"Bull crap!" yelled Bobby, grabbing David and shoving him back against a tall maple tree, as he formed a fist with his right hand and snorted, "This one's got your name on it!"

David felt blood gushing from his nose. Then he felt a sharp pain in his lower abdomen as he bent forward from the impact of Bobby's second punch, only to double over as Bobby kneed him in the groin. Crumpling to the ground, he wondered if Bobby would proceed to kick him senseless.

"Leave him alone, you big bully!" came a sudden warning.

"Ow! My ankle, you little bitch!" yelled Bobby.

"Banzai!" came a fierce war cry, with Bobby receiving a karate kick to his solar plexus. This knocked the breath out of him and he staggered back to consider his attackers, fully noticing that they had tossed their books on the sidewalk.

A boy and girl, each with brown hair and freckles, pressed toward him. The girl had long curly brown hair and a determined look in her eyes. The boy, no doubt her brother, stood two inches taller. He was lankier than his sister, his short hair sporting a military look, and what was even more troubling than the stealth of his approach was the fierceness in his eyes, as he led with his arms in preparation for another strike. Bobby gasped when he saw absolutely no fear in those eyes.

"Here's another kick for your bully little ankle," announced the boy, as his foot impacted its target.

"Shit!" yelled Bobby, riveted by pain and startled at so direct an assault. Hadn't these underlings heard of Bobby Perkins, the only one in school who no one ever messed with?

Bobby shook his ankle as if to throw off the pain, panting. "You're as good as dead, you little runt."

"Bring it on, Jack!" grinned the boy, "I've got a brown belt in karate. Come and get it!" Shifting to what was obviously a offensive

138

position, and waiting for Bobby to advance, the boy once again shouted his challenge, "Come and get it, Jack!"

Bobby was not dumb and, as he stood there panting, he vividly remembered how he had just gotten his breath knocked out of him, yet he couldn't imagine retreating in the face of an attack from what appeared to be a mere, albeit hostile, seventh grader. Trying to catch his breath, he began to point his finger at the boy when his adversary suddenly shrieked, "Oy!", again advancing and kicking him even harder in his solar plexus. Wheezing for breath, Bobby lurched around and stumbled off as fast as he could limp, his ankle still smarting.

David was still on the ground, and all of the foregoing hostilities had seemed a blur above and near his head. Then he felt his head being lifted and cradled by the girl, who said, "Sean, give me your handkerchief. I'll try to stop this bleeding."

Her brother obeyed immediately and added, "Here's some juice I didn't finish for lunch."

"Not yet. We need to stop the blood first. I'm sure you'll be okay," she added, looking at David with a reassuring smile.

"Do you think his nose is broken?" asked the boy.

"Shh. I don't know. Let's just stop the bleeding."

The girl looked at David kindly, "What's your name?"

"David Andrews. I live with my Great Aunt about five blocks from here over on Biggs Street."

"I'm Mary Potter. This is my brother Sean. We're new to Midville, so we don't know exactly where Biggs Street is. Can you sit up?"

David considered the question. "I think so." As he did, David felt dizzy and his head began to throb. He now saw blood all over his shirt as well as on the grass, and he could only imagine how ugly his face looked, puffy nose and all.

"Here. Try a little juice," offered Sean.

David accepted the thermos cup and welcomed the tangy liquid coursing down his throat, which had become very dry.

"Do you know that bully?" asked Mary.

"Yes. His name is Bobby Perkins. He's always getting into scrapes, and I think he has it in for me for some reason."

"Not any more," jeered Sean. "Just let him try something else and we'll take care of him. Right, Sis?"

Mary nodded.

"We may only be in the seventh grade," explained Sean, "but we're tough. It comes from years of kicking each other under the dinner table. It's not easy to take a direct hit in your ankle and not flinch."

"Why do you do that?" asked David.

"Oh, Sean used to make some nasty comment or other," said Mary, "and it was always innocent enough in my parents' hearing. It's just that we *really* know what the other one means, although the words may seem harmless on the surface."

"Yeah, if Mary were my brother, I would 've killed her a *long* time ago," said Sean. "But you know how it is, you can't beat up the girl, and it's always the *boy* who gets punished."

"Is not!" said Mary.

"Is too!" rejoined Sean.

"David, do you have any brothers or sisters?" asked Mary.

"No," said David. "I am an only child, and my parents were killed in an automobile accident last January."

"Oh, gosh! We're really sorry," said the twins, looking at David, shaking their heads. An awkward silence followed.

"I think I'm ready to walk home now," said David. "Thank you."

"What do you mean 'Thank you'?" said Mary. "We're coming with you."

"Yeah. Just in case Jack Nobody tries any more funny stuff."

"Bobby," corrected Mary, "Bobby Perkins."

"Whatever," said Sean. "Still a first class jerk by any name."

"Thanks for coming along," said David.

Sean picked up David's books as David led the way.

"There's still blood caked around your eyes," said Sean. "When you can see better, you will see that I'm the much better looking twin."

"Only in a pig's eye" rejoined Mary, lamming into Sean with a sisterly punch.

After she turned, Sean looked at David and rolled his eyes, as much as to say, "See, you're lucky not to have to put up with a sister."

* * * * *

"You're lucky it's not broken, David," concluded Dr. Smith, examining David's nose. David was stretched out on Aunt Lillian's reclining chair in the music room. Dr. Smith had pulled the piano bench over to probe the damage Bobby had done.

"Thank the good Lord," sighed Aunt Lillian.

Mary and Sean sat on a divan next to the side entrance.

"Twins," inquired Aunt Lillian, momentarily forgetting their names in her concern for David, "did you see the whole fight?"

"No," began Sean. "We had just turned the corner when we saw Perkins knee David in the groin."

"We were only about thirty feet away," continued Mary, "so we tossed our books on the sidewalk and ran to the rescue."

Aunt Lillian closed her eyes.

"And I can kick pretty well in an emergency," Mary added, smiling at Sean, who gave her a dirty look.

"I'm not bad at karate," Sean rejoined, eyeing Mary, "and it's amazing the number of emergencies that come up."

David wondered if the twins would have kicked each other in the ankles had everyone been seated at the dining room table.

The doorbell rang. "Ah, that must be Mr. Ferlinghausen. When I called him, he insisted on coming over immediately."

Otto Ferlinghausen, hearing the collective stories, was incensed. He and Dr. Smith left immediately to pay a visit to Bobby's father at the garage Edward Perkins operated near the outskirts of town.

Father and son were in residence, and a full report of the incident was given. Bobby was suspended from school for a week and, unknown to the principal and physician, received a severe beating from his father after they left. Mr. Ferlinghausen further arranged that until the Christmas holiday, Bobby would be escorted each day to the detention hall from his last period class.

Aunt Lillian, meanwhile, invited the twins to stay for dinner.

"We'd love to," said Mary, "but first we must call and let POTS know."

"Who is ... Pots?"

"POTS is our nickname for our old nanny," answered Mary.

"I mean, we're too old for a nanny, but she's stayed on anyway," explained Sean.

"She's really become part of the family, and she can be with us when our parents are working."

"Well, please call her to see if it's okay to stay, and then why don't you go up with David to his room. He can rest for a while in his own bed with this ice pack, and you can get better acquainted," suggested Aunt Lillian.

* * * * *

Dinner proved to be Aunt Lillian's celebrated meatloaf, whipped potatoes, and Brussel sprouts.

"You said your nanny's name is Pots? Is that because she's good at dishes?"

"Oh, no," Mary smiled.

"Her nickname is an acronym. POTS means," here Sean prompted Mary with his eyes, "Poor Old Thing, Shame!"

Aunt Lillian considered the acronym and suddenly started laughing. The twins were amused their nickname had gone over so well. David managed a smile.

"It's not as awful as it sounds," Mary explained. "POTS's real name is Muriel Mullarney. When we were young and got in trouble, she would snatch us away from whatever we were doing and scold us, saying, 'Shame!' Now that we've grown up, we've turned the tables, so when we're upset with her, or are sorry for her because she has borne the brunt of one of our silly gags, we think to ourselves: —Poor Old Thing, Shame! And it can be either shame on us, or shame on her, or shame on all of us."

"Does she mind being called POTS?"

"Oh, we'd *never* call her POTS to her face. That would be rude," said Mary, adding, "Well, Sean might, because he doesn't know any better."

"Are you kidding?" exclaimed Sean, "She'd kill us dead!"

"Well, you're the one who named her," said Mary.

"How did you do that, Sean?" asked Aunt Lillian.

Sean looked a little sheepish.

"Go on," prompted Mary, "Tell them; or I will."

"Well, this was years ago when Dad was teaching at Harvard and M.I.T., and one of the English universities wanted to confer an honorary degree on Dad. So Mom and Dad had flown off to England. Our parents don't let us watch very much television and POTS had gone out to get some groceries for dinner. I saw the *TV GUIDE* on the table, and was starting to browse through it, when I noticed there was a listing for a really cool war movie, so I turned it on. The only trouble was that POTS came back and caught me. She sent me to my room and said I wouldn't have any more television for two whole weeks! I was *really* mad, and I started jumping up and down on my bed, yelling 'POTS, POTS, POTS, POTS', when suddenly she stuck her big ugly head in the door, wearing a scowl that would turn milk into Limburger cheese. 'What's that?' she growled. 'Are ye daring to be fresh with me, laddie?' And I said, 'No, oh, no! I was just yelling STOP backwards—see, it spells POTS.' 'Oh, all right then,' she said, and I was off scot-free."

"Sean leads a charmed life," explained Mary, rolling her eyes.

"Anyway," Sean smiled, "She let us stay for dinner tonight. Dad's still working at the university and Mom's working the swing shift at the hospital."

"Is your Mother a nurse?" asked David, noticing Aunt Lillian raising her left eyebrow at him.

"No," smiled Sean, "She's an emergency room physician. Has to work twelve hour shifts."

"That must be very demanding work," said Aunt Lillian.

"It is," agreed Mary, "But she says the reason she went into emergency room work was so she could say 'Good bye' to Sean, because she's sure he will arrive there some day on his death bed."

David and Aunt Lillian looked at Sean to consider Mary's prediction, which had carried with it just a tad bit of ironic wishful thinking.

"Mom *thinks* I'm wild," confessed Sean.

"She's RIGHT," said Mary, before any disclaimer could be offered by David or Aunt Lillian.

Sean glared at Mary, who continued blithely, "Oh, it's not just the wildness, you know. You'd expect that in a boy his age. He's crazy about guns and knives and violence, and my parents have restricted him to a sheath knife for scouts and a BB gun for targets."

"What does your father do?" asked Aunt Lillian, hoping to take the onus of attention off Sean.

"He's a visiting professor of mathematics and physics at Cornell," said Mary.

"In both fields?" exclaimed Aunt Lillian.

"Yes," said Sean. "He's got a Ph.D. in mathematics from Princeton and a Ph.D. in physics from Harvard."

"Goodness!" said Aunt Lillian.

"Yeah," said Sean, "He's forty-five but he looks thirty. A lot of people mistake him for an absent-minded graduate student."

"Has he taught at Cornell very long?" asked Aunt Lillian.

"No. This is his first year. He was teaching at Harvard and M.I.T, but some of his students came here to Cornell to teach. Then they needed his help to pursue something they all had been working on at Harvard. So Cornell created a special University Professorship for him so he can do whatever he wants, either in the physics or in the math departments. That way everybody wins and nobody gets mad."

"What's he working on?" asked Aunt Lillian.

"Mostly nothing," explained Sean. "He thinks and works on his computer at home, and then he goes and talks to his former students, or they come over to our house. They're *all* a little peculiar, if you ask me. All they do is go on and on, yap, yap, yap — times this, times that — Bach this, Bach that — always talking about time and Bach."

"Everyone can't play computer games," Mary observed dryly.

"Shut up!" snapped Sean.

"Young people, we will have no harsh words at this table. Is that understood?"

Both twins nodded contritely.

"I wonder why they talk about Bach?" inquired Aunt Lillian.

The twins looked at each other, and Mary sighed, explaining, "Sean sometimes says more than he should. We don't really know. They always seem to be listening to Bach's music. Somehow they seem to think that it's very important to their figuring out what time is all about. Dad even plays Bach on the piano—and he's *really* good."

"I don't recall reading about your father's coming to work at Cornell this year in the university newsletter. They generally list all the new faculty."

The twins looked at each other sheepishly, deciding who would explain this anomaly. Finally, everyone looked at Sean, who put his right index finger up to his lips.

"Hush, hush," he said.

"Hush, hush?" squinted Aunt Lillian.

"Low profile. The project he's working on is government related and is highly classified. The fewer who know he's here, the better."

"Is he that well-known?" asked David.

"In his two fields he's considered tops. He even turned down an offer to take up permanent residence at the Institute for Advanced Study in Princeton."

"And he's not just two doctors," added Mary. "He's really eight doctors."

"Eight doctors!" exclaimed Aunt Lillian.

"Two earned doctorates, and six honorary degrees," said Sean, proudly. "Cambridge University in England gave him an honorary Doctor of Science degree five years ago. Before that it was Cal Tech and the University of Chicago, and before that it was the University of Basel over in Switzerland, and there were two others before that. You should see some of the funny outfits he can wear at academic functions. Usually, though, he's just too busy thinking, or maybe typing something really intensely on the computer."

"So there are nine doctors in your family," said David, smiling at Sean, "and only one waiting for you to die."

"Poor Old Thing is waiting, too," chimed Mary, "and on some days she's probably even hoping."

A muffled whomp was heard under the table.

"Let's do the dishes before we lose anyone tonight," Aunt Lillian quickly suggested.

The Potter twins, with their freckles and deep hazel eyes, were proving themselves to be most unusual children in their own right.

* * * * *

Aunt Lillian tucked David into bed that night, brushing back his front locks of red hair and kissing his forehead.

"The Potter twins are obviously extremely bright and very articulate," Aunt Lillian observed to David after they had left. "It seems that you have two new friends. I like them, and I am very grateful to them for driving Bobby Perkins away."

"I'm sure they'll be back. Sean was really impressed by my computer and laser printer. Said he was jealous, something about they were the shoemaker's children. He said he and Mary only have a feeble, little clone. I'm sure he'll be over to play with my chess game."

"They *are* delightful young people, but I bet POTS has her hands full."

"It will be fun to get to know them," agreed David. "They eat during the same lunch period as Lisa and I do, so I invited them to join us tomorrow. Lisa won't mind. Maybe they can all help me figure out some way of having a positive relationship with Bobby Perkins."

"I am more than a little worried about you, David."

"Please don't, Aunt Lillian," said David. "I'll be okay. I promise. I'll try to figure out some way so Bobby Perkins won't hate me. I've never done anything to him. I don't understand what's going on."

"It's more than likely Bobby Perkins hates himself, David," said Aunt Lillian, kissing David good night and turning out the lamp on the table next to his bed. Aunt Lillian began to say special prayers that night for David's safety.

Chapter Eleven
New Friends over Food

The recurrent dream that had haunted David's summer returned in full force, yet with a new twist. Familiar images persisted: his parents in their old car in the snow and ice and wind, the dark truck running the stop sign, the memorial service, Aunt Lillian driving over late that night, and Max whimpering all night. Most upsetting and startling to David was that the mysterious face in the truck's cab had come clear, revealing none other than the unhappy and panicked face of Bobby Perkins peering through the windows of the cab. The dream made no sense, but the images and detail were so vivid that David knew that his relationship to Bobby Perkins was somehow important to his parents' deaths.

THE RUSTLING OF DAVID'S FEET in the fallen leaves on the sidewalk announced his otherwise stealthy approach to Midville Middle School in the chill of a crisp October morning. David contemplated his present situation. Word of his troubles with Bobby would quickly spread among the students, and he hoped no one would ask too many questions.

Lisa had been a kindred spirit from the beginning, and each had sought refuge in the other's shyness. They were both imaginative and inquisitive, yet quiet and reserved by nature. In one crucial way they were different. If facing injustice, Lisa tended to retreat, whereas David would go on the offensive. David smiled as he thought of the Potter twins.

Knowing them was the bright spot on the horizon. Their joy seemed irrepressible—or perhaps it was Sean who seemed irrepressible. As he contemplated their joining Lisa and him for lunch, David realized how very much he liked them. The twins had admired his library, each borrowing a book, although David suspected they lived in a home that also had hundreds if not thousands of books.

David wondered what new adventures and wit they would bring to the lunch table. He was sure that Lisa would like them as much as he did.

The school doors, now open, exuded an institutional warmth and protection against the morning cold and overcast sky.

"David! Oh, I'm so sorry about what happened!"

"Lisa!"

"I've been waiting here since I got off my bus hoping to see you," announced Lisa.

"Thanks. I'm okay, although I'm still a little ugly to look at, and my nose still aches. Believe it or not, I actually feel better than I look."

"I wish I could have been there to help."

"I know. You're a good and true friend. Thanks. And speaking of friends, I invited the Potter twins to join us for lunch."

"The ones who rescued you?"

David flinched at the word 'rescue', but replied, "Yes."

The three minute warning bell jangled. Students began to disperse for their homerooms.

"See you next period for history," said Lisa, as she turned to report to her homeroom.

"Today at lunch I'll be waiting for you inside," called David. "I'm leaving English a little early to report to the nurse for some aspirin. I even have an official doctor's note."

* * * * *

David looked ruefully at his plate as Lisa sat down with her bag lunch and milk.

"Hot dogs and green beans again," sighed David. "Like clockwork. Every Monday it's the same lunch. You'd think someone would try to vary the routine a little."

"Gets a little boring, doesn't it?" commiserated Lisa.

"Here—"

"We—"

"ARE!"

David and Lisa looked up and saw the Potter twins standing before them, trays in hands, eyes fired with delight.

"Twins," David began, "this is Lisa."

"But I want to buy her," punned Sean.

A brief silence followed as the twins seated themselves before Lisa started laughing.

"No one's ever made a pun of my name before," she said to Sean.

"Hang on," cautioned Mary. "It only goes downhill from here. I propose we restrict Sean's puns to Mondays and fine him if makes any for the remainder of the week."

"I can't help it," explained Sean, "they just come out."

"Sean," asked David, "Why did you say you were the shoemaker's children last night? Your dad is a professor."

"I wasn't being literal. What do they always say about the shoemaker's children?"

"That he never has time to make decent shoes for them," said Lisa.

"Right," said Sean. "Dad gets to use the fancy supercomputer at the university from his special secure substation at home and all Mary and I get is a stinking little clone."

"Why don't you shake him down for a better one?"

"Because he's a nerd," answered Sean.

"No, a *cheap* nerd," corrected Mary. "Whenever we've tried to get a better computer, he says to us 'Oh, you don't need anything more complicated than what you've already got to do your school papers."

"On a stinking cheap dot-matrix printer, to boot," echoed Sean.

"Was that another pun?" asked Lisa.

Sean thought a moment, answering, "Yes."

"Liar," chided David, "it was unconscious and it wasn't bad, but because you tried to take credit for it, you really are 'soleless', as you admitted earlier."

Lisa laughed again. "David, you don't miss a trick, do you?"

"Nor do our new cohorts."

"At least I have a games computer," said Sean.

"Yeah," echoed Mary. "Tell them how you got it."

Sean gave Mary a dirty look, as David and Lisa looked at Sean for his explanation.

"Well, I suppose it won't hurt to tell, as long as you promise it goes no further."

David and Lisa nodded.

"Our dad has total access codes to at least several huge supercomputers, including one at the Pentagon."

"No kidding!" exclaimed David. "Does he work for the CIA?"

"No," said Sean. "He's too absent-minded for that. All we can ever tell anyone is that he does consulting work for the government."

Sean put his hand up next to his mouth so Mary and Lisa wouldn't hear and confided to David, "And *please* don't ask me if he has any privileged connections to the National Security Agency."

"Sean!" said Mary, slapping his hand down.

"I didn't say anything."

"Implying *can* be saying."

"Well, let's just say he does occasional work for the government and that he is also a special university professor at Cornell for as long as it suits him," dead-panned Sean.

An awkward silence followed, until David said, "Well, Mary, why don't you tell us how Sean got his games computer?"

Mary looked at Sean and nodded, "Well, dad was on an extended trip to Washington, D.C.—"

"The Pentagon—" interrupted Sean.

"Shh! Let *me* tell the story," said Mary. "Anyway, Sean decided that he wanted to try to get into dad's supercomputer, but there were some security codes that needed to be broken. The funny thing is that Sean managed to break several of them which, of course, set off all kinds of warnings and alarms both at the university and at the Pentagon. Dad called within minutes to see what was going on. Sean fessed up over the phone. When dad came home he created a whole new subroutine that screens out everyone except some math genius, like himself, who knows all these complex Greek formulas and complicated passwords. He also warned Sean *never* to touch his computer again. Oh, I almost forgot: he gave us two Latin nicknames. Mine is *HONESTUS* because I minded my own business. Sean's is *CURIOSUS*."

"But how does all that fit in with Sean's getting his computer?" asked David.

"That's the funniest part—"

"Maybe to you," interrupted Sean.

"*Excuse* me," chided Mary, continuing, "A few days after Dad got home, a tall man in a gray suit came to the door one night. He showed us his badge and identification and said Professor Potter had been told to expect him. He said he was investigating an incident of tampering with government property—meaning Dad's computer. He asked to see all of us together, but most especially he wanted to see Sean."

"I bet you were nervous," David grinned, looking at Sean.

"Nervous-smervous," yawned Sean. "He was only a gray suit to me."

"Why did you ask to see his badge and gun right away, then?" asked Mary.

"Because I wanted to see if he was legit," said Sean. "And he didn't have a badge. They don't give them badges at the NSA, but he did have a *really* nice 9mm, seventeen shot Glock."

"Anyway," continued Mary, "the man talked about how important it was to stay away from Dad's computer terminal. He and Dad asked Sean what it would take to keep him out of the way, and he said a games computer. The government man took him right out and bought him one. Can you believe it?"

"Yeah. It was the most expensive one on the shelves. Still one of the nicest you can get."

"Our tax dollars! A bribe with our tax dollars!" kidded David.

"It wasn't a bribe. It was ... a gift. Give me a break, anyway. I saw my advantage and took it. I never would 've gotten it any other way. The guy gave me his card, too, and said he thought I was a natural for joining their organization. I asked him if the 9mm Glock was standard issue. He said choice of weapon was personal preference. Anyway, I'm keeping the card in a *very* special, *very* secret, and *extremely* secure place where *NO* twin can find it."

"It's wedged under the right side of the mirror hanging over the family room fireplace," said Mary, looking slyly at David, " and it still has peanut butter on it."

Sean's mouth dropped open in disbelief. "You ... you ... ."

"Don't worry. I don't want your silly little card."

A sturdy whomp could be heard under the table as Mary grimaced.

David looked sad, and Lisa said, "David, what's wrong?"

"Oh, I was just thinking how lucky it is to have parents."

A short silence followed.

"We're really sorry about their accident," said Sean.

"You still have your Aunt," added Mary.

"She's great, I admit. But I still miss Mom and Dad."

"I still have mine," volunteered Lisa, "but I hardly ever see them. They're always at the restaurant. I wish they would let me go help them, but no, they say, 'Work hard on your studies, Lisa. We never even graduated high school and we want *you* to go to college.' So I spend my time reading and getting good grades."

"We can *all* share Poor Old Thing," brightened Mary, adding, "there's plenty of Poor Old Thing to go around."

"Poor Old Thing?" asked Lisa.

"Their once and future Nanny," explained David. "I'll fill you in later."

Lisa looked perplexed.

"Speaking of restaurants," said David, "I wish your parents would contract to run the school's food service. There's nothing worse than these rubberized hot dogs on cold, stale buns."

"Oh, yeah?" challenged Sean. "How about steak doorstops?"

"Steak what?" inquired David.

"Steak doorstops. Mary and I went to a private, residential school near Boston last spring when our parents were in Europe. Dad was doing some very special research and collaboration, and Mom wanted a vacation. Since we all knew we would be coming to Midville in the summer, they clapped us into this preppie school for kids of the really rich and famous."

"It was very put on, if you know what I mean," confided Mary.

"I'm dying to hear about the doorstops," said Lisa.

"Well," began Sean, "the name of the school was Brentwood, and they were so cheap they would serve steak only twice a month. The worst of it was that the steak was so dry and tough, you couldn't even chew it. Well, there was this feisty little kid named Byron Mathis Hawkins, from Providence, who refused to eat his steak one night. Instead, he put it in his napkin and took it up to his room and used it as a doorstop for almost a month. It finally began to disintegrate and attract bugs."

"Gross," said Lisa.

"Well, Byron wrote a sob letter to his old man who was some big-shot banker in Providence. His father called the Headmaster, who then called the food service on the carpet and, believe it or not, the food got better for a while. Instead of steak, they started giving us London Broil, which was still tough, but tasted better."

"The important thing is that you got good results," said David. "I admire that."

"Well Byron did, by ratting to his old man," reflected Sean. "His old man would 've choked to death on the cheap stuff that food service had the gall to dish out on to our plates. It was so bad it even made me miss Poor Old Thing's cooking which, in truth, is *really* quite good. But she had to go back to Ireland to nurse her great-great-great-great-great something or other. No one believes me when I tell them that Poor Old Thing was born the very day after William the Conqueror invaded England, but she *was!*"

"You're really brave when POTS can't hear you," observed Mary.

"Well, that Byron kid knew how to shake the tree down," David said, hastening to change the conversation before someone's shin got kicked.

"Sean, we should have asked Byron how to rattle a new computer out of Dad," said Mary.

"No use," said Sean, "All Dad says is, 'Oh, I never had anything as good as what you've got when I was your age; remember it's not the machine—it's the mind behind it that's the important thing."

"What do you say to that, Mary?" asked David, fascinated with this glimpse into the deliberations of the Potter household.

"My last argument," said Mary, "was that the technology is changing so fast that we can barely hope to keep up with it."

"What did your Dad say?" asked Lisa.

"Oh, he started in about life in Midville, and how he had grown up in a small town, and how he wanted us to know what it's like, and that he didn't want us jaded from all of the academic environments we've been exposed to, and how computers would always be there waiting for us," sighed Mary.

"He doesn't realize the world is different today," said Sean.

"How so?" asked David.

Sean frowned at him. "This is the information-communications age and technology rules the day. No longer do people wait for the Wells Fargo wagon to bring in the week old newspapers. I'm glad my parents agreed with us that Brentwood was too preppie, and I'm even glad POTS could come back to us, but I'm not sure that middle America is where we want to be, either. We can only see six hours of television a week, so instead of frying our brains that way, we read books and make feeble assaults on a dilapidated computer."

"How about your games computer, Sean," asked David.

"Well, it was great at first but, after a while, even it got boring," confided Sean.

"My brother's got a photographic memory, and he *never* forgets anything. Doesn't that just make you sick?" sighed Mary.

"Yeah," agreed Sean, "things get boring really fast."

"You twins can share my computer," offered David.

"Really?" exclaimed Mary.

"Wow!" said Sean, adding, "That's great!"

"Sure. Why not?"

"Well, then," said Mary, grinning, "*We* will share Poor Old Thing with you, David."

"It's ironic," said David, "that I have a fancy computer and my problems are getting along with people, whereas you twins get along well with people but don't have a fancy computer."

"People are not a problem," said Sean. "All you do is shoot the ones you don't like."

"My brother, the outlaw," sighed Mary, throwing her hand toward Sean.

"David," said Lisa, "you get along with everyone except Bobby Perkins, and he's nothing but a bully. I've heard his father isn't very nice to him. He's probably just taking it out on you and the world, the way he's always shoving people around."

"For some reason he seems to have a grudge against *me*. I never did anything to him that I can remember. Even with the warning of expulsion from Ferlinghausen, I've got a feeling that he's going to be waiting for me somewhere. I hate walking around under a shadow."

"Why don't we drop a wheelbarrow on him?" suggested Sean.

"David doesn't believe in violence, Sean," explained Lisa.

"But that's not violence," objected Sean. "It's just a minor accident, a wheelbarrow of cement falling on him from a work platform."

"Please ignore my bloodthirsty brother," sighed Mary.

"What's wrong with that?" asked Sean.

"I just think there must be a better way," said David. "Sometimes after you get to know people, you come to understand them, even if you don't like them."

"How's that?" mumbled Sean, with a mouth full of hot dog bun and mustard.

"I said if you get to know people, then you might not dislike them," repeated David.

"What if you dislike them even more?" asked Sean.

"Always the optimist," sighed Mary.

"Well, at least you would have tried something positive," said David.

"We could *shoot* him," offered Sean. "I've got a BB gun."

David looked at Sean in wonder. "I don't think you understand my position, Sean. Nothing violent, understand? I want to avoid a broken nose and crumpled face. I'm sure there must be a positive way ... somewhere ... somehow."

"I still think we should shoot him," said Sean. "It would be fun."

David sat thinking to himself. "Some answer will turn up. I'm sure I'll think of something. By the way, I wonder if we could plan to have lunch every day and, if so, we need a name for our group. How about the Gang of Four?"

Lisa assented by laughing, Mary smiled and nodded, and Sean was thrilled finally to be part of a gang of any sort.

* * * * *

The next day at lunch David waited until everyone was seated and then drew a crumpled piece of paper out of his pocket.

"I found this in my locker at the beginning of school this morning. I suspect one of Bobby's friends, probably Zeke Minturn, stuffed it through the vents for him. I want each of you to read it. Here, Lisa and Mary, you first, then Sean."

To Mr. Howdy-Deudy,

Aint gonna waist your time or mine with a lot of hooey. I aint supposed to lay a fingur on you again. Well, I wont.

And I wont never forget how much truble you got me in. IOU. Remember, I will always be watchin you. STAY OUT OF MY WAY.

Youll be sory if you dont. I Aint warnin you agin. Dont dare show this to nobody, OR ELSE!

Bobby Perkins

P.s. - I'm glad I aint got school this week cuz its the 1st week of huntin season.

Lisa and the twins read the note.

"Golly," exclaimed Sean, "it's a good thing we didn't try to shoot him. He's probably got a .22!"

David looked at Lisa, and asked, "Well, what do you think?"

"He's certainly going to hang on to that grudge, David."

"I think he'll be looking for any chance to get you," said Mary.

"He's a lousy speller," said Sean.

"No, no. I mean, yes, all that you say is true, but don't you see? He went to the trouble to communicate with me. He even bothered to write something. That means in *some* way he really cares, and that he's also taking a big chance that I don't go right down and show this note to Mr. Ferlinghausen."

"Unless he *wants* to get expelled," said Sean.

"That *may* be, but I'd rather think he feels a little guilty about what he did to me because I know Mr. Ferlinghausen and Dr. Smith talked to him and his father about my belief in non-violence."

"And Ferlinghausen can *really* lay it on thick when he wants to," said Lisa.

"Do you think Bobby's trying to say he's sorry?" asked Lisa.

"I don't know. I suspect he's all muddled up inside. Bullies usually are. You know, not much clarity, but lots of macho spinning off. I really think he may be expecting an answer, but I don't know what to write."

"Say 'SCREW YOU!'" said Sean. "He's already communicated with his fists and his knee. I say we should ambush him and his gang somewhere."

"You've been watching too many westerns, Sean," said Mary.

"I prefer war movies. And I've been reading a lot of good books on World War I and World War II."

"My hopelessly-bloodthirsty brother," lamented Mary. "We were both born on April 14, under the sign of Aries. Mars rules our charts."

"Mary, there's a really neat book on torture in the library," Sean retorted.

A whomp under the table left Sean with a tight-lipped smile.

Lisa studied David's concern.

"David," she began, "I know you would like to patch up the rift between you and Bobby but sometimes the other person just doesn't have enough grace to come along."

"I don't know how to approach him," said David. "There must be a back door where I can get in."

"Yeah, we could use an Uzi or MAC 10," said gleefully.

David rolled his eyes and looked at Mary.

"I'm sorry, David. All he thinks about is shooting people."

"I'm a *warrior*," proclaimed Sean.

"Maybe he'll grow out of it and become a policeman or a criminal or something," sighed Mary.

"I hope it's a criminal," said Sean. "That would be more fun."

161

"If you become a criminal, you can't be much of a 'worrier', since you would obviously have no conscience."

Sean took his knife and held it toward David in a mock-fighting posture.

"Sean is just jealous you made a good pun," said Mary, adding, "but for everyone's sake, let's ban them from our table talk."

"I'll have your liver and heart out," Sean announced to David.

"Lunch wasn't *that* bad, was it?" David quipped.

David studied Sean.

"Why are you looking at me like that?" asked Sean.

"I was just thinking," said David. "Have you ever heard the expression that 'Sport is the moral equivalent to war'?"

"Yeah," said Sean, "but I think war is more exciting."

"Fortunately, many more people believe that those who would make war do much better when they compete through sports or games. *That's* our answer. Sean, would you be willing to approach Bobby as my representative?"

"Sure."

"You, too, Mary, since it was the pair of you who sent him packing when he was beating me up."

"I'll help any way I can," offered Mary.

"Thanks. Now all we need are titles, formats, competitions, and tradition. You both will be my plenipotentiaries."

"What's that?" asked Sean.

"A fancy word for 'representatives'," explained Lisa.

"Does it mean I can bring my BB gun?"

David ignored Sean's question and continued, "We will wait until Bobby returns to school, and then you two will confront him on the stairwell where he roughed me up—that gives us a week to plan and to rehearse."

"Rehearse what?" asked Sean.

"The challenge. We're going to challenge Bobby to a competition that doesn't involve violence."

The passing bell rang, and the Gang of Four regarded each other in surprise. Everyone had forgotten the time.

"Oops! We're gonna be late for next class!" said Sean.

"Here. Stack your plates on my tray. I'll take them in so you can be on time," offered David.

"Thanks," said the twins, rushing off.

"Good luck, David," said Lisa.

* * * * *

Tuesday's pizza was undercooked and soggy.

"Not the best lunch," Lisa observed, "Maybe we should organize against the cafeteria services."

"We don't have a high-powered banker to call the headmaster," sighed Mary.

"Maybe we could get Audrey Vanderkamp to complain to her father. He's a big shot lawyer and has lots of clout," grinned David. "But let's save that cause for a later occasion."

"She's a lost cause, David," said Lisa. "She's only interested in boys and makeup."

"Did you come up with anything, David?" asked Sean, as he tried to take a bite of his stringy pizza, half of which fell off on his plate.

David regarded his fellow gang members and smiled, "I think I figured out what Bobby Perkins wants."

"What?" asked Lisa.

"Me."

"You?"

"Bobby wants to understand me. Something about me bothers him and he wants to figure me out. The only way he knows is by beating me up. We're going to give him a different opportunity."

Lisa, Mary, and Sean listened attentively as David continued.

"We will challenge Bobby to a contest of some sort, winner take all. The prize will be that the loser will serve as the winner's Slave for a Day."

"Do you think he'll go for it?"

"Perhaps. If we stage it in just the right way, I don't think he'll be able to resist the chance of having me as his slave for a whole day. For *that* he'd agree to almost any sort of contest," explained David.

"Yeah," quipped Sean, "like seeing who could kick someone's brains in the fastest."

"*No* violence!" said David firmly. "We are offering him an alternative to violence. That's the whole point. Maybe he'll begin to see there are other ways of dealing with people."

"Yeah. Like a showdown," said Sean. "Why don't we have a showdown to see who can shoot the other first."

"Sean, *please* forget it. And remember, in a showdown, *I'd* lose. You're supposed to be on my side, so *please* forget shooting people and focus instead on helping me."

Sean turned a little red with embarrassment, muttering, "Sorry, David."

"Good," continued David. "Now here is what I want you and Mary to do. When Bobby returns to school this Monday, I want you to meet him in the hallway where he roughed me up and give him this note. The note says that I have an important message for him, if he has the guts to listen to it, and that it will only be delivered in the library workroom."

"How will we get in there?" asked Mary.

"I've already arranged it with Mr. Lowery. The library will be closed during that lunch period, but he will wait for you and let you into the workroom. Then he'll leave for lunch. All you have to do is slam the door when you leave."

"Gosh! How did you get him to agree to help?"

"I'll explain that some other time. Now, if Bobby takes the bait and follows you to the library, Mr. Lowery will nod in the direction of the workroom and leave. You two will escort Bobby into the workroom and close the door. Mary, you'll be in front of Bobby, holding this scroll; Sean, you'll be behind him, so you'll shut the door. Mary, as soon as Sean shuts the door, you turn around to face Bobby and take out a glove and give Bobby a whack across his right cheek."

"Are you crazy, David?" asked Mary.

"No, he's got it," interrupted Sean. "Don't you see, it's the formal way gentlemen challenge someone to a duel. David, I knew you'd come through for a duel. You can borrow my gun."

"It's not going to be a traditional duel. We're going to meet at a later time with witnesses from both sides and spin a dial and take whatever competition or game comes up. I'll explain more about that later."

"What if he gets violent?" asked Mary.

"He won't. Remember, you both drove him off when he was beating me up, so there's a history of defeat there. What's more important, Mary, is that you're a girl, and I'm willing to gamble that even Bobby wouldn't strike a girl."

"That doesn't stop Sean."

A heavy thud moved the table two inches toward Mary.

"Lucky," muttered Sean, looking at Mary, "Hit the table leg." Turning to David, Sean pleaded, "*Please*, David, let me take a little pocket derringer in with me?"

David rolled his eyes and cradled his head in his hands.

Lisa reached over and gently rubbed the back of his neck.

"What did I say?" asked Sean. "What did I say?"

"Sean, somehow I think David's non-violent message is *not* getting through to you," answered Lisa.

"It's only a little pocket derringer," Sean persisted.

David groaned, shaking his head.

"It's only a toy," Sean pleaded.

"Mary, I wonder if you could get your mom to get us a few of those gloves you see doctors using in the emergency room," David asked, ignoring Sean.

"No problem," said Mary. "As good as done."

"Those gloves are made of latex and can really snap," said Sean, brightening.

"Mary will slap Bobby, Sean, and that's final," rejoined David.

Chapter Twelve
A Challenge with an Offer too Tempting

F RIDAY AFTERNOON WAS UNSEASONABLY WARM, the wind carrying the fragrance of fallen leaves through the open windows. As school was dismissed, most of the students left Midville Middle School with one accord: to get outdoors and enjoy the lingering rays of Indian summer. Not so the Gang of Four, for they were embarking upon a different kind of adventure. They found themselves entering the library work area to rehearse the twins' encounter with Bobby Perkins on Monday.

"David," asked Lisa, "how did you manage to get Mr. Lowery to let us use the library workroom during his lunch hour on Monday?"

With a twinkle in his eye, David casually whispered, "I probably shouldn't tell you this, but he and I are fellow gang members." David moved his face inches from Lisa's, studied her wide innocent eyes and continued, "There's a secret confraternity among librarians and the children of deceased librarians. After all, my parents were very active members in the librarians' gang before their deaths."

"REALLY?" exclaimed Sean, his mouth hanging open.

"Ssshhh!" cautioned David, "It's so secret that it's never talked about! Even the secret is a secret!"

"Golly!" said Sean.

"Oh, Sean," David sighed, "I forgot my notepad. Would you please go get my clipboard? It's sitting on top of my locker and I may need to make some notes during our rehearsal."

"Sure. Anything—be right back."

After her brother left, Mary looked dubiously at David, "Librarians' Secret Society?"

"All right. So I fibbed. I thought it might spice things up a little for Sean, since we've taken all the violence out of it."

"It only encourages him," scolded Mary.

"We still have the glove slap," Lisa reminded her.

"Yes," David responded, "but that's high drama instead of violence. I think we will need to play that card right on through to the end. Bobby probably has never experienced the awe and majesty of high drama."

"David, you're being silly again," teased Lisa.

"No, not now. We're doing something out of the ordinary, which makes our goal *extraordinary,* and we want to get *extraordinary* results from our efforts. That means we have to use *extraordinary* means to get Bobby where we want him."

"And where's that?" asked Lisa wryly, "in jail?"

"Unfortunately he's probably a good candidate for jail if he keeps up his anti-social behavior," said Mary.

"That's right," David agreed. "This plan offers him a real alternative to the patterns that he's locked into."

"You mean fighting," said Lisa.

Sean returned and joined the table, handing David his notepad.

"Yes. We want Bobby to discover that he can relate to others without violence. Eventually, we may even become friends."

"I think violence can be *extremely* positive," said Sean.

David quelled Sean with a look and asked Lisa, "Do you think it will work?"

"I don't know. I hope so. It's certainly worth a try."

"If it doesn't work, it could be an awful mess."

"Yeah," echoed Sean, "Wall-to-wall blood."

"Need I remind you, Sean, that you and Mary are the first contacts?"

"Wall-to-wall Mary's blood," Sean corrected.

A whomp shook the table as Sean's smile faded.

"Mr. Lowery said we could have this room until three-thirty. That still gives us about forty minutes. Let rehearse for Monday. Places please," announced David.

Lisa remained at the table as an observer. David would pretend to be Bobby and left the workroom for the library with the twins. Suddenly Sean raced back to shut the door.

A moment later Mary opened the door and led David into the workroom with Sean bringing up the rear. The procession stopped. Mary took the latex glove from her pocket, wheeled around suddenly, and slapped David across his right cheek, proclaiming, "Bobby Perkins, know ye now that David Andrews, Esquire, challenges you to a competition, the nature of which shall be determined by chance, to see who is the master and who is the slave. Do you accept this challenge or do you cower?"

David stood still, pretending to the thunderstruck, and murmured, "Uh ... uh ... yes."

"The sacred scroll, Underling," intoned Mary to Sean.

For the shortest moment Sean looked as if he would like to clobber Mary over the head with the scroll, but keeping to the script, he handed her the long sheet of white paper elegantly tied with a gold ribbon. Mary received it with great solemnity, untied the ribbon, unrolled it, and read, "Bobby Perkins, you are enjoined to take competition with David Andrews, Esquire, in the form of a game to be determined by the spinning of a dial. This will be some sort of competitive game with NO VIOLENCE ALLOWED. Once the nature of the competition is determined, both parties will be given five to six weeks to prepare themselves for this contest, to see who the better adversary is, with the winner taking all. The winner will win for himself the loser as Slave For A Day, on a date to be determined at the winner's convenience. If ye do accept these terms, ye may spin the dial on the game selector that we will bring to this very place this coming Friday at the exact same hour. Ye may also bring thy gang as witnesses. I truly hope thou art not a coward and that thou will muster within thee enough pluck to try thy hand against me. —[signed] David Andrews, Esquire."

Mary then handed David the scroll who, pretending to be Bobby, made a careful study of it.

"Ya mean I can bring Zeke and Danny?" asked David.

"Ye may. To serve as witnesses."

"Thems rules as fair as can be."

"Very well," announced Mary, trying to restrain her laughter at David's imitation of Bobby's syntax. "The form of this competition will be chosen from the royal game board this Friday, at the appointed hour, the beginning of this lunch period. Ye may take this challenge to study it."

David took the scroll, and the three of them exited the room. Lisa clapped her enthusiastic approval. The others returned with bows and grins.

"That was wonderful," said Lisa. "I hope it goes that well Monday."

"It should, provided we keep our heads and don't go off the deep end," David added, looking at Sean who now appeared sad.

Sean looked at David, and then at the floor.

"Sean, did we offend thee in any way?" asked David.

"It's ... just ... that I think *I* should be the one who strikes Bobby across the cheek with the glove. I'm only here to hand Mary that lousy scroll."

David rubbed his chin. "I see," he said. "Do you know, Sean, you *really* have the most difficult job of all."

"I do?"

"Yes. It's your job to shore up any problems that might happen if things don't go according to script. Mary will need your total support. The pressure is really on *you*; we need our strongest player on that base."

"Don't worry, David," Sean brightened, "I'll be prepared for *anything*."

"Just don't muck it up, little brother," cautioned Mary.

"Did I?" asked Sean. "Did I, today?"

"No," complimented David. "You were terrific; you were *all* just excellent. Say, Mary, why do you call Sean 'little brother' if you're fraternal twins?"

"We *are* fraternal twins," Mary announced proudly, "but *guess* who was born first."

"Well, BULLY FOR YOU," retorted Sean.

"David, why don't you come over this weekend and help us rehearse our parts for Monday?" invited Sean, adding, "that is, if you don't mind losing at chess afterwards."

"Thanks. I'd love to come," said David. "How about Saturday afternoon? Aunt Lillian could bring me."

"That'll be fine, but you could always walk over. We don't live all that far from you. I'll give you directions."

* * * * *

Mary thought Monday would never arrive. She and Sean and David had rehearsed their parts in this great experiment *ad nauseam*, largely at Sean's insistence. After all, from Sean's trusting point of view, the entire affair was connected to a worldwide, top secret, and no doubt nefarious librarians' cloak and dagger confraternity. Sean's dreams were slowly becoming reality, not, of course, that he himself would ever consider becoming a librarian. Librarians were all right, he was beginning to discover, and although they might be tough as nails underneath their placid façades, their public *personas* seemed a little too feeble for a worthy warrior.

David was careful to keep a very low profile in English class, not so much as looking at Bobby throughout the entire period. The twins succeeded in meeting Bobby just as he headed down the west stairwell for lunch where he had once pinned David against the wall. David had thought this subtle 'mirroring' of their past encounter might be helpful. The twins stood boldly in Bobby's way, refusing to let him pass.

"Well," he growled warily, "what do you two creeps want? A medal or a chest to pin it on?"

"I've got a chest," snapped Sean, "I want the—OW!"

Here Mary had jabbed him in the ribs lest their larger mission be lost. Clearing her throat she announced, "We have a message for you from David Andrews and we can deliver it to you only in a secluded place. Will you come with us?"

"Ya gotta be kiddin'," laughed Bobby. "What a wimp ... sendin' little rug rat brats to do his dirty work."

Sean jumped in Bobby's face, saying, "We're not rug rat brats, Jack, OW!"

"Do you want the message or don't you?" demanded Mary, slyly adding, "It's a fair and good challenge, and we all expected that you would back down."

At the words 'back down', Bobby flared and stepped toward Mary, who now knew her instinct had been correct. Lifting her right hand, she proclaimed, "Stop! No more until we read David's petition to you. Follow me."

By now Bobby was completely hooked, as he grumbled, "Me? Back down? From that little wimp? Let's go."

Mr. Lowery nodded toward the workroom door as they entered, and then left for lunch. Sean had signed up for library during his first period study hall and had winked at Mr. Lowery when leaving, to which Mr. Lowery gave a surreptitious nod. After all, Sean had proven himself one of Lowery's best clients, especially when it came to checking out books on guns, the Old West, gangsters, criminals, World Wars I & II, and the fine points of Medieval torture.

Bobby was surprised to be escorted into the library, especially when it was just closing. This was only the second time he had ever entered that room, the first being the initial mandatory tour required for all seventh graders. He was even more surprised when Mary led him into the library workroom, normally reserved for faculty, with Sean bringing up the rear and closing the door.

As Mary stopped, Sean's heart was pounding with excitement. He saw her reach for the latex glove in her purse, and then heard the sharp smack of the glove striking Bobby's cheek as Mary turned to confront him.

"Bobby Perkins," Mary began—

"What the hell!" Bobby blurted in dismay.

Sean's heart skipped a beat now that their well-rehearsed script was going awry. His response was as instinctive as it was instantaneous. In that brief millisecond there united in Sean Patrick Potter a sum far greater than all of the individual parts. Drastic action was called for in this emergency, lest Bobby strike Mary back. Sean's superior faculty of mind and memory seized on every western, every war movie, every gangster film he had ever seen, these indelible images combining to form the greater locus of his attention. Faster than words, he pulled out a small toy metal derringer from his right pocket and thrust it into the small of Bobby's back, shouting, "REACH OR I'LL PLUG YOU!"

Sean's shout would have evacuated the library had it been in session, and it was most fortunate that the heavy workroom door had been closed. For the briefest instant, Sean believed he was in fact holding a real derringer to Bobby's back, and since he himself was convinced, so too was Bobby.

Is it any surprise that in the heat of this instant Bobby Perkins raised his arms, indeed, raised them as high as he could reach?

"Don't move, Jack, or I'll splatter your guts all over the front of your shirt. Mary, move aside. These aren't hollow point slugs and they'll go right through him."

This last tidbit of detail galvanized Bobby in to a statue, his face now the color of a bleached bedsheet. Only his eyes grew in size as, frozen in place, he gulped and panted.

Sean kept the barrel of the toy derringer pressed tightly against the Bobby's lower back. Not only was Sean playing out his fantasy, he was vindicating the beating Bobby had given to David. And as he thought of the pain Bobby had inflicted on David, he twisted the barrel of the gun even harder into Bobby's back, whispering, "Yeah. It's only a little-two-shot derringer, Jack, but it's a .38, and if you make me plug you through your guts, I guarantee you my second shot will be where it hurts a lot more—especially after what you did to David. I hope you don't dare move a muscle, because you aren't worth a lousy murder rap."

Mary watched Bobby's face becoming very gray at Sean's graphic threats and became alarmed that he might faint. "Bobby, *please* listen to me. Take long, deep breaths but don't move, because my brother means what he says and he has a very itchy trigger finger."

Bobby gasped as beads of perspiration dripped down his forehead. His eyes were glazed and wild with panic.

To her credit Mary knew there could be no turning back now. Sean's instant action, thanks to his having watched hundreds of blood and guts movies, had caused an intense suspension of disbelief, and the situation was as real now as if her brother actually held a real derringer to the bully's back. She suspected that if Sean were to yell 'Bang!' that Bobby would drop dead from fright alone.

Summoning her courage, she dispensed with the planned preliminaries since the situation had now taken a more dramatic turn. It seemed unlikely Bobby would refuse David's challenge, especially with a gun shoved into his back.

Clearing her throat, Mary demanded, "The sacred scroll, Underling!" This was a brilliant strategy on her part for it gave her new authority over Bobby since she had now demonstrated that the individual shoving the gun into his back was somehow in her service.

Bobby probably never played the game 'Statues' as a child. Even so, today he would have earned an A+ for his considerable efforts, not to mention his stiff muscles, for Sean was acting like a gunman very close to pulling the trigger. All of Sean's focused psychic energy made this scene larger than life, and heartbeats raced wildly.

Bobby listened to the *Proclamation of Challenge* and appeared to understand it. His mouth was dry and still hanging open, although he had stopped gasping.

"Do you understand this *Proclamation?*" asked Mary when she had finished reading it.

It was not that Bobby was afraid to answer, but more that he was afraid to move even the slightest muscle lest he feel the impact of a .38 slug tearing through his lower abdomen. The best he could manage under these strained circumstances was to move the bottom of his open mouth ever so slightly, giving one the impression that he had just contracted some form of palsy. A slight rush of air from his mouth further gave what could be taken as an non-vocalized assent, his eyes still wide.

The silence seemed an eternity, but lasted less than a minute.

Mary finally said, "Okay, we have a solemn agreement to a competition. You'd better not back out of it, if you want to stay healthy." David, unbeknownst to Sean, had orchestrated this warning as a parallel to the one Bobby had given him and Mary had conveyed it well. The message proved to have enormous staying power thanks to the pressure Sean was still applying to Bobby's back.

Not wanting to be outdone, Sean withdrew the toy derringer from Bobby's back and pressed it against the nape of his neck, saying, "And you'd better never tell anyone about this meeting or about my gun or I'll blast you fast to kingdom come." Pleased with the rhyme, he was about to add 'before the sun is done', but Mary's icy glare made him realize that they had played their scenario out. Sean returned the toy derringer to his pocket.

"Do you understand and agree?" Mary asked Bobby.

Bobby, with his hands still lifted in the air, said, "Uh huh, uh huh. Wa,wa,wa."

"What's that you're trying to say?" asked Mary.

"Wa, wa, wa, water ... mouth dry ... need a drink."

"Well, stop and get one on your way to lunch. You may go. And put your silly arms down." Bobby wasn't sure he would ever be able to move them again, but they did come down, albeit stiffly.

"Remember," cautioned Mary, "NOT A WORD TO *ANYONE!*"

Bobby, staring straight down at the floor, fled through the door and out of the library.

Mary looked at Sean who was giving her a smug smile. "Guess we showed him," he said, patting the toy gun in his pocket.

"Sean, David will be furious when he hears what happened. How could you?"

"Look, I saved the situation and saved you from getting clobbered. After Bobby said 'What the hell' what did you expect me to do? He might have hit you."

"Well, if he *ever* finds out it was only a toy gun, you'll be growing grass in the churchyard."

"Guess he better never find out, then," said Sean.

"Right. But we've *got* to tell David and Lisa."

"Maybe I could get a real derringer somewhere," said Sean.

"Sean, you're hopeless," said Mary.

"No, I'm hopeful. I'm hopeful that some day I'll have a real derringer, not to mention an Uzi, a MAC 10, a .357, a P-38, a 9mm Cobra ... "

Mary walked out of the library, refusing to listen to a further listing of her brother's future arsenal. Sean ran to catch her, knowing she was going to lunch and not wanting to be late in sitting down with David and Lisa.

As it worked out, Sean was earlier than Mary. He ran to a stairwell that brought him by the front of the lunch line, whereas Mary took the west stairs and came up from the rear. In passing the lunch line, Sean saw Zeke Minturn make a place for him. Because Zeke kept staring at Sean's right hand pocket, Sean rightly intuited that Bobby, before fleeing to the bathroom to regain his wits, had put out the word to his gang to give the little man with the derringer a wide berth. Mary was stuck at the end of the line. When she finally took her seat among the Gang of Four, David looked up, smiled, saying, "Sean said it went very well and that you both were terrific and that you will give Lisa and me a complete replay after school."

Sean winked at Mary who, in turn, gave David a weak smile and found she couldn't eat any lunch. She only wondered what David would say when he heard what had happened.

After school the Gang of Four gathered in the library workroom. With their characteristic élan, Mary and Sean re-enacted the reading of the *Proclamation of Competition* to Bobby, and no one was more surprised than Mary to see David rolling on the floor with laughter.

Chapter Thirteen
Incontrovertible Logic

L ISA MET DAVID AT HIS LOCKER the next morning at the beginning of school.

"I really like the twins," Lisa confided to David, who had just opened his locker. "Look what I brought for us for lunch today, some tuna fish salad from the restaurant."

David smiled, "Hmm. Salad looks great. We won't have much time to read now that we'll be meeting a lot in the library workroom during lunch. I know it's different now, Lisa, but I think we have been *twinned.* We can always read at other times than lunch. How often does one have the opportunity to get to know such unusual personalities, and twins besides?"

"As much as they squabble, I suppose each would defend the other to the death if the other were attacked."

"Lisa," David grinned, "With all of the excitement yesterday, I never got to tell you about Saturday."

"Saturday?" asked Lisa blankly.

"Yes! When I visited the twins. *I* got to meet POTS!"

"Really?"

"Aunt Lillian drove me over and had about half a dozen cups of tea with POTS. They got along like two lost sisters. I even got to meet Dr. Potter."

"Which one?"

"The two-doctor Potter. He was holding some sort of seminar for several of the university faculty. He came out to get a book and Sean introduced me. Then his dad wanted to meet Aunt Lillian, who was very flattered by the experience, because he told her how pleased he is that Sean and I have become friends. He said something to Aunt Lillian about Sean really needing an older brother. And he's amazing looking; he and Sean have the same deep hazel eyes, the kind that peer right through you ... but where Sean's hair is on the short side in sort of a military way, his dad has long brown hair flowing almost down to his shoulders. As Sean once said, I'm sure his dad could pass himself off as a graduate student, except maybe for the wrinkles around his eyes. I wonder if he's discovered the fountain of youth, and just isn't telling anybody?"

"David, I'm jealous! It must have been like meeting Albert Einstein."

"Sort of, I guess, although Sean said his dad has to avoid publicity because of his hush-hush government work. He could have been on the cover of *Time* magazine three years ago, but he refused and suggested they interview a friend of his who teaches at Princeton."

"What's their house like?"

"It's huge and wonderful and old and they must have a million books, all over the house! Shelves everywhere! I thought my parents had a lot of books, but the Potters put us to shame."

"Well, your parents devoted their lives to looking after other people's books, which is even more important."

"Yeah, I suppose so. Anyway, Sean's mom was working at the emergency room, so I haven't met her yet. POTS told Aunt Lillian that the twins' mom, they call her the *real* doctor because she's a physician, has an unbelievably erratic schedule. She works twelve hour shifts on any one of three rotating time blocks. It's like a roller coaster. POTS said Mrs. Potter told her that they would have had to give Sean and Mary away if they didn't have her to crack the whip."

"I'm sure she was only kidding," said Lisa. "Why does she work so many hours?"

"That's just part of being a doctor, though POTS said Sean's mom has occasionally told him, 'The only reason, Sean, that I am at the emergency room so much is that when they bring you in, I want to be able to say 'goodbye' to you, or say 'I'm sorry' to your victims."

"Sean's not that wild, is he?"

"Well, the door to his bedroom has a skull and crossbones poster on it and a blood red script which reads: *ENTER FOOLISH MORTAL, AND DIE!*"

"That sounds like Sean, doesn't it? What's his room like? Did you dare to enter?"

"It's a really neat room. Sean has a large collection of computer games, the kind of games where you can shoot a lot of electronic villains. When I admired all the computer equipment, Mary reminded me that its very presence and installation had been the government's bribe to keep Sean off his dad's computer. Sean also has a large collection of books on military history, wars, and battles, medieval torture, the wild west, and firearms. There's also a sizable collection of fiction—mostly war stories, westerns, and mysteries. There's also a dart board. Mary suggested that I ask Sean how he got the dart board at lunch today, but when I did, he said to 'forget it.' Oh, he also has the most unusual chess set, comprised of military action figures holding different kinds of guns. Mary said that the set was a gift to Sean from someone *really* high up in Washington."

"Sean will probably end up in the FBI or CIA," said Lisa.

"No doubt. By the way, we'll meet in the workroom during lunch to lay plans for the spinning board. Thanks for bringing the tuna salad. See you next period," said David.

* * * * *

Lunch that day for the Gang of Four had taken a necessary turn. It marked the beginning of their concerted efforts to lay the foundation for the competition between Bobby and David. It also heralded a much finer culinary offering, thanks to Lisa's parents' donations. David and Lisa were already seated at the work table when they heard the twins enter.

"Greetings twins," said David.

"Greetings," answered Sean.

Mary smiled and bowed to them, announcing, "Now it's my turn. Lisa, as you know, Sean invited David over last Saturday. Would you please do us the honor of coming for a visit this coming Saturday?"

"I'd love to," beamed Lisa.

"If you're parents are working at the restaurant," said Mary, "POTS will pick you up and take you home. I've already checked."

"That's very thoughtful. David's been telling me all about last Saturday."

"Did you tell Lisa about our Burmese connection?" asked Mary.

"No. I hadn't even gotten to that. Why don't you?"

"Well, we have six Burmese cats," smiled Mary.

"Oh! I adore cats. Why Burmese?" asked Lisa.

"Because of Sean's persistence. He wanted a dog, specifically an Irish wolfhound. My dad said that they were wonderful dogs, but too much trouble for a family with our kinds of obligations and lifestyles. He also said that POTS had her hands full dealing with us much less adding a huge dog."

"So ... " prompted David. "What happened?"

"Well, Sean started shaking down our mother like a tree. He knows who to shake down to get what he wants—"

"So do you," interrupted Sean.

"And finally she made some inquiries and came home and said, 'Sean, cats would be easier pets for us to have and I'm told that Burmese cats have the personalities of dogs. So I ordered one for you and one for your sister,'" Mary explained.

"But you now have six," said David.

"Well, we sort of got a boy and a girl," explained Sean.

"And we've always been able to sell any of the kittens we don't want to keep. It gives Mary and me occasional pocket money."

"Besides our allowances," added Mary.

"What kind of allowance do you get?" asked Lisa.

"We each get ten dollars a week," said Sean.

"My parents only give me five," said Lisa.

"You should negotiate for more," said Mary.

"I wouldn't dare," said Lisa.

"Well, friends, we'd better get down to business," said David.

"David, it sure was nice of Mr. Lowery to allow us to use his library annex during our lunch period to work together on this project," said Lisa.

"He wasn't being nice," corrected Sean, shaking his head and placing his right index finger up to his lips. "He's honor-bound by secret code. Shhh."

David smiled at Sean and surveyed the materials that lay in front of them, noting, "It was really nice of Mr. Besio to give us this plywood. He edged it so it can be put together easily. All we have to do is brace this part with these two parts. But we still need a spinner."

"You can have one of the arrows from my archery set," offered Sean. "It would look really lethal as a spinner."

"It's only an arrow with one of those rubber suction tips," sighed Mary.

"So we'll take off the rubber tip and shave down the point," said Sean.

"No, we'd better try something else. Mr. Besio probably has something. He liked my spinner board design. I bet he could furnish us with a pointer in less than twenty minutes. Now we have to come up with competitive games, one for most letters of the alphabet," said David, munching an apple.

"What if David can't compete well?" asked Mary.

"Fair is fair," said Lisa. "Bobby will have the same disadvantage."

"Why not A for ARCHERY?" suggested Sean. "You can use my set, David. Wow! Maybe you and Bobby could see who could shoot Mary in the forehead first."

"Very funny," said Mary. "Just wait until I get my bearings, little underling brother."

"B is for ... " David began.

"Backgammon," said Mary.

"I doubt if Bobby knows anything about backgammon," said Lisa. "Why not bowling?"

"David and Bobby will each have the same number of weeks to get ready, with our encouragement and help. We should pick unusual categories so they each have to learn the selected category," said Mary.

"Lisa, please look through that Hoyle's book on games. We're going to need it," said David. "Maybe we should re-think the A for archery, too."

"But we can't have only card games," objected Sean.

"Okay," David assented. "Keep archery and bowling. What can we put for C?"

Lisa started thumbing through the game book.

"C is for CHESS," said Sean.

"No," said Mary.

"Why not?" asked Sean.

"David, do you play chess?"

"Yes. My dad and I used to play a lot."

"Do you think Bobby ever has?" Mary continued.

David thought for a moment.

"No. You're right. It would be unfair."

"Why not C for CANASTA?" offered Lisa, looking up from the book.

"Isn't that a card game little old ladies used to play?" asked Sean.

"Why not?" said David. "Let's keep it. We don't have much time. Let's go around in order and each of us will contribute. Sean, you're next. D is for … "

"DARTS," Sean said. "You can use my board, David. Mary can hold it."

"Okay," said David. "Thanks, Mary."

"May I please see the book, Lisa?" said Mary.

The book was passed.

As it worked out, the Gang of Four selected E for EUCHRE, F for FENCING, G for GOING TO BOSTON {a dice game}, H for HANDBALL, I for I DOUBT IT, J for JAVELIN THROWING, K for KLONDIKE, L for LANSQUENET, M for MUGGINS {a form of dominoes}, N for NINE MEN'S MORRIS, O for OLD MAID, P for POKER, Q for QUINZE, R for REVERSI although Sean had pushed his hardest for Russian roulette, offering Mary's head, but in denying Sean this prize, the group was obligated to award his choice S for

SHOOTING, then followed T for TABLE TENNIS, U for UNDER AND OVER SEVEN, and finally W for WEIGHT LIFTING in a contest of duration pressing fifty pounds.

"I could shoot Bobby, you know where, after he lifts the bar," offered Sean.

"Someone may shoot you if you don't watch it," warned David.

"BB guns aren't that loud and we could play loud music and I could hide at least fifty feet away ... "

"Sean, please remember, the rules explicitly state that there will be no violence," Mary reminded him.

"But it wouldn't exactly be violence, Mary. I mean, if I didn't know the gun was loaded and was just checking the accuracy of my sights and ease of the trigger pull and suddenly ... ."

David buried his head in his arms.

"Sean, hush up," said Mary. "Lunch period is almost over and you've given David another headache with your jabbering. Let's adjourn. Lisa, will you please do the calligraphy on the board tonight?"

"What did I say?" Sean asked Lisa.

David lifted his head and looked at Lisa, "Can you get the board home conveniently on the bus?"

"Sure. It stops right by my door. No problem. See you tomorrow."

* * * * *

Wednesday at lunch the Gang of Four eagerly watched as Lisa unwrapped the spinning board that she had created.

"Wow!"

"Great!"

"Super!"

"I added YAHTZE and VAULTING to get an even twenty-four categories," Lisa explained with obvious pride, "six for each quadrant of the circle. I measured it all off and inserted the lines and then used calligraphy inks and then varnished it twice."

"Watch," groaned David. "It will come up VAULTING."

"Let's attach this pointer Mr. Besio made for us. Maybe Lisa could take it home and varnish it so it goes with the game spinning board," suggested David.

"I can bring it back tomorrow so everything will be ready for the big meeting," said Lisa.

The next day at lunch period Lisa returned with the newly varnished pointer. The Gang of Four fastened it onto the game spinning board, and Sean gave it a test spin. It worked so well that the others all took turns spinning it.

"I wonder which one will come up?" wondered Sean.

"Who knows?" said Lisa.

"That's not *my* worry," grinned David.

"What's your worry?" asked Mary.

"I'm worried that *I* might think of what you did to Bobby the other day when you brought him in," said David. "If I do, I just know I'm going to fall down laughing."

"Well, if *you* do, so will *I*," said Lisa. "That way, Bobby will think we're *both* crazy."

"I could bring the derringer, and we could ask Bobby to do it all over again for you," said Sean slyly, tempting David.

"For consideration of your life, I think it best if Bobby never know the true nature of your bluff on Monday," cautioned David.

"Okay," assented Sean, "but it *really* was sweet. It was my finest hour."

"And if Bobby finds out, Sean, it may be your last," added David.

"Bobby will know sooner or later," said Mary. "Sean is an open book. He couldn't keep a secret if his life depended on it."

"Well, his life *might* well depend on keeping this one," said Lisa.

"PLEASE *DON'T* remind me about it, at least not until after our meeting tomorrow," said David.

* * * * *

Thursday's lunch period brought the greatly anticipated meeting with Bobby and his gang, although any meeting would be anticlimactic compared with Mary and Sean's rather dramatic encounter with Bobby on Monday.

Mary and Sean ushered Bobby, Zeke, Danny, and Joe into the library workroom. They were very subdued, as all eight signed a document indicating they were witnesses to the formal spinning of the dial. Mr. Lowery had chosen to remain to eat his brown bag lunch in the workroom, and he sat quietly in the corner. The document named Bobby and David as sole competitors, but all others as approved support team members to help organize and administer the eventual competition. Each student read the document and signed it in silence.

The spinning board had been covered with a peacock blue silk scarf borrowed from the bottom of Lisa's mother's hope chest. Lisa unveiled the game spinning board with a flourish. Bobby and his gang were obviously impressed by the high standard of workmanship of the board, and Mr. Lowery looked over at the unveiling and murmured, "Very nice".

From the very same pocket where he had packed his derringer on Monday, Sean took a quarter and flipped it in the air. "Okay, Bobby, you call," he said.

Bobby called, "Heads wins."

Sean opened the palm of his hand, and the image of President George Washington greeted the witnesses.

Sean nodded to Bobby, and gestured toward the game spinning board.

Bobby stepped forward and twirled the dial.

Around the dial spun, with all eyes riveted on its movement.

It began to slow, slowed, and stopped ... at C for CANASTA.

Bobby looked at his gang blankly, who were in turn looking at him in confusion. Having decided, however, that some sort of action was required in the face of all this drama, Bobby promptly turned and strode out the workroom door, causing his three gang members to race after him in an effort to bring up the rear.

The Gang of Four was also disconcerted, for somehow each had been anticipating more, yet no one had known quite what to expect. The high drama and potential fireworks of Monday's encounter had snuffed out like a fizzling sparkler. Still, the Gang of Four and Mr. Lowery were yet to be rewarded, after a fashion.

Suddenly they heard the library door fly open and the rapid approach of steps. Zeke Minturn stood at the workroom door, pausing to catch his breath, looking at them in embarrassment.

"Yes?" asked David. "What is it?"

"What the hell is canasta?"

"A card game, a form of rummy, " answered Lisa.

"Thanks," said Zeke as he turned to rejoin his gang.

After he had left, David looked at Lisa and said, "I've got a question, too."

"Yes?" said Lisa.

"What the hell is canasta?"

Whereupon all four raced to retrieve the book of card games.

* * * * *

Cheese steak sandwiches brought the Gang of Four back to the cafeteria on Friday. After everyone was seated and eating, Sean revealed that Zeke Minturn had sought him out before homeroom period to ask for his telephone number, which Sean had volunteered.

"He came into my homeroom," explained Sean, "and said, 'Hey, Little Dude, what are ya packin'?' I put my finger up to sshh him. Then I said, 'I warned Bobby not to tell anyone about the derringer.' Then he said, 'Hey, like cool man.'"

"You may have warned Bobby, Sean, but you also convinced him you had a *real* derringer, and in a village school like this that's BIG news," explained Lisa.

"You're becoming a gangster in your own time, Underling," laughed Mary. "Maybe Zeke should start calling you Little Caesar instead of Little Dude."

Sean made a fist toward Mary's face, warning, "Shut up, or I'll give *you* a Little Caesar!"

"Twins!" pleaded David, "We're friends, I hope, and we're also the Gang of Four. Now Sean, did Zeke give you any reason for asking for your phone number?"

"No. He just said he thought he might need it."

"Are you afraid he might call your father to tell him you had a gun in school?" asked Lisa.

Sean's eyes suddenly doubled in size.

"That would be the end of Sean," laughed Mary. "He had enough trouble getting a BB gun."

"That was because of Mother and all you women who are afraid of guns," retorted Sean. "Dad didn't care. He used to have one, too."

"I don't think there's anything we can do except wait," said David. "Why don't we brainstorm our team's next move."

"I think it would be best if the four of us learned how to play canasta," suggested Lisa. "I can bone up on the game and maybe we can meet at David's house to begin learning the rules."

"Okay with me," said David. "Let me check with Aunt Lillian and I'll call you."

"Sunday is best for me, David," added Lisa, "because the restaurant is closed and my mom can bring me over."

"Better make it Sunday afternoon for us," said Sean, "because Mary and I have MYF in the evening."

"What's MYF?" asked David.

"Methodist Youth Fellowship," said Mary, adding, "and it's a pretty wild group, mainly because Sean is in it."

"Yeah," agreed Sean. "Mom told me a long time ago that since I was wild, anyway, I might as well be a wild Methodist."

"Our family happens to be Methodist," said Mary, "but the group is for any young people who want to come."

"My Aunt Lillian is Episcopalian, although we don't go to church very much. She says she put in overtime all those years when she was an organist, so now she's enjoying retirement compensation. In fact, she sometimes refers to herself as a 'retired Episcopalian'. My parents were Attenders at Quaker Meeting," explained David. "I don't know, maybe I'll come along with you sometime."

"They soft pedal the religion part because they know it's *really* boring," said Sean blithely. "We usually have a great time. You could come, too, Lisa."

"We're not really much of anything, although my dad was born a Catholic. I don't think my parents would mind if I tried it."

"Actually, for a lark, you should come to Sunday School on one of the Sundays we have Mr. Lytle," suggested Mary. "He's the husband of our youth choir director. Our youth choir sings one Sunday, and then Mr. Lytle blathers at us on alternate Sundays.

"Yeah, and I *really* prefer choir, even though I don't like to sing," said Sean. "I'd take old Skunk Head any day to Mr. Little Bantam Rooster."

"Skunk Head?" inquired David.

"Mrs. Lytle has a really white streak of hair growing back from the left center of her forehead," explained Mary.

"She looks *just* like a skunk!" said Sean. "Smells like one, too. She wears so much perfume, it could knock an elephant over at a hundred yards."

"And you said something about Bantam rooster?" David asked Sean.

"Yeah," explained Sean. "Her husband reminds me of one of those little Bantam roosters. He's not more than five feet tall, and he's always preaching at us. It's really sickening. He brings in the local section from the Sunday paper, and then he paws through the pages and announces something like, 'Ah, I see Mrs. Jones has been elected president of the historical society, and children, THIS IS *GOOD*, because Mrs. Jones is a *CHREEStian*."

"It wouldn't be so bad if he didn't emphasize the first part of the word CHREEStian. It's like getting hit with a sledgehammer, again and again," Mary continued.

"We even begged our parents to spare us Mr. Lytle," continued Sean, "but they said the world is full of fascinating individuals, and that we should experience as large a diversity as possible. And I said, 'I don't see you sitting in there with us, taking the whammy every other week', and they said, 'We have enough of our own'."

"Mom always says, 'Actions are a lot louder than words, especially when goodness is the issue,'" said Mary.

"Yeah, one time Mary and I were coming into the church from the fellowship hall after services, and Mrs. Lytle was coming out the door with all this music bundled in her arms, and we heard Mr. Lytle say, 'Since you're going to the car, Elvira, take my Bible'. And he plops this really *huge* Bible right on top of all her music, and she totters a little this way and then a little that way, and suddenly the Bible slips off and hits the sill of the doorwell. Now to most people, that wouldn't be a big deal, but not to Mr. Lytle. You'd had thought someone had just burned the Constitution. He starts this big production, yelling at her, 'How could you drop the *Holy Book?! The Precious Book!* Oh, Good Lord, deliver us!' with poor Mrs. Lytle tottering there, trying not to drop all her music. Suddenly WHOOSH, and the music goes flying all over the place. This happened just after we first arrived in July. Then little Mr. Bantam starts shouting at her to be more careful."

"I wish she had pasted him a good one right across the kisser," said Mary, "but she's a very reserved lady."

"Anyway, please come to MYF sometime, we'd love for you to come as our guests. You should also come to Sunday school and choir just to see the productions, especially the one Lytle's gets away with. It's an awful, dreadful class. It's enough to make anyone want to throw up right in his face, or maybe even to become an atheist," encouraged Sean.

"Little brother, you make it sound *so* inviting. How could anyone possibly refuse?" sighed Mary.

"I'm sure Aunt Lillian wouldn't mind if I came with you sometime. As I said before, she was organist at the Episcopal church forever, and now she says that she doesn't like showing up there too often—because it would be like Marley's ghost returning to visit Scrooge—so we generally read to each other Sunday mornings," said David. "But I think I want to get this whole Bobby Perkins business behind me first before I try anything new. Maybe I'll come sometime after Christmas."

"Me, too," said Lisa. "I'll wait until David comes."

"Sounds good," said Sean.

"Now, in way of preparing for the upcoming canasta competition, why don't you all plan to come to over about one o'clock this Sunday afternoon. I'll call you tonight to see if that time works for everybody."

* * * * *

David was relaxing on the living room sofa, reading the Sunday comics. Aunt Lillian was in the kitchen preparing a Sunday brunch which had become their tradition after their Sunday morning reading.

The telephone rang.

"I'll get it," yelled David. "Hello?"

"David, this is Mary. Sean and I are going to be a little late. Poor Old Thing can't bring us around until one-thirty or so. Is that all right?"

"Sure, no problem. Mary, guess what? My Aunt Lillian is an *expert* on canasta!"

"You're kidding."

"No. Do you remember how Sean said it was a game that little old ladies play? Well, Aunt Lillian was *one* of those little old ladies."

"Cool! It'll be like learning from Houdini."

"I guess so. I never thought of it quite like that, although I don't think Aunt Lillian is half as tall as Houdini was."

"Oh, David, please don't tell Sean I mentioned this, but just wait until you see him. He's hardly slept all weekend because he's worried sick that Zeke Minturn will call at any minute to report to Dad that Sean took a real derringer to school. You should see the circles under his eyes. He looks like a raccoon!"

"Maybe that's better for you, Mary. You know ... maybe he won't be so ... bloodthirsty."

194

"Are you kidding? Whenever he gets this tired, he stops talking about shooting people, and then starts pretending to thrust stilettos in people's backs and bellies, always twisting the blades. He's probably assassinated over half of the professors in the university's math and physics departments, not to mention any number of distinguished guests who frequently stop by to visit with my dad."

"Well, at least he keeps them on their guard," David smiled.

"Yeah, watch it Mr. High Official, you're about to get murdered. I sometimes wonder if I'll wake up in the middle of the night with Sean standing next to my bed holding a knife to my throat."

"No way. Sean is not stealthy, he's just a warrior, albeit an irrepressible warrior. It will all stand him in good stead some day."

"Yeah. Right in the middle of some jail cell."

"No way. You'll see. He'll surprise you. And remember, no matter what, he *is* your brother. That's more kin than Lisa or I have."

"I never quite thought of it that way. Would you like to *share* him?"

"Why not? In fact, we already *are* sharing him. Remember how I got him going on this secret confraternity of librarians ruse? That held him at bay for a while, didn't it?"

"Yes. He's already renewed his card twice at Melrose Library."

"See, Mary, now he'll be checking out more books."

"Yeah. He's just discovered a whole new section on war crimes and torture, not to mention gangsters and mobsters."

"Well, at least his interests remain consistent."

"Straight as an arrow."

"Honestly, Mary, what's it like to have a twin?"

"It has its moments."

"But remember, he's your *raccoon* twin today. It's fun to play games like seeing what kinds of animals different people remind you of.

Because of your long, curly hair, which I admire, you remind me of a fastidious Persian cat."

"David, you should become a diplomat."

"Well, it's true. Oh, I think I hear Aunt Lillian calling me to our Sunday brunch. See you around one-thirty. Thanks for calling."

* * * * *

Sean looked so much like a raccoon when he arrived at one-thirty that David could hardly keep from laughing. He had related his conversation with Mary to Lisa, and as Sean entered the dining room, Lisa could not contain herself from breaking into hysterics.

"What's so funny," asked Sean.

"Uh ... well, uh ... well, I don't think you'd get it."

"Hey!" retorted Sean. "Aren't we members of the same gang, the Gang of Four, which has special ties to an international secret confraternity? That means none of us gets left out of anything, doesn't it? So what gives?"

David was plumbing the depths. He didn't want to hurt Sean, but he couldn't think of a joke as timely or as funny as Lisa's laughter. —Perhaps a kernel of truth will save the day, he gambled.

"Well, Sean, I was explaining a game to Mary on the telephone where we see what kinds of animals people remind us of. She reminds me of a fastidious Persian cat."

At this announcement, Lisa burst into laughter.

"What do I remind you of, David?" asked Sean.

Before David could answer, Mary blurted out, "A tired raccoon. Just look at those eyes. Jeepers creepers!"

Lisa, David, and Mary all laughed.

"Better than a spiny anteater," Sean scowled at Mary and sat down.

The telephone rang. Aunt Lillian appeared and beckoned to Sean, "Your father is on the telephone for you. Something about a message from Zeke somebody, and your dad needs to talk to you right away."

Sean now suddenly resembled a tired whitewashed raccoon hung out to dry. He looked at his comrades, gulped, and advanced to the kitchen to take the call.

Sean reappeared shortly, looking greatly relieved and smiling, "David, Zeke said Bobby needs to talk to you in the worst way. I've got Zeke's number so you can call him. Zeke has fingered me as the go between. That's why he wanted my telephone number. My dad was just relaying the message."

David went to the kitchen and called Zeke.

He emerged several minutes later with a puzzled expression on his face.

"Anything wrong?" asked Lisa.

"I don't know," said David. "All Zeke would say was that Bobby desperately needs to talk to me tomorrow in the library workroom at the beginning of lunch period. After I see him, I'll tell you all at lunch what he wants. Sean, Zeke also said to tell the Little Dude good night."

"You mean the Little Raccoon," laughed Mary. "Sean, maybe you could win first place in a raccoon-look-alike contest."

"Maybe you could fall off a curb going home and skin your knee," growled Sean.

Aunt Lillian entered from the kitchen with two decks of cards and a plastic card tray. "We can begin the canasta instruction anytime you'd like. I propose we move to the dining room and use the larger table."

After the Gang of Four had seated itself, Aunt Lillian looked solemnly at Sean and said, "I feel it only fair to warn all of you that this is a game that can easily get in your blood, and that it might well keep you awake at night."

"Why?" asked Lisa.

"Because, especially in its two-handed form, it can become incredibly competitive and cut-throat," explained Aunt Lillian.

"Sweet!" exulted Sean, suddenly becoming all attention.

"Anyone want out?" continued Aunt Lillian.

No one moved.

"Very well, but please don't say I didn't warn you. Canasta had its origins in South America, and it is a form of rummy. Some authorities maintain all the revolutions, rebellions, and bloodshed we have seen in South America these last forty years, or so, may be traced back to one grand canasta game, and that the resulting feud has been fought ever since."

"Excellent!" rejoiced Sean.

"I caution to suggest," Aunt Lillian continued, "that *that* theory is a bit of an exaggeration of the power of canasta, but there may be some basis for it, especially in two-handed canasta, where a player may suddenly lose a huge discard pile of cards and wildcards to his opponent."

"Awesome!" Sean said.

"First," Aunt Lillian smiled, "let's begin by learning card values and functions. Then we will review general rules as well as several specific strategies. Finally, we will play several open hands."

The Gang of Four sat at full attention for the next two hours.

* * * * *

David went to the library to do some independent research during his English class, a privilege which had become his contractual right as long as he maintained a 98% average. To wait for Bobby in the library workroom, rather than to walk to the library after English class, would put David in a much stronger psychological position. Bobby would be entering David's territory, thanks to Mr. Lowery's allowing David to use the workroom space. In fact, Mr. Lowery beckoned to David when he entered the library, and motioned for him to stop at the desk.

"David," said Mr. Lowery, "I want you to know that whatever project you and your friends are up to, it has already had an amazing effect on Bobby Perkins."

"It has?"

"Yes. This morning during his third period study hall, Bobby came to the library from study hall for the first time since he's been at this school. He asked my help in locating books about card games, especially canasta. Then he checked out *two*! That's a *real* first."

"Gee, that's great, Mr. Lowery! I hope it opens some new doors to him. He's coming here to meet with me briefly at the beginning of next period lunch. Is that okay?"

"Yes. What are you working on?"

"I can't give too many details now, but the four of us are working on a positive way to have a friendly relationship with Bobby without having it deteriorate into violence."

"Very laudable. If I can help, let me know."

"You already are helping. Thanks."

* * * * *

David paced the library workroom. Five minutes had passed since the passing bells had rung, and David was beginning to wonder if Bobby was going to show up. Finally, he sat down at the desk.

Suddenly there was a knock on the workroom door.

"Come in," invited David.

When Bobby Perkins entered, David immediately wondered how much sleep *he* had gotten over the weekend for Bobby was in a dead heat with Sean in the raccoon-look-alike department.

Ill at ease, fidgeting with his hands, Bobby looked uneasily at David, waiting to be prompted.

"Yes, Bobby. What did you want to see me about?"

Bobby glanced at the floor, and then out the windows, and then at the worktable, taking time to organize his thoughts. Finally, he began, "This canasta business. I looked into it a little and, you know, it's a card game that little old ladies used to play. Seems to me we ain't got no good competition between us but, instead, a really *weak* sister. I mean, I'm the toughest kid here in school, and if word *ever* gets out that I'm playin' canasta, I'll be the total laughin' stock."

"I won't tell anyone, Bobby," promised David.

"Well, it's not exactly *you* I'm worried 'bout. You're not doin' no solo on this affair, you know."

David reflected, then said, "Ah, you think Sean will spill the beans?"

"I ain't know nothin' about no beans, but I did me some checkin', and what I hear is that kid is always talking, I mean *always!*"

"We can try to keep our competition completely secret, Bobby," offered David. "I can ask my team not to tell anyone."

"That's as well as may be, but in the heat of the moment, with that little magpie jabberin' away for all he's worth, you never know what might come out. I mean, he might say whatever comes into his foolish little head, if you know what I mean."

"Why don't we plan to have the competition at my house?"

Bobby looked at David dubiously, and then with averted glance said, "Your old dame aunt ain't never gonna forgive me what I done to you."

"I'm sure she's already forgiven you, Bobby."

Bobby thought a while, and then said, "Even if we don't play cards here in school, if word ever got out I was even playin', I'd still be the total laughin' stock, if you know what I'm trying to say? That jabbering little magpie doesn't seem to restrict his talk to school stuff, if you know what I mean?"

David repressed a smile, asking, "I wonder if we could get Sean's attention diverted to something else that would minimize the risk of his telling others about our canasta competition?"

"Beats me," said Bobby, shaking his head.

"Do you know," brightened David, "I bet my Gang of Four could successfully divert the school's attention with some sort of ruse so that absolutely *no one* will ever find out about our canasta competition."

"What's a ruse?"

"A kind of trick. We'll capture everybody's attention on some trumped up issue here at school. It will be so diverting that no one will even venture to notice what we're doing on the side."

"That may be as well as it goes, but I ain't never learned how to play no card games, and I can't make no sense out of the books I looked at. They was Greek to me. I ain't gonna be able to learn it."

"As it works out, my Aunt Lillian is somewhat of an expert on canasta, and she began teaching me and my team last night. I'm sure she'd be delighted to teach you and your team. Maybe you could come over on Saturday afternoons. On the Saturdays that you come, I will plan to go over to Sean's house."

"So you'd be gone, right?"

"Yes."

Bobby gave David a worried look, and asked, "Do you *really* think your Aunt has forgiven me?"

"I'm sure she already has. You must remember, after all, that she *is* an Episcopalian."

This explanation seemed to make sense to Bobby, and he bought it, even though it was obvious he didn't have the slightest clue what an Episcopalian was.

"Okay, then, by me and my gang if she will teach us. Darn decent of her to put up with us. I bet she can really deal them cards."

"As a matter of fact, she really can. Why don't you and your gang plan to come for your first lesson this Saturday afternoon from one to four?"

"We'll be there," said Bobby firmly.

David nodded his approval.

Bobby kept standing in front of him, looking at the floor as if he wanted to say something else.

—Perhaps a little more prompting will help, thought David.

"Yes, Bobby. Is there anything else?"

Bobby surveyed the room and took a deep breath. "I did me some checkin' up on them two Bobsey Twins of yours. They came to Midville in June from Boston, which is a mighty powerful city and has lots of schools where kids of all ages are on drugs and have guns, if you know what I mean."

"Certainly not like Midville. Boston, I would say, would be much wilder," said David, biting his tongue.

"*Deadlier* wilder, if you catch my meaning. I'm warnin' you, David, that little beggar Sean ain't what he appears to be; I'm tellin' you, he ain't no tame Bobsey Twin, but a little hoodlum, that's what he is. And it ain't right, but what's done is done."

David now bit his tongue much, much harder.

Bobby gave a heavy sigh, and taking a deep breath, he continued, "A week ago today, mind ya, in this *very* room, my life passed right before my eyes, and I swear I'm a new Bobby Perkins for the trauma of it. But don't you never dare cross that little hoodlum, or you might find yourself pushin' up daisies."

David tried his best to look grim. The knowledge that his tongue was bleeding helped him convey an air of grave concern.

"Thanks, Bobby, I'll be careful."

Bobby's sincerity and goodwill had carried the day and David's tongue had saved him from hysterics, although it was sore for a week.

* * * * *

Bobby's note in David's locker next morning read:

> We all talkd it over and want to come
> lern how play canasta, but want all of
> this kept absolutly TOP SECRETE!

Saturday would mark Bobby's gang's indoctrination into the much neglected and sometimes thrilling game of canasta. David began to think there might well be light at the end of this tunnel. The new problem would be to silence Sean, as well as find a ruse that would succeed in diverting the attention of the entire school lest anyone breathe word of the canasta competition. David had promised to protect Bobby from becoming a laughing stock, and he wanted to prove true to his word.

Chapter Fourteen
Ruses in the Making

ALL MEMBERS OF THE GANG OF FOUR HAD FINISHED their bag lunches in the library workroom and were considering how they could insure that David's and Bobby's canasta competition be kept secret, therefore sparing Bobby the public embarrassment and humiliation of playing a 'little old lady's game'.

"If we could put tape over Sean's mouth until after the competition, people wouldn't know about it until after the fact," said Mary.

Sean looked at her threateningly.

David then related how Bobby had warned him about Sean's bellicose nature. Mary pealed with laughter, announcing, "You've been baptized by a bully, Sean. From now on, I may take to calling you Little Hoodlum."

"And I may take to coming into your bedroom tonight and gouging your eyes out," snarled Sean. Little Caesar had been bad enough, but Little Hoodlum?

"Shhh," said David. "I'm thinking."

Silence followed.

David brightened and said, "Achilles' heel."

"What's that, David?" asked Lisa.

"Achilles' heel," repeated David. "We've got to find an Achilles' heel."

"Who's heel?" asked Sean.

"The school's, of course," answered David. "It's from Greek mythology, from Homer's *The Iliad*, where during the Trojan War, Achilles was killed by Paris with an arrow shot through his heel—"

"Cool!" interrupted Sean, "That would have really hurt, but it shouldn't have killed him."

"It was Achilles' only vulnerable spot. And someone's Achilles' heel has since come to mean someone's or something's weakness," explained David.

"I don't quite understand," said Mary.

"We need some sort of ruse that will divert the attention of the school so no one gets wind of the canasta competition. I promised Bobby he wouldn't lose face and that we would keep the competition totally secret. So we need to find one of the school's vulnerable areas, and then make an issue out of it, something like a policy not being enforced, or that sort of thing."

"But no one will find out about the canasta competition, will they?" asked Lisa.

Mary and David looked at Sean, as David answered, "I wouldn't bet on that. Some people can't seem to keep secrets."

"Don't look at *me*" remonstrated Sean. "I won't say a word to *anyone*, not even to POTS."

"Well, if Sean keeps his word, we're ninety percent sure we can keep it quiet," said David, "but we also must remember that in a small school like this, any change of pattern is sure to be noticed, even if the activity involved isn't happening on school grounds. If anyone sees Bobby and his gang arriving at Aunt Lillian's, there may be questions. Others will certainly notice a change in Bobby's behavior. People are naturally curious. I suppose we could just ignore any questions."

"If they're curious, we can shoot them," said Sean, forgetting that his own father had ascribed to him the accolade CURIOSUS.

"Sean, you're sick," said Mary.

"Better sick than dead," retorted her brother.

"Sshh," said David.

Silence followed.

David slammed his fist on the table, startling Lisa.

"We need information on school procedures. That should give us one or two areas of attack. I wonder if there is anything in this room. Let's look over on those shelves. Sean, what's over there?"

"A lot of old faculty handbooks."

"Excellent," said David. "Let me see one of the oldest ones."

Sean passed the handbook dated *1963* to David.

As David pored through the manual, Sean said, "We could have a burglary."

"Be quiet, Little Hoodlum," scolded Mary.

"I wish I had my sheath knife with me," said Sean.

"Sean, pass me last year's faculty manual, please. I think I may have found something."

Sean passed the manual and David thumbed quickly to the page he wanted.

"Just as I suspected," concluded David. "I've found a remnant from the sixties."

"What's that?" asked Sean.

"Something that was done years ago, but is no longer done today. I think it's something they forgot to delete from the handbook. No one ever bothered to take it out, so it just slipped through unnoticed."

"What are you talking about?" asked Lisa.

"Here, let me quote. It's the same in both books: 'State law requires that all schools conduct twelve fire drills and three air raid drills each year. Eight fire drills will be conducted prior to the first day of

December of each school year, so as to familiarize faculty and students with the appropriate evacuation protocols.'"

"So?" asked Sean.

David grinned and looked at Lisa.

"Lisa, you were a student here last year. Were there any air raid drills?"

"Not when I was here, and I only missed two days for the flu."

"See?" David grinned.

"See what?" said Sean.

"The school handbook mandates three air raid drills a year, but I bet they haven't had any air raid practices since the late sixties or early seventies."

"Why did they have them in the early sixties?" asked Lisa.

"Well, I suspect the Cuban missile crisis, and the nuclear scare, and the nuclear arms race caused people to worry about atom bombs falling. Fortunately, that's all in the past now. The original need is no longer there, so the air raid drill protocol is no longer necessary, even though it's still on the books."

"But why get so excited about someone forgetting some stupid old air raid drills?" asked Lisa.

"Because *that* will be our complaint. We promised Bobby that no one would find out about the canasta competition. Accordingly, we need to create a diversion that will capture everyone's attention and maybe even rally the entire school's support for our cause. Our mandate will be to: 'Bring back the air raid drill!'"

"David, you *can't* be serious," Lisa smiled.

"I most certainly am," grinned David. "*This* will be a perfect ruse for bonding the entire student body together. I wonder who's been teaching here the longest?"

"Why not check the old yearbooks? They're over there next to the faculty manuals."

After a cursory examination of yearbooks, it was generally concluded that the life expectancy of middle school teachers fell far short of national averages, but Miss Kirkpatrick, home economics teacher, won the prize for having taught at Midville Middle School and the former Midville High School for thirty-five years.

"Lisa, do you know Miss Kirkpatrick?"

"Yes. I had her last year."

"Would you please stop next period and ask her if she ever remembers having air raid drills in this school?"

"Sure," said Lisa.

"Great. Then we'll have a sense of history about when they stopped observing the protocols."

"Why would students care about bringing back air raid drills?" asked Lisa.

"Because it's a waste of time," said Sean.

"Right!" agreed David. "It's also sort of exciting."

David read a little further in the *1962* faculty manual.

"I'll be a monkey's uncle," smiled David.

"If you can't find a monkey, how about a raccoon named Sean Potter?" asked Mary.

Sean pelted his apple core at Mary, striking her on the forehead.

"Hey!" shouted Mary.

"Sshh," scolded David. "You asked for it, Mary."

Mary glowered at Sean.

"Listen," said David, "They also had one GO HOME drill a year in the early sixties."

"Now *that's* what the students would *really* go for," said Lisa.

"I bet they probably count early dismissals because of blizzards as GO HOME drills these days, if they still even think about it," added Sean.

"What we're dealing with here is a protocol that was once necessary, but after the need to enforce it fell away, no one remembered to delete it from the published regulations," said David.

"Too bad murder isn't like that," said Sean as he looked wistfully at his sister.

"It's obvious this part of the faculty handbook hasn't been updated in years," observed David. "Air raid alerts fell through the cracks a long time ago."

"How does that help us, David?" asked Lisa, breaking open her banana.

"Well, we have found an incongruity. We can lobby for air raid drills for the common preparation and defense of the school community. Silly as it is, it might prove a reliable way to rally the entire school together. We've already lamented about how dull and droll Midville Middle School is. Here is a little something that will spice things up, something to make one day different from the next."

"I don't know," said Lisa. "It seems pretty farfetched."

"It is," agreed David, "but the challenge for us will be to pull off this ruse *so* well that it will divert everyone's notice from what Bobby's doing to prepare for the big canasta showdown. All that we need now is a way to call attention to this incongruity of policy. I bet we could use *Bare Fax* to take our case to the entire school community."

"How about going to Mr. Ferlinghausen?" asked Mary.

"No. He's a really good guy. I don't want him to be the patsy," said David.

"The patsy?" asked Mary.

"Yes, some unsuspecting victim on the faculty whom we can lure into our web, so we can create a conduit of concern to force this issue," said David.

"But how do we force the issue?" asked Lisa.

"By shooting people," interjected Sean.

"By a much greater power," said David. "The power of the press. We'll stage an interview with our pigeon and then let the presses roll."

"Who will be our pigeon?" asked Mary.

* * * * *

The dismissal bell had rung and students were leaving the building to board their buses. Melvin Dandy sat in his office reading *The New York Times*. He did this religiously, and accordingly had become accomplished at playing trivia games. But reading *The Times* was only one of Melvin Dandy's gifts, for he also had become an expert at what is classically known as 'laying down the law'.

The intercom buzzed.

"Yes?" said the counselor.

"Mr. Dandy," said Mrs. Fullerton, "David Andrews would like to see you."

Melvin Dandy closed his eyes, deciding upon a course of action. Folding *The Times* and placing it in the bottom right hand drawer of his desk, Dandy walked to his office door, threw it open, saying, "David, David, do come in. How nice of you to stop by, and I see you have brought a friend."

"Mr. Dandy, this is Lisa Jones. We wonder if you would be willing to grant an interview to the school's alternative newspaper *Bare Fax*? Would you mind if we asked you a few questions?"

"Not at all, not at all. Always happy to oblige the press," smirked Dandy, adding smugly, "come in and sit down. Tape recorders are permitted as well as notes."

Dandy was somewhat startled and disconcerted to see David pull out a small tape recorder and turn it on.

Lisa opened her notebook, looked at the counselor, and said, "Mr. Dandy, we are here to get your views on the importance of following school regulations and mandated procedures. Would you please give us your opinion?"

"Ahem. Well, following the rules is very, *very* important, although I do not expect that many of our impressionable young people appreciate the full burdens and consequences of such rigorous discipline. Ahem. You may attribute their lack of appreciation to their lack of experience. One learns, as one grows older, that rules *help* us rather than hurt us."

Dandy gave a forced smile, as if he had been speaking into a television camera, and patted the crown of his toupee.

"Would you, therefore, Mr. Dandy, believe it important that all rules be followed?" asked David.

"Oh, my, my, but most definitely. Civilization *itself* depends on such discipline," responded the counselor emphatically.

"Do you believe the schools are effective in teaching students to follow rules?" asked Lisa.

Dandy stroked his chin for effect, for he was almost always on stage. "Yes ... and no. Most students cooperate and uphold the general welfare in their decision to adhere to the regulations. A few, unfortunately, flaunt the rules and make it hard on everyone else. Largely, I would say, rules are written for the very few who have trouble knowing the acceptable limits of civilized behavior."

"Mr. Dandy, do you believe that it is fair, then, to have lots of rules for students who demonstrate responsible behavior?" asked David.

David's question made Melvin Dandy visibly wary, for he had come to respect the enormous intelligence that lay beneath those freckles.

Stroking his chin even longer than before and frowning for effect, Melvin Dandy finally sidestepped David's question, "Fairness is a red herring. Rules are only helpful if obeyed by everyone. If not, anarchy would reign."

"But you just said rules were written for the very few who have trouble knowing how to behave," challenged David. "And, anyway, there are some who don't obey the present rules, and anarchy hardly reigns."

Melvin Dandy became very flushed, and sputtered, "Never mind what I just said, and don't you dare go trying to put words into my mouth, young man! You know what I meant, or you *should* have known what I meant. Let me try it again: rules are written to help those who need more discipline."

"Mr. Dandy," asked Lisa, "do you believe the school should serve as a role model in this whole matter of following rules and regulations?"

"Absolutely! Absolutely! It must begin here in school as well as at home, or all is lost."

"How about rules and regulations regarding the general welfare and safety of our school community?" asked David.

"Those are definitely the *most important* rules and regulations we are given to follow," answered Dandy.

"And does our school follow all such rules and regulations?" baited David.

"My dear students," exhorted Dandy, "if such rules and regulations were not followed to the letter, our school district would be in very serious trouble with the State Education Department, which oversees all matters pertaining to the general and specific welfare of each student, as well as the safety of the entire school community. You have my *personal* guarantee: Midville School District adheres to all regulations and rules incumbent on it to follow, both those required by the State Education Department as well as those that obtain from time-honored local norms. And you can *quote me*!"

"Thank you very, very much for your help, Mr. Dandy. We will no doubt quote you, and we appreciate your taking time from your busy schedule to see us."

Dandy looked down surreptitiously at the drawer where he had hidden *The New York Times*, saying, "Not at all. Not at all."

As David and Lisa left the office, the rustle of newspaper could be heard behind the counselor's closed door.

"We got it, Lisa, although I'm a little disappointed," confided David.

"Disappointed?" questioned Lisa. "I thought it was *terribly exciting*."

"To me it seemed a little too easy, that's all," reflected David. "It was like taking candy from—"

"His name *is* Dandy— "

"And, yes," replied David, "it rhymes with candy."

"David" asked Lisa, "are all ruses this exciting? What's next?"

"Well, if the twins can stop squabbling with each other, I will ask them to canvass as many seventh graders as possible to see if students who have transferred here from other schools remember ever having had air raid drills. Maybe some precedent can be suggested from discovering the current practices of other school districts. I will also ask them to collect signatures on a petition that demands the reinstitution of air raid drills here at Midville Middle School. We'll meet them tomorrow in the cafeteria since they're serving dried up hamburgers and soggy french fries. Sean begged me, saying it was better than the health food Poor Old Thing gives them when they brown bag it."

"Maybe we should have organized a student protest over the quality of food in our cafeteria," suggested Lisa.

"Yeah, but everyone *knows* it's lousy," said David. "Anyway, would you ever trade that interview we just had with Mr. Dandy?"

Lisa thought a moment. "No, never. Not for anything."

"It was a classic, wasn't it?"

"Yes," agreed Lisa.

"Let's run with it, then."

* * * * *

The next day during lunch period the Gang of Four began planning for its Extra edition of *Bare Fax*. Mary reviewed a page of notes made when she and Sean consulted with seventh graders the day before.

"We canvassed a lot of seventh graders, and even some eighth graders," reported Mary, "and of the nine students who have transferred here to Midville in the last two years from within New York State, only one came from a school district that still conducted air raid drills."

"That would confirm that there was, at one time at least, a state requirement for such drills," concluded David.

"The kid who told us was Mark Bennett," added Sean. "He said that air raid drills in his former school were almost a joke. The school used a high pitched electronic siren on the intercom to give the alert."

"Why was that almost a joke?" asked Lisa.

"Well, Mark said the intercom speakers were so cheap that they made the electronic siren sound pretty feeble. Kids would be laughing through the whole thing as they braced themselves up against the lockers in the hallways."

"Tenetia Edwards moved here from Kansas two years ago," reported Mary, "and she said they had 'duck and cover' drills because of all the tornados."

"Yeah, but we don't have many tornados around here, do we?" asked Sean.

"Thank God, no," said David. "Let's go for the air raid drill."

"Errrnnnnnn," Sean imitated a siren as the others laughed.

* * * * *

On Friday the Extra edition of *Bare Fax* was distributed to homerooms, and pinned to most bulletin boards. Students who eagerly clustered to read the latest news were treated to the following headline:

SCHOOL OFFICIAL IN ERROR; ALL PROTOCOLS NOT FOLLOWED!

Students read the lead article with surprise and glee. Perhaps it would lead to one, or two, or even three air raid drills which, of course, would take a few minutes away from precious 'instructional time'. The newspaper, in the interest of accurate reporting, had transcribed and printed Lisa's and David's entire interview with Mr. Melvin Dandy, as well as the air raid drill protocols from the current faculty handbook. Mention was also made that several students, who had transferred to the Midville School District, clearly remembered having had similar drills as standard practice in other districts.

* * * * *

After students had passed to their first period classes, Melvin Dandy arrived at Midville Middle School, at which time his secretary notified him that Mr. Ferlinghausen requested his immediate presence in the principal's office. Melvin Dandy's face was a taut crimson as he crumpled a copy of *Bare Fax* in his right fist.

"I'll never say a damn word to that rag again," sputtered the counselor.

David always delivered copies of his paper to the office, and Mr. Ferlinghausen had summoned Melvin Dandy, perhaps in hope of staving off an attack of apoplexy.

"Melvin, you *really* put your foot in your mouth, didn't you?" laughed Otto, adjusting his blue and white tie.

"How could *I* know they were after air raid drills? I said all protocols were strictly followed because *someone* has to hold the line around here on all these smart-assed upstarts," Dandy blurted defensively.

"Now, Melvin, calm down. It's not the end of the world."

"I've been made into a laughing stock," grimaced Dandy, "and let me just tell you, for two cents, I'd give that damn rag a quote or two, if such things were printable. If they ever *tried* to put my real thoughts about their lousy rag into print, it would singe their copier to a crisp."

Otto Ferlinghausen studied his red-faced colleague with compassion, gently admonishing him, "Melvin, I'm telling you that it's not the end of the world."

"Oh, yes it is. What else is an air raid but the end of the world?"

"Now, calm down. The kids have had a little fun, admittedly at your expense, but I'm sure they will apologize."

"I don't want an apology from anyone, least of all those two. I said what I said and I stick by it: *someone* has to hold the line and keep a lid on these foolish shenanigans."

Otto Ferlinghausen smiled. "Melvin, when you work with middle school youth, you've got to know which lines are worth holding and which are worth sacrificing."

"No you *don't*! I'm of the old school, and if you give them an inch, they'll jolly well gobble up the whole goddam mile. Before long, they'll waltz right in here to your office and demand to run the entire school. And just you guess who'll be leading the horde?"

"Melvin, you're very flushed, and I suspect your blood pressure is topping off near the stroking point. Why don't you take the day off and go home and relax?"

Melvin momentarily considered the offer until he realized he had left his *New York Times* in his office.

"No," he answered. "I won't abandon you to fend off that horde by yourself."

"There is no *horde* to fend off. Get some perspective, man!" said Otto.

"Eh. The Mongols, that's what they are. Latter-day Mongols, and that damned freckled-face-redhead upstart is Genghis Khan!"

"Now Melvin, it's Friday, and we've had a long week. I am *ordering* you to go immediately to your car and to drive home for a very deserved rest. Is that clear?"

Dandy sputtered and fumed, considering the relative loss of an unread *New York Times*. Otto looked at him sternly.

"Oh, all right," Dandy conceded. "What will *you* do after I've gone?"

"Nothing."

"Nothing?"

"Nothing."

Shaking his head, Melvin Dandy could only say, "Good day, Otto," as he stalked out of Otto's office through the main office, and into the corridor.

As fate would have it, Sean Potter was just then entering the office in order to repay a loan for lunch money borrowed earlier in the week.

217

Upon noticing the unhappy counselor, Sean couldn't resist stepping up to the paper's most recent interviewee.

"Mr. Dandy, Mr. Dandy," Sean implored.

"Eh? What do you want?" growled Dandy.

"What is your opinion of today's issue of *Bare Fax*?"

Sean had never seen anyone become quite so agitated and crimson-faced, or heard anyone sputter with such intensity, but thanks to Sean's impeccable memory, the Gang of Four was able to use a new lead banner for their extra special Monday edition.

* * * * *

MR. DANDY CALLS PAPER 'SCANDAL SHEET'; STUDENTS SUBMIT PETITION FOR DRILLS; 'SCHOOL HAS NO SIREN ALARM' SAYS PRIN.!

As Monday's Extra edition was circulated and posted throughout Midville Middle School, the banner headline caught the interest and imagination of faculty and students alike. Ironically, this surge of interest confirmed Dandy's prediction of descending hordes, for students elbowed themselves into position to read the news. The unfolding drama had taken on a life of its own; the ruse was sprung.

Chapter Fifteen
What is Canasta, Anyway?

SUNDAY AFTERNOON FOUND THE GANG OF FOUR at David's seated with Aunt Lillian around the dining room table. Max lay beneath Sean's chair, for Sean had romped with him earlier, revealing to his comrades, "I miss having a dog, but our parents say we are more cat people and that we can't do justice to having a dog. I know *I'd* do justice, especially to a wonderful dog like Max. You're really lucky, David. Let's toss the sponge ball back and forth so Max can try to catch it. He just loves jumping for it, and he's getting better each week."

"That would be fun. I'm glad Max has fit in here, even though it took him a while to realize that Her Majesty rules this roost," said David, looking at the card tray in front of him. "By the way, Aunt Lillian, it's really good of you to teach us canasta."

"I hope you will thank me *after* I've done so, and that no one regrets it," Aunt Lillian replied.

Lisa smiled and Mary asked, "Why do you say that?"

"Canasta can be an extremely competitive game," observed Aunt Lillian.

"I think it is especially good of you to teach Bobby and his gang," added Lisa.

"They're really not bad boys at heart," said Aunt Lillian, "although our first session yesterday got off to an awkward start."

"How so?" asked Mary.

"Bobby was embarrassed about the way he had abused David, and he didn't know how to apologize. But I admire him for wanting to put all that behind us. I helped him along as he blurted it out. He came half an hour before his friends and, as it worked out, we had just enough time to forge a new beginning."

"What did he say?" asked David.

"He said that he was sorry he had hurt you and that he hoped he would be forgiven," said Aunt Lillian, adding, "and I said, 'I *do* forgive you, Bobby. It is often things inside of us that cause us to hurt others, rather than something in those people we hurt.'"

"What did he say to that?" asked David.

"He thought about it for a little while, and he finally said that he thought I was most probably a very wise, old lady, quickly amending his words, saying, 'beggin' your pardon Ma'am, old meaning sort of elderly and well-preserved, if you catch my meanin'.'"

The Gang of Four laughed.

"How did Bobby and his gang do with canasta yesterday?" asked Sean.

"I'm sorry, Sean, but you *know* I'm sworn to complete silence by both sides. So I'm afraid I can't tell you anything more; perhaps I've already said too much."

"I bet he had a wicked time of it," baited Sean, "because he isn't especially quick, is he?"

"Sean Potter, I will *not* fall prey to your bait. But I do suggest that you not write Bobby Perkins off as the slow type, because it's simply not true. I suspect he's potentially quite bright although, unfortunately, he hasn't had many of the advantages all of you have enjoyed."

"We could lend him Poor Old Thing for a couple of months," said Sean cheerily.

"For sure," agreed Mary. "She'd be an education all in herself."

"I wonder if Poor Old Thing ever thinks of trading you both in?" asked David.

"Not me," said Mary, "but I suspect she's always praying for a happy death for Sean."

Sean made a face at Mary, and Mary, in turn, winked at her brother, as if to add 'just kidding.'

"Now, my young friends, full attention must be given to learning canasta. Lisa, you look unhappy. Is anything wrong?"

Lisa had been looking at the pile of books next to Aunt Lillian's reading chair in the music room.

"I just wish my parents would do something other than work in their restaurant. I sometimes wish they would show a little interest in reading, or music, or plays, or things like that. All they do is work, day in and day out."

Aunt Lillian listened carefully, nodding her head occasionally.

"I know they feel their options have been limited because of so little education," Lisa continued, "and I know that's probably very true. But just for once, I wish they'd close the restaurant so we could take a family vacation to New York City to see the museums and shows."

"That would be an *expensive* vacation," suggested Aunt Lillian.

"I know, but why save money *all* the time?" continued Lisa. "Why not spend it occasionally? They are always putting anything extra into my college fund. I don't even know if I want to go to college."

"All in good time," Aunt Lillian smiled, "and as much as college can change a person, I must warn you that if you continue to learn canasta, it may have the dark potential of changing you even more."

"What do you mean? *You're* baiting us now," asked David.

"If you continue to learn canasta," answered Aunt Lillian, "you will never be the same people again. It's as if a dark, evil, and competitive veil falls over your whole character."

"Cool!" said Sean.

"I don't believe it for a moment," laughed David, "because you learned it yourself, and you're one of the most decent people I know."

"Most of the time, perhaps," smiled Aunt Lillian, "but when I play canasta, I become absolutely ruthless. It is extremely competitive, especially the two-handed variety. Shall we have a review lesson from our last session? I think that I can now continue in good conscience since I have warned you again that you might become very, *very* cut-throat."

"Excellent!" rejoiced Sean. David had beaten Sean in chess on Saturday afternoon, and Sean was now hoping for revenge.

"Now, please watch and listen," announced Aunt Lillian, "as I demonstrate with these cards. I will start again from the beginning. Canasta is played with two decks of cards, including jokers, like these. When only two players are playing, one player shuffles at least half a dozen times and the other cuts. Each player is dealt fifteen cards."

"Is that when the 'other' cuts his opponent's throat?" asked Sean hopefully, looking at Mary.

Aunt Lillian smiled, answering, "Sean, David has told me about your love for blood and adventure, and I'm sorry to disappoint you by saying that I was not speaking literally about throat-cutting. The only literal cutting in canasta is with cards."

"Too bad," said Sean, looking at Mary and making a slash across his throat.

"Well, to continue: the object of the game is to acquire at least two canastas and to go out, which means melding all of your cards on the playing board. Canastas must contain at least seven cards and are either naturals or mixed. If they are naturals, it means they are all of one kind of card, queens for example. A natural or straight canasta is worth 500 points."

"Wow!" said Sean.

"Mixed canastas are worth 300 points," Aunt Lillian continued, "and must have at least four of one kind of card with the remaining cards being wild cards, which are jokers or deuces. Remember you must have at least seven cards to make a canasta. Wild cards are jokers, which are worth fifty points, and deuces, which are worth twenty. At least three cards must be melded on the board at one time, and the number of wild cards may equal, but never exceed, the corresponding number of cards melded. For example, you could meld with two tens and two jokers, but never with two tens and three jokers," continued Aunt Lillian. As she spoke, she grouped different combinations of cards together in illustration.

"After you've picked up and arranged your hand," continued Aunt Lillian, who had arranged single cards on the left, wild cards in the center, and pairs and larger sets on the right of her hand, "if you are the player who cut, you draw first. Draw two cards and discard one. That way your hand accumulates more and more cards."

"And so does the discard pile," observed Sean.

"Yes, how does one get the pile?" asked Mary.

"If you have not melded or if the pack is frozen, you need two of the same card discarded in order to pick the pack. But you also must meld when you pick the pack, if you haven't melded already."

"What's melding?" asked Sean, who had decided that if any pack was going to be picked up, he would be the one doing it.

"If your score is between five points and 1495, you meld 50 points worth of cards on the board. You can always meld more than the minimum required, although it's usually very hard to meld 120 without wild cards, especially jokers. Please remind me to review the relative value of cards after we discuss more about amounts required for melding. A score of 1500 to 2995 requires a meld of 90. Any score of

3,000 or above requires a meld of 120 points. Values for each card are the following: an ace is worth 20 points as is a deuce, the latter of which is wild. Jokers are also wild and count 50. Threes vary depending on color, with red threes being worth 100 points when melded. Each red three brings the privilege of drawing a replacement card. Four reds together are worth 800. Any red three in your hand, should someone go out, counts 200 against you; thus, if you have all four red threes in your hand, and someone goes out, you lose 1600 points."

"Awesome!" said Sean, devouring every word.

Aunt Lillian studied Sean briefly and observed, "I would highly recommend melding any red threes as soon as possible."

Sean nodded.

"How much are the black threes worth?" asked David.

"Only 5 points each," said Aunt Lillian, "but they carry the advantage of being a safe discard that cannot be picked up. They are quite handy in keeping the pack away from your opponent. Any questions so far?"

The Gang of Four looked at each other and at Aunt Lillian and shook their heads.

Aunt Lillian was about to continue when Lisa suddenly asked, "Could you please explain melding again?"

"Melding is placing cards on the board in order to qualify for picking the pack. Think of it as a sort of obstacle. It's usually very easy to meld 50, but 90 is sometimes rough, and 120 is often very unforgiving, especially if you don't have any wild cards. Let me continue about the point value of cards. Fours through sevens are worth five points each while eights through kings are worth ten points. Aces are worth 20 points each. Now remember, melding gives you the privilege of taking the pack. You can meld in the same turn that you pick up the pack. If it is not your first pick, and if the discard pile is not already frozen, which means someone has placed one or more wild cards in the discard tray, you may then pick up the pack with only one of the same kind of card that has been discarded together with a joker or deuce. It's called 'taking the pack with one and a wild'."

"Doesn't a black three freeze the pack?" asked Sean.

"No. Only deuces and jokers can do that. But a black three guarantees that your opponent will not be able to pick the pack on that draw. Think of its as the ultimate discard, Sean."

"Yeah," said Sean, looking at Mary. "It stops your enemy dead. I think I'm going to like black threes."

"Remember Sean," cautioned Aunt Lillian, "a wild card can keep the pack from your opponent, but discarding it is a greater risk because it is so useful in making canastas."

"Aunt Lillian," began Lisa, for all of the Gang of Four were now calling her 'Aunt', "isn't it possible that you'll get the discarded card back again?"

"Most definitely," smiled Aunt Lillian. "If the game becomes a simple vying for a large pack, and two-handed canasta sometimes goes that way, the player who gets the huge pack often wins."

"Cool!" said Sean.

Aunt Lillian smiled and continued, "That player wins because he has amassed the greater wealth in cards and, in general, the more cards you have, the more you can do, including making canastas. That reminds me. Canasta scores are determined by adding two different tallies. The first is called Basic, which counts how many canastas and red threes you have on the board when the game is over or after someone goes out. The second is called Count, which is the simple addition of point value on the board, whether the cards are in canastas or not. Also, you must subtract whatever points you have in your hand at the end of the game. I know this is probably all quite confusing. It takes a little time for the strategy of this game and the rules to take root. Ah, yes, I almost forgot the concealed hand."

"What's that?" asked David.

"It's surprising your opponent by suddenly going out without having melded. It doesn't happen often, but it's great for flummoxing your opponent."

"Just like an ambush!" said Sean.

"Yes, I suppose so," said Aunt Lillian, "especially if you catch him off guard and with lots of points in his hand."

"Has anyone ever gotten shot for going out with a concealed hand?" asked Sean.

Aunt Lillian smiled. "I don't know, Sean. What do you think?"

"I think it's very probable."

"Well, it wouldn't surprise me," said Aunt Lillian. "Canasta tends to be the kind of game that gets the blood up."

A wide grin appeared on Sean's face, as he announced, "I think I'm going to *love* this game. Let's play!"

"All right," agreed Aunt Lillian. "Lisa and I will play an open hand and I will explain the various options as we go along. Then why don't we let David and Sean play a game, with Mary and Lisa watching David's hand while I'll watch and help Sean."

"Remember, we're blood relatives," said David.

"I know, dear, but it's only fair to help our guest the best we know how," said Aunt Lillian.

"Somehow I don't think Sean is going to need much help," said David.

"The Little Hoodlum has a photographic memory," said Mary.

"Aunt Lillian, wouldn't you rather play on my side?" asked David.

"Not today, David. Do your best," encouraged Aunt Lillian, adding, "now, remember, in two-handed canasta each player receives how many cards?"

"Fifteen," said Sean.

"Right. Let's deal."

The open hand was played slowly and deliberately with many questions being asked by David, Sean, and Mary. Lisa got the first pack, but Aunt Lillian froze the pack and got an even bigger pile before the end of the game, which enabled her to make six canastas.

"You're a little out of my league," said Lisa to Aunt Lillian.

"Remember, I've been playing for at least forty years longer than you have," said Aunt Lillian, "and you'll get better as you play more."

"I can't wait to cream David," said Sean. "He beat me at chess yesterday."

"That's only because you don't take your time," said David.

Aunt Lillian sat shuffling the cards as the Gang of Four squared off for their first real game of canasta, two to witness, one to win, and one to lose.

Lisa wasn't entirely pleased with the hand dealt to David because it only had one wild card, although at least that one was a joker. Aunt Lillian smiled when she saw Sean pick up among his dealt hand four aces, three tens, three deuces, one joker, and two black threes.

Both players were extremely cautious and deliberate in their play, drawing cards slowly, considering each potential discard, and which cards to keep. Neither David nor Sean melded for fear that such cards as would be placed on the board would give advantage to the opposing side.

By his sixth draw the Little Hoodlum had collected five aces, three tens, four deuces, two jokers, and still had two black threes. But the discard pile was now looking more and more attractive because it contained a dozen cards, almost a hand in itself, and Sean decided with his whole being that he wanted this discard pile more than anything. His declaration of war was plopping down a prized black three, thus thwarting any possibility of David's taking the stash.

David had a black three to discard after drawing, and Sean followed suit. David followed by discarding a deuce and Sean again followed suit. David then parted with his Joker, and Sean plopped down another deuce, smiling, waiting to pounce.

David drew and sighed, for he realized he must take a chance on his next discard. Sean had, since the beginning of the game, acquired several new pairs, and he was hoping David would plop down a ten, for now he had four. But David instead took a chance with a five and Sean did indeed have a pair.

Suddenly shouting, "BANZAI!", Sean slammed his right hand down, clawlike, onto the pile.

Mary jumped several inches and rolled her eyes at Lisa, who said, "Not so fast! Meld your fifty points first."

Sean smugly melded his two fives, followed by the four tens, and took the five at the top of the discard pile and placed it with the two on the board, adding next to it four aces. Perhaps Sean was arrogant to put down such a splendid meld of 115 points; certainly it was overkill, but such nuances bothered Sean's thinking not at all. What was important was that his meld, together with his taking the discard pile, had rattled David, and he now fingered his new trove of cards like a miser apprizing his gold.

A certain innocence had departed from the eyes of both players. As David had witnessed the loss of a discard pile that he had desperately wanted, he felt within himself a new resolve to get the next pack.

Both boys' spirits had kindled to canasta in its most ruthless, dog-eat-dog form, and all present were witnessing only the preliminaries.

Chapter Sixteen
Escapades on Halloween

THE FOLLOWING TUESDAY WAS HALLOWEEN, and the atmosphere of Midville Middle School bustled with excitement and anticipation. Paper pumpkins, black witches and eerie moons dotted bulletin boards, door windows, and chalkboards.

The Gang of Four had seated itself for lunch at a corner table in the cafeteria. Its departure from eating lunch in the library workroom owed to Sean's wanting to try the cafeteria's pumpkin pie as well as the complimentary orange and black candies that were dispensed to students in small paper cups.

David examined a note that Sean had just handed him from Zeke Minturn, but written by Bobby, which read: 'Meet us at the groshurey store on 3rd and Elm at 9—tonites the night!'

"So Zeke Minturn gave you this note from Bobby, and he really wants us to meet him in trick or treat costumes at the grocery store on 3rd and Elm? I was going to help Aunt Lillian pass out candy. Were you going out tonight?"

"Of course. This is the night of all nights," said Sean.

"I tried to convince Sean not to dress in costume tonight," said Mary. "That way he can simply go as a little hoodlum."

Sean grinned at Mary, saying, "You rejected my suggestion, too. I wanted us to go *together*. I'd be the horse's front and Mary would be the—"

"Sean, please don't start," said David.

"Me? What do you mean me? Mary started it!"

"Sean's right, Mary," said Lisa.

"Don't let her get your goat, Sean. That's what she wants, you know. Just ignore it. She'll get bored and lay off, right Mary?" suggested David.

"Why don't you mind your own business, Mr. Smarty Pants," retorted Mary, laughing.

"See, Sean, we're on to her," David encouraged.

"I just wish she'd lay off this little hoodlum business," said Sean.

"Where would the fun be then?" asked Mary.

Sean abruptly lifted his nose in the air, as if to say, "No matter what you say from now on, it won't bother *me*."

David waved Bobby's note in front Sean, wanting more explanation.

"Zeke just gave me the note," explained Sean, "and said it was really important for you and me to meet them at 3rd and Elm Street at nine o'clock sharp."

"What does that little P.S. on Bobby's note say, David?" asked Lisa.

"It says 'I guarantee you a complete truce with full cooperation tonight.'"

"Well, at least he doesn't want to pick a fight with you any more, David," said Lisa, adding, "Mary, why don't you come over and help me give out candy since my parents will be at the restaurant? Halloween gives me the creeps when I'm alone."

"Okay, but I'll have to make sure Poor Old Thing can bring me," said Mary.

"I can give out candy when Poor Old Thing takes you," offered Sean.

Sean returned to the cafeteria line to get an ice cream sandwich.

"You know, Lisa, it isn't Halloween that gives me the creeps," said Mary.

"What does, then?"

"Sometimes it's my brother, that's who."

"He's all right," said David, "although maybe a little eccentric about some things."

"Yeah," said Mary, "like murder, torture, killing, shooting—"

"Just a phase," said David.

"It's been a pretty long phase. And you know, when he threatens me, I sometimes wonder if there isn't a part of him that is really planning to do something."

"Mary! He's your *own* twin brother. It's male banter, that's all," said David.

"Mom says a part of Sean would have liked a brother, especially a younger brother. I suppose they could have fought it out. But here he is with only a sister. And he can be *very* intense," lamented Mary.

"Well, what did Freud once suggest, 'That the thought is father of the deed'?"

"Thanks a *million*, David," sighed Mary.

"Look, I'll try to be a brother to Sean, how's that?"

"Good luck. You'll have my prayers."

Sean returned to the table, tearing open the wrapper of his ice cream sandwich.

"Anybody want some of this?" he asked.

"Sure," said David. "thanks. By the way, what are you going as tonight? Mary made it clear when we sat down that you're not going as a gangster."

"That's right," smiled Sean. "I'm going as something tonight that might soon become relevant to my dear sister's future."

"And what's that?" asked Lisa.

"Death," smiled Sean.

"Death? How are you going to go as Death?" marveled David.

"Easy. I got Poor Old Thing to give me a worn bedsheet which I cut up so it goes over me, and then I got a mask that looks like a real skull. It looks awesome! Best of all, I found a rusty old scythe. It's kind of unwieldy, but I'm going to lug it along."

"Where did you find the scythe?" asked David.

"In the barn behind our house. Somebody left it there a long time ago. The blade was really dull, but it sharpened up nicely."

"Spare us," sighed Mary.

"The others, yes," answered Sean, "but not you." He made as if to slash with the scythe across Mary's neck, adding, "*You*, Mary Potter, are marked."

"And you, my little brother, are nuts."

"David, what are you going as?" asked Lisa.

"I don't know. I wasn't planning to go out at all, but this note from Bobby presents a new problem. I can't think of any costume right now."

"Zeke said Bobby *really* wants us there, David. We've *got* to go," said Sean, brightening, "I've got it. I'll go as Death and you go as my victim. We can get some red paint and splash it all over you and then you could stumble up to the doorbell, ring it, and when they answer, you slump down dead and I jump out from one side, yelling, "Got *another*, who's next?"

"See Mary," said David, "It's *not* just you."

"Sean, you're sick," lamented Mary.

"No, I'm Death. And you'd better watch out."

"Well, I think my Aunt Lillian is having a positive effect on Bobby and his gang," said David, changing the subject, "otherwise I doubt that Sean and I would be invited out for Halloween with them."

"Does she say anything about her Saturday afternoons with Bobby and the others?" asked Lisa.

"Not a word," said David. "She is completely neutral. And I *do* try to get information out of her, but she's pretty cagey and only tells me not to underestimate Bobby and his gang. I think she's becoming fond of them. She calls them her 'Diamonds in the rough'. Anyway, I think the most diplomatic thing to do is to accept Bobby's and Zeke's invitation at face value. What do you say, Sean?"

"Count me in," said Sean. "I'll walk over to your house after Poor Old Thing gets back from taking Mary to Lisa's house."

* * * * *

A light snow had fallen late in the afternoon and, with the falling temperatures, it now crunched underfoot. The air was as clean and crisp and cold as a florist's cooler. Two costumed figures, one carrying a scythe over its shoulder, approached the grocery store on the corner of 3rd and Elm just as the Methodist Church tower bell struck nine o'clock.

"Psst!" called Zeke Minturn's voice, "Psst! Over here, behind the tree. Pretend you don't hear me. Come over and duck down real quick."

The costumed figures obeyed, and soon found themselves face to face with Bobby and Zeke. They eyed each others' garb.

"Where are the others?" asked David.

"Danny and the others are providin' us with an alibi in case we need one," said Bobby.

"Sweet!" exclaimed Sean, "What are you two guys supposed to be anyway?"

Bobby and Zeke, with soot blackened faces, looked like two tramps dressed in all sorts of ragged and mismatched clothing.

"Chimney sweeps, same as always, like in *Mary Poppins*," said Bobby, adding, "and don't never mock our outfits 'cause Zeke's Mom labored somethin' terrible over them."

Sean and David nodded.

"What are you two supposed to be?" asked Zeke.

"Sean is one of them Druids from England, or France, or some place like that from the ancient times," guessed Bobby.

"*No* WAY!" shouted Sean.

"Ssshh. Calm down, Sean, calm down. We need to keep it really cool tonight," cautioned Zeke.

"What do *you* think I am?" Sean asked Zeke.

Zeke wasn't quite sure, but he didn't want to risk another outburst. Taking his cue from David who was standing behind Sean and pretending to strangle himself, Zeke said, "Something really awesome, if you ask me. Maybe like the Boston Strangler?"

Sean was so pleased with a compliment however indirectly related to death, that he blurted out, "You almost got it, Zeke. I'm Death."

"Death?" questioned Bobby.

"Yes. As in dead, dying, done gone, and buried. DEATH!"

David wondered how far Sean was going to push the prestige he had secured with his rumored derringer. He certainly was showing a lot of pluck against these two brawny brutes who together could have as easily twisted him into a pretzel as look at him. Of course, one would always have to weigh his black belts and fierceness into any mix of force. The insight that Sean would never be bested crossed David's mind, and he decided that the Little Hoodlum was probably protected by angels and miraculously impervious to harm.

"Ssshh. Okay, okay, so you're Death. That's cool," agreed Zeke. "You can be anything you want, just take it easy. You ain't packin', are ya, Little Dude?"

"Not tonight," answered Sean.

"And just look at David the clown," Bobby laughed.

"Not exactly a clown," David explained. "You see, I didn't really have a costume, so I had to come as something not unlike myself. Look," he said, assuming a mannequin posture, "It's Howdy-Doody time!"

Bobby's mouth dropped open as he fell to the ground laughing, much to the surprise and disapproval of Zeke. It was the first time David or Sean, or Zeke for that matter, had ever heard Bobby laugh so freely.

"Hey, Boss, I never heard you laugh like that before," said Zeke. "Quiet down before the fuzz spots us."

Bobby wiped away tears trickling down his cheeks and looked up at David, "Hey, Howdy Doody, you sure can take a joke, and I ain't justa kiddin'."

"Hey, what's the scam anyway," Sean asked impatiently, for the scythe was feeling heavier on his shoulder.

"Come in to the center of these bushes and I'll explain," said Bobby. The four boys drew closer into their circle and Bobby continued, "I done some research on you, Davie Boy, and I find out you had it out with that dame Coachman, and she tried to give ya hell and you slung it right back into her big, ugly, pig-faced puss."

It was clear that Bobby was not a fan of Gertrude Coachman, and David admitted, "I guess you could say that."

"Well, I ain't never liked her 'cause as far as I can figure out she's nothin' but a 'Do as I say, not as I do' dame. I was in her study hall last year, and she comes walzin' in like the Queen of Sheba every day, and the first week yelled her ugly head off at anyone who was even whisperin'. Then she'd preach to us about keepin' quiet and havin' manners and workin' hard and showin' respect to our elders, enough to make ya want to puke. But words is cheap, and after a couple of weeks, she comes in and slams her books down real hard and starts talkin' to herself and laughin' to herself. It made me so mad I could see red, just like the deep blood red on the Little Dude's Death outfit. And mind ya, I knew I was gettin' outa line, but I was just fed up with her lordin' it over everyone, so I says, 'What's so funny? Why ya laughin'? I don't see no mirror.' Then her ugly puss darkens worse than a thundercloud, and suddenly there's a real fish-hate look in her eyes, and the room is ten degrees colder, and she tells me to mind my own beeswax, or she'll box my ears to learn me some manners. So I tell her to box away, 'cause there be lawyers in the world for somethin' other than to make loads of money, and I ain't gonna stand for any of her crap. Then she turns real red ugly in that puss she calls a face, and looks just like old farmer Robinson's great big sow, the one he kept for five years before it died of overweight, and she looks daggers at me and jumps up and yells to me that I'm in some sub or anthill—"

"Insubordinate?" asked David.

"Yeah, that's it. Hey, Davie Boy, and I wish you could 've been there to help me pay 'er out for what she did to me and to you. Well, study hall got worse and worse and worse until I couldn't stand it no more, like a black curse hangin' over my head. And then the grand day arrives where I got suspended for five days, but it was worth it not to have to look at her ugly puss every day of the week."

"Gosh, what happened?" asked Sean, who was spellbound.

"Well, on that day she swaggers in and slams her books on the desk, and they all go crashin' to the floor. Everybody laughs and suddenly the old sow jumps up and starts yellin' about manners. I couldn't stand it no more. So I stands up and say, 'Your books ain't have fallen on the floor if you'd hadn't slammed them so hard on the desk.' Then she says, 'Well, if it isn't Mr. Know-it-all himself.' And I says, 'I don't know it all, and I don't *pretend* to know it all,' and that's where I gave her the evil eye to make my point, 'but I do know enough not to slam my books on the desk if I don't want them to go flyin'.' Then she says, 'I did it on purpose to get your attention,' and I says, 'I don't believe you.' 'Cause I saw how surprised she looked when all the books tumbled down. Then she says to me, 'I got a lot of psychology trainin', and I knows how to deal with the likes of you and your crowd,' and I says, 'Just what is the likes of me and my crowd?' and she says, 'You're rude and ignorant and don't know any manners,' and I says, 'At least we don't knock our books off our desks,' and everybody in the study hall cheers me. This made her real mad 'cause she puffs her self up and peers down at me from her stinkin' little podium and says, 'You look more and more the fool in this argument, just like that jackass that ain't got 'nough sense to come in outa the rain.' So I says, 'Even a jackass knows when it's raining,' and she flies off her podium and rushes down to me, with all those great big jowls shakin' like an earthquake, and she grabs me by the back of my hair, but she has to reach up 'cause she's such a short little runt of a sow, and she gasps, 'I think I pulled a muscle,' and I says, 'Serves ya right to put your hands where they don't belong,' and she says, as she tries to pull my head down to her runt level, 'I'm gonna teach you some manners, you dirty rotten little scum,' and I looks down and see those big ugly jowls of hers shakin' up in my face and I lose my head and lip off, 'How could a pig like you teach anyone manners?' and she slaps my face real hard, and I feel the pain in my cracked tooth and see red, so I kick her in her left leg and she starts hoppin' back to the podium cryin' 'Help, murder, police,' and I walks out of the study hall and turns myself in to old Ferlinghausen who suspends me 'cause I kicked her, and I ain't arguin' that I didn't deserve all I got. Then when I gets back to school, I go into study hall to find a new teacher who

237

treats us all normal and decent like and human, and that was fine with me."

"Did anything happen to Mrs. Coachman?" asked David, wide-eyed.

"The old pig was outa school for three weeks 'cause she said she couldn't walk right 'cause of where I kicked her, but I didn't kick her that hard. She was pullin' my hair so hard I was seein' stars. And I heard later someone had seen her ugly puss out late and goin' lickety split, so she could really walk just fine."

"Let's shoot her!" yelled Sean.

Zeke Minturn threw his left arm around Sean's chest, clasping his right hand over the little dude's mouth. As Sean struggled, Bobby continued, "Shootin's too good for the likes of her, 'cause she's no normal dame; she's some sort of witch in human clothin'. Maybe that's what they do where you come from, little dude, but we ain't gonna do that here. Anyway, five will get ya ten that the devil his own self doesn't want her stinkin' sow-faced soul yet."

David's heart went out to Bobby, and the rough sort of poetry that sprang from the bottom of Bobby's soul. Bobby's joke about the devil was obviously one he had heard from someone about someone else. Under the circumstances, especially in the face of Bobby's dead-pan sincerity, the joke *was* genuinely funny. David smiled, as he asked, "So, what's the plan?"

"Well," continued Bobby, "I've been checkin' on that dame and she's the town's worst miser, she is, I swear to God. Guess what she gives out to the little kids on Halloween?"

"Warts," said Sean.

"Sssh," gestured Zeke.

"She gives out mean, little pennies, one to a customer, that's what she does. An' more and more kids don't even bother stoppin' there 'cause they know her lousy sow trick. Too cheap to giv 'em candy, that's what she is. So she puts a little penny in every kid's bag, saying, 'A penny saved is a penny earned' and 'Alms to the poor, alms to the poor.' I ain't bright enough to know what 'alms to the poor' means, but I bet ya ten to one it ain't very nice, and I'd like to shove a whole bunch of mean little pennies down her cheap, rotten throat."

David listened intently. He was beginning to see in Bobby what Aunt Lillian had already sensed, namely an unrefined but rather accurate and keen intelligence, girded with a primitive sense of justice. The Bobby Perkins who beat people up was making less and less sense to David, yet Bobby's reputation as town bully and scrapper had become near legend in Midville.

"The plan?" demanded Sean, impatiently.

"The plan is we got some special tricks for that old bag and we gotta be careful and quiet or the police will nab us. They almost got us last year. So follow us real quiet like and do as we tell ya, okay?"

While David had never contemplated participation in such a clandestine adventure, Sean had always dreamt of doing so. Both boys nodded assent, David reluctantly, Sean eagerly.

Bobby looked at Sean's scythe, saying, "Ya better ditch that here in the bushes in case we have to run." Sean obeyed instantly. Bobby then gestured for David and Sean to follow his and Zeke's lead. Wisps of dark clouds were scudding across an almost full moon as snow crunched under their boots. They ducked stealthily behind bushes and trees as they went.

When they arrived in the middle of Elm Street park, they found cover behind a small hedge. Bobby and Zeke pointed to a Victorian house and moved back and forth.

"What are you guys doing?" asked Sean.

"We're lining up our aim at her house."

"Cool!" said Sean.

"Whose house?" asked David naively.

"That old pig Coachman, who do ya think?" answered Bobby.

David felt a chill coursing up and down his spine.

Sean retrieved a handkerchief under his costume with which to blow his nose, which was running, only to feel his arm quickly stayed by Zeke Minturn, "Go easy little partner," cautioned Zeke, "we're under a truce tonight and all on the same side. We can't risk any noise 'cause it might blow our cover. Don't blow your nose. Just wipe it."

Sean promptly obeyed.

David felt slightly dizzy, with a sinking feeling in his stomach. He began to breathe more deeply.

"What are we going to do?" asked Sean, as he watched Zeke and Bobby unpacking the sack they had been carrying.

"We're gonna lob all kinds of stuff at that old pig's house," answered Bobby.

"That's at least a hundred yards away. You can't throw stuff that far," said David.

"We ain't gonna throw it," explained Bobby. "Zeke, bring out 'The Flying Ace'. Show 'em how high tech we are."

Zeke smiled as he lifted an enormous slingshot out of their burlap bag.

"Golly," asked Sean, "it must be the mother of all slingshots! How long is that huge rubber band?"

"It can be stretched back six feet or more. Two of us have to hold the slingshot steady while two of us pull it back and let 'er rip," said Zeke.

David stood speechless, feeling an intense conflict rising inside himself. Part of him wanted to lob anything available, including rocks, at Gertrude Coachman's house, yet part of him felt such an assault to

240

be an act of senseless violence. However, Gertrude Coachman lived in the perpetual punishment of her own company, condemned to listen to the shadow of her own strained laughter and pathetic monologues; her singular manner seemed to invite this crude, rough justice that Bobby proposed. David cleared his throat and asked, "Is there any chance we'll hit an innocent bystander?"

"Are you kiddin?" retorted Bobby. "All the kids know how cheap she is. They avoid her house like the plague on Halloween. She made her cheap tricks, so now she deserves a few treats from us."

"Let's shoot something at her house," rejoiced Sean.

"First," said Bobby, inspecting their burlap sack, "rotten apples to get the old pig out of bed. Zeke, you and Sean hold the slingshot while David and I'll load it up and let 'er rip."

David felt the cold rubber tighten around his fingers as he pulled the sling back, the formidable aroma of rotten apples wafting over the band. Bobby aimed the shot and whispered, "Now!"

There was the softest whoosh and then silence.

"We missed!" lamented Sean.

Suddenly a thunk, thunk, thunk, thunk, thunk could be heard on the stones of the dark Victorian house. The boys repeated another volley of apples. A light appeared in an upstairs window.

"Now we got the pig up," said Bobby, grinning at Zeke. "Time for the rotten eggs. David and I'll hold the sling, and you and Sean shoot."

In his eagerness to shoot, Sean slipped on some leaves as he pulled back the sling. Zeke instinctively pulled back a little harder and released the sling before Bobby could give the signal, for fear they would waste an entire load of eggs. Again there was silence, and then splat, splat, splat, splat, splat.

"Thanks a bunch," snapped David, who had taken the lowest flung egg in the back of his skull. It was smeared all into his hair, and his head was throbbing, not to mention smelling to high heaven.

"Sorry," said Sean. "Are you all right?"

"My head hurts like a door hit it, and I have stinking egg goo in my hair," growled David, "but I *think* I'll live."

"First casualty of war," Sean grinned, adding, "Don't worry. I'll finish you off later."

"And from friendly fire, too," David grumped.

Bobby lifted up the top of the burlap sack and wiped the back of David's head the best he could manage.

"Let's shoot the rest of the eggs before the cops come," said Bobby.

"Are the cops really coming?" asked David.

"Probably already on their way. She called 'em out right away last year," said Zeke.

"Cool," whispered Sean, his eyes dancing with excitement.

The second volley of eggs brought on the porch lights. The boys could see Gertrude Coachman's rather considerable silhouette behind the colored glass of her front door.

"Now for the marshmallows to bring the old pig out," said Bobby.

"It drew 'er out last year," explained Zeke.

Two full bags of marshmallows were prepared and slung. An eerie silence and the faintest crackle against the old Victorian house. A flashlight could be seen inspecting Gertrude Coachman's front yard.

"See, I told you it'd bring the old pig out for dessert," said Bobby.

"Now let's finish with the sticky marshmallow-cereal-peanut-butter bomb," said Zeke as he removed a concoction the size of a large grapefruit from the burlap bag. Sean and David held the slingshot, and Bobby and Zeke pulled back the sling and aimed. Two more flashlights had joined the first one on Gertrude Coachman's lawn, and the boys heard Coachman's voice, "Now they're shooting marshmallows, officer."

"The Fuzz!" whispered Bobby. "Probably parked a few houses down hoping to surprise us. Let fly and run! Follow me!"

As the boys made their hasty retreat, they heard the telltale crash of a window pane.

"Hey, over there, HALT!" shouted a deep authoritarian voice. "This way Larry."

The race had been joined, the pursuit begun.

David's heart was throbbing faster than it ever had in his entire life. It almost seemed to be in his throat. His mouth was dry and ached as he ran. The boys raced along behind bushes, under fences, and through driveways. They could still hear their pursuers.

"We shouldn't be running from the police," David panted to Sean.

"We're not *running*," Sean panted back, "we're *eluding*."

"Down that driveway!" whispered Bobby as the boys ran down a plowed driveway, taking cover under a row boat that leaned up against the side of a garage.

They waited under the boat, looking out into the clear, cool moonlight, their hearts thumping in their heads, sweat trickling down the inside of their costumes.

A flashlight could be seen near the street as a policeman searched each driveway and hedge. "They're out there on the sidewalk," whispered Sean. "We'd better make a break for it."

"Sshh. No," whispered Bobby. "That's what they want. Sit tight as ya can and no heavy breathin'."

The squad car drove up to where the tall policeman stood, its rack lights flashing, and suddenly it shone its spotlight down the driveway. Gasping, the boys lay hidden beneath the cold, wet boat, as red and white flashes glistened off the snow, spiraling into the moist, black velvet sky. David closed his eyes and waited. Sean, however, peeked out from under the boat, wishing he had an Uzi with which to spray the Fuzz should they venture down the driveway.

Suddenly Gertrude Coachman herself joined the officer standing near the patrol car, and the boys craned their heads to hear their conversation.

"Any sign of them?" came her stentorian voice as she limped up to the patrol car, panting in her pajamas and bathrobe, her iron gray hair adorned in bobby pins. She took the liberty of leaning against the patrol car for support. After all, it was village property, and she always paid her taxes on time.

"We thought we saw those boys duck down this driveway, Ma'am. At least, this is where the footprints end. We're just checking it out with our spotlight."

A dog several houses away began to bark. David felt chills running up and down his spine.

The officer in the patrol car was making out some sort of report. Looking up at Gertrude Coachman, he asked, "What broke your window, Ma'am?"

"They shot some sort of gooey, marshmallow, peanut butterball that broke the shade on my favorite reading lamp. It was my favorite, but that's all right. I hope it's insured, although my deductible probably won't cover it, but the broken window will count, too."

"Did you get hurt, Ma'am?"

"I stubbed my big toe, and it's pretty chilly tonight and I'm beginning to feel a little coldie, so I probably won't be able to go to school for a couple of days. We intellectuals need our rest if we're to mold young minds."

"Yes, Ma'am," said the officer standing by the patrol car.

"Would you boys care to try these marshmallows?" asked Gertrude Coachman, offering her hand toward the officers. "They're actually not too bad, and shouldn't go to waste, you know."

This last was too much for Sean. Forgetting his situation, and the predicament of his comrades, he exclaimed indignantly, "Geeze, what a greedy *pig*!"

"What was that?" asked the officer in the patrol car.

"I heard them," cried Coachman, "They're over there, under that boat. After them!"

"Abandon ship!" shouted Bobby as the boys darted from underneath the boat and ran into the back of the adjacent yard. Another dog started barking as several house lights flashed on.

"After them! Stop, hooligans! Stop!" cried the Coachman, raising the hue and cry as the officers pursued their quarry.

David had never felt his heart throbbing in his head before, and his throat was as parched as if he had been walking in a desert.

"Climb that fence," whispered Bobby, scaling the boards easily and reaching down to help David up and over. Sean and Zeke were already clear.

"This way," panted Bobby. "Keep running, don't look back, don't slow down." He led the fugitives down an alley that fetched out onto Maple Street. The boys ran across the street, into a second driveway, and behind its garage, noisily knocking over some garbage cans as they ran. Lights began to illuminate in that house, and the boys could now hear the officers in close pursuit as more dogs began to bark at the shrillness of a police whistle.

Coming to a chain link fence, the boys quickly scrambled up and over, finding themselves in a meadow. The moon shone down as the stars blazed in the heavens. Snow had dusted the long grass, and the whole place smelled damp and wild. A massive dark shadow, a giant alien presence, cast itself across the field.

"Look, there's the water tower," urged Bobby. "We can run past it to the dirt road by the old Evans' farm, and through their field and up by their brook, and then hide in the low grass until its safe to work our way back to the center of the village. The cruiser 'll never reach us up there."

David intuited that Bobby Perkins was a master strategist, and wanting, for the moment, to remain a fugitive from justice, David followed as fast as he could run, feeling an intense pain in his side from running so hard. As they crossed under the water tower, however, they could hear the officers approaching the side of the field they had just left, and they automatically relaxed their pace, knowing that their pursuers could now not catch them.

* * * * *

David returned home near midnight, wet and tired and shivering to the bone. The boys had had to double back several times on their route home because of a certain persistent squad car that kept circling the Coachman neighborhood and the adjacent environs. Without barking Max met David at the kitchen door, giving him a welcoming nuzzle. Grateful that Aunt Lillian's light was out when he entered, he shed his wet sneakers, removed his torn and soaked Howdy Doody costume, went to his room and changed into his pajamas. His bed was warm where Max had been lying on it, waiting for him. He wondered if he would have dreams of being a fugitive from justice, diligently pursued by the law. This was the first time in his life he had ever experienced such adventure, and his face was hot and his heart still raced with excitement. The thrill of the chase was in his blood, and he would never be the same David Andrews again. Bobby had succeeded in bringing a juvenile justice to the wrongs that he and David had suffered at the hands of an ignorant and uncaring fool, and now they shared the special bond of avenged victims.

David could still feel and hear broken egg shell in his hair when he put his head on his pillow, and his conscience briefly pricked him for the broken window and lamp shade. But his blood was still up and, to his surprise, he found that he did not regret the evening's adventures. Not for anything! More pointedly, he relished them. Bobby had baptized him into the world of hooliganism, and David had tasted some of the delicious thrills it offered, including the sulphurous stench of rotten eggs. At this moment, however, every muscle in his body ached, so stroking Max's fur, he soon closed his eyes and fell asleep.

Sean arrived home shortly after midnight, stealthily slipping into his bedroom unobserved, although he saw the light was still on in his father's office, and he could hear the strains of one of J. S. Bach's *Brandenburg* concertos echoing underneath the study door.

Sean had long known the thrill of Halloween escapades, but never one of such magnitude, and never one involving the law. This night of all nights had offered him anew an unforgettable foray into secret dangers worthy only of a true warrior. He felt no remorse for the old witch's broken window and lampshade, and his heart was still racing and riding on the glory of the night's adventures when, in sublime satisfaction, he closed his eyes and slept the sleep of lions.

Chapter Seventeen
Bring Back the Air Raid Drill!

THE FRIDAY EDITION OF *BARE FAX* could well have been an EXTRA edition for its banner unabashedly demanded:

BRING BACK THE AIR RAID DRILL!

A second lead headline in a separate article lower on the page read:

DANDY SLAMS DOOR IN REPORTER'S FACE

"Melvin, get a hold over yourself," urged Otto Ferlinghausen.

"Get a hold over myself? Every little thing I do or say gets plastered all over the front page of that damn scandal sheet. If I were principal, I'd ban that rag so fast your ears would sizzle. Nothing but trouble, if you ask me!" remonstrated the counselor, who stood before his principal in an olive green suit and a garish, scarlet bow tie.

Otto Ferlinghausen smiled at his high-strung guidance counselor, hoping to persuade him to a larger view, "Melvin, the kids are only trying to have a little fun. Can you imagine the headlines that would follow any ban? NEWSPAPER BANNED; FREE EXPRESSION SILENCED: BILL OF RIGHTS IGNORED! And the very banning would not double, but rather triple the interest in the paper's news.

David Andrews is a *very* adept adversary when he decides he wants something."

Melvin Dandy scowled at the mention of David's name and stared daggers at the wastepaper basket next to Otto's desk, as if he hoped he'd find David in it.

After a moment's pause, Dandy asked his principal, "Well, Otto, what are you going to do?"

"I'm going to give him his air raid drills."

"You *can't* mean it! I'm *shocked* to hear you say it!"

"Look, Melvin, we are committed to it *de facto*. The air raid drill protocols are printed in the faculty handbook. They remain there because twenty years ago nobody had enough foresight to delete them. Our very hypocrisy is being thrown back into our faces. So, what is the harm in going ahead and giving them an air raid drill or two?"

"Well, why don't you go ahead and do it and get the damn thing over with?"

"I still haven't figured out how we can signal the emergency. Florence Kirkpatrick was teaching here when they used to have air raid drills, but she forgets what they used for the alarm. She vaguely remembers some sort of siren or horn. She also remembers that with all the student problems they had in the late sixties and early seventies, things like air raid drills got forgotten pretty quickly."

"Otto, I believe you're making a grave error in humoring these kids. There's no telling what it will lead to. Giv 'em an inch and they'll take ten miles."

"No, Melvin. I am resolved to go ahead with it. I plan to tell David as soon as I've found a way to signal the alert. Maybe you could help me with that. I'm open to suggestions. Think on it over the weekend and let me know on Monday."

After Mr. Dandy left the office, he nearly had a stroke when he passed the art room and noticed that Mrs. Jones' art class was making paper air raid helmets and wearing them in support of air raid drills. Suddenly feeling faint, he veered from his chosen path, which had been to the faculty lounge, ultimately walking back to his office where he growled at Mrs. Fullerton, "Cancel my morning appointments. I've got a splitting headache."

Mrs. Fullerton could discern only a faint rustling of a newspaper from the inner office throughout the remainder of the morning.

* * * * *

The Gang of Four had reverted to meeting in the cafeteria, and today's bill of fare included fish sandwiches. Sean and Mary joined David and Lisa at their table.

"Here, take this paper helmet and put it on," David announced. He and Lisa demonstrated how to do it.

"Mrs. Jones' class made some extras for us and for the other students who decide to support our cause. Nifty idea, isn't it?"

"Yeah," said Sean, blandly. "I've got a better army helmet at home for when I play war. I'd rather wear that, but I could take this one down to Mr. Dandy."

"Oh, I wouldn't do that, if I were you," cautioned Lisa. "Eric Morton told me Mr. Dandy canceled all of his morning appointments because of a headache. I think this morning's edition of *Bare Fax* may have contributed to that headache. And the past editions can't be helping. Maybe we should lay off a little, David. What do you think?"

"Maybe we should. I wouldn't want to be responsible for anyone's stroke."

"Why not?" Sean chomped on his fish sandwich.

Mary glowered at him.

"I'm afraid Mr. Dandy is wrapped a little too tight to be working with middle school kids," continued David, adding, "He doesn't have much of a sense of humor. Maybe we could invite him to play along with us. He really needs to play more. It would keep him young."

"He was *old* the day he was born," laughed Lisa. "Let's face it; the man has major issues."

"We need to help him to have a little fun," urged David.

"Why not write him a short little note saying we hope he'll throw his support to our side?" asked Mary.

"No. He's probably too suspicious of us because of that first interview and article. Lisa and I quoted everything he said."

"Then how do we get him on our side?" wondered Lisa.

"Look for a weakness," said David. "Ah! I've got it. Vanity. Mr. Dandy is very vain."

"How do you know that?" asked Lisa.

"I saw some old pictures of him in his office. His hair line is a lot lower on the recent ones."

"You really mean it?" laughed Lisa.

"Yes," smiled David. "He wears a toupee."

"You're kidding," said Mary.

"No, I'm not," said David. "And it's probably a very expensive one, but still it's still not his hair."

"You've got to be kiddin'," said Sean. "It looks like—"

"Sean, no swearing!" admonished Mary.

"I wasn't going to swear, Mary. All I was going to say is that Dandy-Pandy's hairpiece makes him look like a flying squirrel just landed on his head."

David cradled his head in his arms.

"Well," reflected Sean, "we only have two choices then."

"Two choices?" inquired Mary.

"Yeah. Either we place a bounty on it, or we blackmail hi—OW!"

"And deserved, too," said David, nodding to Mary.

"Let's ignore the hairpiece and butter him up," said Lisa.

"But why?" asked Mary.

"Because we'll say we really *need* him," beamed David.

"Need him?" said Sean, "We don't need him a bit, or want him."

"True," said David, "but if he *thinks* he's needed, maybe he'll help agree to help us."

"That's right," said Lisa. "Everyone likes to feel needed. Let's write him a different kind of note and see what he does."

David read the final draft to the group:

> Dear Mr. Dandy,
>
> We need your help in insuring that air raid drill protocols are followed. Although an air raid in the sense of an atomic attack is only a remote possibility, many people forget that gas trucks can sometimes overturn near school buildings. We have voted unanimously to have you named the school's CHIEF AIR RAID WARDEN, and we hope that you will join with us in affording the Midville Middle School community the protection it deserves.
>
> Sincerely,
>> The Gang of Four . . . *and then our names*

"Do you think we should describe ourselves as a Gang?" asked Lisa, tugging behind her back to straighten her pony tail.

"I'm sure Mr. Dandy has called us much worse," David smiled.

"Do you think it will work? After all, he probably has apoplexy every time anyone mentions *Bare Fax*," asked Mary.

"Only one way to find out. I'll drop it off at his office when we leave the cafeteria. I suspect that our nomination of Mr. Dandy to be Chief Air Raid Warden will clinch the whole arrangement. I'm sure Mr.

Ferlinghausen doesn't care who the Chief Air Raid Warden is, and if it gives Mr. Dandy a little something to be proud of, what's the harm?"

"Has Mr. Ferlinghausen said anything to you about our lobbying to have air raid drills, David?" asked Lisa.

"I saw him this morning when I dropped off today's issue. He laughed when he saw it, and said we'd get our air raid drills as soon as he could arrange for some sort of alarm, which reminds me, Sean, any luck on the siren module?"

"Siren module?" asked Lisa.

"Last Saturday when I was over at Sean's playing chess and canasta, Sean suggested we build a siren module that interfaces with the school's intercom for the air raid alarm. It shouldn't be too hard to do. You just build something that sends a signal over the speakers."

"Wow! Do you know how to build something like that, Sean?" asked Lisa.

"Not exactly. But I knew how to *arrange* for it," said Sean proudly.

Lisa's raised her eyebrows.

"It's the same way he gets everything he wants," sighed Mary.

"Hush," Sean scolded Mary. "I wait for the right moment. I knew my dad would be consulting with three post-doctoral students Saturday evening. They often come over to the house. So I waited until they were in Dad's office, and then I barged in and asked if anyone could help me build a siren module."

"That takes a *lot* of nerve," said David.

"Well, I knew they'd do *anything* to get rid of me, especially since all they ever want to do is talk about time—time this, time that, Bach this, Bach that, yap, yap, yap—and it's all supposed to be so hush, hush, and who could give a hoot? Anyway, Daniel, one of the post-docs, said right off that he has always enjoyed tinkering with electronics and modules, and that he would get the materials and would build it for us no later than Thanksgiving Day. They're all coming over for dinner on Thanksgiving."

"What a stroke of luck!" David admired, "and nerve."

"I also told Daniel we didn't want any sissy siren, but one that would wake the dead. So he said we would try for a low, double frequency, oscillating one that will catch people's attention right away. It's supposed to sound as if all the graves have been opened."

"Well, everything seems to be going according to schedule," David smiled.

"Until we get the real siren module," Sean suggested, "we could ask Mr. Dandy to get on the P.A. and yell 'Air Raid! Air Raid! Take cover before you're all blown to smithereens!'"

"That would go stale after the first time," said David.

"Well, then maybe he could just blow his nose," suggested Sean.

David, Lisa, and even Mary burst into laughter.

"What did I say that was so funny?" asked Sean.

"Oh, it's just *you*," said Mary with reluctant fondness.

* * * * *

Upon receiving the note from the Gang of Four, Mr. Dandy canceled all of his afternoon appointments and remained sequestered in his office.

"Mrs. Fullerton?" inquired Mr. Dandy's voice from his office intercom at 2:30 p.m..

"Yes, Mr. Dandy, are you all right?"

"Of course I'm all right."

"How's your headache?"

"Never mind the headache. It's gone. What I want to ask you is this: wasn't it Mrs. Bowen who took a cruise with her husband last Christmas vacation?"

"Yes. It was."

"Good. Please send a note up to her room saying that I *must* see her before she leaves the building today. And please bring me some fresh copies of the school's floor plan."

* * * * *

The following Monday Otto Ferlinghausen, having talked with David Andrews after school on Friday, was not in the least surprised to receive a telephone call from Melvin Dandy just after the beginning of first period.

"Otto, could you please come here to my office? I have a surprise for you."

"Very well, Melvin. I'll be there in about fifteen minutes."

When Otto Ferlinghausen entered the Guidance Office, a visibly nervous Mrs. Fullerton sighed with relief at his arrival, saying, "I'm so glad you're here. I'm really worried about Melvin. He's wearing a plastic gray rain coat under the strangest white helmet you ever saw."

The principal entered Dandy's office. There the counselor sat proudly behind his desk, wearing a civilian air raid helmet that was adorned with a light blue triangle and CD, for Civil Defense.

"Have a seat, Otto," Melvin smiled. "I see you gawking at my helmet. Got it from my uncle. The authentic article, not like those foolish little paper imitation helmets Mrs. Jones' art class fabricated."

Otto considered his counselor. Not wanting to let on that he had been clued in to the whole affair, he asked, "Melvin, are you okay?"

"Never better, Otto. Finally, that little Gang of Four outfit came to its senses by seeing that the only way to get this air raid drill nonsense to work was to tap the support of the strongest leader in the school, with your permission, of course."

Otto Ferlinghausen looked quizzically at the counselor.

255

"The long and short of it, Otto," continued Melvin Dandy, "is that they have asked *me* to assume the position of Chief Air Raid Warden. Since they've obviously come to their senses, and have politely asked for my help, I've decided to show them how such things are properly done. I'm sure it will prove an enduring lesson for them."

"Fine with me," rejoined Otto. David's prediction was becoming a reality. "This seems a very sudden about-face regarding our young friends. What happened?"

"As I just explained, they sent me a polite letter on Friday which, indirectly, acknowledged that I'm the only one around who could help them pull off their little scheme. Since then, I've wasted no time in preparing for our air raid drills. There's a lot of checking and arranging, you know."

"Checking and arranging?"

"Yes. I compared all existing protocols to our school map, and in two places students had been instructed to brace themselves against lockers that have been turned into trophy cases." The counselor moved his face toward Melvin's confidentially, and whispered, "Trophy cases with glass in them. If anyone had gotten cut, there would have been some ridiculous law suit. I also checked with Liz Bowen."

"What on earth for?"

"She and her husband went on that cruise to the Bahamas last Christmas vacation so I asked her after school on Friday what kind of alarm they used when they mustered the passengers for the mandatory life boat drill. She vaguely remembered it had been some kind of horn blasting away, and I'm surprised she remembered that much for all the partying they did."

"Why did you ask her about the ship protocols?"

"Well, I was thinking about this whole business Friday afternoon, and it suddenly occurred to me that our building is very rectangular and massive, a little like a huge cruise ship, if you don't mind stretching a point or two. I mean, it's monolithic by modern standards. The brick chimney adds to the effect, too."

"I suppose you could stretch the point in way of metaphor ... "

"I knew you'd see it, too. Well, we won't be abandoning ship, but rather securing the ship by having students brace themselves against the lockers and walls for protection from the impact of the explosion."

"What explosion?"

"Why the overturned gas truck, of course."

Otto finally burst out laughing.

"Now, don't laugh, Otto. That's rude, you know. Someone has to think through the potential hazards and emergencies that our school community might face. For heaven's sake, we stand *in loco parentis*. Thank the good Lord we will probably never have to face a nuclear threat, but the scenario of an overturned gas truck next to the school, waiting to explode, is one I find most daunting. We've *got* to be prepared. No matter how *unlikely* such a situation is, it *still* could happen. We are responsible for protecting faculty and students from harm's way. I've reviewed the school floor plans and have updated all classroom protocols for air raid drill procedures. Faculty will be required to look on, to make sure proper decorum is maintained. Mrs. Fullerton is typing a complete list of updated room protocols right now."

"What about the air raid signal, Melvin? We still don't have a proper alarm, short of asking a fire truck to drive by and sound its siren," said Otto.

Dandy gave Otto an exasperated look, chiding, "Right and we'd really have time to do that if a gas truck were overturned next to the school! NO! We need something in house and on the ready. Liz Bowen gave me an idea about that last Friday when she mentioned a horn. Close your eyes, Otto, I have a surprise for you."

Otto closed his eyes. He heard Melvin rumbling through his desk. "Okay, open wide!"

Otto opened his eyes and saw Melvin Dandy holding his hands toward him, each one containing a portable compressed air boat horn.

"Well, here are our signals. Since my office looks onto the cafeteria auditorium, I can blast away there and you can take the girls' gym. We should blast down each of the long corridors, too, so we'll have to run back and forth a little. But that way most of the school will hear the alarm. We'll probably still have to alert the shops and boys' gym by telephone or intercom."

"Why don't we just blast away over the public address system?" suggested the principal.

Suddenly indignant, Dandy brought himself up, intoning, "Now I'll have NONE of that. What if the electricity were somehow cut off? No, these have to stand on their own. If necessary, we can send a couple of runners to the distant areas of the building."

"Will these be loud enough? It *is* a huge building," asked Otto.

"Of course they will. We'll announce the time of the first drill so everybody will be listening for it—then wait for five minutes past the time everyone expects it to happen and then blast away," said Dandy.

"But if it were a real air raid alert, they wouldn't be listening, would they?"

"Now, Otto," chided the counselor, his eyes ablaze, "let's not muddy the waters. I think we've got clear sailing now, but we have to figure out a proper code. The fire alarm is four gongs and a pause, and then it repeats itself twenty or thirty times. Why don't we give three short blasts on these horns and then one very, very long one, and repeat that sequence twice? That should get everybody up and out and braced against the walls."

"Melvin, you astound me that you have endorsed this enterprise?"

"Well, you told me the other day, 'If you can't beat 'em, join 'em.' I didn't quite understand what you meant, but now I think I do. And all joking aside, it's because of that desperate letter that trouble-making outfit sent to me. It finally dawned on them that they needed someone in *authority* to pull off their little drill, so I decided to follow your advice, Otto, and join 'em. And I suddenly saw that I could do something positive to help prepare for a potentially dangerous situation. They opened my eyes when they talked about the possibility of an overturned gas truck. Then it all fell into place, and I became determined to do what's best for our school."

Otto couldn't help thinking that Melvin might also be doing what was best for Melvin, or at least the unconscious needs of Melvin's personality, but what harm could it do? A little play might well be just the thing for him.

Smiling, Otto cleared his throat, and announced, "Melvin Dandy, I hereby appoint you Chief Air Raid Warden of Midville Middle School."

* * * * *

The next day at lunch the Gang of Four sat in joyous triumph.

"Mr. Ferlinghausen called me in to tell me that he has appointed Mr. Dandy as the school's Chief Air Raid Warden and that there will be an air raid drill at two o'clock on the Wednesday before Thanksgiving vacation."

"Gosh," said Sean, "that's getting really close. Do you think we'll be ready? I mean, the siren module won't be ready until Thanksgiving Day at the earliest."

"It doesn't matter," said David. "*They* are obviously ready—so we've won! And, best of all, we've distracted the school's attention so no one will get wind of our Canasta Showdown. Bobby's reputation will not be tarnished in any way."

"I can't believe Mr. Ferlinghausen went along with the scheme, David," said Lisa.

"He's really a good egg," David confided, "and he can take these things in stride. By the way, what are the preparations we have outlined so far?"

Lisa peered at her small flip-top notebook. "This is what I've scribbled down from our previous brainstorming sessions: 1. Have Mrs. Jones' art class make arm bands for the Junior Wardens showing the circle with the letters CD for Civil Defense on the inside. Mary and I agree that these arm bands should be blue and white, and so does Mrs. Nelson."

David nodded.

"How are we going to pick the Junior Wardens?" asked Sean.

"We'll have to find student volunteers who resemble the newly appointed Chief Air Raid Warden," said David, smiling.

"Oh, what a horrible thought," said Lisa. "Do you really think there may be some miniature Mr. Dandys running around, David?"

"Lots of them. All we'll need to do to get them to come out of the woodwork is to offer them a little power," answered David.

"But how will we know them?" asked Mary.

"By their beady little eyes," said Sean, squinting to take aim and adding a very loud "POW!"

A sudden veil of silence enveloped the cafeteria. Zeke Minturn was among those who looked rapidly toward the Gang of Four's table.

Mary put her head in her hands, saying, "I am *so* embarrassed. Sean, when will you grow up?"

"Never!" retorted Sean.

"Twins, come on!" David scolded. "We need to cooperate if we're going to pull this ruse off. Now let's start looking for Junior Air Raid Wardens in our classes this afternoon and don't forget to ask around."

"Who are we looking for?" asked Lisa.

"Anyone who is emotionally tight-laced, who wears a frozen face, who seems a little too dignified, and who would be in absolute glory to order other people around during an emergency—or any other time, for that matter," answered David.

"Sounds *just* like Dandy-Pandy," said Sean.

"Dandy-Pandy?" asked David.

"Yeah," explained Sean, "that's what the seventh graders call him. He came into all the seventh grade English classes the second week of school, announcing, 'My name is Dandy; it rhymes with candy.'"

"Yes, I've heard that," said David.

"Then he launches into a spiel about how we're now out of grade school and have to put our noses to the grindstone, or else no college will even look at us. So I raised my hand that day and said, 'But Mr. Dandy, my dad never worked in middle school or high school or even very much in college, and now he's got two Ph.D.'s.'"

"What did he say?" asked David.

"He coughed a bit, and then said, 'There are always a few exceptions to the time-honored rule that hard work equals success. Then he asked my name, and scrawled it down in a little black book. Now he always seems to avoid me whenever he sees me."

"Dandy-Pandy," laughed David, shaking his head.

"I've heard the ninth graders call him far worse," said Lisa.

"What do they say?" asked Sean.

"It's not for your young ears," said Lisa, putting her index finger up to her lips.

"I sort of feel sorry for him," said David. "He comes across as a pathetic figure, always standing on his dignity."

"Just like our Sunday School teacher Mr. Lytle," said Sean, as he and Mary began laughing.

"Maybe they're related," said Mary.

David shrugged, saying, "People can surprise us if given the chance; look how he's embraced our air raid drill ruse."

"Or maybe *he's* just the first one out of the woodwork," said Lisa. "If it doesn't work out, he'll turn on us. You'll see."

"But what could go wrong?" asked David.

"I don't know. Anything that would make him look bad. That's the danger, making him look bad."

"Make Mr. Dandy look bad?"

"Dandy-PANDY," corrected Sean.

"What will Junior Air Raid Wardens do?" asked Mary.

"Look official," laughed David.

"No, they need to do something more than that," said Lisa.

"How about pulling the window shades and shutting off the lights," said Mary.

"What good would that do in an air raid?" asked Sean.

"None," said Mary. "But we've made our case with the scenario of an overturned gasoline truck, so we'd better stick with it."

David looked at the others and smiled, "The whole school will be talking about this until Christmas, well after our very secret Canasta Showdown. This air raid diversion will save face for Bobby because nobody will ever find out he's playing a little old ladies' game ... that's downright ruthless."

"When is the canasta playoff?" asked Mary.

"I'm leaving that to Sean," announced David.

"Why Sean?" asked Lisa.

"Bobby has appointed Zeke Minturn as his official go-between, and I have appointed Sean in a similar capacity. We all shared a sort of bonding on Halloween. Here's Zeke now," said David.

"Hey, everyone," said Zeke, having just returned his lunch tray. "Hey, little partner, how about taking a stroll to the men's room so we can discuss when the big game will be?"

"Right after I return my tray," said Sean.

"Here, I'll take it up for you," offered Lisa.

"Thanks," said Sean.

The two left the cafeteria, looking very purposeful in their gait.

"Do you think that was wise?" asked Mary.

David smiled. "I asked Sean to think about a good date for the game after Zeke inquired about it last week. We agreed it should be sometime after Thanksgiving, but well before Christmas vacation."

"Sean is going to mess it up," said Mary.

"No, he's not. He'll be just fine," David smiled. "You'll see."

* * * * *

Zeke and Sean entered the lavatory, its faded green tile waiting to lend an eerie echo to their words.

"Bobby thinks he'll be ready to face David by the week before Christmas," Zeke whispered, a little daunted by their new acoustic.

"No way, Jose!" countered Sean, jarring the room with his voice.

Zeke stared in amazement at such conviction in so young a person, albeit one who carried a .38 derringer in his pocket.

"Hey, be cool, little partner. Why not?"

"Because it's *got* to be on December seventh," Sean explained, "because that's the day Japan bombed Pearl Harbor."

"Oh," said Zeke, as if this reasoning made perfect sense, "I guess that's what it'll be, then."

263

"No *better* day to have it than on December seventh, and it's on a Thursday, so the loser can be the slave for the winner on Saturday, December ninth," Sean continued. "Having it early is also added protection just in this case if the air raid jive rolls off everyone's back before Christmas. Do ya get my drift?"

Here Sean had assumed his best gangster stance, with his lower lip dipping to the right, just enough to emphasize the small scar under his right eye.

"Okay, okay, Dude," said Zeke, "Keep it cool, keep it cool. You've got it."

* * * * *

Returning triumphant to the lunch table, Sean offered a full description of all that had transpired.

Mary laughed, "And do you know how he got that scar, David?"

David shook his head.

Sean looked at him and said, "Would you believe in a knife fight?"

David continued to shake his head.

"When we lived in Boston, Sean helped a neighbor lady carry a heavy box up this huge flight of stairs to her house," explained Mary, "but he slipped on a patch of ice, and fell all the way down the concrete steps. Blood was everywhere."

"It was an *awful* sight!" Sean rejoined.

"Any more questions on our air raid drill protocols?" asked David.

"I wonder what kind of alarm they'll come up with?" said Sean.

"It'll be fun to see what they do. Let's finish our 'Student in the Corridor' interviews for tomorrow's special edition of *Bare Fax*."

Chapter Eighteen
An Air Raid and an Accident

TUESDAY'S EXTRA EDITION OF *BARE FAX* carried a surprise banner:

DANDY NAMED SCHOOL'S CHIEF AIR RAID WARDEN

The feature article included choice quotes from an interview with the new Chief Warden, wherein he recounted a compelling scenario of a large gas truck overturning next to the school, and the need to marshal students and faculty into school corridors where they would brace themselves against the walls in anticipation of a severe explosion.

A special message box appeared at the top of the front page headline, giving the following information:

AS WE GO TO PRESS: Mr. Melvin Dandy, Midville Middle School's new Chief Air Raid Warden, announced late yesterday that the first air raid drill of the school year will be conducted on the WEDNESDAY PRIOR to the Thanksgiving vacation, beginning at PRECISELY 2:00 P.M..

A special addendum to the paper outlined revised air raid drill protocols, making adequate note that the complex planning and revision had been executed by the Chief Air Raid Warden himself. Faculty members were asked to review regulations in their classes to insure all members of the school community would be fully apprized of proper procedure in the event of an air raid alert, announced or unannounced.

Faculty and students were invited to submit their questions, comments, and observations to *Bare Fax* for a forthcoming special issue to be headlined:

SCHOOL COMMUNITY GIRDS ITSELF FOR FIRST AIR RAID DRILL IN MANY YEARS!
* * * * *

David sat in the middle school office waiting to see Mr. Ferling-hausen. Having already secured permission to make extra copies of Tuesday's *Bare Fax*, since the paper had taken the initiative to publish the newly revised air raid drill protocols, David's next proposal seemed a logical step. Tuesday's edition had been one of the largest printings, with copies delivered to all faculty members, student council members, as well as the usual homeroom and corridor bulletin boards.

"Ah, David. Come in, please," Mr. Ferlinghausen said as he opened the door to his office. "What can I do for you?"

"I wonder if you would consider giving me the privilege of printing future copies of my newspaper *Bare Fax* on the office copy machine? Most students are eager to read each new issue, especially with the air raid drill news, and we try to save paper by posting copies on bulletin boards. We also try to keep each edition down to three pages."

"I think we can manage that," answered Mr. Ferlinghausen.

"Thank you. We will have an edition ready on Thursday afternoon for Friday morning distribution, if we could please bring it in for copying after school?"

"Certainly, I'll ask Mrs. Dixon to run as many copies as you need."

"Thank you. Do you think maybe we could also start using colored paper? It dresses things up a little."

"I don't see why not. I must say I am very pleased with what you have managed with your paper, David. You have successfully attracted the interest of most of our school, faculty and students alike. And I take to heart that so many of your readers are also becoming interested in knowledge for its own fascination and sake. I doubt if many here knew that bats account for one quarter of all mammalian species, or that they represent a family of mammals over 50 millions years old. You manage to find intriguing facts that pique a reader's curiosity and ignite the imagination. I salute you."

"Thank you."

"How are you and Bobby Perkins getting along?"

"Quite well, actually."

"So Mr. Lowery has told me. I find that very encouraging and very interesting."

David smiled his own approval of this improved situation.

"One thing does bother me, though, about all this air raid drill folderol."

David gulped, managing to say, "And what is that, sir?"

"I get the uneasy feeling that it may well be a smoke screen for something else, a sort of planned diversion to steer everyone's thoughts in one way. I worry a little about when the other proverbial shoe might fall."

Sighing with relief, David took a deep breath, and said, "Mr. Ferlinghausen, we have an open and honest relationship which I value, and regarding our lobbying for an air raid drill, I can only say this: on one level, it is exactly as you suggest, but I promise you that what is being obscured from view is nothing wrong or untoward. On another level, it is a way to unite our entire school community to focus on something beyond the humdrum of our daily routines. I predict good will come from both pursuits, but I am sworn to secrecy regarding the private matter, which has absolutely nothing to do with school."

"So I had suspected. David, I have come to respect and trust you. Can you tell me anything more?"

"I'm sorry, but no. I *can* assure you that what is being hidden is no longer happening here in school and that it is designed to repair a relationship. The secrecy is to save potential embarrassment."

Mr. Ferlinghausen looked puzzled.

David smiled and sat silent.

"I've also learned that your distinguished Gang of Four is cooperating with Bobby Perkins and his friends regarding some special project."

David continued to smile and sit silent.

"May I infer from your silence that this project is what you are trying to keep a secret?"

"One should never infer too much from Quaker silence, Mr. Ferlinghausen."

"I'm a Lutheran myself, but I hold a long and deep respect for Quakers. They enjoy a rich tradition of successfully translating their values into good deeds."

"My parents were Attenders of a Quaker meeting. I certainly like a lot of what the Quakers are about, but right now I'm keeping my distance from organized religion."

Mr. Ferlinghausen raised an eyebrow.

"I still wonder why God let my parents get killed by that drunken driver," blurted David. "It just wasn't fair, and I don't see why they or I should get such a raw deal."

"Have you and your Aunt talked much about this?"

"A little, although it's mostly my problem. She doesn't push me. She's a retired Episcopalian who served as her church's organist for many years. She goes to church now about once every two months. I went with her once after I got here and it just didn't feel right. I don't really feel I was able to open myself to thank God. Aunt Lillian said she understood my reasons for staying away. She said she's also trying to enjoy some of those holiday Sundays she missed for so many years when serving as the church's organist. Anyway, I'm not very pleased with God just now."

Mr. Ferlinghausen closed his eyes, nodding, "I think I can understand why you feel that way, especially in the wake of your loss. My wife and I lost two children shortly after they were born. Please hear this one suggestion, though: God gives us free will, so we may make choices and do what *we* choose to do. As a result, we do much evil and harm to each other, but God scarcely creates or condones it."

David pondered the insight.

"I know it's only words, David. You've suffered an irreparable loss, and words come cheaply. But these words may some time lead you to greater light."

"The Quakers talk a lot about light," interjected David.

"Yes. So I've heard."

David rose to go.

"David, just one more thing before you go."

"Yes, sir?"

"I have heard an unsettling rumor about one of our students; in fact, he is a young and rather bellicose associate of yours. I have heard that he brought a small gun to school."

"Mr. Ferlinghausen, I can say with absolute certainty that no *real* gun has ever been brought into our school by anyone I know," answered David.

"Just as I thought," laughed the principal. "Just as I thought. Thank you."

* * * * *

Friday's *Bare Fax* created a stir among the school community since many of the faculty and students were quoted in their response to the following question: 'Do you believe Midville Middle School is better or worse off for finally adhering to its air raid drill policy?'

A sampling of the array of quotations follows:

Mrs. Jones, art instructor, "It has given my students a practical application for their art designs and projects, such as the protest helmets and now the Civil Defense arm bands that were created for our recently appointed student wardens."

Mr. Diehl, history teacher and veteran, "Our nation learned an enduring lesson at Pearl Harbor of the need to be prepared for all eventualities; I hope these practices never prove necessary for real emergencies, but it's the kind of insurance that brings peace of mind."

Mrs. Coachman, English teacher, "NO COMMENT!"

Mr. Winters, math teacher, "It's all balderdash."

Mrs. Prentice, reading tutor, "It is helping the students to understand potential events larger than their immediate classroom concerns."

Mrs. Maxwell, music teacher, "I really don't see the sense in it, and I personally would rather have the time for rehearsal because students don't practice enough as it is. But the air raid drill protocols also shouldn't appear in the faculty handbook if they aren't going to be exercised and observed."

Miss Kirkpatrick, home economics teacher, "We have reviewed the kinds of canned food that would be helpful for survival, should we ever be deprived of our conveniences for any length of time."

Mr. Lowery, librarian, "There has been a surprising surge of interest in air raid procedures during World War II and the early Cold War. Library usage is up by twenty percent."

Mr. Pennythorpe, history instructor, "It should be great fun and informative as well. Having lived through many wars, I am convinced that *preparedness* should remain our watchword. Good luck everyone."

Audrey Vanderkamp, student council representative, "Well, if the boys are willing to go out and brace themselves up against those ugly walls, it's only right that we girls should go out and support them."

Theodore Hummel, student warden, "We'll have to have lots of drills to get our new responsibilities in good working order. It's a lot of work to pull shades, and usher students, and secure lights. ORDER, remember, ORDER is ESSENTIAL—and I mean NO LAUGHING!"

Hilda Edwards, student warden, "If students could only come off their perpetual party and realize lives are at stake during an air raid alert, then maybe people will see there's more to life than party, party, party. To be prepared, is to be ready, is to be alert!"

Mr. Amos Walker, custodian, "I remember when we had the air raid alerts in the sixties, although I was working at a different school. We don't seem to need them today, but this overturned gas truck theory has some merit to it, God forbid it should ever happen."

Mrs. Nellis Oliver, cafeteria manager, "Thank God they scheduled the drill for two o'clock. What a mess the cafeteria would have been if it had occurred during lunch period! It would have looked like a bomb really *had* hit the place. Worse than Dresden."

* * * * *

David refilled the dinner glasses. The onions and chives in the beef stew had made Aunt Lillian and him thirstier than usual. Max waited hopefully next to his chair, following his every move and gesture with undivided attention and mournful brown eyes.

"I can't wait for the turkey the day after tomorrow," said David eagerly.

"It's a small bird, but it promises to be delicious. I will make your favorite: mashed potatoes made with cream cheese. It will be the first Thanksgiving I've celebrated here in years, and just for the two of us," said Aunt Lillian, adding, "I fondly remember so many wonderful Thanksgivings at your parents' place."

"What did you do when you didn't come to us?"

"On those years I couldn't come, I went with some friends to one of the local restaurants."

David looked at Aunt Lillian wistfully, "Holidays can bring back memories that are painful."

Aunt Lillian reflected for a moment. She took a long sip of water.

"Yes. Painful because of the loss of loved ones. I remember how hard holidays were for me the first few years after I had lost my father. I was quite out of sorts the first year. I was only six when my mother died, so that was not quite the same."

"Why are holidays so intense?" asked David.

"We seem to draw closer to our loved ones, to take special time to be with them."

David stared at his water glass.

"Why did *they* have to die, Aunt Lillian?"

"I don't know, my love," Aunt Lillian answered, shaking her head, "I'm sorry, but I just don't know."

David stood up to clear the table. Wagging his tail expectantly, Max followed him to the kitchen.

* * * * *

At last! The day of the air raid drill had finally arrived, or more specifically, the day on which air raid drills would be reinstituted at Midville Middle School. A fever of expectation coursed through the corridors prior to homeroom, and after the morning announcements were read by Mrs. Dixon, Mr. Ferlinghausen spoke to the school community: "Attention all faculty and students. There will be an air raid drill this afternoon at two o'clock. Teachers, please review regulations with your classes throughout the day so that all students will be informed as to the proper procedures. Students may now pass to their first period classes."

Throughout the day speculation grew as to how the administration would signal the air raid alert. Some said it would be by siren, others said by horn, yet others slyly implied that Mr. Dandy would blow his nose over the public address system. If it had been the latter, Midville Middle School students would rightfully have felt themselves royally cheated. An alarm has to have a little pizzazz if it is going to do any good. Such was the unconscious opinion held by a majority of Midville Middle School students, who also amply demonstrated a natural affinity for bells, whistles, sirens, horns, firecrackers, gunshots, screams, shrieks, wails, moans, yells, and any other sort of general hysteria. As the fateful hour approached, an expectant tension grew among faculty and students alike. The entire school community became as one ear, harkening for a new sound.

At twenty minutes 'til two o'clock, a confident Melvin Dandy strode into Otto Ferlinghausen's office, carrying a small box and wearing his uncle's air raid helmet.

273

"Hello, Melvin, what have you there?"

"Our air raid horns, but I thought it best to conceal them until we use them. Students are pretty nosy about such things, and I think it will serve us better to keep them in the dark until we spring the surprise. I practiced last night when my wife was doing the dishes, and I am sorry to report to you that our china set is now down to nine plates."

"Melvin, why don't we simply blast one of these horns over the public address system? It would be far easier then running back and forth blasting down those long hallways."

"No way! What if the power were to go out? What if the gas truck toppled the power lines near the building? No, we've got to be prepared to signal the emergency independently of the intercom," insisted the counselor.

"It seems like a lot of unnecessary fuss," sighed the principal, momentarily identifying himself with the infamous Dr. Frankenstein, for had he not unwittingly created this Dandy monster standing before him, dressed in a navy double-breasted suit, replete with vest? —At least the monster is well dressed for once, thought Otto.

"Look, Otto," replied his monstrous air raid warden creation, "it will be much better this way, I promise. You blast away here outside the office, maybe giving the signal twice to each corridor, and then repeating it. I'll do the same thing upstairs. You only have to walk back and forth next to the girls' gym rail, whereas I will have to negotiate the entire cafeteria."

"What about the third floor?" asked Otto.

"Oh, dear, me! I forgot all about the third floor. I'll have to run up one of the stairwells, and so will you. Why don't I take the east stairwell, while you take the west. Run up to the third floor on the west stairwell after you've blasted each hallway twice. The music rooms will hear you from here. I'll run up to the third floor on the east stairwell.

You have one more floor to run, but you're more athletic than I am. Then, let's signal the third floor again, and then we'll return to where we started, and repeat the original sequence," instructed the counselor.

"Melvin—"

"Yes, Otto?"

"Let's start blasting away at one fifty-eight, just to catch them off their guard."

Melvin Dandy looked in genuine admiration at Otto and smiled, "You give the sure sign of an experienced principal, Otto," he nodded, adding, "almost as good as springing a fire drill when classes are passing. Okay, one fifty-eight it is. Just wait for my first blast before you begin."

Otto nodded.

Melvin Dandy pranced upstairs to his office, which faced onto the cafeteria.

Otto strolled the railing that overlooked the girls' gym, which was sunk beneath the level of the corridor. Moving to the east hallway, he held his boat horn out with his right hand, waiting.

Suddenly from the cafeteria above came the first resonant blast from Dandy's air horn. Otto began his sequence, repeated it, and then crossed to the west corridor and repeated the whole thing. Then the principal ran up the stairwell to the third floor, walking to the west corridor that faced onto the cafeteria-auditorium balcony, and repeated the sequence. Turning and racing down the west stairwell and rounding the corner leading to the first floor, Otto slipped. His ankle suddenly felt as if it were on fire, and a sharp pain cascaded up his leg as he felt himself falling to the brick floor.

Melvin Dandy, oblivious to this real emergency, continued to blast away on the floor above, obviously having forgotten the prearranged code. So much for practice.

It was fortunate that Miss Forsythe, whose gym students were bracing themselves around the girls' gym, heard Mr. Ferlinghausen crying for help. She examined the ankle, helped make him comfortable, and ordered him not to move until the ambulance personnel had arrived. She then notified Mrs. Dixon, who immediately summoned the ambulance.

Meanwhile, Melvin Dandy continued to blast away in the cafeteria. All students and faculty were now in the corridors, and the small boat horn could be heard quite distinctly on both the second and third floors, and even as far away as the computer room. Melvin Dandy kept blasting away, partially because of an internal psychic spasm similar to dim-witted dogs that bark continuously at the wind, and partially because no plan had been discussed on how to silence the alert. *I blast, therefore I am.* After about two minutes of this racket, faculty and students began to wonder if there weren't indeed some sort of real emergency afoot, and how right they were, and how wrong Dandy was. Finally, the counselor, who was perspiring profusely from his forehead and face, dropped his horn on the floor, exclaiming, "Whew! What a workout!"

Mr. Winters approached the counselor and growled, "Dandy, you've had your fun. Now send us back to class so we get ready to pack everyone out of here. The buses will be here any minute."

Melvin Dandy, as was his custom, looked blankly at so sensible a suggestion. "Buses?" he said vaguely. "Are the buses coming?"

"They're probably already outside waiting, you idiot. Let's get a move on, so we can all get out of here." It would be insensitive to mention that Mr. & Mrs. Winters had tickets for a holiday cruise, and were flying from the regional airport at five thirty. Mr. Winters liked to avoid the winter as much as possible, and had purchased a condominium in Florida for his Christmas and February holidays. But this

Thanksgiving was a special anniversary cruise, and he didn't want to miss it. Peering into Melvin Dandy's eyes, and quickly concluding that there was no one really in charge, Mr. Winters turned to the students and faculty clustered around the walls of the cafeteria and shouted, "All right, folks, the drill is over. Back to your classes until you're dismissed."

As students and teachers returned to their classrooms, they heard Mrs. Dixon's frantic voice on the public address system: "Would all students and faculty please return to their classrooms. The air raid drill is over. Please return to your classrooms. Teachers, please DO NOT, I REPEAT, DO NOT DISMISS ANY STUDENTS, INCLUDING WALKERS, UNTIL YOU ARE INSTRUCTED TO DO SO BY THE OFFICE."

An ambulance's siren could be heard in the distance.

Chapter Nineteen
The Law Laid Down

AUNT LILLIAN GRIPPED THE TELEPHONE receiver tightly; her eyes wandered from the telephone table to the floor. "You say Mr. Ferlinghausen got a badly sprained ankle when he ran down the stairwell during the air raid drill? And he's already home. Good. And will he be out of school very long? I see. Mrs. Ferlinghausen, please tell your husband that the Gang of Four is very sorry for his accident, and that they will do anything they can to help him. Thank you. Goodbye."

Aunt Lillian turned to Sean, Mary, Lisa, and David.

"Mrs. Ferlinghausen says he's already home, but that he will have to stay off his ankle for at least ten days, maybe two weeks."

"I feel awful," said Lisa. "If we hadn't pushed this air raid business, none of this would have happened."

"It's really too bad," agreed Mary.

Sean looked disconsolately at the table, stroking Max who had placed his head in Sean's lap.

"I don't think you should blame yourselves," said Aunt Lillian. "After all, accidents do happen, and don't forget: it was Mr. Ferlinghausen, himself, who embraced the whole idea of reinstituting the air raid drills."

"Well, I think it did help to pull the school community together, if only for a short while," said David.

"I'm still going to have that siren built, just in case Mr. Ferlinghausen ever wants to spring another air raid. All he'll have to do is flip a switch, and then a really low and intense blood-curdling siren will drone over the P.A. system," announced Sean.

"I doubt if we'll *ever* have an air raid drill again," sighed Lisa.

"Let's not be negative. The air raid phenomenon has helped us to focus the school's attention away from our big canasta showdown which is coming in a couple of weeks. That was part of the bargain we made with Bobby, to create a suitable diversion."

"I just wish there were something we could *do*," said Lisa.

"How about sending an arrangement of flowers?" suggested Mary.

"Great idea," David brightened. "I can put twenty dollars in, since I'm getting more allowance than the rest of you. Let's call a florist right now. I wonder if anyone is open this late?"

"I'll also put in twenty, David," announced Aunt Lillian. "If you all don't mind, I would like to order the arrangement from Gunther's Flowers at the Mall. They don't close until nine o'clock, and Spunk used to be one of my piano students. We'll have it delivered to the Ferlinghausen's home tomorrow morning. How do you want the card to read?"

"Wishing you a speedy recovery, —The Gang of Four," said David.

"The Gang of Four AND AUNT LILLIAN!" Sean corrected, frowning at David, adding, "David, may I please take Max outside and give him some of those dog biscuits he loves?"

"Sure."

"Oops. Sorry Aunt Lillian. I guess I take you too much for granted sometimes," David apologized, after Sean had taken Max.

"Maybe she doesn't want her good name to be associated with us after everything that's happened," said Lisa.

Aunt Lillian smiled, and said, "I don't think I have much choice in the matter, but my answer is that I most certainly want to be associated with all of you! You shouldn't blame yourselves for Mr. Ferlinghausen's accident."

Aunt Lillian left to fetch her credit card and to telephone Spunk Gunther for the flower arrangement.

* * * * *

Thanksgiving Day dinner chez Lillian Biggs was scrumptious and succulent in the most traditional and delicious of ways.

"I just love this dressing and gravy," said David, "and the turkey is done to perfection."

"Thank you, David. You're a Grand Nephew," beamed Aunt Lillian.

"And you're a Grand Great Aunt!"

"I'm a little sorry that Bobby and his friends and your Gang of Four are taking the Thanksgiving weekend off from canasta. Bobby is becoming a formidable player, just as you are, and I wish you both the very best when you have your canasta showdown. I have come to look forward to Saturday and Sunday afternoons that resonate with canasta and laughter."

"I know you are sworn to secrecy, Aunt Lillian. But this is Thanksgiving and God will forgive you, especially after you made such a wonderful feast."

Aunt Lillian raised her left eyebrow as David continued.

"Confidentially, who's the best canasta player?"

Aunt Lillian reflected and smiled.

"David, I can tell you honestly, without breaking any oath: the best canasta player among all of you is Sean."

"That's not what I meant! You know that, too," David laughed. "Anyway, Sean is always romping on the floor with Max. I'm surprised the Little Hoodlum hasn't turned into a real canine yet."

"Nevertheless, he *is* the finest player among you."

"Probably because he's the most cutthroat," sighed David.

"It also might have something to do with his remarkable memory," rejoined Aunt Lillian.

"Well," persisted David, "between Bobby and me, who's the better player?"

"You'll not wheedle that information out me, my dear. You'll have to ask Max, or perhaps even 'Her Majesty'."

"I would, if I could," said David, leaning down to stroke Max's mane, and tickling him behind his ears.

"It's going to be different on weekends after the great showdown," said Aunt Lillian.

"What will we do?" asked David.

"I thought we might consider picking a couple of good books to read to each other, much as we did last August," suggested Aunt Lillian.

"I loved it when we did that. I'm sorry we haven't had as much time since school started, except on Sunday mornings. Sometimes I feel that I learn more from you and Mr. Pennythorpe than from all my other teachers combined."

"School *is* important, David. But don't forget, I learn a great deal from you and your friends," observed Aunt Lillian.

"The wisest folks often feel they know the least, like Socrates," said David. "That's the sort of feeling I get from Mr. Pennythorpe. He knows so much, and he really loves learning, yet he's truly modest. He's *really* ancient, too."

"His secret, David, is that he remains young at *heart*," smiled Aunt Lillian.

Silence ensued.

David looked at the candles gloomily, confiding, "I'm really sorry that Mr. Ferlinghausen hurt his ankle."

"Now you must *stop* blaming yourself for Mr. Ferlinghausen's accident. It's certainly unfortunate, but there's nothing more we can do now, except keep him in our prayers."

"Do you believe in prayer?"

"I most certainly do. Why do you ask?"

"Well, you don't go to church much these days since you stopped playing the organ, and I wondered how you were feeling about God and all that," said David.

"Oh, I feel my relationship with God is quite healthy, and I certainly don't feel that attendance at church necessarily furthers my spiritual growth. I know that you are still mad at God, David, because your parents were killed. I can't say that I wouldn't feel the same way. You got a raw deal; no question about it. I'd be mad at God, too."

"But you're not, are you? And they were family to you, too," David chided.

"Yes. Very dear family," said Aunt Lillian slowly. "Your parents were and *are* family, David. They continue elsewhere, just as we continue here together. I do miss them terribly, more than words can say. We had so many good times together, full of laughter and love. But I'm not mad at God for what happened to them, because I don't believe God was responsible for their accident. That drunken driver was. God gave him free will, just as he has given us all free will. With that freedom comes a heavy responsibility. That poor driver was probably an alcoholic, and we know today that such people react differently to alcohol than do most of us. They can't help their dependency, but it takes an enormous courage for them to confront their addiction. Some call alcoholism the disease of denial, and they certainly have a point.

That man's drinking, together with his foolish decision to drive that night, created a horrible tragedy, and the pain from tragedy will haunt us, and everyone who knew your parents, forever. How I wish we could bring them back, but we can't. We have to move on, as best we know how."

David sat staring into the candles, his face a mask of stone.

Aunt Lillian shook her head sadly, adding, "Forgive me, David. Perhaps I say a little too much sometimes, and here we are celebrating Thanksgiving."

"Sometimes I feel a hollow, empty pit in my stomach when I think about what happened to Mom and Dad. I hate that man who killed them," said David.

"Yes. I can understand that. He died, too. I suppose he would have been burdened with their deaths for the rest of his life if he had lived. But you must try to forgive him, David."

"No way! I don't even *want* to forgive him. How do you forgive someone who's killed your parents?"

"I suppose by asking God to help you to want to forgive," said Aunt Lillian.

"But I don't," said David. "I'd like to rip the man's face off."

"You've been listening too much to Sean," said Aunt Lillian.

"No. Sean would shoot him. But I'd love to hurt him. It would feel so good to hurt him. I know it would."

"He certainly hurt you, didn't he? And me, as well. And even if you could hurt him, it would only feel good for a moment. What then? How would it feel after that?"

"I don't know. I just don't know."

"David, I've tried to be a good person my whole life. I sympathize with your feelings, but you're only hurting yourself by refusing to forgive this man you hate so much."

"I just can't, Aunt Lillian. I don't even *want* to."

"Then your pain will fester and fester until you do, my dear. I truly don't know any other way but forgiveness, certainly for your sake as well as for his. Hm, I wonder. Do you know what day of the week you were born on?"

"Thursday," replied David.

"How very curious. Remember the old rhyme? 'Monday's child is fair of face; Tuesday's child is full of grace; Wednesday's child is full of woe; Thursday's child has far to go. David, my dear, it would seem that you *do* have far to go."

"How far is forgiveness? One light year or two, or does it stretch to the edge of the universe itself?"

"Forgiveness stretches far *beyond* the limits of the universe, David," smiled Aunt Lillian, adding in a whisper, "So does love."

They cleared the table and washed the dishes in silence.

* * * * *

An hour later Aunt Lillian and David were reading quietly in the music room. The telephone rang.

"I'll get it," said David. "Hello?"

"Hello, David? This is ... Lisa."

"Lisa, are you okay? Have you been crying?"

"Yes. We had a terrible scene here at the restaurant just a little while ago," confided Lisa.

"With your parents?"

"No. Oh, no. With Bobby Perkins' father. He and Bobby came for our Thanksgiving Day dinner. I think Bobby wanted to surprise me. He looked really washed up and combed down, if you know what I mean. Anyway, his dad started drinking one whiskey after another. Then when he got his dinner, he stood up and yelled out that his dinner wasn't cooked properly and that he wasn't going to pay for lousy food. He accused my dad of trying to poison him. My dad threatened to call the police, and that's when Mr. Perkins grabbed poor Bobby by the nape of his neck and dragged him out the door. I tried to put Bobby's dinner in a doggie bag, but his dad grabbed it and stomped on it, saying it wasn't fit for a dog. It was an awful scene."

"How was Bobby?" asked David.

"He was so embarrassed he wouldn't even look at me after all the commotion started. I know he must have been just sick about it," said Lisa.

"I'm really sorry, Lisa. What did your mom and dad do?"

"Do? What *could* they do? They just shook their heads, and then my dad said Mr. Perkins was never to be allowed in the restaurant again."

"I'm sorry, Lisa. Both for you and your parents, and also for Bobby," said David. "Thanks for calling."

David returned to the music room and looked at Aunt Lillian.

"Anything wrong?"

"Bobby Perkins' dad made an awful scene at the Jones' restaurant. Said their Thanksgiving food was unfit for a dog to eat. Drank too much and stormed out, dragging Bobby behind him."

"How's Bobby?" asked Aunt Lillian.

"Lisa said he was in tears when he left."

"Can we call him?"

"They don't have a telephone. I asked Lisa to have Zeke go over and check on him tomorrow. I don't know what more we can do. Do you?"

Aunt Lillian shook her head thoughtfully, "Nothing that wouldn't make it a lot worse for Bobby. I am just sick for that boy's situation. I wish we had thought to invite him to come for dinner here."

"Aunt Lillian, has Bobby ever talked much about his father?"

"Never. It's no secret in this village, though, that Edward Perkins is an alcoholic. Everyone chooses to look the other way. It can't be very pleasant at home for Bobby. Perhaps that's why he seems so pleased to come here on Saturdays to play canasta. And do you know David, when Bobby plays canasta, he's very focused? In fact, he's becoming a very formidable player, although Sean is the best of all. The only thing I think Sean loves more than playing canasta is romping with Max."

"You're right about that. What does Bobby talk about?"

"Mostly about you."

"Me?"

"Yes. Now that he's gotten to know you, he has discovered that he admires you very much. He also says he's glad you have a nice big house to live in and that our library books are not wasted on you. Then he'll get a little red in the face and suggest that there *are* some in the world on whom our books would be wasted, even on a few who think they can teach English." Aunt Lillian smiled, adding, "Bobby doesn't have a very high opinion of Gertrude Coachman, does he?"

David gulped, wondering if the truth of Halloween would out.

Aunt Lillian smiled again. "I gather," she continued, "that you and Bobby are becoming friends, after a fashion."

"I hope so. That was the original reason for all this folderol, and it sure is better than getting beaten up."

"I'm glad for your success David. Perhaps Bobby will learn, through you, that there are *real alternatives* to violence," said Aunt Lillian. "I suspect that he hides all of his home life under an enormous basket, hoping that the world will never peer in."

"I would be embarrassed too, if my father acted like his," said David.

Aunt Lillian shook her head, "And if that's what he does in a public restaurant, what goes on at home, I wonder?"

"What do you mean?"

"I mean, David, that I am beginning to fear for Bobby's well being."

"Do you think he's in danger?"

"Probably only when his father is in some drunken rage or other. I begin to wonder—"

"What can we do?"

"We should continue to do what we are already doing because it brings Bobby here on Saturdays. Perhaps we will be able to do more, if a situation presents itself where decisive action can be taken," concluded Aunt Lillian.

"That doesn't sound very hopeful, does it?"

"We can also pray, David."

* * * * *

Melvin Dandy entered Otto Ferlinghausen's office at seven fifteen Monday morning, sat down in the leather swivel chair, and reflected on the meeting he planned to have, after announcements, with that measly little Gang of Four. Dandy displayed due diligence in the application of what has become a common commodity in our modern world, namely, a *convenient memory*. What the counselor *now* remembered, in light of his fallen principal's unfortunate accident, was that the Gang of Four had forced the counselor, the principal, and the entire school community to capitulate to all that silly nonsense about air raid drills, persisting until a drill was finally conducted, much to the wise counselor's vehement objections. As Melvin Dandy sat very high on top of his dignity in the principal's chair, he conveniently forgot that it was he, himself, who had insisted on using separate air horns for the air raid signal. Had he agreed to blast the alert over the intercom, Otto would never have twisted his ankle. And for that mishap, someone must accept blame. Justice, mused a dignified Dandy, would soon be served up to a particular little Gang of Four and, as he assumed his new duties as acting principal, he rubbed his hands with relish as he anticipated the dressing down that he would soon launch on that measly gang's misdirected energies.

Hearing the office door open, Melvin Dandy called out, "Mrs. Dixon, when you have finished with the morning announcements, will you please announce that I have a special announcement to make before students pass to their first period classes?"

Mrs. Dixon nodded her assent.

When Melvin Dandy's moment arrived, he took the microphone from the secretary and began, "Faculty, students, and staff of Midville Middle School, this is Acting Principal Melvin Dandy speaking. I report to you with deep relief that our leader, Mr. Ferlinghausen, is now at home recuperating from his most unfortunate accident of last Wednesday. He hopes to resume his duties within a week or two. I promise that, during my tenure as acting principal, this school will have a dignified decorum and that I will not tolerate any little foolish escapades. Pertinent to Mr. Ferlinghausen's very unnecessary accident, and to the changes I will momentarily implement, I now want to see the following students in my office IMMEDIATELY: David Andrews, Lisa Jones, Sean Potter, and Mary Potter. Students may pass to their first period classes when the bells sound." Thus, through one misinformed announcement, from one very convenient memory, had Melvin Dandy conveyed to the school community the erroneous impression that the Gang of Four had been directly, if not diabolically, responsible for Mr. Ferlinghausen's accident.

Seating himself in the principal's chair, Melvin Dandy eagerly rubbed his hands as he sat waiting to lambast the Gang of Four. Not having the morning *Times* to read, he didn't quite know what to do with himself. Taking a pencil out the top center desk drawer, he started tapping it nervously as he waited for the victims of his wrath. Gratifying his curiosity, he proceeded to paw through Otto's desk, wondering what it would be like to be a real principal. He fidgeted in Otto's chair, which felt much too large for comfort, as he endeavored to untangle some paper clips.

The office telephone rang. Mrs. Dixon answered it, and stepped to the doorwell, announcing, "Mr. Dandy, the students you wanted to see are at the Guidance Office."

"What!" yelled Dandy, his face darkening. "Order them down here at once!"

Melvin Dandy slammed the door to his office.

Mrs. Dixon picked up the receiver and conveyed the acting principal's request.

The Gang of Four heard the counselor's rage over the telephone as they stood in the Guidance Office. Their stroll to the main office offered valuable time for strategic planning.

"I told you he'd turn against us if it went sour," said Lisa.

"You sure were right," said Mary.

"We're really in for it," said Sean.

"No, we're not," said David, confidently. "We just have to listen to him rant and rave at us for a bit," said David.

"But it's a bum rap," Sean objected.

"Yes, it is," agreed David. "But let's wait to see where we can turn this situation to our advantage."

"Good luck," sighed Lisa.

"Leave it to me," said David. "Let's let Mr. Dandy talk himself into a royal hole. Just be polite and look at him. Try not to think of one of those little bantam roosters that's on the strut to the outhouse. If you begin to laugh, look down at the floor. Let's make sure his insults roll off our backs like water, and let me do all the talking."

The others agreed and, after their short walk, they entered the Main Office.

"So they're *finally* here, are they?" Dandy bellowed into the intercom in answer to Mrs. Dixon's announcement. "Send them in."

The Gang of Four entered and stood solemnly in front of Mr. Ferlinghausen's desk, studying the interloper who had seized authority to run things properly. Poor Melvin, he looked much too small for the chair he was now occupying. In fact, he looked rather silly, just like an insignificant little bantam rooster that was puffing itself up in a failed effort to imitate a majestic eagle.

The students stood in silence, waiting to receive the first salvo from this rather ruffled blunderbuss.

"Well, my little, reliable trouble makers, are you all quite satisfied with the disarray you have caused?"

The Gang stood silent, and this only encouraged the acting principal.

"Mr. Ferlinghausen is now sitting at home, when he might well have been here, except for his most unfortunate accident. Are you satisfied? Or do you hope to topple some other high official?"

Although the Gang of Four could scarcely conceive of Melvin Dandy as a high official, the idea of toppling him seemed very attractive, especially to Sean, who began to wish that he had brought his derringer.

"You have every reason to be silent in the face of my authority, and my asking you these questions no doubt embarrasses you," continued Melvin Dandy. "In fact, I'm surprised you had the nerve to come to school at all today. But now that you have, LISTEN UP! I'M LAYING THE LAW DOWN! There will be no more editions of that foolish little paper until Mr. Ferlinghausen gets back. All it does is stir everyone up. If he wants to play those games, that's his own choice and his own funeral. *I* will not have it! So don't you dare test me, or you'll be out on your ears. There will also be no more injunctions for air raid drills by your precious little gang. We've had enough of that foolishness, and we'll have NO MORE!"

Here Melvin Dandy gave his best evil eye to the four youth, who stood before him in silence. In his mind's eye, he saw himself as an avenging eagle, holding the famous Maginot line; however, from the perspective of the Gang of Four, he resembled a pathetic, cranky, miserable, and undernourished vulture.

Having exhausted his over-rehearsed speech, Dandy concluded, "Well, what have you to say for yourselves? And why are all of you looking down at the floor. Did somebody drop some money?"

An interval of silence followed, and it is probably a good thing that Melvin Dandy did not know that the students had been trying not to burst into laughter. Had they done so, their mirth might well have netted the acting principal a major stroke, or them early graves.

"Well? Say something!" Dandy commanded.

"Flowers, sir," said David.

"Flowers?" asked a perplexed acting principal. "Flowers? What flowers?"

"Did you send flowers, sir?"

"Flowers? Flowers to whom?"

"To Mr. Ferlinghausen, of course, sir," said David.

Now Melvin Dandy sat embarrassed. Never having served as acting principal, he hadn't a clue as to whether he should have sent flowers to Otto. It certainly seemed the decent thing to do.

Coughing a little, and pulling at his shirt collar, Dandy said, "No. I was too busy trying to bring order out of that awful mess you all caused on Wednesday." An unkind smile passed his lips as he added, "Did *you* send flowers?"

"Yes, sir," said David. "Fifty dollars worth."

Dandy slammed his fist down on the desk, harder, in fact, than he had intended, snarling, "You can't buy kind thoughts and forgiveness out of bad deeds!"

A short silence followed as Dandy, holding his hand, scowled fiercely at the Gang of Four.

Lisa began to cough to keep from laughing. To cover her, David stepped forward, saying, "Sir, permission to speak, sir."

Dandy nodded, and looked at Lisa, saying, "Please step back a little, my dear. You may be getting a cold. With Mr. Ferlinghausen now indisposed, it goes without saying that all precautions should be taken to insure my continued good health, lest I be unable to serve as acting principal. I am vital to Midville Middle School's returning to some semblance of sanity."

David, noticing that Sean was beginning to open his mouth, no doubt to say that he would be glad to put to rest in the most permanent of ways any question about Dandy's 'continued good health', poked the little hoodlum and announced: "Flowers have *already* been sent, sir. The school should do something else."

"And what should the school do?"

"A card, sir."

"And how can five hundred and sixty-seven students send a card, pray tell?

"By asking Mrs. Jones to create an enormous card, and then inviting everyone sign it, sir," said David.

Dandy mulled over the idea. It was a very original idea, but he didn't want the Gang of Four to get credit for it. He also had no clue as to how to manage the logistics of having so many students sign such a card. Looking at David, he asked, "And how would you have the students sign such a card?"

"Mrs. Jones could probably have it ready by seventh period. Why not make that period a signing period, and have each class report to the cafeteria to sign their names? Then someone, like yourself sir, could drop it over to Mr. Ferlinghausen after school."

"And that someone *will* be *me*, young man. Don't put on airs. I will look into all of this, thank you. You suggest having each class come to the cafeteria to sign the card. Why not have everyone do it at lunch?"

"Too messy, sir. Food and drink all over the card. More dignified this way, more purposeful."

"Oh, I didn't think of that. More dignified, but at the expense of a lost class period."

"Sir," said David, straightening himself tall, "only *you* have the authority to cancel classes. The card, by your order, sir, could be ready and waiting to be signed by the seventh period."

This final appeal to authority struck the Napoleonic vanity of the acting principal, who immediately embraced the proposal. Yet still not wanting to give any credit to the Gang of Four for the idea, Dandy merely replied, "Well, perhaps I will look into it. You may all go now."

After the Gang of Four left the office, Lisa asked David, "Do you think he'll go for the card?"

"I guarantee it," David smiled. "We had him in the palm of our hands. Did you see the glint in his eyes when I suggested to him that only *he* had authority to cancel classes?"

"Not so you'd notice," said Sean.

"Beneath the appearances," said David. "I predict there will be a general announcement about the card signing sometime next period."

David was wrong. Melvin Dandy's general announcement came at the end of the third period. The announcement had three essential points: the first point was that he, Mr. Dandy, was acting principal and had sole authority to cancel classes; the second point was that he, as acting principal, was canceling seventh period instruction to allow students to proceed to the cafeteria, in an "orderly and dignified" fashion as instructed to do so by the office, that they might "inscribe their names" on an enormous card Mrs. Jones' art classes were making for Mr. Ferlinghausen; the third point was that he, Mr. Dandy, was acting principal and had sole authority to cancel classes.

The signing plan would have worked as smoothly as a Swiss watch had Melvin Dandy stayed sequestered in Otto's office. Although no protocol had ever been devised for such a card signing activity, it was determined that Mrs. Dixon would call students by their respective classroom numbers over the public address system, and those classes would proceed to the cafeteria when instructed to do so. What was to complicate the card signing was Melvin's retreat to his own office late that morning to read *The New York Times*. He felt he had already done a full day's work, and that he should best save his energies, the better to supervise the card signing arrangements later that day.

Midville Middle School, an old brick rectangle of a building, had stairwells near each of its four corners. The two stairwells on the west side of the building were designated as DOWN stairwells while the two on the east side of the building were reserved for traffic going UP. On this particular day, Miss Freeman, Mr. White's student teacher, was teaching ninth grade mathematics for Mr. White, who had called in sick and was enjoying what he fancied as a 'mental health' day. Miss Freeman was only vaguely aware of the stairwell protocols and, when her class was summoned, she directed her students to proceed *down* the UP stairwell on the east side of the cafeteria. From Miss Freeman's third floor classroom, this stairwell provided the most direct route to the cafeteria below. At this particular juncture of time, Melvin Dandy was strutting about the cafeteria, attempting to appear 'dignified and in authority', as he attempted to preside over the card signing. "Now, move along, move along after you've signed," he intoned. "We don't have all day, you know."

When the acting principal noticed Miss Freeman's students advancing *down* the UP staircase, he nearly suffered a stroke, for another class that had already signed Mr. Ferlinghausen's card and was just beginning to ascend the same stairwell. In truth, the stairwell was more than ample to accommodate each class passing the other in single file, and that very minor task was about to be accomplished, when Melvin Dandy shouted to the first student in Miss Freeman's class, who was on the landing between floors, "That's an UP staircase; you're going in the wrong direction! Turn around and go back up, and then come down on the other side of the cafeteria next to my office!"

Miss Freeman was, herself, now beginning to descend the wrong stairwell from the third floor. When she heard the obnoxious shouting, she assumed that one of her students had gotten into trouble. When she saw her students turn to come back up the stairwell, clearly not yet having signed Mr. Ferlinghausen's card, she ordered them to turn around and proceed back down to the cafeteria as originally instructed. Melvin Dandy, now standing at the corresponding spot on the second floor, noticed that the students he had just ordered to return upstairs were now turning once again to proceed down this *verboten* stairwell, thus slowing up two classes that were patiently waiting to ascend what was becoming the prized staircase.

"What do you *mean* by turning around? I ordered you to go back upstairs!" the acting principal sputtered at Derek Wilson, who was the leader of Miss Freeman's class. "If a donkey can turn around, so can you. Now turn around, and march yourself *up* that staircase. There are two classes down here waiting to return to their rooms."

"Don't be impertinent to me, young man," Miss Freeman scolded Brad Davies, who had just made an about face, and was trying to return *up* the stairwell. "You turn around and walk right down there the way we were instructed and sign that card. Now MARCH!"

The poor line of students turned again to return to the cafeteria.

"What do you mean turning around on me again?!" yelled Melvin Dandy. "I don't care who's up there, even if it's the Queen herself. *I'M* the one in charge here. Now we have *three* classes waiting to return upstairs, and you're holding up the whole lot! Now get going! What if this were a fire drill? We'd be in poor shape, wouldn't we, all burned to a crisp!"

"What's that?" asked Audrey Vanderkamp, as she put her makeup kit back in her purse, for, after all, she had been following the very muscular Derek down to the cafeteria, thinking only about boys and nothing else.

Melvin Dandy's face darkened as he scowled up at Audrey, shouting at the top of his lungs, "I said WE'D ALL BE BURNED TO A CRISP!"

Audrey's face turned white as she shouted, in turn, up to Miss Freeman, "Mr. Dandy says we'll all be burned to a crisp!" For what followed, we can singularly credit Audrey's vast experience as a gossip, together with her long habit of changing a message's original tense from the subjunctive to the future.

It is also amazing how much panic such a small change in tense can occasion in a student teacher. Miss Freeman, a naive yet well-meaning college senior, had been brought up ever eager to do the *right* thing. The present panic that seized her imagination quickened her normal response time, as she suddenly noticed that she was standing in front of one of the school's ancient fire alarm boxes, the kind that is so old that after one breaks the glass, one prays *something* will happen. Audrey's scrambled communication had convinced Miss Freeman, in the deepest recesses of her idealistic soul—for most college students can still afford the luxury of ideals—that *some* sort of fire or emergency was afoot, and having enjoyed for years the reputation of being a quick study, at least in college, she promptly removed her right shoe and gave the fire alarm box a resounding crack.

CLANG, CLANG, CLANG, CLANG sounded the fire bells.

During the short interval between the first and second series of gongs, Melvin Dandy could be heard to shout, "Judas Priest!"

CLANG, CLANG, CLANG, CLANG repeated the sequence.

Students were now beginning to emerge from all of the second and third floor classrooms that faced on to the auditorium-cafeteria.

CLANG, CLANG, CLANG, CLANG the bells continued.

Melvin Dandy could be seen running faster than a sprinter, his arms held straight and stiff at his sides, *down* the upstairs stairwell {for shame!}, in hope that he might quickly get to the Main Office and telephone the village fire department *not* to respond.

CLANG, CLANG, CLANG, CLANG echoed the bells.

Entering the main office, Dandy saw a confused Mrs. Dixon telling the custodian over the intercom, "No, Mr. Walker, it's not a drill. Please come to the office to help us find out what's going on!"

"Call the fire department!" ordered the acting principal.

Mrs. Dixon complied, announcing, "Ringing, sir."

CLANG, CLANG, CLANG, CLANG continued the bells.

Melvin Dandy grabbed the phone receiver, "Hello, this is Melvin Dandy, acting principal of Midville Middle School. We've just had an accident with our alarm system and there is *no* fire, I repeat, *NO* fire, so *PLEASE* don't send any fire trucks. What?! You've already dispatched three trucks?! Can you call them back? No. Okay, I'll run out and flag them down."

CLANG, CLANG, CLANG, CLANG repeated the bells.

Students and faculty who had already evacuated the building, and there were many, suddenly saw their acting principal running as fast as he could, his arms still hugging his sides, toward the side of the school where the buses were now pulling in to wait for the students' dismissal. Sirens could be heard careening around the Maple Street corner, and three fire trucks suddenly appeared, lights flashing, sirens wailing.

Acting Principal Dandy ran toward the lead bus, trying to flag it down so as to make room for the advancing fire trucks. Instead he created a traffic jam, and soon three fire trucks were hopelessly blocked by ten buses.

"Make way, make way!" shouted the acting principal.

CLANG, CLANG, CLANG, CLANG echoed the bells from inside the school.

"Is there a fire?" asked Mrs. Logan who drove the first bus.

"What?" scowled the acting principal.

"Is there a fire?"

"Of course there isn't a fire," came the acting principal's labored reply. "Move over to let the trucks through."

This contradictory response led Mrs. Logan to conclude that there might indeed be a real fire, and she pulled her bus up over the curb, thereby almost running over her own acting principal's right foot, causing him to jump fleetingly out of the way. Her example was followed by the other drivers. The fire trucks now began to clear their way toward Mrs. Logan's bus, where Mr. Dandy was now yelling harshly at the poor driver, "Damn it! You nearly killed me, you fool. And you made me stub my toe."

Producing a handkerchief, and alternately wiping his face and waving it at the faculty and students who stared in amazement at the spectacle, the acting principal sputtered, "Back, I say, back. Go back into the building!"

CLANG, CLANG, CLANG, CLANG echoed the bells.

"But the bells are still ringing," shouted Mrs. Wagner.

"I know they're still ringing, damn it! I've got two ears in my head. Go back in, I say! There's no fire."

"Where's the fire?" called the assistant fire chief from the first fire truck, which had now pulled along side Mrs. Logan's bus.

"There *is* no fire," shouted Dandy. "We've had a false alarm."

"Jerry," the assistant fire chief instructed his driver, "you pull the trucks out and take them back to the station. I'll stay here to investigate. Call Detective Maynard and have him come over to help me with the investigation."

"It wasn't that kind of false alarm! It was a misunderstanding, a simple little accident," screamed Dandy, failing to endear himself to the assistant fire chief.

"Is there a fire?" asked the assistant chief.

"NO!" yelled Dandy.

CLANG, CLANG, CLANG, CLANG persisted the bells.

"Are the alarm bells ringing?" asked the assistant chief.

"Yes. Can't you hear them?" said the exasperated acting principal.

"Then there *HAS BEEN* a false alarm!" countered the assistant fire chief, smugly taking out his notebook.

In face of such compelling logic, Melvin Dandy paled with anger and rage and, turning, ran back toward the building. Racing up the cement stairs he reached the outer doorwell, pausing to lift his handkerchief to wipe the sweat from his brow. Those watching suddenly perceived something black fly from his head. Quickly ducking down, Dandy picked that something up and, clutching it at the crown of his head with both hands, ran into the building.

Students and faculty became increasingly astonished as they witnessed these extraordinary proceedings.

"*Who* was that *funny* little man?" the assistant fire chief asked Mrs. Logan.

"Acting Principal Melvin Dandy," she sighed.

"He's a dandy, all right," grumbled the assistant chief, looking at his watch, and adding, "and he won't be getting home in time for his supper tonight, I'll guarantee you that."

The afternoon's decorous card signing had deteriorated into a fiasco the likes of which the school would never forget. The fire bells were finally silenced, and students returned to the their classrooms to prepare for a late dismissal. Mrs. Dixon took the responsibility to dismiss classes, since Mr. Dandy had been summarily confined to Mr. Ferlinghausen's office for an extended interview with the assistant fire chief and the newly arrived Detective Maynard. As the acting principal attempted to explain the afternoon's foibles, he won no sympathy from the investigators. That most of his sentences began with "That saucy little Gang of Four" and "Those miserable little trouble makers" and "Those damn rabble rousers" should not be held against a man in so desperate a state. During the interview, Detective Maynard sat in Otto Ferling-hausen's chair, for he had quickly intuited *someone* had to assume authority. Melvin Dandy sat across from him, sputtering away, while the assistant fire chief lumbered around the office.

More than a few of the Midville Middle School faculty wondered if the card, designed to cheer Mr. Ferlinghausen, was worth the price of the afternoon's confusion; for all of the students, however, it had proved nothing less than a grand and glorious spectacle, the likes of which happened perhaps only once every second generation. The master plan had been partially accomplished, as well, for over half of the students had inscribed their signatures on Mr. Ferlinghausen's card prior to the unplanned evacuation.

On his way home, Melvin Dandy, exhausted and depressed, dropped the enormous get well card off at the Ferlinghausens' home, thrusting it quickly into Mrs. Ferlinghausen's hands, while declining her invitation to enter to greet Otto saying, "Ask me no questions, I'll tell you no lies."

Arriving home a short while later, an exhausted Melvin Dandy crept in his house, brushed by his wife with the same message he had accorded to Mrs. Ferlinghausen, promptly took four aspirin, poured himself a double scotch, which he downed in one large gulp, and proceeded to fall into bed, clothes and all.

Chapter Twenty
Conversations and Preparations

THE NEXT MORNING, which was the Tuesday after Thanksgiving, Mrs. Dixon entered the main office of Midville Middle School at her usual time of seven fifteen. No lights were on in either the main office or Mr. Ferlinghausen's office. As was her custom, she went into Mr. Ferlinghausen's office to open the Venetian blinds and turn on the lights.

Opening his office door, she gave a great start and a little shriek. In front of her, in Mr. Ferlinghausen's chair, wearing dark glasses, sat Melvin Dandy, acting principal.

"Sir, I ... I didn't think anyone was in here because the lights were off. Are you all right, Mr. Dandy?"

Dandy sat in the chair rubbing his hands as if he had not heard her question.

"Are you all right, Mr. Dandy?" Mrs. Dixon repeated.

A glimmer of recognition penetrated the acting principal's dark glasses as he sat in that very dark office. He looked up at Mrs. Dixon and said, "I'm not sure, Mrs. Dixon. I'm not sure. I think I *will* be, but right now, I'm not sure."

"Do you want me to call someone to help?"

"I believe we did enough of that yesterday, don't you? No. I need to ask you an enormous personal favor, if you don't mind."

"Anything, sir. Just name it. What can I do for you?"

"SHIELD me."

"I beg your pardon?"

"SHIELD me. Protect me. Hide me."

"From what?"

"From that insidious, odious, little snot-nosed Gang of Four and from any other kind of menace that might increase my status as the school's laughing stock. I need to keep a very low profile between now and the time Mr. Ferlinghausen returns."

"Mr. Dandy, why don't you just go home? Perhaps you could take a few days off—"

"What? My presence in this school is *vital* until Otto returns, but I don't want to see anyone, for *any* reason."

A forlorn Melvin Dandy took out a handkerchief and wiped his brow. Removing his glasses and rubbing his eyes, he continued, "Mrs. Dixon, to be very, very frank with you, before you sits a broken man."

"A what?"

"A broken man. My spirit, Mrs. Dixon, is crushed, shattered. I'm but a shadow of my former, robust self. I'm afraid I've lost my nerve, and I don't know if I'll *ever* get it back."

"Sir, I think you should go home for a good rest," said Mrs. Dixon.

"No! Absolutely not! I won't hear of it! I can sit here for Otto until he returns. I can do *that* much, but no more. You would not believe me, Mrs. Dixon, if I described the awful ordeal I endured in this very office yesterday after school, with that horrid assistant fire chief and his henchman buddy Police Detective Maynard."

"Did it go badly, sir?"

"Well, I wouldn't exactly describe us as having gotten along like three peas in a pod."

"As what?"

"Mrs. Dixon, have you ever heard of the Spanish Inquisition?"

"Yes. I think so."

"Well, Mrs. Dixon, I need someone to talk to because *I* can now say that I know what it must have felt like to have been interrogated during the Spanish Inquisition. I have *never* been more humiliated in all my life. These investigators, you know, always get their way with you. They can jolly well have it any way they want it. Don't forget that if you should ever bear this cross. One of them, that irritating assistant fire chief, was fuming and snorting over the false alarm, while the police detective was being as sweet and nice as candy and apple pie as he asked all kinds of innocuous questions. Then, when I thought I had finally gotten my bearings, the nice one suddenly turned on me and shoved his big bulbous nose in my face, asking me if I knew that causing a false alarm was a misdemeanor. Then the assistant fire chief had the audacity to ask me if I had any credentials to serve as acting principal. What a lousy knock! He didn't even say 'principal'—'*acting* principal' was all he said. I feel like such a damn also-ran."

"What are you going to do, sir?"

A hint of smile appeared on Melvin Dandy's lips. "Nothing," he said.

"I beg your pardon?"

"Nothing. Absolutely nothing. Otto caught on quicker than I did about how that rotten little Gang of Four succeeds in making fools out of people. My first mistake was when I crossed swords with that little red-haired infidel. I've learned my lesson. I'm going to sit here all day with that door closed and weather the storm. Then I'm going to slink out of here at exactly six o'clock this evening, after *everyone* has gone home except, of course, the night cleaning staff. Meanwhile, I'm not available for *any* telephone calls, interviews, discipline problems, or anything else. I don't care who telephones, even if it's the District Superintendent himself. Tell everyone I'm very busy, and that Otto will get back to them after he returns. Write down the day and time of call, and then put a memo in Ferlinghausen's mailbox. Let him deal with it when he gets back."

"What are you going to do in here all day long with the blinds drawn and the lights off?" asked a perplexed Mrs. Dixon.

Melvin Dandy had not yet considered this dilemma. His morning habit was to peruse the *New York Times*. The library's copy of the *Times* had been delivered first to his office for many years because of Dandy's insistence that faculty deserved a few privileges for their unrewarded labors. The *Times* spent the better part of the morning in Mr. Dandy's office before being taken to the library. Now Melvin Dandy faced a conundrum: if he were to ask Mrs. Dixon to go the guidance office to fetch the *Times* for him, he would signal her that it was business as usual. This revelation would fly in the face of his desperately expressed need to be 'shielded' from all external forces, most especially the Gang of Four. As sorely tempted as he was to request the newspaper, Melvin girded himself against temptation, resigned to forego his usual daily pleasure.

Gazing at Mrs. Dixon with great solemnity, Mr. Dandy announced, "I will *think*."

"You will think, sir?"

"Yes. I will think. And when I think, I think I will think, when I think, about retirement. Perhaps I could manage it in eight years if they make me a generous offer. Now, please turn the lights off and shut that door, and don't bother me again for *any* reason."

* * * * *

The Gang of Four had joined the lunch line together, made their necessary purchases, and had now seated themselves together at a table toward the east side of the cafeteria. From their common vantage point, they gazed briefly at the singular stairwell where Mr. Dandy had created his own private and noisy Waterloo the previous day.

"What a day!" exclaimed Sean.

"Pure melée," David agreed. "I dropped into the office this morning to see what had happened to the card we signed, and Mrs. Dixon said she thought Mr. Dandy took it over to Mr. Ferlinghausen last night. There was something very odd going on, though, because I didn't see him in the office. I asked when he would be in, and Mrs. Dixon said he was already in Mr. Ferlinghausen's office, but that he didn't want to be consulted or disturbed for *any* reason."

"That doesn't sound like Mr. Dandy," said Lisa. "I wonder if he's well?"

"He's probably *really* embarrassed," said Mary.

"Let's go ask him for an interview about yesterday," suggested Sean.

"Sean," scolded Mary, "have a little decency."

"Sorry," quipped Sean, "can't afford it."

"Look," persisted Mary, "I know Mr. Dandy is a little much to take, but he probably feels like a worm after creating all that confusion and disorder yesterday."

"He *did* have a little help from Dear Audrey," said Lisa.

"Yes, but he wouldn't have flustered her if he hadn't had such a stroke about Miss Freeman's class coming down the wrong stairwell," said David.

"But it was a math class," grinned Sean, "and they're obligated to do everything precisely."

"I bet poor Mr. Dandy wishes he could begin yesterday all over again," said Mary.

"Well, he can't," said David unsympathetically, "and I'm not so sure that this may not have helped all of us more than we know."

"How so?" asked Lisa.

"Mr. Dandy is a very authoritarian personality ... " David began.

"Yeah," agreed Sean, "let's plug 'im."

"Sshh!" scolded Mary, who wanted to listen.

"Well, if Dandy's drawn in his horns because of this fiasco," David continued, "it means he won't be shoving his nose into everybody's business. That works to our advantage, since he tends to place himself in an adversarial position with us."

"And loses, for all his trouble," said Sean, adding, "let's call yesterday DANDY'S FOLLY, in Friday's edition of *Bare Fax*."

"That would be cruel," said Mary.

"So?" shrugged Sean.

"How would you feel if it had happened to you?" Lisa asked Sean.

"I would love to have been Miss Freeman," said Sean. "It must have been fun setting off all the fire bells. Oh, by the way, the siren module is almost finished, and I think we'll have it as a 'welcome back' surprise for Mr. Ferlinghausen by the BIG DAY."

"That's right!" exclaimed Lisa. "The big canasta tourney is only nine days off. I'm counting the days on my calendar. Are you happy you got your way, Sean? December seventh will be remembered for more than Pearl Harbor after next week."

"Yeah!" Sean enthused. "The day David sank Bobby's ship of cards."

"I don't know," said David, shaking his head, "Aunt Lillian says Bobby's getting better and better at the game. She also says you're the best of all of us, Sean. I can never beat you at canasta, only at chess, and then only when you make impulsive moves."

"Canasta is awesome!" said Sean.

"Especially if you're winning," grumbled David.

"It's real easy if you get the wild cards," continued Sean.

"As you *usually* do," lamented Mary.

"Well, all I know is that I'll need to practice a lot between today and the seventh," said David. "Sean, can you come over tonight, and we'll play a couple of games?"

"For sure. It'll give me another chance to *slaughter* you for all the times you've creamed me in chess."

"Chess is a thinking man's game," said Lisa, "whereas canasta is brutal and bloodthirsty."

"Right on!" agreed Sean.

"Sean, you can't go tonight," scolded Mary. "Old Thing said you were grounded until you clean up your room and all the mess you made shooting at those toy soldiers with your BB gun."

"I put papers behind the soldiers so I wouldn't hit the wall like last time," explained Sean.

"Yeah, and now there are all these little fragments of newspaper all over the floor," said Mary.

"Hey, David, why not tomorrow night?" asked Sean.

"Okay," said David. "Could you please explain something to me? Why do you take all those chances discarding so many wild cards? It drives me nuts."

"I go for broke," Sean explained. "I love getting the pack, and I especially love it when I can build it up to a gigantic stack. That's when the game is *really* awesome. It makes the game a lot more exciting."

"The Canasta Showdown will be exciting," said Lisa, adding, "and school will be relatively quiet if Mr. Dandy stays cooped up in Mr. Ferlinghausen's office."

"It will be a very uneventful week and a half," predicted David, "but it will give us a chance to concentrate on winning the Big Canasta Showdown. Mrs. Dixon took me aside before I left the office this morning and told me Mr. Ferlinghausen plans to come back on December seventh. She also told me that Mr. Dandy keeps his door shut and his blinds closed all day, and has a whole row of different kinds of pills on his desk. She said it looks like a small pharmacy. She asked if we would please consider *not* publishing *Bare Fax* until after Mr. Ferlinghausen gets back on the seventh. I said, 'No problem'."

"Dandy-Pandy's nerves must be really shot," said Sean.

"Probably," said David. "It's surprising what happens to some people when they suddenly come into a little power or money."

"How's that?" asked Lisa.

"Aunt Lillian says an excellent test of character is to give people a little power or a little money, and then watch what they do with it," explained David.

Mary glowered at Sean, saying, "*Some* are probably selfish pigs and go out and spend it all on themselves."

"And *some* are probably jealous that they don't have any money," retorted Sean.

"Mr. Dandy got real intense about his power when he became acting principal, the way he tried to blame *us* for Mr. Ferlinghausen's accident," said Lisa.

"Well, now he's had a taste of that bitter pill himself," said David. "I suspect that's why he's keeping out of sight. Probably not a bad thing. A little knowledge can be a dangerous thing. You puff yourself up and fancy that you're qualified to do something like run a school, only then to discover maybe you're not quite as hot as you think."

"Mr. Ferlinghausen probably never has to think about how to be principal. He just *is*," said Lisa.

"Like in canasta," said Sean, slamming a clawlike hand on the table. "Just grab that old pack after it's loaded up with wild cards."

David smiled weakly at Sean. —I wonder if I'll be that successful, he thought, contemplating the impending Canasta Showdown. The canasta competition had proven to be the best kept secret of the year, and David was sure Bobby hoped it would remain that way. The positive side of it was that the preparations for the showdown had brought Bobby and David together without violence. They were becoming friends, with the first break in that direction having arrived, at Bobby's initiative, on Halloween with the visit they had paid to Gertrude Coachman. David still got goosebumps when he thought of it.

"So what do you think, David?" asked Lisa.

"Eh? Sorry. I was thinking about something else," David apologized.

"Can Mary and I come over to watch you and Sean play tomorrow night?"

"Sure, why not? How about seven o'clock? That is," David added, "if you want to see Sean lose."

Sean picked up his knife from the tray and playfully thrust it in David's direction, challenging, "Bring 'em on! Bring 'em on!"

"Boys," sighed Mary. "Always posturing."

"And sometimes fighting, too," added Lisa.

* * * * *

As it worked out, Sean didn't lose on Wednesday evening. In a sense this was only fair, for David had recently bested Sean in chess several Saturdays in a row. But in canasta, Sean reigned as undisputed master, in part because David was the more conservative player, whereas Sean never shrank from taking chances. Lisa and Mary sat as witnesses to see David go down in defeat once again. With the Great Canasta Showdown soon approaching, an uneasy tension had clouded this evening's game. Devoted to his master as he was, Max would nevertheless come and lie each evening beside Sean's chair, lending canine moral support, perhaps in reciprocity for their frequent romps together. 'Her Majesty' presided with equanimity over the canasta proceedings by perching her royal self on top of the silver chest, which sat on top of the nearby serving table.

After Sean had picked up an enormous pack, loaded with juicy wild cards, David slammed his cards on the table, growling, "I quit!"

Sean looked up in dismay. "You can't *quit*. I just got the pack."

"I know. *That's* precisely *why* I quit. You *always* get the pack. It's no fun getting smeared day after day."

"Gee, David. You don't have to be a sore loser," said Sean.

"I'm *not* a sore loser. I'm just *tired* of losing."

Lisa coughed and cleared her throat, "I think I know how David is feeling, Sean. It's depressing to meet wave after wave of defeat; after a certain point, one entirely gives up any hope of winning. Even *you*, Sean, must get tired of winning all the time."

Mary fell out of her chair laughing as Sean matter-of-factly replied, "Not really."

"Maybe it would help to analyze the game," Lisa continued. "Sean, you go first."

"Well, I risked a lot of my wild cards by placing them on the discard pile, and since I had a straight in fives, I baited David with fives. Then, when he finally discarded a five, I pounced for the whole pile and slaughtered him."

David groaned.

"You're the living soul of diplomacy itself, Sean," sighed Lisa. "David, you play a good game, but you're too trusting."

"Because Sean suckered me for fives?"

Lisa nodded.

"Well," grumped David, "I can't help it. I probably *am* too trusting. I don't play expecting to get a knife in the back."

"It wasn't a knife in the back," Sean protested. "It was a knife in the gut. I fooled you into thinking I wasn't interested in fives. I had to discard five to do it, but then you put one down and I let you have it. Going out with a concealed hand would have been a knife in the back."

"Sneaky, but effective," said Lisa, shaking her head.

David buried his head in his hands. "I'll *never* beat Bobby."

"Nonsense, David," said Lisa. "You're already a good player. It's just that Sean is better."

"You have to be *really* warped to play the way Sean does," said Mary, hoping to cheer David.

"Let's play darts, Mary," said Sean.

Max nuzzled his head in David's lap, offering a consoling trill of affection and sympathy.

"Thanks, Max," said David. "Even if I lose, I've still got you."

"Why don't we switch players," suggested Mary. "Lisa, you be David's partner until the Great Canasta Showdown. Sean can be a silent observer."

"That might help restore a little of my confidence," said David.

"BORRRing," said Sean. "I'll romp with Max, instead."

"No you *won't*," corrected Mary, much to her later regret.

The change of partners *did* help David because he and Lisa were more evenly matched. Yet Sean was hardly a silent observer. Whenever David was on the verge of making what Sean perceived to be a mistake in strategy, Sean would cough, tap on the table, grunt or groan. This back seat driving served only to increase David's tension and drove him nuts. Finally, he insisted that Sean lay off. Almost immediately following, he ended up giving Lisa an enormous pack because his concentration was shot. At this sad juncture in the game, Sean fell to the floor, pounding the carpet with his fists.

"Sean," said Mary, "I think you're going to have to get some manners by the time we have the Great Canasta Showdown."

"I've got it," said Lisa, "Let's have Sean be the Master of the Game?"

"Master of the Game," said Sean.

"Yes," said Lisa. "You'll establish the tone and insure that everything is done fairly and properly. What do you think, David?"

David nodded his assent.

"Terrific!" said Sean. "I'd love to be the Master."

Sean left the dining room to go visit with Aunt Lillian who was reading in the music room. Max followed him and soon he and Sean were romping and playing together on the music room floor.

"Lisa, that was brilliant!" said David, "I hope it works."

"It will," predicted Mary. "Sean can be very focused when he gets a responsibility he wants."

"David, has Aunt Lillian said how Bobby's doing in canasta besides that he's pretty good?" asked Lisa.

"Only that he's getting better and better each week. Unlike *me*."

"You're getting better, David," said Lisa.

"Yeah, at losing."

"Sean is in a different league," said Lisa.

"My brother is from a different planet," sighed Mary.

"Let's play again, David," said Lisa. "This time you'll be able to concentrate."

"Okay."

"And look at it this way, David. No matter what happens Thursday, you've already won."

"How's that, Lisa?"

"Well, the whole goal was to find a non-violent way to relate to Bobby Perkins. That has already been accomplished. The rest is gravy. You're no longer his punching bag."

"December seventh is going to be a special day," said David. "Mary, is Sean all ready with the intercom siren module?"

"Yes. He put a second coat of varnish on it last night. He also stopped to see Mrs. Dixon, to make sure the connectors fit, and they do."

"Great. Won't Mr. Ferlinghausen be surprised?" Lisa smiled.

"I just hope he uses it and forgives us," said David.

* * * * *

At six o'clock, the evening of Wednesday, December sixth, Melvin Dandy's tenure as acting principal of Midville Middle School expired. The most outstanding feature of his term of office was that it had passed by relatively unnoticed, except, of course, for the very first day.

As Mrs. Dixon prepared to leave the main office late that afternoon, Melvin Dandy had called her into Otto's office.

"Yes, sir? Is there anything I can get for you?"

"No, thank you. I just wanted to thank you for shielding me. It has been a most traumatic week and a half and I'm glad Otto is coming back tomorrow, even though his hours are restricted. Nine to one, isn't it?"

Mrs. Dixon nodded, "Yes, for the first two weeks."

"Yes, I thought I remembered that correctly," Dandy continued. "Apparently everyone is eager to have Otto back. I know I am. I've never heard such applause and cheering as when you announced his planned return just before dismissal today. I still feel out of sorts. I will report directly to the guidance office tomorrow, so you can bring Otto on board when he gets here."

"He will have his work cut out for him," Mrs. Dixon observed, looking at the mountain of mail and memos on the principal's desk.

"Well, he's had a sort of vacation, and he will be jolly well ready to jump in fresh. I wish *I* could take a vacation, but vacations cost money. This has been a *very* expensive week for me."

"I'm sure you'll get some rest, sir," encouraged the loyal secretary.

Mrs. Dixon had assumed Melvin Dandy was talking about the emotional toll taken on his psyche when, in reality, he had been lamenting having to purchase his own copy of *The New York Times* in the early morning on the way to school, but he did not disabuse her of her perception or her concern.

Chapter Twenty-One
The Great Day Arrives

AT PRECISELY NINE O'CLOCK THE NEXT MORNING, a dapper and rested Otto Ferlinghausen entered the main office, smiling at Mrs. Dixon and asking, with a twinkle in his eye, "Well, did *anybody* miss me?"

"We *all* missed you, sir. Welcome back!"

The light snow that had been falling still sparkled on Otto's mountaineering hat, the one he had purchased in Bavaria several summers ago when he had journeyed there to trace his family origins. The feathers glistened from the melting snowflakes.

"Mrs. Dixon, any mail or messages?" asked the principal.

"Quite a lot, I'm afraid, and they're all on your desk, sir."

Surveying the mountain of paper on his desk, Otto winced, exclaiming, "Good heavens! I see I am about to pay for my inadvertent vacation. But it's a fair trade, because it was the first real vacation I've had in years. I've never felt better. I could climb a mountain, and I happen to be wearing just the hat for it."

"So I noticed. It does become you."

"Well, I never guessed I'd be wearing it when I climbed through a mountain of paper. I'd better get to it. Did Melvin tackle any of it?"

"No, sir. I'm afraid he just sat in your office with the door closed and the lights off. He says he has lost his nerve."

"Lost his nerve? Now that doesn't sound like the Melvin Dandy I know. What on earth has happened?"

"It's a long story, sir. It has a little to do with the Gang of Four, and a lot to do with Mr. Dandy's insistence on following protocols to the very last letter."

Otto nodded sympathetically. "Melvin doesn't typically leave room for surprises, does he?"

"Well, he *was* surprised, sir. In fact, he was flabbergasted."

Mrs. Dixon recounted Melvin Dandy's contretemps with the fire department. A knowing grin emerged on Otto's face.

Otto shook his head in conclusion, observing, "Poor Melvin. He must have been horribly embarrassed. I'm sure he was doing his best, but he's a little high strung and too easily rattled. I must go down later and tell him how much I appreciated that very fine card. By the way, what's that sitting over there on top of the intercom system?"

"Oh, I almost forgot, sir. The Gang of Four brought that in, right after school opened this morning. It's supposed to be some sort of welcome back surprise for you. That young boy, Sean Potter, the one who's father is the famous scientist, asked if he could plug it into our general intercom system. I told him I didn't know anything about that, and he'd have to talk to you. Then he inspected the intercom system and said it would be fine, and that he would connect it so you could use it. I asked him if he knew what he was doing, and he said something about not having two Ph.D.'s, but that he would try his best to attach the device the right way. Just then his sister kicked him, and David Andrews scolded her, and then they all thanked me and left."

"Those Potter twins are quite remarkable," said Otto. "I suspect that their combined I.Q. scores easily reach well into the three hundreds. Let's go see what they brought us."

Otto and Mrs. Dixon approached the object sitting on top of the intercom, Otto unveiling the purple cloth cover. Beneath the cloth lay a handsome, varnished wooden box, with two large toggle switches on the front, one red, the other blue. A bronze plaque on top was engraved as follows:

To Mr. Otto Ferlinghausen, Principal

upon his return to Midville Middle School

we present Greetings & Felicitations together with

this Air Raid - Take Cover Siren Module.

This module connects to the public address system.

Air Raid = Red; All Clear = Blue

Affectionately, the Gang of Four

"Just look at that! The engraving alone must have cost them a young fortune!" exclaimed Otto.

"How thoughtful!" said Mrs. Dixon, "I wonder if it works?"

Otto gave a sly smile. "There's only one way to find out. I suspect there are four students out there waiting for my 'thank you'. And this is December seventh, isn't it? The anniversary of the attack on Pearl Harbor? How *very* appropriate. I suppose the date is a fortunate coincidence, although I wouldn't put anything past that Gang of Four. I also once knew a spirited Baptist lady who, under these circumstances, would say, 'Let 'er rip.' So, Mrs. Dixon, what do you say?"

Mrs. Dixon, giving one of her engaging smiles and looking very much the Baptist lady indeed, answered, "I agree, sir. Let 'er rip."

"As soon as I've thrown this toggle switch, please call Mrs. Fullerton at the guidance office. Ask her to tell Mr. Dandy that a surprise air raid drill is afoot, and that we desperately need his help in notifying the members of our school community."

Without further ado, Otto threw the switch.

* * * * * *

In a phrase, Sean's siren module proved 'most awesome'. With dissonant pitches set at blood-curdling low frequencies, no hearer could confuse its eerie wail with anything but the announcement of the apocalypse itself. Rising slowly from the depths, it crested, falling slowly, only to rise again. Puzzled faculty peered from their classrooms. Curious and perplexed, Mr. Dandy, who had been hiding in his office reading the library's *New York Times,* emerged from his office, and then strode through the outer office's door into the cafeteria.

"Mr. Dandy! Mr. Dandy!" cried a frantic Mrs. Fullerton, "the office is on the phone. This is a surprise air raid drill, and they say they need your help in notifying everyone! What are we to do?"

Melvin Dandy now stood near the apex of his next to finest hour.

"Air ... raid ... drill?" he stammered, for he had enough of drills of all kinds.

"Yes! A sneak alert like the sneak attack on Pearl Harbor! Today is December seventh! It's the anniversary of that attack."

A fleeting, decisiveness entered into Melvin Dandy's eyes. "Mrs. Fullerton, you go door to door on the first floor announcing the alert. I'll announce it to the classrooms facing on to the cafeteria."

Running back to his office, Mr. Dandy emerged, momentarily, sporting his antiquated air raid helmet.

"Air raid! Air raid!" he shouted, hoping to rouse responses from faculty and students in the classrooms surrounding the auditorium-cafeteria. Faculty members, however, continued to stare from their classroom doors in confusion. Wasn't this the very same Dandy who had cried 'wolf-fire' little more than a week ago? The haunting siren continued its eerie song, rising and falling like death itself.

Meanwhile, Melvin Dandy continued to stand in the center of the cafeteria shouting to his colleagues, "Air raid! Air raid! Are you all deaf?" Dandy himself would later describe their inaction, stating that they had remained as 'stiff as pokers'.

Running back into his office, Melvin Dandy emerged again with a boat horn in each hand, both horns blazing away. In the confusions of that critical moment, one honk was worth a thousand words. Faculty members, remembering the last air raid drill and signal, promptly ordered their students into the hallways to brace themselves against all available lockers and walls.

Mrs. Fullerton, still talking with her hands, had by this time successfully alerted classes on the first floor, as well as faculty and students in the north wing by the library, which was on the second floor, and had now returned to the cafeteria to see Melvin Dandy still honking away. It soon became apparent that only the counselor was now sounding the alert, since the school's new siren had ceased its dramatic wailing. And the only way Mrs. Fullerton could silence Melvin Dandy was to go up and forcibly pull his right arm down to his waist.

"Eh? What are you doing? There's an air raid on," scolded the counselor.

"Sir, the main office has stopped signaling. Why don't we stop to see if they will make an announcement about the drill's being over?"

"Eh? Very well. Maybe we should call them. Go call them."

Mrs. Fullerton left to telephone the Main Office.

An eerie silence predominated in the cafeteria-auditorium, with students braced against the walls and in some places even layered on top of each other. It is amazing how long a few seconds can seem under such circumstances.

Mrs. Fullerton approached Mr. Dandy and whispered, "They're going to signal the 'All clear', sir."

Suddenly the sound of an electronic horn with oscillating pitches broke the silence. "All clear," shouted the counselor. "All clear, All clear. Return to your classes!"

After the signal stopped, Otto Ferlinghausen's voice could be heard on the public address system, "All students and faculty may now return to their classes. I want to extend my congratulations and thanks to the entire school community for its most resourceful response to this surprise air raid alert. I also say a hearty 'thank you' to all of you for the lovely card you sent to me during my recent convalescence."

David and the other members of the Gang of Four worked very hard during lunch period to prepare a special edition of *Bare Fax* for the next morning. David had been excused from two of his morning classes to prepare articles for the paper. —Under such circumstances, he mused to himself, —it doesn't hurt to have a 98% average.

In the special edition being prepared, Audrey Vanderkamp was quoted thus, "Oh! That dreadful siren was just horrible, and it gave me the worst goose bumps. But the All Clear signal sounded like those European police cars you see only in the most expensive movies, and all of the boys were *so* brave, and now I hope we can still have our school dance on Friday." Gertrude Coachman said, "I was very shocked by the drill, and still feel very, very queasy." She was unable to see her words in print on Friday, for she had begun to feel 'coldie' Thursday night and had called Mr. Ferlinghausen at four o'clock in the morning to say she wouldn't be able to meet her classes. Mr. White was quoted as grumbling, "It's all folderol, but the *one* thing that would improve it would be to get rid of all that wretched honking."

Despite this slight to the well-intentioned efforts of Melvin Dandy, banner headlines were written to transform the counselor from a laughing stock into the Counselor-Who-Saved-The-Day, thereby helping him to restore an iota of his lost nerve together with a ton of his dignity. The *Bare Fax Special Edition* headlines proclaimed:

SURPRISE AIR RAID DRILL CONFUSES ENTIRE SCHOOL; COUNSELOR DANDY SAVES DAY BY NOTIFYING FACULTY AND STUDENTS BY QUICK AND DECISIVE HONKING!

Smaller leads for additional articles read: 'New Siren Supersedes Primitive Boat Horns' and 'New Alarm Signals Donated by Sean Potter'. Sean received six orders that same day for identical alarm modules from six of Midville Middle School's more rapacious students.

After school The Gang of Four finished copying and stapling the pages of Friday's special edition of *Bare Fax,* leaving school at three forty-five. They were pleased that Mr. Ferlinghausen had embraced his surprise gift. Although they were exhausted, they now faced the Great Canasta Showdown, for Bobby, Zeke, and Danny Taylor would soon be arriving at Aunt Lillian's for the long anticipated contest.

* * * * *

The competition between David and Bobby, begun in October with a formal, white glove challenge, proceeded to a sober and focused conclusion. A canasta playoff would seem an anticlimax for those not personally acquainted with the vagaries of the game, but to the seven adolescents who sat around Lillian Biggs' dining room table, a moment of shared truth and inner triumph had arrived.

Bobby and David had done their best to master what innumerable lucid seers, on their very deathbeds, have described as 'that awful little game'. Both boys were very intuitive, and this would stand each in good stead as the game unfolded. As for the general and relative degree of bloodthirstiness indigenous to each player, for many adolescents are naturally inclined in that direction, David and Bobby, on a scale of one to ten, would weigh in at three and six, respectively, with Sean, their junior partner-in-crime weighing in at a robust thirteen.

Aunt Lillian, who had taken counsel with the Gang of Four, had acceded to their request that this Canasta Showdown be played around her dining room table, since it was both formal and large. Bobby and David sat across from each other, closest to the kitchen, with Sean sitting next to them at the end of the table. Sean, the irrepressible, had been appointed Game Master, in hope that any title, however fatuous, might serve the better to bridle him.

Aunt Lillian, for all now called her that, sat a little farther down the table, next to Bobby. Lisa and Mary sat behind David, with Zeke and Danny sitting behind Bobby. Since Sean had been appointed Game Master, Zeke had also been appointed Official Monitor, presumably to watch the Game Master lest he pull out any sort of firearm and proceed to threaten the assembly.

Sean's natural instinct for canasta, as well as his mastery of the game, made him the perfect choice for Game Master. He was charged with seeing that the cards would be shuffled at least eight times and that the proper number of cards would be dealt. Additionally, Sean, in consultation with Aunt Lillian, would decide all manner of disputes and disagreements that might arise from the game.

"The game will now begin," proclaimed Sean, standing in front of his chair. "Players, please assume your positions."

Sean stood solemnly, as if he were holding a knight's sword, until David and Bobby shook hands and sat down.

Without saying a word, Sean stepped over to Zeke and let him examine a coin. Zeke nodded his approval. Sean returned to his place and remained standing, "We will now flip for first deal," said Sean. "Bobby, you call it."

"Heads," said Bobby.

Sean flipped the quarter with ease. "Heads wins it," he announced, showing the quarter to everyone. Even Max and 'Her Majesty' bore witness to the toss.

Taking the two decks, Bobby began to shuffle them as Sean sat down.

An expectant silence had fallen over the group. After eight shuffles, David cut the deck, and Bobby carefully dealt out two piles of fifteen cards each.

"Gentlemen, you may pick up your hands and begin the game," said Sean.

David felt a sinking feeling in his stomach as Sean uttered these words and wondered why. It wasn't that the long awaited game was finally a reality. There was something more. As he organized his hand, David glanced occasionally at the Little Hoodlum seated to his right. In Sean's countenance he saw, more clearly than ever, a young and noble warrior. It was clear, that in accepting the office of Game Master, Sean had embraced the obligatory honor among thieves' position of uncompromising neutrality.

As he apprehended this, David suddenly felt an acute sense of loss. Yes, it was exasperating to recall how many times Sean had beaten him in this 'awful little game'. David had grimly accepted this continual bludgeoning, though, in hope of some day he might win. But now, something was different, even though Sean was still most capable of bludgeoning whomever or whatever he pleased. No, it was something else. Sean was *very* good at whatever he chose to do, and he was *very* passionate. Was it his neutrality? That must have something to do with it. Sean had been named to the position of Game Master the better to bridle his sometimes dramatic responses to the progress of any canasta game. David had, from this strategy, lost Sean's loyalty. *That* was what was missing. David now desperately missed that support, which he had counted on more than he had known, if only for distraction's sake. He now realized a sobering insight—that, as Game Master, Sean was being, and would remain, absolutely neutral.

This troubling perception rattled David. In so cut-throat a game as canasta, Sean had demonstrated himself to be *very* capable of cutting his opponent's throat, even relishing the opportunity. If dire push came to shove, canasta notwithstanding, and it fell to Sean to cut David's throat, David was sure that Sean would most probably practice on Bobby's and Zeke's throats first, to insure that he gave David's throat the very best slash. Then he would probably cut Mary's throat as an afterthought, sorry that he hadn't thought to cut it just before Zeke's, for more practice. David now saw how much he had really been depending on Sean to save him from defeat, and how shortsighted he had been to assent to Sean's being named Game Master. But the die was cast. —I've cooked my own goose, thought David. And what did this say about David's sense of justice and fair play? Before David could fathom this new dilemma, a voice called to him.

"Okay, David, it's your play," announced Sean. "Draw two cards."

David looked at Sean, who was smiling at him, but who had also smiled the same way when he had instructed Bobby to shuffle.

"Go ahead," Sean encouraged.

David drew. Two red threes! And with one in his hand already, David melded the three red threes, drawing three bonus cards. Everyone gasped, and Bobby gulped. David then drew a four and two deuces to replace the red threes. —What a fine beginning, thought David, as he discarded the four.

Bobby melded his one red three, thoroughly destroying any hope David may have had for acquiring all four red threes and the eight hundred bonus points that came with them. Bobby discarded a five.

Each player continued to draw and discard for a long time. David had a lot of wild cards, but few pairs. Bobby had a number of pairs, but very few wild cards. The discard pile became increasingly attractive. Finally, Bobby smiled as he melded three aces, and then discarded a black three. David drew, and discarded a six. Suddenly, Bobby's hand clamped with such vigor on top of the discard pile that Lisa jumped. The growing tension was broken, and there were several sighs and whispers.

"I guess I got that one," said Bobby, as he melded a joker and a six.

"The old one and a wild trick," observed Sean, dispassionately.

David sighed. He had been foolish not to remember how easy it was to meld with a deuce and one card, provided the discard pile was not frozen and one had already melded. Bobby had not forgotten, and had gotten himself an admirable haul. The game continued, with David making two mixed canastas and laying down several pairs with his many wild cards. Bobby made two natural canastas and one mixed, owing to his vast accumulation of cards. David was finally able to go out. As both boys tallied their scores for Basic and Count, Sean watched like a hawk, for he was also Official Scorekeeper.

"Fourteen hundred and seventy-five," said David

Bobby smiled. "Eighteen hundred twenty," he announced proudly.

"David, you will have to meld only fifty during this next hand. Bobby, you will have to meld ninety," said Sean.

Max, who had been lying under Sean's chair, crawled over under David's chair and offered an affectionate nudge.

David shuffled the cards eight times, Bobby cut, and David dealt the second hand.

Bobby now encountered difficulty because he held many cards of low count. David took full advantage of this, using several high pairs to pick three small packs, and thus lay out an impressive board for himself. Bobby was finally able to meld, using a joker and two aces. Bobby then froze the discard pile, hoping it would prevent David from taking more cards. David had five aces in his hand and discarded three of them. Bobby discarded two black threes and a deuce. David countered with a deuce. Then Bobby drew an ace and, thinking all of the aces were out, discarded it to David, who promptly seized the pack. Again sighs and coughs broke the tension that had pervaded the room. This turned out to be David's hand, for with four mixed canastas and one red three, together with an impressive count, he added 1,760 points to his score for a running total of 3,235. Bobby could only manage one mixed canasta and two red threes, thus adding 830 points to his score for a running total of 2,650.

"We will now take a fifteen minute break," announced Sean.

Suddenly the room erupted in conversation.

"Guess you're ahead," said Bobby to David.

"For now. But this game changes like the weather," David encouraged.

"It's rainin' for me right now," said Bobby.

"Yes. But you've got the advantage of only having to meld 90 next hand, where I've got to come up with 120. It isn't easy to come up with all those points if you don't have a couple of jokers."

"Here, have some soda," said Sean, handing glasses of cola to Bobby and David.

"Thanks," said Bobby.

David accepted the soda from Sean with a mild bow.

"It ain't no ordinary game, you know," said Bobby, making a sweeping gesture to the two piles of cards on the table.

"No. I sometimes wish I'd never learned how to play," said David, looking at Sean. "What I hate most is having potentially good cards but no wild cards to go with them."

"It ain't right when one player hogs all the wild cards," agreed Bobby.

"But it's the way the game sometimes goes," said David, adding, "and I think there are a few people who must have magnets in them that draw wild cards. Sean is very lucky that way."

Sean looked a little abashed, and this was the more remarkable since he very rarely, if ever, felt embarrassed. "I've had some good hands," he said, "but now it's time to get back to the Canasta Showdown. Gentlemen, good luck to you both."

The three boys shook hands and sat down. Sean picked up the little silver table bell that Aunt Lillian had lent to him, ringing it to signal the recommencement of the game.

After five draws, Bobby was able to make a solid meld of 90, using three aces and three tens. David had cards of mostly lower denominations and couldn't meld, thus lamenting his earlier prophecy about how hard it might be to meld 120. Bobby took several packs and melded two red threes. David drew and melded two red threes and drew twice more, shouting, "All right!"

Everyone around the table wondered if David had drawn two jokers.

David smiled as he promptly melded two jokers and five fives, thus melding and making a canasta at the same time. Bobby countered by adding two deuces to his five tens, and then two deuces and a joker to his four aces. Several turns later David laid most of his cards down, including five eights, to which he added two deuces. Bobby drew, and gave a great sigh, and then promptly placed an entire natural canasta of fours on the board. David went out the following turn.

The running scores after both Basic and Count were added were: Bobby, 4615; David, 4310.

The game was very close, and everyone knew that anything could happen, for David was little more than a mixed canasta behind Bobby. Sean declared a five minute recess. Bobby left the table and went to the bathroom. David stood up, pacing nervously back and forth in front of the bay windows, as Lisa walked beside him.

"I didn't think the game would be so close," she began.

"I'm grateful to be holding my own," answered David. "Playing with Sean has certainly prepared me for losing. And Bobby is *really* good at this game. Aunt Lillian wasn't kidding when she said he was a quick study."

"David, no matter what happens, you've already won," said Lisa.

"Thanks. I think so, too. Any suggestions for the final round?"

"Concentrate and don't be distracted," said Lisa.

"You're right," said David. "I *am* a little rattled."

Sean rang the table bell with surprising majesty, and all returned to their chairs.

David shuffled the cards, Bobby cut, and then David dealt out the two piles of fifteen. Both boys drew and discarded for half a dozen turns, each drawing and melding two red threes. Finally, Bobby, after drawing, gave a broad smile and melded six aces. David's eyes widened, and two turns later he melded with a joker with four kings and three eights.

"David," Bobby began, "remember the fun we had on Halloween? I ain't never gonna forget that night, and I bet Zeke and Sean ain't gonna forget it neither."

David felt himself flush in embarrassment, and wondered how red his face was getting. Aunt Lillian, who was sitting to the right of Bobby, didn't seem to take notice.

"Best part of that night," Bobby continued, "was when we lobbed those marshmallows at the old dame's house, and then she struts off the porch and begins eatin' 'em like the fat, old pig she really is."

Zeke laughed in recollection. David felt perspiration on his forehead and neck. He melded some queens, jacks, and nines, finishing his kings, making a mixed canasta. "Guess I got the high cards this hand," he said, desperately hoping to change the subject.

But Sean's blood was up, now that Bobby had recounted some of their glorious exploits, and the Game Master added, "The best part of Halloween for me was when that gritty honey-marshmallow bomb sailed right through the old bag's cheap window. Crash! And then all of us hiding under that ratty old boat when that police cruiser came down the street, and then those two officers chasing us up over the hedge when we broke for the water tower."

David looked sheepishly at Aunt Lillian, who was smiling at him as if she had not heard a single word Sean had just uttered. Mary, however, was frowning at her brother, trying to get his attention.

Discarding a seven, David said, "Looks as if I'm ahead, doesn't it?"

Bobby slammed his hand down so hard on the table that everyone, except Sean, jumped. All eyes followed Bobby's hand, as it shaped itself into a claw and picked up the enormous discard pile.

"Not any more, you ain't," said Bobby. "Just look at my pack!"

Bobby proceeded to meld most of his cards and finished the aces with a deuce. He had six sevens and five fives and finished both as mixed canastas by adding deuces.

"That's all my wild cards 'cept one I'm savin'," said Bobby, giving David a black three.

David, by now, had lost his concentration and general orientation and decided he should try to put down as many cards as possible. He melded most of his wild cards and high cards, and then discarded a nine to Bobby.

Drawing, Bobby gave a joyful yelp. Aunt Lillian had heard this sound before, and she knew the game would soon be over.

Suddenly, all of Bobby's cards were on the table. He had gone out.

David sat dumbstruck. The multiple recountings of their Halloween escapades had not exactly helped him to concentrate. He had not played this last hand to advantage, but Bobby certainly had.

Looking into Bobby's eyes, David suddenly realized that he had been had. The Halloween references had been Bobby's ace in the hole all along, should the game prove close. And Bobby had planned his strategy well, and had played his hand like an expert.

Sean rang the table bell again, announcing, "The official final score is: Bobby Perkins: 5845; David Andrews, 5260. I hereby declare Bobby Perkins the winner of this Canasta Showdown!"

After an enthusiastic round of applause, hands were shaken all around, perhaps the very way hands are shaken in the secret enclaves of the Supreme Court just before *they* sit down to play canasta.

Cheese twists and sodas were brought out, and the room erupted in conversation.

"Bobby, when do you want David to be your slave?" asked Sean.

This question appeared to flummox Bobby, who seemed to have forgotten the prize promised to the winner of the Canasta Showdown.

"Slave?" he said blankly.

"Yes," reminded Sean, "You've won the Canasta Showdown. So, now, David must, according to the rules, serve as your slave for an *entire* day. How about this Saturday?"

"Saturday?" asked Bobby.

"Yes," continued Sean, gleefully, "David could come over to your house really early and wait on you hand and foot all day long. You could live like a king for a whole day."

Sean stopped short when he noticed David's icy glare.

Bobby looked at David, saying, "Guess I forgot all 'bout the slave stuff, since I was so busy learnin' the game. Never expected I'd win, anyway."

"Well, you won," said David. "By hook, or by crook, you sure did. When do you want me to come? Saturday okay?"

Bobby seemed to consult an internal calendar.

"Okay," he said, "but come about eleven."

"All right," said David. "It's the gas station on the east side of town, about four miles from here?"

"Yes. That's the place. We live in the little buildin' behind it. My dad doesn't work on weekends. So come around eleven. Okay?"

"I'll be there," said David, shaking hands with Bobby once again, adding, "Good game."

"Thanks," said Bobby.

* * * * *

After everyone had left, David looked at Aunt Lillian.

"I'm planning to make restitution to Mrs. Coachman for her broken window at Christmas, in an anonymous sort of way," he announced.

"Some things are best done anonymously," smiled Aunt Lillian.

"You didn't seem surprised to hear about our Halloween adventures," said David.

"I wasn't. Bobby told me all about your adventures long ago."

"That little stinker," David frowned.

"Remember, David, I told you Bobby has become very trusting of me, and he has told me everything about himself from the beginning, everything except his home life, that is. *You'll* discover that."

Chapter Twenty-Two
Slave for a Day

O N SATURDAY, DECEMBER 9, A DUSTING OF SNOW had delicately covered bushes and trees. The wafting wind was crisp and cold enough for David to don his wool scarf and ski hat along with his winter jacket. As David approached the Perkins' Garage, he saw Bobby standing out in front, waiting for him. The garage was built of white brick, to which a wood extension had been attached, almost as an afterthought, and David guessed this was where Bobby and his father lived. White posterboard appeared in the garage window, with red letters scrawled on it: **NO GAS SOLD HERE** and below that **CLOSED ON WEAKENDS AND HOLIDAYS**.

David wondered whether Bobby or his father had made the sign.

"Hey, Slave!" Bobby said cheerfully, waving.

David waved in return, saying, "Good morning," as he approached.

"My dad's asleep so I says let's David and me go into town and mess around. How's that sound?"

"Fine with me," said David.

"I ain't never had a slave before so you got to show me the particulars," said Bobby.

"I've never *been* a slave before," said David. "What do you want me to do for you today?"

"Just be with me. I ain't much good at makin' up fun, but I guess we could always play more canasta, if reduced that low."

David's spirit soared. Bobby not only had a genuine sense of humor, he also had the tact to smooth over David's defeat in the Canasta Showdown. David wondered briefly what Sean might have required of a slave. His imagination conjured up a scene of some poor devil tied to a chair, waiting to be impaled with numerous arrows and then roundly riddled with bullets.

"I hope I ain't got you in no trouble over spillin' the beans about what we did to that old pig Coachman," continued Bobby.

"After you left, Aunt Lillian told me that you spilled those beans to her right after Halloween," answered David.

"But strictly confidential, so you wouldn't be the goat," Bobby hastened to clarify. "Strictly confidential."

"I wasn't the goat, but I still feel a little guilty about the broken window."

"Ain't a good window that breaks so fragile-like anyway," said Bobby.

"Well, I've decided to send the old hag a Christmas present," announced David.

"Don't do that! She'll know who did it! And once she gets on your back, she ain't never gonna get off again. Like a big fat beemoth suffocatin' your lungs."

"Behemoth," David corrected.

"Behemoth," repeated Bobby. "Anyway, what are ya gonna send her, maybe some pig slop? She'd really go nuts over that."

"No. I've ordered a special book that's out-of-print. It's a collection of poems by Mr. Vachel Lindsay, her favorite poet. He was a poet who killed himself."

"Must've been right after he met the old pig," said Bobby, adding, "I always thought she was her own favorite poet."

"That may be true in a deeper sense," said David, weighing the wisdom of Bobby's insight. "You know, you're smart. You just haven't read very many books."

"I ain't smart, and I ain't a brain, but I think on my feet," said Bobby.

"You sure thought on your feet yesterday when you started talking about Halloween, making me lose my concentration and all. I should have won that last hand."

Bobby grinned. "I know. See, I knew I probably couldn't beat you fair and square, but all's fair in love and war, they say, don't they?"

"I guess so," David said grudgingly. Then he laughed.

"Why ya laughing?"

"At you. You're a slyboots," said David.

"Nobody never called me a slyboots before," said Bobby. "What does that mean?"

"It means you think on your feet," said David.

"Oh, well, I guess I'm a slyboots then," said Bobby. "You hungry?"

"Sort of. I had breakfast around eight," said David.

"I ain't had no breakfast. Never do. But I got some dough an' it's tellin' me we could eat decent at the diner near the bus station. How 'bout it?"

"I don't have any money ... " began David.

"*I* have money," Bobby proudly proclaimed, "an' since you're my slave, I got to take care of you, ain't I? I ain't no ne'er-do-well."

The diner was not crowded, and the boys sat in one of its tacky and tattered booths, whose plastic upholstery was cracked. It was obvious the gum chewing waitress knew Bobby, because she brought David a menu and asked Bobby, "Who's your new buddy?"

"This is David," said Bobby, "and David, this is Shirley. She always lets me have the straight scoop on what's good and what's rotten. What's decent today?"

"Well, our regular hot turkey sandwich with gravy and fries is a fair bet, and we just got in some new hamburger buns. The chili's not bad. But stay away from the pot roast, it's three days old and has whiskers on it."

Bobby looked at David, who was studying the menu.

"I think I'd like a cheeseburger, with fries, if that's okay?" David said, looking at Bobby for approval.

"And why not two big colas, too? I'll take the hot turkey sandwich, which is *my* favorite, with extra gravy on the fries an' a side order of peas."

After Shirley left, David surveyed the diner. It appeared to be a reasonably clean place, although a greasy film colored the Formica table. The faded yellow curtains protected plastic plants, and the jukebox was playing country western music. Three men guzzled coffee as they draped themselves over the diner's counter, while two women gossiped in a booth next to the rest rooms.

"You come here often?" David asked Bobby.

"Yeah. Almost ev'ry Saturday and Sunday. My Dad sleeps a lot on weekends, so I come here to eat."

"Do they treat you well?"

"Yeah. It ain't too bad. They're pretty nice here. The food ain't the Taj Mahal, but it ain't skid row, neither."

"Does your dad give you the money to come?"

"Sorta. He ain't really aware I come. He's usually asleep. Outa sight, outa mind, you know."

David wasn't at all sure that he knew.

"Gentlemen, your lunch is served. *Bon appetit*," said Shirley, placing their respective plates in front of them.

After she left, Bobby whispered, "She always says that 'bonpeteet', and it drives me nuts, 'cause I ain't got no inklin' as to what she's drivin' at, an' I ain't gonna show her I got no culture."

"*Bon appetit* is French for 'good appetite'," David explained. "It means she hopes we enjoy our food."

"Hey, David, you can eat in two languages, and probably a lot more," Bobby admired.

The food was delicious. David thought he had never tasted a better cheeseburger anywhere, and acknowledged his gratitude to Bobby, saying, "The food here is great!"

"Ain't much of a dump to look at, but who comes to look? They's in the eatin' business an' knows how to crank it out, and it ain't dirt cheap, but it ain't the world, either," said Bobby.

"Thanks for treating me to lunch, Bobby. I wish I had brought some money to help," said David.

"Hey! You're my slave, ain't you? I got to take care of you 'til I free you, which will be sometime this afternoon, so don't have regrets, just enjoy bein' a slave for a while," said Bobby.

"What do you want to do now?" asked David.

Bobby had just left a dollar tip and looked up.

"Well, I see in the paper there's a good flick at the theater. I still have 'nough dough for a show an' popcorn. How 'bout it?"

"What's the show?" asked David.

"Somethin' by Disney. I like everythin' by Disney 'cause I know it's all gonna turn out okay, and the bad guys are gonna get theirs, and the good guys are gonna end up happy."

David nodded assent and thought, as they headed for the theater, how ironic it was that the school's most notorious bully would prefer

Disney movies to the violent fare generally offered to teen audiences. Sean, in contrast, would no doubt prefer to see the bloodiest and most violent of movies, especially if they involved shooting.

The movie turned out to be *The Fox and the Hound*. The boys stopped at a bakery on their way back to Bobby's, and Bobby bought half a dozen sugar donuts for them to eat. There were small tables available and Bobby also ordered two glasses of milk before they sat down and gorged themselves.

"Great movie," said Bobby.

"Yeah," agreed David, adding "I'd never seen it before."

"It's been around before. Ya know, in a way, it reminds me of us," said Bobby.

"How so?"

"Well, I sorta look like the little hound, with my flat nose and dog ears. And you look a little like the young fox, with your red hair, freckles, and nose. Anyway, the movie reminded me of us."

"Yeah, you're right. People sometimes resemble animals, don't they?" agreed David.

"Yeah. Like that dame Coachman. She's the queen of the pigs, if there ever was one," Bobby grinned.

"How about Mr. Dandy?" asked David.

Bobby's face suddenly darkened in contempt.

"What did I say?" asked David.

"Wouldn't insult *no* animal by comparin' it to that n'er-do-well," said Bobby.

David was again astounded at Bobby's keen perception of people, especially since it seemed so uncannily accurate.

"How about Mr. Ferlinghausen?" asked David.

Bobby thought a minute, then said, "A bear for sure. He ain't as hairy as a real bear 'cause he's bald, but he walks like one and he's pretty jolly. Any bears bald?"

"I don't think so," said David. "Maybe in Australia. I've heard they've got almost everything imaginable over there."

"It'd be *great* to go over there!" said Bobby, his eyes brightening. David nodded.

"Why don't we? We could run away together. I ain't kiddin'. With your brains and my brawn, we could make a killin'."

"I think I'd just as soon finish my schooling first," said David. "They say there's more opportunity the more schooling you have."

"Yeah. Tell me. You'll be sittin' on the Supreme Court makin' a bundle, and I'll be sweepin' the streets here in Midville. I can't fault ya. I even hope ya make good, David."

"You'll make good, too, Bobby," David encouraged.

"Naw. I'm stupid. Dandy-Pandy told me so when I went in for my career talk with him last May. Said I should plan to quit school at sixteen and join the service. 'That will be your salvation'," Bobby intoned in imitation of the counselor, repeating, 'That will be your salvation.' I was so mad, I saw red. I may not be smart, but I know I'm not dumb, 'specially if you're comparin' me to the likes of him. What a joke! So I tells him as much, and he yells, 'In the old days, they would 've thrown you into prison just on your looks alone', so I says, 'And *you* into the nuthouse'. Then he gets really hot, and jumps up on his little high horse, and shoots out from behind his desk and pushes me up against his file cabinet, tryin' to look the tough man he's not. Then he squints those beady eyes at me, and waves his little crooked finger up into my face, and tells me he has three degrees and is dignified and deserves respect. And I says I shows respect to wise people, not fools. And he says I should shut my mouth, or he'll shut it for me, and I says,

'Try it, buster, and I'll twist you into a pretzel and serve you for breakfast.' And he pulls back to hit me a good crack across my face, and I ain't sayin' I ain't deserved it, but I just steps back, and WHAM!, he slams his hand into the file cabinet and screams, 'I'm kilt! Oh, mercy mild! Call a doctor!' Then his flitty secretary runs in and looks at me like I just shot 'im, and sometimes I wish I had, but I never even laid a finger on 'im, although, mind ya, I was just itchin' to. I only steps back a little. And then, holdin' his hurt little hand with his left paw as if it was broke, he goes runnin' up and down that stinkin' little hole he calls his office, makin' quite the spectacle of himself, yellin' that he'll have me in reform school by nightfall, and that prison is too good for me."

David's eyes were wide with amazement. Although a diamond in the rough, Bobby was a raconteur of the first order, a real storyteller.

"Gosh! What did you do then?" asked David.

"I done the only reasonable thing a person could do. I walks out and slams the door real hard."

"What happened?"

"Ferlinghausen catches up with me later that period an' tells me to follow 'im to his office, and, as I go in, I notice that little runt Dandy-Pandy cowerin' behind Ferlinghausen's chair, like he's afraid I'm gonna go after 'im. And Ferlinghausen asks me what happened, and I tells him straight out. Then Dandy-Pandy gets his swig at it. Then Ferlinghausen says I should show some respect to faculty. And then I says I don't give no hoot who's faculty, or who's student, or who's the man in the moon, but I tries to show respect to thems as deserve respect. And then I glare real hard at that little Rumpelstiltskin, cowering behind the *real* man's chair. But my speech makes Dandy-Pandy turn red in the face, and he puffs up like a little hen and holds his nose up high an' says he's too dignified to be talked to like that an' deserves an apology. And then he says he wants me to call 'im doctor. Then I notice Ferlinghausen groaning and holding his head, so I looks at Dandy-Pandy and says, '*Are* you a doctor?' And he says, 'I didn't finish my list oration—'"

"Dissertation—" David corrected.

"Dissertation. See, David. *You're* really smart, not like that Dandy-Pandy fop," said Bobby grinning, adding, "I learned 'fop' from when our class read Shakespeare, which I really liked, what I understood. Anyway, I puts it to Dandy-Pandy real formal like, '*Are* you a doctor, or are you *not* a doctor?' I puts it to him plain and simple. And he says, 'I've fifty hours.' And I says, 'I don't wanna know the time. Are you a doctor and, if so, what kind of doctor?'"

"Gosh, what'd he say?"

"He puffs himself up even more than before and says, 'I'm almost a Doctor of Education.' Then he gives all this bull about never finishing his his … disser … ta..tion 'cause he was too dedicated to his students an' wasn't gonna shortchange nobody. And I says, it's a good thing he's not a doctor, and he says, 'Why?' And I says, ''Cause callin' *you* a doctor is like callin' a teddy bear a grizzly.'"

David's mouth dropped open in astonishment.

"Then I gets to see his Dandy-Pandy face fall and see his double chin jiggle up and down, and he turns to Ferlinghausen and says, '*See* the incidence—'"

"Insolence," said David.

"Maybe that was it," continued Bobby, "which I take to mean no respect, 'cause I ain't got no respect for that little weasel, beggin' the pardon of real weasels everywhere, who are truly graceful and beautiful creatures. So Ferlinghausen stands up and says he's declarin' a truce between us, and that I am to take two weeks detention for my attitude."

"Did that end it?"

"Kinda. Dandy-Pandy and I keep our distance. Sorta like nitro and glycerin. I go *straight* to Ferlinghausen when I gotta problem. He's all right."

"Yeah, I think so, too. These donuts were great!"

"I still have a little money. Want some more?" asked Bobby.

"No thanks. I'm really stuffed. Thanks just the same."

"Well, it's almost three-thirty. I need to be gettin' back," said Bobby.

"But I haven't even been your slave yet," David objected.

"Nah. Don't worry 'bout it. We had a good time anyway."

"At least let me walk back with you," said David. "I'd really like to meet your dad."

"He don't let me bring no friends home," Bobby confided.

"No friends! Why not?"

"I dunno. He usually needs to sleep on weekends, and he doesn't want no noise. But I got somethin' to give ya, and I forgot it. Let's go back, and you can wait for me outside."

When the boys arrived at the gas station, Mr. Perkins' tow truck was gone.

"He's out for a spell, but I bet he'll be back soon. Let's hurry in, and then you can go," said Bobby.

The apartment behind the gas station was small, its paint peeling. The connecting passage was neither plumb nor centered. The metal door urgently needed oiling and the apartment itself was strewn with magazines, dirty clothes, chipped dishes, and broken tools.

"A *real* bachelor pad, eh?" said Bobby sarcastically.

"Who has to pick up?" asked David.

"My dad's girlfriend used to before she bolted. Got fed up with my old man. He has a nasty streak," Bobby explained.

David hesitated, but asked, "How ... how about your mother?"

"Never knew my mother. I'm a first-class bastard. She and my old man had it out, so he broke her nose and ran her off."

"Without you?" asked David in disbelief.

"She was afraid to come back 'cause my dad threatened her," said Bobby.

"How do you know that?" asked David.

"'Cause a nice woman across the street told me when I got to be ten years old. She was gettin' pretty old, and she died a year later. I really miss her. Her name was Dorothy. Only mother I'll ever know, I guess. She treated me real decent, like I was worth somethin'."

David thought how true that must have been, for Bobby's treatment of David as a slave had been one of total solicitude. Bobby Perkins' image as bully was, in fact, David now decided, quite false. But why, David wondered, did a kid as sensitive and good-hearted as Bobby get into all the scrapes for which he was so famous?

A loud screech of brakes was heard. Panic filled Bobby's eyes.

"Dad! David, go hide in that little bathroom 'til I can sneak you outa here. He'll kill me if he finds you here!"

David promptly obeyed, his heart pounding hard in his chest. From where he hid in the small bathroom, he could still see into the living room.

A boorish, brutish man, of ungainly girth and enormous neck, suddenly stood menacingly before Bobby. His clothes were crumpled and sloppy and he wore a two day old beard.

"So you're back, after all, you filthy little cheat," accused Edward Perkins, his voice straining in anger.

"Ain't no good to call me no cheat," said Bobby.

"There's two twenties missing from my wallet, and I got a mind you took 'em. Ain't I right?"

"Yeah," said Bobby, "you're right."

"Curse you!" shouted Edward Perkins as he struck Bobby hard across the face, knocking him to his knees. "Curse you to hell and back again!"

David was so afraid that his legs quivered like jelly and he found himself short of breath.

"Hittin' me ain't gonna bring no dough back," yelled Bobby.

"What d'ya squander it on?"

"Ain't none of your business. I keep the garage runnin' when I ain't in school, no thanks to you, 'cause all you can do is sit in the back room swillin' up the booze and givin' me nothin' but shit and dirt for my trouble. I figure I got it comin' to me."

"An' how long have ya been robbin' me blind?"

"Don't go callin' it no robbin' you blind 'cause it ain't. An' the more I take, the less you have to get loaded on."

This observation was almost an afterthought on Bobby's part, and he soon regretted it, for his father's hand promptly struck him full in the face, causing a burst of blood from his nose.

"Don't *never* say that to me agin!" yelled Edward Perkins. "I got to the liquor store, and couldn't buy me nothin' worth drinkin' 'cause I opens my wallet and sees a sick little fiver. And nothin' left in the house, neither! So, now, it's gonna come outa your lousy little hide! Where's my big belt buckle?"

Edward Perkins stumbled to the bedroom which lay across the living room from the bathroom. Bobby ran to the bathroom door, trying to stop the blood gushing from his nose. Looking fearfully at David, he whispered, "Go!"

David started toward the door but froze when he noticed the form of Edward Perkins blocking his path. Holding a sinister looking leather belt with a huge silver buckle, Edward Perkins regarded David in disbelief and then looked at Bobby and said, "Ain't I said I *never* want ya bringin' ya little vermin friends around here?"

"He ain't no vermin," said Bobby obstinately, adding, "This here is 'tween you and me. Leave 'im out of it."

"Who are you, you little pup?" glared Edward Perkins at David.

"My name is David Andrews," said David with more conviction that he had thought possible.

"I never knew no Andrews in Midville," said a puzzled Perkins, eyeing David suspiciously.

"I'm living with my aunt, Lillian Biggs, who lives on Biggs Street."

"Ah, the one related to the old judge?"

"Yes," said David.

"The music teacher?"

"Yes," said David.

"I know where you live, you little pup," said Edward Perkins, tightening the belt in his hands.

Although he was trembling, David took a deep breath, and said, "Mr. Perkins, I have to go home now, and I promised Aunt Lillian that Bobby would come home with me for dinner."

"The hell," said Edward Perkins, scowling at Bobby.

"She's expecting *both* of us," David persisted.

"You saucy little pup," growled Edward Perkins, "he ain't gonna go nowhere, especially with *you*."

David looked at Bobby in appeal, hoping a way could be found to escape.

"In fact, I ain't takin' a fancy to either of ya leavin' 'til I've teached ya some respect," said Edward Perkins. "I'll tan both of ya, I will," he continued, advancing on the boys, raising the belt over his head.

David's knees were sinking, and he felt sick at the sight of Bobby's bruised and bloody face. Yet as Edward Perkins advanced, Bobby automatically grabbed a small wooden crate which had served as a makeshift table, thrusting it against the senior Perkins' kneecaps.

"Ow! My knees! You little bastard," swore the senior Perkins, teetering to retain his balance. David seized the opportunity to kick the crate at him as hard as he could, causing Edward Perkins to fall to the floor. David yelled, "Come on, Bobby! Let's get out of here!"

The boys ran out of the shack, hearing drunken threats and curses as they left.

"The truck. Let's take the keys out, in case he tries to follow us," said David.

The keys were in the ignition, and the boys removed them and ran for cover behind some bushes. David felt his heart thumping wildly as they watched Edward Perkins stumble out of the shack, stagger to his truck, cursing loudly when he found the keys were gone. Returning to the garage, he picked up a rock, smashed the pane of glass next to the front door handle, and reached in to open it.

"Gonna get his second set of keys," said Bobby.

"We've got to warn Aunt Lillian," said David. "Let's go!"

Both boys followed the shortest route to Biggs Street, racing through several fields, many back yards, and over several fences. Finally, with Aunt Lillian's house in sight, both boys burst through the kitchen door, panting loudly. Aunt Lillian had been knitting in the library when she heard the noise.

"David? Is that you? Is anything wrong?" she asked

Entering the kitchen and turning the light on, she saw Bobby's swollen and bloody face, and exclaimed, "Good Lord! What's going on? Bobby, you're a mess! David, get some bandages."

"No time," panted David. "Bobby's dad's on his way here to tan us both, and he's drunk as a skunk."

Aunt Lillian's face became very stern, and she looked with great determination at the boys. Very deliberately she said, "Now listen to me carefully: *both* of you go upstairs with Max. Don't come down, no matter what happens! David, start cleaning up Bobby's face with the towels in the upstairs bathroom. Keep the bathroom door locked."

"But Aunt Lillian," protested David.

"*Don't* argue with me! *This* is an emergency. Now go! I need to make one phone call, and then I will turn out all the lights after which I will wait here in the kitchen should Mr. Perkins be foolish enough to break into our house. Now GO!"

The boys obeyed, and Max ran upstairs between their feet.

As David cleaned up Bobby's face, the boys listened for the drone of Edward Perkins' tow truck. The anticipation of his arrival brought an eerie silence. Max nuzzled his head in Bobby's lap, seeking to comfort him.

The distant rumble of the tow truck could finally be heard, and its troubled engine got louder as it got closer. Then it stopped. David clamped his hands over Max's mouth to prevent him from barking as they heard the slam of the cab door. Suddenly, a heavy pounding could be heard on the front door. Max whimpered, wanting to bark, but David quieted him. The pounding grew louder. A short pause followed. Then there was the sound of shattered glass.

"He's broken the glass in the door," said David to Bobby.

Bobby trembled in fear.

Edward Perkins reached through the broken glass, unlocked the front door, and stumbled into the foyer. Suddenly the front hall lights blazed on, causing Edward Perkins to stagger back and squint his eyes. Aunt Lillian stepped into the foyer.

Although the light still hurt his eyes, Edward Perkins looked at Aunt Lillian, growling, "Who the devil are you?"

348

"I'm Lillian Biggs, and the house into which you have just broken happens to be mine. You are now trespassing."

Edward Perkins stared stupidly at Aunt Lillian as if he couldn't comprehend her words.

"Ma boy. I know you have ma boy. He just come here with that little red-haired pup."

Aunt Lillian said nothing, but stared icily at Edward Perkins.

Suddenly he shouted, "I WANT MA BOY!"

David's hand slipped, and Max started barking.

Edward Perkins heard the sound from upstairs, and turned toward the stairwell.

"Do not go any farther," warned Aunt Lillian, stepping in front of the stairwell.

Perkins paused to consider the challenge, looking around the foyer. He noticed a large, heavy cane in the umbrella rack that had once belonged to Judge Biggs. He stepped back, grabbed it and, lifting it over his head, shouted to Aunt Lillian, "Move, woman, while ya still can!"

"I've *got* to help Aunt Lillian," said David, opening the bathroom door. As the boys reached the top of the stairs, there was a very ugly sight below. Edward Perkins had a large cane raised over Aunt Lillian's head as he advanced toward the stairwell. He grabbed her arm to shove her out of the way and, as she began to resist, he shoved her to the floor.

An ominous growl caught his attention. He looked up the stairwell to see Max hurtling toward him. Max leapt from the fifth step and, as they collided, Edward Perkins brought down the judge's cane like a thunderbolt.

David screamed, "NO!", racing down the stairs to tackle the senior Perkins, knocking him off his feet and slamming his head against the side of the front door which still lay open to the winter cold. Perkins eyes went wide and his mouth opened. He breathed hard for a few seconds, and then turned on his side, attempting to get up.

David couldn't understand why Max hadn't advanced to corner the fallen Perkins. Instinctively, David reached for the judge's cane, raising it over Edward Perkin's head, "If you get up, so help me, I'll smash your brains in!"

"Everyone *freeze* in the name of the law!" commanded an authoritarian voice. David looked up to see Midville's Chief of Police Gordon Craig training his revolver on Edward Perkins.

Edward Perkins was now sober enough to raise his hands.

David turned to make sure Aunt Lillian was all right, his heart going cold as he saw her and Bobby kneeling beside Max, blood staining the carpet near Max's mouth.

As Gordon Craig handcuffed Edward Perkins, David knelt by Max, lifting up the Husky-Collie's limp head, tears welling in his eyes as he stared in disbelief.

"Lillian, could you come meet me at the station after I book him?" asked Gordon Craig.

David looked up and saw a sullen Edward Perkins: Max's murderer. Suddenly an anger, a rage, raced through him that he had never felt before. Like a great dam bursting, every pore of his body cried for vengeance, and he didn't care about the consequences. Raising the judge's cane above his head and screaming with pain, he hurled himself toward Edward Perkins, who was looking glumly at Gordon Craig.

"Pa! Look out!" cried Bobby.

The last thing that Edward Perkins saw that evening was the crook of a huge cane advancing toward his eyes, hitting him square in the forehead. He crumpled to the floor like a sack of flour.

"Pa!" cried Bobby, racing to his unconscious father.

David would probably have hit the senior Perkins again had not Gordon Craig grabbed the cane from his hand and thrust him back onto the stairwell. David began to weep. Aunt Lillian knelt beside him, hugging him as he wept.

Chapter Twenty-Three
The Mirror Comes Clear

AUNT LILLIAN RETURNED FROM THE POLICE STATION after midnight. She saw that David and Bobby had placed a blanket over Max's body and had wiped the blood from the hall carpet. The house was silent, except for the sound of shuffling cards that could be heard from the kitchen.

"Oh, hi Aunt Lillian," said David, as Lillian entered the kitchen.

"Hello David, Bobby," she answered.

David looked up at his aunt, noticing for the first time that she had wrinkles in her face. She had stayed with him and Bobby for half an hour before she went to file charges against Bobby's father. They had talked for a short while about how wonderful and loving a dog Max had been. There was no way to bring him back, and he had given his life to protect Lillian and David from harm. Perhaps it was because David had already suffered grave loss, but it was Bobby, not David, who had wept the whole time the three talked. Leaving the boys with the practical task of covering Max and cleaning up the mess made by Bobby's father, Lillian had felt confident that she would be away no longer than an hour. But that hour had stretched into many hours.

"We almost called the police station to see if you were okay," said David, "but Bobby said if anybody on earth could take care of herself, it was you. What kept you?"

"A small reunion," said Aunt Lillian, smiling.

"A reunion?" asked David.

"Yes. Many decisions had to be made tonight regarding Bobby's father, as well as Bobby himself, and a substantial number of people needed to become actively involved." Aunt Lillian sighed and managed a small smile and, somehow, didn't look as tired as she had when she had first entered the kitchen.

Sitting down next to the boys, she laughed to herself, explaining, "I am most fortunate to have had the Mayor, the Police Chief, the Director of Social Services, the District Attorney, Dr. Smith, and the Family Court Judge as former piano students. All of them good hearted, too. First the Family Court Judge was called to see if I could become a temporary foster parent to Bobby. She drove to the police station immediately when she realized what had happened, and then all kinds of telephone calls were made to the others and, before long, much of Midville's power elite sat with me in Gordon Craig's office. I never dreamed I was so, what do they say, 'well connected'. We talked about the problems at hand, about old times, and about the future. It was a wonderful reunion. It was also the most amazing exercise at cutting through bureaucratic red tape that I have *ever* witnessed."

Aunt Lillian paused, then looked directly at Bobby and continued, "Bobby, you are now in my protective custody and have been assigned to me as a temporary foster child. I hope I did not assume too much in making that arrangement. David and I would be most honored if you consented to moving in here to live with us."

Bobby's eyes glistened as he nodded his assent.

"Your father's future presents a more difficult problem, and we have to wait to see what *he* decides. He has been given a choice, via a letter from me as well a much stronger letter from Judge Robert Ayers. Essentially, he must choose between rehabilitation and jail. Funds have been found, thanks to my former piano students, to pay for his rehabilitative treatment at a private medical facility near Rochester for a maximum of one hundred and twenty days. We all agreed that one month would be little more than a lost effort, in view of your father's history, Bobby. So now he must choose between drying out in jail or in a place that is equipped to help him."

"I don't put much hope in the choice that he'll make," said Bobby gloomily.

"Well, Dr. Smith and the District Attorney are going to talk with him in the morning, after he has sobered up and has had time to read and consider the two letters. I would be happy to get some sleep, but first I must ask you both to consider some insights I believe I have had regarding your situations."

The boys nodded.

"First of all, Bobby, it is now my assumption that you have been beaten up by your father most of your life."

Bobby nodded.

"It is also my belief, Bobby, that he was the only security you knew, and that you were afraid to lose him, even though he beat you. In order to protect him, you portrayed yourself as a bully at school, as well as in the community, so that any bruises or marks that showed on your person would be written off to what was perceived to be your continual fighting with others. Your father was all you had, and you feared that you'd be totally lost if anything should happen to him. Briefly, you chose to remain in a bad situation, rather than risk getting into an unknown situation."

Bobby nodded once again.

"I can say this with real conviction, because since the very first day you came here to learn canasta, I knew you were not a bully."

Bobby lifted his eyes to meet Aunt Lillian's.

"Call it an old lady's intuition, if you like. But in the words you used and the feelings you expressed, I saw, instead of a bully, a very sensitive and sincere young man. I *still* see that."

Bobby flushed a little.

"I have also been trying to understand why you beat David up, and my best guess is that it is because you were jealous of him."

Bobby nodded once again, looking at David. "I hated that smile of contentment on your face, 'cause I had heard how wonderful your Aunt Lillian was, and I knew how rotten I had it. Every time I thought of you, I saw red, 'cause I wanted to be like you."

David considered Bobby's words carefully, suddenly smiling brightly, saying, "Well, now you *are!*"

"And David," continued Aunt Lillian, turning to her Grand Nephew, "I also perceive a sense of relief in your bearing. I know, my dear, how very much Max meant to you, and I know nothing we can do will bring him back. Still, I wonder if Bobby's father didn't provide you with a flesh and blood vehicle upon which to vent your anger. Max's death unleashed the repressed rage with which you have struggled ever since your parents' deaths."

As he considered Aunt Lillian's insight, David's eyes glistened.

He closed his eyes in contemplation, then opened them and nodded.

"You see, my dears, you are *each* victims of the same disease, both directly and indirectly. That pain and suffering has forged a special bond between you. You have *both* suffered a lot. But you also have *new lives* to live, and the sooner we get to bed," yawned Aunt Lillian, "the better."

"Bobby, David will show you the guest room which will become your room, and no one else's. We can discuss this tomorrow if you like, but we will also need to go over to Bobby's to get the things he needs to move here. We'll know more about all that once we've heard from your father, Bobby. I should think we'll get a response no later than noon tomorrow. Good night, my two young princes. Sleep well. Oh, poor Max, we'll also have to take his body to the vet tomorrow morning. I'll call them early. Dr. Noble used to be one—"

"Of your piano students," said Bobby and David together, grinning at Aunt Lillian.

Aunt Lillian flushed slightly, then added, "Can I help it if I'm well connected?"

* * * * *

The next morning David and Bobby rose to the delectable smell of pancakes and sausage. Aunt Lillian served one of her best spreads. During breakfast, the conversation was largely centered on Max and on what a fine dog he had been.

After breakfast, Max's body was taken to Dr. Noble's animal clinic. It was agreed that he would be cremated, with his ashes returned in the spring for sprinkling on the vegetable garden.

Returning home shortly after 11:00 a.m., they noticed Dr. Smith's car parked outside Aunt Lillian's.

"Have you been waiting long, Wayne?" asked Aunt Lillian.

"Only about ten minutes. I've been reading and rereading this letter that Bobby's dad asked me to deliver to all of you in person. As you know Bobby, he doesn't write very well, so he asked me to take down his words, but to make sure they were still *his* words. I offered to smooth out his language, and he said that would be nice, but to make sure it still sounded like him. I read this version back to him and he approved it, and then he asked me to bring the letter over here to read to all of you."

"Well, do come in, Wayne. I'll prepare us some hot tea."

After everyone was seated around the dining room table, Wayne Smith opened the envelope and began to read:

> *Dear Bobby and Miss Biggs and David,*
>
> *I'm now sober and have learnt what I done. I'm terribly sorry for all the pain I caused. I'm most sorry for killin' the dog, and there's a hundred dollars in my savings account for a new dog. I've given Dr. Smith a separate note so the bank will allow David to get the money. I know this doesn't bring your dog back, boy, but I hope it helps, somehow.*
>
> *I've been given the choice of jail or dryin' out in a special hospital. I've never been in jail, and never intend to sink so low.*
>
> *Bobby, I've been a lousy father to you, even though I do love you. The good lady, Miss Biggs, is gonna be your foster parent. When I get out of this special hospital, I will try to do much better for you. Drinkin' is an awful curse once it's got you by the throat. Then, you're a goner.*
>
> *I do hope the kind lady will bring you, Bobby, to see me now and again.*
>
> *To the kind lady, please, I beg you to take care of my son—raise him the right way, 'cause I ain't up to it.*
>
> *They says good things come out of bad situations and I think these good things are already happenin'.*
>
> *God forgive me, and I beg you all on my knees to forgive me.*
>
> *[signed] Edward Perkins*

Everyone had moist eyes. Wayne Smith looked at Bobby and continued, "Your dad is now on his way to the rehabilitation hospital. I saw him off myself and promised him I would come directly here to read this letter to you and to Lillian and David. I have his address here should you decide to write to him."

"I think we may all want to write to him," said Aunt Lillian.

"Oh, yes, Lillian, Bobby's dad also asked me to give *you* a message."

"Oh?"

"Yes. He said, 'Please tell the kind lady that the Judge's letter was a damn bit sobering, but hers was downright unnerving. I ain't *never* had a letter like that before.'"

"What did you say?" asked David in surprise.

"That, my dears, must remain forever between me and Edward Perkins."

"Aw, come on!" cried Bobby.

But Aunt Lillian had placed her right forefinger to her lips, and the three gentlemen knew the conversation was closed. The content of her letter would remain confidential and downright unnerving, too.

"I wonder what's going to happen now?" said David.

"Christmas," said Aunt Lillian.

"Christmas?" inquired David.

"Yes, Christmas is coming. And I think we should plan to make it a season of thanksgiving and celebration."

"It won't feel much like Christmas without Max bouncing around, wagging his tail," said David sadly.

"It will take us some real time to mourn Max. But I think we shouldn't let the opportunities of this special season ebb away from us even though we've lost a dear pet, not to mention dear family. I've not gone overboard for Christmas in recent years, but something tells me *this* is the year for me to pull out all the stops, speaking as a former organist. After all, this is *our* first Christmas, the three of us together."

"Why so much fuss?" asked David.

"Because, my dear, Christmas love, more than anything, brings out the marvelous child that lives in each of us. It will, I hope, kindle our hearts and allow us to rediscover those inner children, that we might once again trust in ourselves and play together."

So began preparations for a season of celebration and joy.

Acknowledgments from the 1996 Edition, published under the title *Thursday's Child*

Novels are the product of an author's imagination, springing from the ground of particular encounter and daily experience — loose shards of intuition, memory, and insight which gradually coalesce into plots, characters, themes, images, struggles, challenges, triumphs, disappointments, joys, laughter, tears — all of which ultimately add up to a story.

Although writing is inherently a solitary vocation, the product of an author's pen, if it is to be refined and honed, depends on readers who will offer helpful comments and suggestions. It is impossible for an author to know the quality of his or her own work, but every story can be helped enormously by discerning readers who, in their variety of insights and responses, apprise the author of a manuscript's unnoticed pitfalls, mistakes, and inconsistencies, as well as of its strengths and successes.

I express deep gratitude and thanks to my wife, Martha, for her expert editing, perceptive insights, helpful suggestions, and constant affirmation.

Thanks is also given to Sally Cashion, who kindly offered excellent editing suggestions of the book's earliest drafts.

Thanks, especially, is extended to my three daughters — Monica, Lucy, & Sarah — who aided me in making *Thursday's Child* a better novel. I thank them for their insights, affirmation, patience, and love.

David Harbert II and Patrick Tuttle also served as readers, and I thank them for their excellent help.

Grateful thanks and appreciation are also given to readers Annie Billups, Peter & Sherrill Boyce and Mark Boyce, Dana Catherine, Tom & Jane Donahue, Joseph Downing, Thomas Garbrick, Jan Greene, Sandy Hudson {hers, literally, was an eleventh hour review}, Glenn Jacobs, Joshua Koenig, Sheri Swerdfeger, Bethany Trombly, and Kenneth Williams for their very helpful and careful readings of the manuscripts.

A very special thank you is extended to Paul J. F. Howe {*Platypus extraordinaire*}, who, with his keen insights {despite his graduate training at an obscure university in Cambridge, MA}, together with his uncommon acumen and natural gift for literary analysis, probed the novel and offered many excellent and helpful suggestions which I deeply appreciate.

I also wish to acknowledge the great debt of thanks I owe to the two writers with whom it has been my privilege to study.

Poet Lewis Turco, during my undergraduate years, afforded me a durable and lasting foundation in writing poetry as well as a cultivating love for language. Thank you, Lew, for your very helpful *The Book of Forms* {*The Book of Forms,* The University Press of New England, 2000}, for your own poetry, for your love of language, and for fond memories of the writers' guild you so generously sponsored.

Many years later, Madeleine L'Engle taught me how to write fiction as well as how to listen to my intuitive self. Madeleine's many wonderful Writers' Workshops at Holy Cross Monastery in West Park, New York, serve as an enduring encouragement and foundation for my stories. Thank you, Madeleine, for all that you have taught me, for your own illuminating work, for your depth of wisdom, for your love of Story, and for your kind and generous affirmation.

It remains my hope that all who read *Thursday's Child* will feel amply rewarded for their time and trouble, once they have journeyed among these engaging and surprising characters, sharing in their laughter, tears, joys, and sorrows. And their adventures do continue.

Steven Emerson Swerdfeger
Sarasota, Florida

Second Edition — A New Title

To revise or not to revise? That was the question!

Since this novel was accorded Finalist Honors in the 1997 Small Press Book Awards, I felt that only spot revision would be appropriate, although in the process of revision, I have been forced to reach the unlikely conclusion that printers' gremlins actually do exist.

Although writers, especially novelists, are rarely short on the use of the written word, I will be brief here, in the conviction that the work itself should be the prime vehicle of communication. Some might ask why I decided to change this story's title. The title *Thursdsay's Child*, although very applicable to the story's protagonist, has been used over a dozen times, whereas *The Canasta Capers*, which reflects one of the novel's sub-themes, remains unique.

In an age where electronic media hold sway, it is always gratifying to hear from readers. One reader wrote to inquire in what way I had known her high school guidance counselor; this was sobering, since Melvin Dandy is intentionally steeped in hyperbole. Another reader wrote to report that she had encountered a Gertrude Coachman in the form of a high school history teacher. Hopefully, the Thatcher Pennythorpes will balance out all such lacking incarnations of educator.

Surprisingly, our pool attendant reported that he had passed on his copy of the book to a relative in the Midwest, where it was enthusiastically received and read in an adult Sunday school class.

An even larger number of responses from readers has indicated that the book had served as a vehicle of healing for individuals who had lost loved ones in alcohol-related accidents.

I also extend my deepest thanks to Mrs. Sharon Johnston and to her intrepid band of sixth graders who not only loved this book, but also enjoyed the second in the series.

My wife, Martha, is urging me to write a fourth story, wherein the mysterious nature of Mr. Astor will be disclosed. However, science fiction is calling, and I now need to cull from over a decade of research.

STEVEN SWERDFEGER
Scottsdale, Arizona

Companion Volumes to
The Canasta Capers

An Opening of Heart

The adventures continue as Aunt Lillian and David welcome Bobby Perkins into their home and decide to invite neighbors and friends to an Advent Party. Even a raging snow storm cannot prevent the planned celebration, at which Thatcher Pennythorpe recites part of Charles Dickens' *A Christmas Carol*, indicating that he at one time gave holiday readings of that story every year. David becomes determined to have Mr. Pennythorpe renew his custom of public readings, with all ticket proceeds going to the community food back.

The Potters invite Aunt Lillian, David, and Bobby to Christmas Eve services at Midville's Methodist Church, and later in the holiday the young people attend a Watch Night Service on New Year's Eve. During the vacation, Sean Potter also takes David and Bobby to the enigmatic Mr. Astor's shop of curiosities where the boys receive unexpected gifts.

On New Year's Day, Gertrude Coachman discovers that she no longer needs to continue teaching English, and embarks upon a journey that is beleaguered with unexpected frustrations and surprises.

Mr. Ferlinghausen, Midville Middle School's principal, invites David and his cohorts to host an assembly program for Dr. William Gregory, an educator and researcher who comes to speak to the school.

David becomes consumed with his science report on the megafauna, and hopes to upstage Mallory Evans, who is obsessed with the T-Rex as well as the need to be an Alpha male. David does his best to win sympathy for the megafauna during his presentation, and experiences a moment of cosmic consciousness regarding the interconnectedness of all life, which evokes in him a profound vision and transformation.

Finally, after some intentional slights, misunderstandings and mishaps throughout the story, David, Bobby and Sean discover and acknowledge a new sense of friendship and brotherhood.

Because They Think They Can[1]

This is a story about a group of adolescents who encounter a new teacher who refuses to allow them to ignore their school work. At the prospect of failing ninth grade, the class implores classmate David Andrews, a respected advocate, to help them. Mr. Gregory sets as their task the requirement to demonstrate that they 'love learning for learning's sake.' Befuddled by this requirement, the students follow David's advice and form a Learning Club.

The Learning Club invites Mr. Gregory to be its first speaker. He talks about how students learn differently. Owing to Bobby Perkins' disquiet with fallacies, student leaders agree that it would seem most appropriate to invite a psychologist to speak next. Mr. Pennythorpe, the school's affable history teacher, recommends Dr. Clarence Baker, who proves enormously popular. Invited to return, he speaks first on the subject of hypnosis and later leads the club in an experience of guided imagery.

The class is assigned to present its rendering of *Macbeth* to the community, and more bonding results in their frantic efforts to rid themselves of stage jitters. The play is a huge success. An awards dinner follows which recognizes two faculty and the mayor and which distributes ticket proceeds between school and town libraries. Mr. Pennythorpe speaks, but suffers a heart attack before concluding his remarks. As Pennythorpe lies gravely ill, David works through his worry by organizing a welcome home party for his mentor. Cast members join in, and the elderly history teacher returns safely home to conclude his remarks. Pennythorpe, in his final comments about learning, likens it to love, for "the more we can understand, the more we can appreciate, and the more we can appreciate, the more we can love."

[1]The title is taken from a quotation ascribed to Pliny the Elder, who said of young athletes of his day, "They can because they think they can."

Canasta Rules à la Swerdfeger

At least *two* canastas must be made before "going out". Draw two cards, discard one. {When dealing and drawing, rotate clockwise.} Canastas are composed of seven or eight cards, using a minimum of four of a kind, plus the requisite wild cards, should any be used. A mixed canasta, made with wild cards, is worth 300 points. A natural canasta {sometimes called a 'straight'} is composed of seven or eight cards of the same kind. {e.g. 7 kings, 8 fives, etc.} The discard pile may be frozen by a wild card, after which a player needs two of a kind to pick the pack.

Melding: What must be played on the board to lay down initially, based on the number of points already earned.

> Minus to 0 = 15 point meld required
> 5 points to 1495 = 50 point meld required
> 1500 points to 2995 = 90 point meld required
> 3000 points or above = 120 point meld required

Black threes are discards that cannot be picked; as discards, they essentially 'freeze' a pack [discard pile] for that particular turn. Wild cards [jokers and deuces] always freeze the pack for that turn and all subsequent turns until either that pack is picked or the game is over. Red threes are worth 100 points when melded; 800 points for all four! Red threes that are in a player's hand at the game's conclusion incur a 200 point penalty.

With two players the initial deal is fifteen cards; with three players, thirteen cards; and with four players, eleven cards. Consider adding additional decks should more players be included in a game.

Scores are comprised of COUNT and BASIC.

> BASIC is comprised of the points earned from red threes, canastas, and going out.
> COUNT is comprised of the total value of points of cards that a player accumulates.

Card point value determination:

> red threes = 100 points each {800 points for four red threes}
> jokers = fifty points
> aces and deuces = twenty points
> eights through kings = ten points
> black threes through sevens = five points

When the discard pile [pack] is not frozen, a deuce or joker can be used to meld a discard, provided the player has already previously melded cards on the board. A player may meld three or four black threes when going out, as well as place a discard in the discard tray.

Strategy can be helpful, as in baiting a player when the pack is "frozen" by discarding a card yet keeping a pair. In addition, going out with a concealed hand — going out when one first melds — is sure to flummox and raise the ire of one's opponent.

Wild cards offer the opportunity to make canastas and/or to freeze the discard pile.

Regarding CANASTA and its vagaries

Yes, canasta is one of our family games. I first learned it in the 1950's and fondly remember playing it with my parents, sister, and Canadian cousins. For those of you who may be interested in playing canasta, the Swerdfeger "House Rules" are listed above. Today it may also be played on the Internet. Good luck!

HER MAJESTY sends a personal message to all readers:

"I highly recommend canasta and acupuncture."

Since Lucy is commencing her studies in art and illustration at the Minneapolis College of Art and Design this year, we thought it would be appropriate to use two of her portfolio drawings as well as two caricatures for our author/illustrator images.

STEVEN SWERDFEGER was born in Massena, New York, on July 13, 1948. He attended local public schools, later entering the State University of New York at Oswego, where he earned his Bachelor of Arts degree in American literature. He also holds a Master of Arts degree in religious education from Princeton Theological Seminary and a Doctor of Philosophy degree in creative writing from the Union Institute & University in Cincinnati, Ohio.

His various career interests have included child care work, teaching high school English, creative writing, church music, hypnosis & guided imagery, college teaching, and publishing.

He is married to Martha Grout Swerdfeger, a physician who serves as Medical Director for the CrossRoads Clinic in Phoenix, Arizona, and who practices under her maiden name Martha M. Grout.

LUCY SWERDFEGER was born in Syracuse, N.Y., on November 7, 1982. Having begun formal studies in painting at the age of six, she has studied art with Gale Simon Coleman and Michael White, among others.

Lucy will begin her studies for a B.F.A. in illustration at the Minneapolis College of Art and Design in August of 2005. Her interests include illustration and comic art.

She has kindly allowed her parents to adopt Brody, her tiger cat, while she is away at art school.